SO-AXU-165

MASTER OF THE HOUSE

"Lord Sheffield. I am—Miss Wells. Cassandra Wells." She heard herself continue with the lie but was still unsure why she had.

His hand held hers for a brief moment and then released it. "You're traveling alone? What was your family thinking of to allow a girl of your age to travel alone?"

Lifting her chin a trifle, she said, "I am twenty, my lord."

He nodded, gazing at her in a very direct way that was a bit unsettling. "According to your coachman, you suffered a broken axle?"

"My coach did," she murmured.

The hard stare continued for a moment, but then he smiled quite suddenly—and his harsh face was lit with warmth. "I stand corrected, ma'am."

Cassandra felt herself smiling back at him and coping with the oddest sensations. A kind of fluttering near her heart that she had never experienced before . . .

—From "Masquerade"
by Kay Hooper

ROMANCE COLLECTIONS FROM
THE BERKLEY PUBLISHING GROUP

Love Stories for Every Season . . .

SECRET LOVES: Passionate tales of crushes, secret admirers, and other wonders of love, by Constance O'Day Flannery, Wendy Haley, Cheryl Lanham, and Catherine Palmer.

HIGHLAND FLING: The romance of Scottish hearts, captured by Anne Stuart, Caitlin McBride, Jill Barnett, and Linda Shertzer.

HARVEST HEARTS: Heartwarming stories of love's rich bounty, by Kristin Hannah, Rebecca Paisley, Jo Anne Cassity, and Sharon Harlow.

SUMMER MAGIC: Splendid summertime love stories featuring Pamela Morsi, Jean Anne Caldwell, Ann Carberry, and Karen Lockwood.

SWEET HEARTS: Celebrate Cupid's magical matchmaking with Jill Marie Landis, Jodi Thomas, Colleen Quinn, and Kathleen Kane.

A CHRISTMAS TREASURE: Festive tales for a true Regency holiday, by Elizabeth Mansfield, Holly Newman, Sheila Rabe, and Ellen Rawlings.

SUMMERTIME SPLENDOR: A golden celebration of romance, featuring today's most popular Regency authors . . . Marion Chesney, Cynthia Bailey-Pratt, Sarah Eagle, and Melinda Pryce.

LOVING HEARTS: Valentine stories that warm the heart, by Jill Marie Landis, Jodi Thomas, Colleen Quinn, and Maureen Child.

A REGENCY HOLIDAY: Delightful treasures of Christmastime romance, by Elizabeth Mansfield, Monette Cummings, Martha Powers, Judith Nelson, and Sarah Eagle.

HEARTS of GOLD

Kay Hooper
Kathleen Kane
Karen Lockwood
Bonnie K. Winn

JOVE BOOKS, NEW YORK

If you purchased this book without a cover, you should be aware that this
book is stolen property. It was reported as "unsold and destroyed" to the
publisher, and neither the author nor the publisher has received any
payment for this "stripped book."

HEARTS OF GOLD

A Jove Book / published by arrangement with
the authors

PRINTING HISTORY
Jove edition / February 1994

All rights reserved.
Copyright © 1994 by The Berkley Publishing Group.
"Masquerade" copyright © 1994 by Kay Hooper.
"Betrayed Hearts" copyright © 1994 by Maureen Child.
"Perfect Mates" copyright © 1994 by Karen Finnigan.
"Heart of Erin" copyright © 1994 by Bonnie K. Winn.
This book may not be reproduced in whole or in part,
by mimeograph or any other means, without permission.
For information address: The Berkley Publishing Group,
200 Madison Avenue, New York, New York 10016.

ISBN: 0-515-11307-7

A JOVE BOOK®
Jove Books are published by The Berkley Publishing Group,
200 Madison Avenue, New York, New York 10016.
JOVE and the "J" design are
trademarks belonging to Jove Publications, Inc.

PRINTED IN THE UNITED STATES OF AMERICA

10 9 8 7 6 5 4 3 2 1

MASQUERADE

a novella

by

Kay Hooper

Dear Readers,

As some of you may know, I began my writing career with a Regency romance titled *Lady Thief* (currently out of print). The majority of my work since then has consisted of contemporary love stories, with an occasional historical or fantasy romance and two murder mysteries, but I've always had a soft spot for the Regency period.

Novellas provide the perfect opportunity to revisit the world Georgette Heyer painted for me over the years, the world of lords and ladies, of carriages and balls and Almack's—a bright, colorful place filled with romance and adventure. As a writer, I find the combination irresistible.

Valentine's Day, Regency England, and romance—I hope you enjoy the visit as much as I did.

Kay Hooper

ONE

A COLD WIND snatched at her cloak as Cassandra Eden bent forward to peer in the direction of her coachman's pointing finger. She shivered as she looked at the broken axle. It was a *very* broken axle, and she did not require the opinion of an expert coach-builder to perceive that the vehicle was not going anywhere until it was repaired. Cassandra's dismay intensified when fat white flakes of snow began to swirl through the gloom of approaching night.

"Oh, no," she said.

John Potter, her coachman, nodded glumly. "I suspicioned that axle was cracked, miss, and this godforsaken road finished it off right enough. There'll have to be a new one, and where to find aught tonight—"

"Obviously we won't be able to get it repaired tonight," Cassandra said with a sigh. "But we must have shelter. How far to the nearest inn, John?"

The grizzled coachman ruminated with a frown, then said, "That'd be the Boar's Head, miss, and it's all of twenty miles along and back on the main road."

Even a lightweight racing curricle and team of fine horses would have required more than an hour for the journey on such a bad road, but in any case Cassandra had neither. She had a weary team of well-bred but sturdy horses and an elderly, broken coach that should have been left in her uncle's London stables. It was late January, late afternoon, and the leaden sky was a grim indication that the drifting flakes of snow were only the overture to a storm.

Cassandra glanced up at the window of the coach, where her maid's worried face could be seen, then stepped away and surveyed the countryside with considerable—though masked—worry of her own. A damaged bridge some miles back had necessitated this detour from the normal route between London and Bristol; they were presently somewhere in north Berkshire, an area that was almost exclusively patchy forests and endless acres of cultivated or pastured land.

"John, is that a manor house? There—on the edge of that forest across the field?"

The coachman squinted, then nodded slowly. "It appears to be, miss. Haven't seen another place bigger'n a cottage for miles, so stands to reason there'd be an estate of some kind in these parts. Lonesome place, though."

Cassandra agreed silently. In the fading light it was difficult to see clearly, but she thought the distant house looked lonely and more than a little desolate. But that was probably the weather, she told herself sternly.

"We shall go there, then," she said in a decided tone. "Another half mile along this road should bring us to the drive, I think."

"I'll go, Miss Cassie. I'm sure they'd be agreeable an' send a carriage—"

"Oh, nonsense, John. I would much rather walk to the house than huddle in the coach awaiting rescue. We shall not impose upon our host any more than absolutely necessary. Come out, Sarah—we must walk from here."

Her maid, a pretty but apprehensive young woman no more than a few years older than her mistress, left the shelter of the coach reluctantly. "Walk, Miss Cassie?"

Cassandra could hardly help but smile at Sarah's consternation; town bred, the maid considered anything outside London's narrow and bustling streets the wilderness and undoubtedly quaked at the thought of walking any distance at all through this bleak landscape.

"Would you prefer to freeze, Sarah?" She didn't wait for a response but directed the groom to unstrap her smallest bag from the coach and hand it down to her. Since the horses were standing wearily with no need to be held, the lad scrambled atop the coach and did as he was bid.

"I'll carry that, miss," John Potter told her as he reached up for the bag. "Tom can stay with the coach till I bring help from the manor. An' you won't be wantin' to rap on a strange door with no more than this slip of a girl beside you."

Cassandra, who was neither a shy woman nor one who imagined herself threatened where there was no cause, was a little amused as well as resigned by her servant's determined protection. It was one of the reasons her uncle had allowed her to set out from London with only her maid; he knew very well that John Potter was a more trustworthy guard than any number of outriders and could be depended upon to defend as well as advise Cassandra in the event of trouble.

"I very much doubt the manor is filled with desperadoes," she told him in a dry tone.

"Likely not, miss," the coachman returned stolidly. "But Sir Basil would have my head on a platter was I to let you out of my sight before I was sure you'd be in good hands."

Too wise—and too chilled—to bother protesting further, Cassandra merely told Sarah to take care on the uneven surface of the road, then struck out briskly. Unlike her maid, she was country bred and enjoyed daily long walks when she was home, so this trifling distance bothered her not at all.

Her estimation of the distance involved turned out to be

fairly accurate; they came upon the manor's neat driveway a little more than half a mile from the stranded coach, and Sarah had complained of sore feet only once. But the drive itself wound along for another half mile, and it was nearly dark by the time they neared the house.

John Potter seemed much reassured by the condition of the place, commenting once that care and money had been spent here right enough. Cassandra agreed silently. The estate was clearly in excellent shape, the lawns immaculate and the shrubbery pruned, and the manor house itself was neat as a pin, at least on the outside. For the first time she wondered whom it belonged to; the place was a fair distance from London—inconvenient in a country house.

Not that she was in any position to be particular as to the identity of her host, of course. She needed shelter.

With her servants half a step behind her on either side, Cassandra trod up the steps and applied the gleaming brass knocker firmly. When the door was pulled open almost immediately, she had to fight the impulse to step back, and Sarah's gasp was perfectly audible in the startled quiet.

It had become dark enough outside that the only illumination came from inside the house, and in that faint light half of the manservant's grim, swarthy face was visible. Unfortunately for the maid's disordered nerves, that side of his face bore an ugly scar that twisted from the corner of his left eye to the corner of his mouth, and the disfigurement lent him an appearance of menace virtually guaranteed to terrify an imaginative young woman.

"Yes?" he said, his unusually deep voice another shock.

Cassandra's alarm had been momentary, and when she spoke it was pleasantly. "Good evening. I am afraid I have suffered a slight misfortune on the road and require assistance."

The servant's chilly gray eyes looked her up and down

swiftly, and then were veiled by lowered lids. "Indeed, miss? We don't get many travelers out this way."

A little impatient at being kept standing out in the cold and snow by a servant—hardly the kind of treatment to which she was accustomed—Cassandra's voice sharpened. "I don't doubt it. Be assured I would hardly have come this way myself had not a bridge washed out some miles back. Would you kindly be good enough to inform your master of my plight? I have my maid, as you see, and my coachman will require assistance to bring my coach and horses safely off the road."

It was not in her character to be so peremptory, particularly with a servant in a private house, but Cassandra was chilled and tired, and all she wanted was something hot to drink and a brisk fire where she could warm her hands and feet. And she was not pleased by the notion that this manservant regarded her with only thinly disguised disdain.

And, indeed, he hesitated after she spoke just long enough to subtly imply that it was his decision rather than hers to admit her to the house. He stepped back, opening the door wider, and said in a colorless tone, "If you'll step this way, miss, I'll inform His Lordship."

Cassandra came into the entrance hall, which was quite impressive and blessedly warm, and said, "His Lordship?"

"Yes, miss. The Earl of Sheffield. This is Sheffield Hall." He said it as if he seriously doubted she had not been aware of the information.

She heard a quickly indrawn breath from Sarah, and Cassandra felt a bit dismayed herself. The Earl of Sheffield? Though she had never met him—or even seen him, for that matter—two Seasons in London had certainly exposed her to all the talk concerning one of the more infamous rakes of past Seasons.

Stone's his name, stone his heart. That was what they said about Stone Westcott, the Earl of Sheffield. It was always said with a sad shake of the head and an ominous frown, a warning to all young ladies of quality to stay out of the earl's path if they wished to keep their good names—and their hearts. Of course, unmarried young ladies were considered too innocent to hear what sin, precisely, Sheffield was guilty of committing, and so those interested or merely curious were reduced to piecing together whispers and overheard comments and arriving at some conclusion, however unsatisfying.

The facts Cassandra felt reasonably sure of were few. Sheffield sprang from a long line of apparently rakish earls, most of whom had treated their reputations with careless disregard and the rules of society with even less respect. Sportsmen rather than dandies, they had excelled in all the manly pursuits, and among the numerous sporting records gentlemen discussed, many were held by various Westcotts. They seemed to own the finest horseflesh and to drive their racing vehicles farther and faster than anyone else (often merely to win a bet), were famous for their punishing fists in the boxing ring, and were said to be superior marksmen.

And for generations they had seemingly held a powerful, unusual fascination for the women they encountered. Rarely handsome and never famed for their social graces, they nevertheless boasted an astonishing history filled with conquests. It was whispered that more than one lady of quality had abandoned her morals and, many times, a husband and family in order to run off with "one of those Westcotts."

From all Cassandra had heard, this particular Westcott, the current earl, was worse than all his ancestors put together.

All this flashed through her mind as the dour manservant crossed the hall on silent feet and opened the door to the parlor, where she and Sarah would wait, but her hesitation was momentary despite her misgivings. She had little choice, after all.

"What name shall I gave His Lordship, miss?" the servant inquired as he held the door.

Before Cassandra could reply, her maid spoke up in a voice that was higher than usual and definitely frightened. "Wells. She is Miss Wells."

Once again, Cassandra's hesitation was fleeting. *It hardly matters, after all. With luck, the coach can be repaired tomorrow, and I will never see Sheffield after that.* So she didn't correct her maid, allowing the lie to stand.

But as soon as they were alone in the lovely, snug parlor, Cassandra took a chair near the crackling fire, held out her gloved hands toward the flames, and said severely, "Sarah, why on earth did you say such a thing? Wells is your name, not mine."

"You know very well why, Miss Cassie," Sarah retorted with spirit. "They say the earl has run through his fortune and intends to wed an heiress—and you're under his roof unprotected! He's already ruined one lady and only laughed when her brother demanded he marry her *and* nearly killed the brother in the most wicked duel the next day!"

Cassandra's surprise was momentary. Naturally, Sarah would have heard servants' gossip—which was clearly more candid than what was whispered abovestairs. But was it any more truthful?

"Duels in this day and age? Sarah—"

"It's true, Miss Cassie. It was years ago, but it happened. My cousin was groom to—to the young lady's brother, and he swears he saw it with his own eyes. How the earl stood there smiling like a *fiend* and then shot that poor young man, blood everywhere, and then he just walked away. And he was still smiling, Miss Cassie! Like a devil!" Sarah shuddered, obviously finding a ghoulish delight in the retelling of such a dramatic story.

Cassandra was unwillingly impressed but reminded herself silently that gossip—even that supposedly obtained by an eyewitness—could seldom be replied upon to be wholly truthful. Still, it seemed at least probable that a meeting had taken place between the disreputable earl and some man he had grossly insulted, though the cause as well as the meeting itself was doubtless less dramatic than Sarah's cousin had described.

"Be that as it may, you have put me in an awkward position," she told her maid firmly. "Whatever the earl may have been guilty of in his past, there is no reason to suppose he would be anything but courteous to a stranded traveler, and I very much dislike facing him with a lie."

Unrepentant, Sarah said, "Even a saint can be tempted, miss, and tempting a sinner is foolish! Bad enough you're so pretty and look so delicate—if he knew you had a fortune as would make a nabob stare, he'd be after you in a trice!"

Cassandra couldn't help laughing, but she shook her head as well and lapsed into silence as she warmed her hands at the fire. Hiding her identity had not been her doing, and it was not what she wanted, but now that Sarah had taken that step, she was uncertain if she would correct the situation.

She was not afraid of Sheffield, or of being under his roof without the protection of a family member; no matter how black the earl was painted, he was indisputably a gentleman. He might well flaunt the conventions of society, and he might even have compromised a lady and then refused to marry her, but he would no more take advantage of a young lady temporarily under his protection than he would rob a bank.

So it wasn't fear of him that made Cassandra hesitate to offer her true identity. It was, more than anything, a rather weary repugnance for the inevitable response her name evoked in so many of the men she had met. Fortune hunters had dogged her steps since the day she had come out into society, and she was very tired of weighing the sincerity of every compliment and searching each charming smile for signs of duplicity or greed.

At least if Sheffield had no idea she was an heiress, she would be able to relax that particular guard. Not that she expected him to attempt to charm her—despite Sarah's flattering words, Cassandra knew herself to be too dark for fashionable prettiness, too tall, and so pale and fine-boned that she appeared ridiculously fragile—but her social mask had become so fixed that it required a conscious effort to relax.

Which was one reason she had decided to go home for a few weeks.

Cassandra was still undecided about exposing Sarah's lie when the door opened a few moments later and a trim middle-aged woman in sober raiment entered the room carrying a tray.

"Good evening, Miss Wells. I am His Lordship's housekeeper, Mrs. Milton. He'll be down to welcome you shortly but asked that I see to your needs in the meanwhile. Your coachman has gone with some of our men to fetch your coach and horses, and I will take your maid and baggage to the room being prepared for you. We keep country hours here, but supper has been put back to allow you time to warm and refresh yourself."

As she accepted a cup of steaming tea, Cassandra said apologetically, "I am sorry to have disrupted the routine of the household, Mrs. Milton."

Her own tone comfortable and placid, the housekeeper replied, "There's no bother, miss. We have visitors rarely enough, but His Lordship expects things to be done right. Now—I'll take your maid up and see to her, and as soon as the room is ready, I'll be back for you."

"Thank you," Cassandra murmured. Left alone in the warm parlor, she reflected wryly that the moment for confessing Sarah's lie was beginning to recede into the distance. Every time she faced someone as "Miss Wells," it would become more and more difficult to tell the truth.

She removed her gloves and untied the ribbons of her bonnet to remove it as well, having been reassured that she would remain at the Hall at least for tonight. The mirror over the fireplace told her that her dark curls were sadly crushed. She did what she could to restore them but did not worry particularly about it; she was not a vain woman and, moreover, had no desire to present any more than a neat and ladylike appearance to the earl.

She had finished her tea as well as a slice of bread and butter, and was feeling much warmer and more comfortable—and, in fact, a little sleepy—when the door opened a second time and her host strode in.

Cassandra rose to her feet in a response that had less to do with politeness than with something deeper and more basic within her, and her drowsiness vanished.

"How do you do, ma'am?" the earl said in a rather hard, abrupt tone as he came toward her. "I am Sheffield."

She did not know what, precisely, she had expected, but Lord Sheffield surprised her. She doubted he was much past thirty, which was rather young to be so infamous a reprobate. He was an unusually big man, well over six feet tall, with very wide and powerful shoulders, and he moved with an almost eerie, catlike grace. His thick hair was black, his eyes dark and brooding, his complexion tanned; he was not a conventionally handsome man, but he was quite definitely . . . impressive.

Cassandra offered her hand, having to look up to meet his eyes, which was rare for her. "Lord Sheffield. I am—Miss Wells. Cassandra Wells." She heard herself continue with the lie but was still unsure why she had.

His hand, unexpectedly well formed and beautiful, held hers for a brief moment and then released it while his frowning dark eyes looked her over with more censure than admiration—or even curiosity—and his voice was still abrupt when he spoke. "You're traveling alone? What was your family thinking of to allow a girl of your age to travel alone?"

The impatience in his tone did not disturb Cassandra; her uncle was a man of irritable temperament, and she got along quite well with him. Nor was she offended by his assumption of extreme youth; she knew only too well that, despite her height, large eyes, and a childlike voice—which she had attempted in vain to mature—caused her to appear a good four or five years younger than her actual age.

If she had removed her cloak, he would have had no doubt of her maturity; slender virtually everywhere else, her breasts were well formed and generous—the envy of her friends but an attribute with which Cassandra had never been quite comfortable because of the way men looked at her. So while she might, if she wished, have added to the lie and allowed him to believe her much younger, her own body made it unlikely she would be believed.

"I am not a child, my lord, and I often travel alone," she told him, polite and perfectly composed.

He frowned. "How old are you?"

Cassandra had hoped to avoid a direct answer, but the blunt question—however rude—demanded one. Lifting her chin a trifle, she said, "I am twenty, my lord."

His brows lifted in surprise. "You don't look it—or sound it. But I maintain that you should not be traveling alone; twenty is still hardly more than a child. Sit down, ma'am." He stepped away from her to stand with one shoulder idly propped against the mantel. "Have my people seen to your comfort?"

She resumed her seat and replied only to the last rather indifferent question. "Yes, Mrs. Milton has been very kind, and I understand my coach and horses are being fetched."

He nodded, gazing at her in a very direct way that was a

bit unsettling. "They are. According to your coachman, you suffered a broken axle?"

"My coach did," she murmured.

The hard stare continued for a moment, but then he smiled quite suddenly—and his harsh face was lit with warmth. "I stand corrected, ma'am."

Cassandra felt herself smiling back at him and coping with the oddest sensations. A kind of fluttering near her heart that she had never experienced before. It was deeply disturbing, almost frightening, and she was very glad when the sensation faded. She thought there was even a touch of relief in her voice when she spoke to him. "Can it be repaired quickly, my lord? I am expected home tomorrow."

"Your destination is Bristol?"

"Some miles northeast of Bristol, yes."

The earl's smile had been brief, the seemingly habitual frown quickly returning, but his voice seemed less abrupt when he said, "The broken axle is not the problem, ma'am; I would be happy to lend you one of my vehicles and send your coach along later once it is repaired. However, the weather has definitely taken a turn for the worse, and I doubt travel will be possible for at least a few days."

Dismayed, she said, "But there was only a little snow falling when we arrived—"

"There is much more than a little now; it is mixed with sleet as well, and the wind is building steadily. Unless I much mistake the matter, we will be in the midst of a full-blown storm before midnight."

Cassandra's consternation increased, but she was too sensible to struggle fruitlessly against the potent combination of fate and nature. It appeared that her destiny included an enforced stay at Sheffield Hall. Sighing, she said, "I am sorry, my lord, but it seems I must impose upon you for the duration."

He bowed slightly with more courtesy than enthusiasm,

his harsh face immobile. "It is, of course, my pleasure to offer you shelter, ma'am."

She felt one of her eyebrows rise before she could halt the indication of derision at the conventional—and obviously reluctant—offer but was able to respond politely. "Thank you very much, Lord Sheffield."

There was a sudden gleam in his dark eyes, and a faint smile played about the corners of his strong mouth, but before he could say anything the door opened and Mrs. Milton came to convey Cassandra to her room.

Sheffield bowed again, this time with a slightly mocking tilt to his dark head. "I would be honored, ma'am, if you would join me for supper. In an hour?"

Cassandra picked up her gloves and bonnet, rose to her feet, and curtsied with a brevity that held a subtle touch of her own mockery. He could deride the often stiff and formal conventions of polite society if he chose, she decided, but there was no reason why she should pretend she didn't understand his indirect ridicule; she refused to play dumb.

"Thank you, my lord," she replied sweetly. Then she followed the housekeeper from the parlor. She didn't look back at the earl, and so she didn't see his smile—or see it die as he turned his gaze to the bright fire.

TWO

THE ROOM PROVIDED by her host was lovely, and as Cassandra allowed Sara to divest her of her traveling dress, she decided that if Sheffield was indeed in financial difficulties, he had certainly not scrimped on keeping his estate up to snuff. There were no signs of economizing that she had seen: The house was neither chilly nor drafty and appeared to be in excellent repair; none of the main rooms seemed to be closed up in order to avoid having to heat them; brisk and generous fires burned in the grates; and the linens and draperies seemed in excellent condition. Still, Cassandra was completely aware that such things were not necessarily signs of a full purse. Many a noble family had kept up an appearance of prosperity while falling deeper and deeper in debt.

"The velvet gown, Miss Cassie?" Sarah inquired as she brushed out her mistress's raven hair before the dressing table.

Drawn from her musings, Cassandra hesitated. The velvet gown, while elegant and entirely suitable for a winter's evening, was also high-necked and long-sleeved, and not particularly flattering. Sarah, of course, suggested that particular gown because it was imminently *proper,* with no unseemly display of flesh—with which to tempt a sinner.

Cassandra knew she should accept her maid's sensible suggestion and wear the velvet gown, but she kept hearing the earl's brusque voice stating that "twenty is still a child," and she felt ridiculously belligerent about the matter. She was a mature and intelligent woman, and strongly disliked being viewed as a child.

"No," she heard herself say in a disinterested tone. "The blue silk, Sarah. And my lace shawl."

The brush stopped abruptly, and in the mirror Sarah's expression could only be described as appalled. "The blue silk, miss? But—"

Quite gently Cassandra repeated, "The blue silk, Sarah."

Sarah considered her mistress to be one of the kindest possible, but she understood that tone perfectly well and knew better than to argue with a mind made up. Swallowing whatever comments she wanted to offer, she murmured an obedient response, finished arranging the gleaming black hair, and then went to lay out the blue silk gown.

Some minutes later as she considered her reflection in the mirror, Cassandra knew a twinge of doubt. The gown, while perfectly proper for evening dining in a private home, *was* rather revealing. Low-cut, it left her shoulders bare and covered no more than three-quarters of her breasts. The blue silk was drawn up snug beneath her breasts and clung to the remainder of her body with every movement, glimmering slightly as silk did when light played over the material.

Though she could boast a jewel collection to rival any woman in London, Cassandra tended to wear very little ornamentation to even the fanciest dress balls; all she wore tonight were tiny gold earrings and a wide blue velvet ribbon around the base of her throat, to which was pinned a cameo. The lace shawl, beautifully made and very old—it had been her mother's—did not so much cover her bare shoulders as it did cunningly reveal them.

The effect of the outfit was what Cassandra had hoped. While no one could have had the least doubt she was a lady of quality dressed with simple elegance, there was also no doubt she was a woman.

She knew an impulse to change into something less revealing but chided herself sternly. There was absolutely nothing wrong with what she was wearing—it was perfectly proper—and she would *not* behave like a missish female by covering herself in layers of clothing in order to thwart advances the earl certainly had no intention of making!

With that resolve in mind, she left her room with her head held high—and found the grim manservant awaiting her out in the corridor.

His name, Sarah had reported with a shudder, was Anatole. He was neither butler nor valet, but more of a head steward, responsible for making sure the earl's household was run as smoothly as possible. He was not English; Sheffield had apparently found him during a trip abroad several years before, and between the two—according to Sarah—was a relationship quite different from the usual between master and servant.

How it differed was something Sarah had not been able to say beyond remarking that Anatole was reportedly quite blunt in his speech to the earl and that he seemed to "take a great deal upon himself" when it came to running the household. Apparently, there were hostilities of a sort going on between Anatole and the Hall's housekeeper, a long-standing tug of war over who was in charge.

All that flitted through her mind as Cassandra left her room and found Anatole awaiting her, and she couldn't help wondering if there had been a tussle to determine who would escort her down to supper.

The manservant, his scarred face expressionless, bowed to her with more politeness than he had yet shown. "I am Anatole, miss. Most find the Hall difficult to negotiate at first; I will show you the way."

She had a good sense of direction and was confident she

could find her own way, but Cassandra didn't object. Composedly she said, "Thank you, Anatole," and followed him down the hall.

The Hall *was* both unusually large and laid out rather peculiarly, she thought as they made two turns and traversed three short hallways before reaching the main staircase. But there were candles aplenty to light the way, most in sconces, and by the time her escort had bowed her into a pleasant drawing room, Cassandra was confident she had memorized the way.

Lord Sheffield was in the drawing room. He, too, had changed, from the country buckskins he had worn earlier to knee-britches and a long-tailed coat. His coat was cut so that he could shrug himself into it without the aid of his valet, and his cravat was neatly rather than beautifully arranged, but the less dandified dress suited him admirably, Cassandra thought. He was a physically powerful man and would have looked a trifle absurd decked out in the affectations of a town tulip.

"Good evening, ma'am." He bowed as she came toward him, but he did not leave his position by the fire and move to meet her. "I trust your room is—"

Cassandra felt heat rise in her cheeks as his impassive query broke off abruptly. His dark gaze was every bit as direct as it had been earlier, unnervingly direct, and she had the doubtful satisfaction of knowing that the blue silk gown had chased all notions of childishness out of his head.

"My room is quite lovely and entirely comfortable, my lord, thank you," she replied as if he had completed the question, her own voice sedate. She sat down in a chair near the fire, forcing herself to continue meeting that unsettling stare. However, she had not fully considered the earl's characteristic bluntness, and so his next words caught her by surprise.

"I see I am to stand corrected a second time, ma'am.

Twenty is not always a child, after all. You have a magnificent figure."

For a brief moment Cassandra debated whether she should take offense or else pretend he had not said anything that was certainly frank beyond the bounds of what was appropriate; those *were*, after all, the only two acceptable ways of handling such disgraceful bluntness. But as she gazed into his dark eyes, she felt a surge of recklessness inside her. After two Seasons of polite conversation and genteel advances from gentlemen, she found the matter-of-fact admiration in the earl's words and tone curiously refreshing.

"Thank you." Her voice was a bit dry but calm. She frowned slightly. "Though I suppose I am hardly responsible; I am told I very much resemble my mother."

The earl seemed amused, whether by her clear acceptance of his scandalous manners or by her response she could not be certain.

"Indeed? Then I envy your father."

She had asked for the outrageous response, Cassandra decided ruefully. Unable to hide her amusement, she merely said, "Do not be so quick to envy him, my lord; my mother was also infamous for her temper. She was half French, you see, and prone to throw things when she became enraged."

"And do you throw things, ma'am?"

Thoughtfully she replied, "I have not so far become more than irritated, I should say. So there is really no telling what I would do when thoroughly enraged."

The earl was definitely smiling. "While I have no wish to enrage you, I confess I am most curious. I have never seen a lady throw things."

It was most improper, but Cassandra could not help offering him a hint of her sophistication by casually responding, "Perhaps not, but I am sure you have, in the course of your life, seen *some* female in the throes of passion."

"One or two," he retorted without hesitation.

Cassandra felt another blush rise in her cheeks as she suddenly recollected that the word *passion* had many meanings, but she refused to allow the unintended blunder to cause her to retreat back into conventional politeness.

With dignity she said, "I should be much surprised, my lord, if you had *not* observed some female enraged enough to throw things at you. You seem to me a man at whom any female would frequently become *infuriated.*"

He laughed suddenly, and she felt once again that mysterious and alarming flutter inside her. His whole face changed when he laughed, from something hard and rather forbidding into something warmly and unexpectedly attractive. She was curiously breathless for an instant and knew an impulse to rise and touch him—an urge as shocking as it was incredible.

"That is probably quite true, ma'am," he said, concurring somewhat wryly with her charge. "I have a blunt character and a thoughtless tongue—and both have led me into difficulties with the female sex on more than one occasion."

Having recovered her composure, Cassandra said, "As I said, my lord, I cannot have any doubt of that."

Whatever he might have said then was prevented by the opening of the door. Anatole stood there, his gaze on the earl, and bowed slightly before retreating. Cassandra assumed from this that their meal was ready to be served, a guess confirmed when Sheffield stepped toward her and offered his arm.

"Shall we? I understand my cook has exerted himself, delighted by the prospect of a more appreciative audience than I provide."

"So you are a man of plain tastes, my lord?" Cassandra rose and took his arm, very conscious of his nearness and the contact as he escorted her toward the dining room. She was far more accustomed to being on eye level with most gentlemen; the earl's height and evident strength made her aware of him in a way she had never known before.

"When it comes to what I find on my table, yes, ma'am. I have no liking for heavy sauces, and that preference is apparently a knife to the heart of any fine cook."

That may have been so, Cassandra thought much later, but the earl seemed to enjoy his cook's efforts as much as she did herself. The food was excellent—and the company was even more so. After her exhausting day she had thought herself too weary either to care what she ate or to be much interested in conversation, but both beliefs were in error.

When the meal was finished, Sheffield suggested that she forgo the custom of withdrawing while he enjoyed his port in lonely splendor, and she was pleased to accept; in her uncle's house that practice was confined to evenings in which there were no guests present, and she had always enjoyed the relaxed and casual conversation with her aunt and uncle.

In the earl's snug dining room it seemed to her just as comfortable. He drank his port, she leaned her elbows on the table, and they talked on in the frank manner so quickly established between them, discussing subjects ranging from the treacherous unpredictability of the weather this time of year to the war with France.

He seemed quite interested in her opinions even when they disagreed with his, and never once treated her as anything other than an equal with an intelligent mind fine enough to challenge his own. Cassandra had encountered that unusual attitude in only one other man, her uncle, and she responded to Sheffield with a pleased freedom from constraint that made her virtually glow.

The conversation turned eventually to the social scene. The earl laughed often, much entertained by her perceptive and pungent descriptions of society, particularly when she became somewhat indignant on the subject of young girls "married off to the highest bidder"—that being her opinion of London's glittering social Season.

"When did you come out, ma'am?" he asked her.

"Last Season. I was presented at Court, of course, and *that* was interesting enough, but the rest tried my patience sorely."

"Balls and routs? Dancing at Almack's? Theater parties?" His voice was matter-of-fact.

Cassandra, who knew that the earl was welcome at any private social event as well as Almack's should he happen to grace London with his presence, felt curious as to why he had for years—to her knowledge—avoided such events. While many in society clearly still disapproved of him, and mothers of marriageable daughters quailed at the mere mention of his name, he undoubtedly had friends and connections who urged him to attend their social gatherings.

But she shied away from asking the question, reluctant to bring up the subject of his place in society both because she did not want to betray what knowledge she had and because she was afraid the discussion would change the frank and easy manner between them. So she merely answered his questions.

"Yes. And visits of ceremony, and rides in the park where one cannot even shake the fidgets out of one's mount with a brisk gallop. The necessity of changing one's clothing half a dozen times each day. Having one's toes crushed at least twice each evening by an unwary step, and being forced to suffer both the sly digs of matchmaking mamas with daughters to settle and the measuring scrutiny of gentlemen silently debating one's attributes and possibilities."

Sheffield chuckled. "I daresay you encountered quite a number of the latter, ma'am."

Since she wanted to avoid any mention of the fortune

hunters who had dangled after her, Cassandra merely said briskly, "According to the current standards of beauty, I am both too dark and too tall to be accounted any more than passably attractive, my lord, as you well know. However, I must say that a number of gentlemen seemed to believe that my possibilities were worth their interest."

"Yes, there must be a few intelligent men among the town bucks," the earl stated casually. "Doubtless you have received several offers. Then why are you unattached, ma'am? If this has been your second Season, you must be conscious of the usual pressure brought to bear upon young ladies expected to become betrothed quickly to a suitable candidate."

Cassandra hesitated, but then answered truthfully. "I have a blessed advantage most of my contemporaries lack. My uncle—who has been my guardian for fifteen years—has the novel idea that I might like to decide my own future. To that end, he has left the decision of marriage—whom I wed and, in fact, whether I choose to do so at all—up to me."

"And so far, no aspirant to your hand has persuaded you to abandon your independence?"

Surprised at his understanding, she nodded a bit hesitantly. But then, lest he believe she was boasting of conquests, she said with a touch of wry humor, "My aunt tells me that I have stuffed my head with too many romantic notions, but I must say the thought of accepting a sensible and cold-blooded arrangement to spend the rest of my life with a virtual stranger is something I simply cannot support."

"Then you're holding out for a love-match?"

Cassandra was surprised again, this time that there seemed to be no mockery in his question. And her surprise led her to reply more honestly than she might otherwise have done. "I—I suppose that is what I want. Perhaps it is a foolishly romantic desire, but I know myself too well to believe I would be happy with anything else." She looked at him curiously, bothered by an elusive note in his voice that she couldn't define. "Do . . . you believe in love-matches, my lord?"

For the first time that evening, his gaze fell away from hers, and he studied his glass of port as if the shimmering liquid held secrets. His mouth was hard, a little twisted, his voice suddenly bored and yet a bit harsh when he answered.

"I believe, ma'am, that whatever the wishes of we mere mortals, the pressure of those around us is often impossible to resist. As I have no doubt you will discover—the first time someone refers to you as an unmarriageable spinster."

Cassandra felt a twinge of hurt, yet at the same time she had the odd idea that he was telling her something far more important than his words indicated. Was his absence from the social scene these past years less a matter of his supposed sins than his animosity toward society? And, if so, what had caused it? Was there more to the tale of a young lady's good name scandalously ruined than Cassandra knew or could imagine?

She wanted to ask, but the earl's closed, brooding expression warned her that this was not the time. Instead, suddenly weary and aware of how late it had grown while they had sat talking, Cassandra pushed back her chair and rose to her feet.

"If you will permit me, my lord, I will retire. It has been a very long and eventful day."

He rose as well, and his voice remained bored, the earlier relaxation and enjoyment completely gone. "Of course, ma'am. If you require an escort—"

"No, I believe I can find my way. Thank you very much, my lord, for your aid and hospitality as well as a very pleasant evening. Good night."

"Good night, ma'am."

She felt his gaze on her as she left the dining room, but Cassandra did not look back at him.

"The port decanter is empty, my lord. Should I refill it?"

The emotionless voice roused Sheffield, and he thrust his empty glass away from him in a gesture of controlled violence. "No," he replied shortly.

"Very good, my lord."

"What's the time?"

"Nearly midnight, my lord."

"As late as that?" The earl frowned down at the polished table but made no move to rise.

Silent, Anatole removed the decanter and glass. He then knelt to put more wood on the fire, which leapt up eagerly to snatch at the new fuel and brightened the snug room with its renewed energy. With that task completed, the manservant rose and pinched out a guttering candle, then polished the gleaming sideboard and adjusted two of the chairs at the table.

The earl scowled at him. "Would you have the goodness to leave me in peace? Your endless fidgeting would try the patience of a saint!"

Anatole stood by the table, still expressionless. "Of course, my lord." He did not move.

Sheffield, staring broodingly down at the gleaming table once again, muttered, "She is very young."

"If I may say so, my lord, not in her self-assurance and manner. Quite an intelligent young lady, and not at all flighty unless I miss my guess. It was pleasing to hear Your Lordship so enjoy the evening."

"She has a—an engaging frankness. And amusement rather than missish dismay when I respond in kind."

"An excellent attribute, my lord."

"She's lovely as well. 'Too dark and too tall to be

accounted more than passably attractive,' indeed! As if any man with a particle of sense would prefer some ordinary female with pale hair and washed-out eyes to her glorious raven curls and smoky eyes. And however childlike her voice, her splendid shape proclaims her most definitely a woman."

Anatole preserved a diplomatic silence.

Sheffield swore beneath his breath. "I am being a fool even to entertain thoughts of . . . We met only hours ago, I cannot possibly feel . . ." He stopped, then said stolidly, "In a day or so the weather will improve, and she will be gone."

"I believe, my lord, that the storm will be a severe one, and native members of the staff agree. Travel may not be possible for a week or longer."

"A week." There was a silence, and then the earl said, "I have been alone too long."

"Perhaps it would be more accurate, my lord, to say that you have been alone long enough."

After a moment the earl looked up at his manservant. He was frowning once again. "If you for one moment suppose that I am so lost to all sense of decency as to take advantage of a young lady under my protection—"

"No, of course not, my lord," Anatole soothed. "But to spend time with the young lady here, where all is peaceful and where there are no . . . difficulties . . . surely that is a *situation* of which to take advantage."

Sheffield's scowl faded but did not entirely disappear, and he did not reply to the comment. Instead, he pushed back his chair, rose, and spoke abruptly. "Have we supplies enough to weather the storm?"

"Yes, my lord."

The earl nodded, hesitated, then sighed a bit wearily. "I am going to bed. See that I am awakened at first light."

Scarred face still impassive, Anatole bowed. When his master had gone, he banked the fire for the night and began extinguishing candles. The building wind of the storm outside made itself heard for the first time, and as he paused to listen to the eerie sound, Anatole smiled to himself.

Cassandra slept well, though when she awoke the next morning, she had the discomfiting awareness that her dreams had been highly sensual ones. She did not remember specifics, but found it oddly embarrassing that she woke smiling.

Sarah did not seem to notice anything amiss. While Cassandra drank her morning coffee, Sarah chattered on as usual, commenting on various members of the household staff and offering her opinion that Anatole would win the conflict with Mrs. Milton, because the housekeeper had stated her intention of leaving the post she had held since the earl was a boy.

"Leaving?" Cassandra frowned at her maid. "When?"

"By spring, she said, Miss Cassie. She's all upset about it but says she can't have Anatole taking over her job, not and hold her head up."

Cassandra thought about that as she finished her coffee. It wasn't her place, of course, and the earl would probably not thank her for interfering, but she had experience directing a large household staff and was reasonably sure she could soothe Mrs. Milton's territorial spirit. She was less certain of Anatole but thought shrewdly that he would not object to her suggestions so long as he remained head of the household staff.

She rose and dressed, choosing today a subdued dress of gray merino that was rather plain but suited her coloring and figure most admirably and which was one of her warmer dresses; though the temperature inside remained comfortable, the wind could be heard from time to time, and its howling had a chilling effect upon the mind. She had ventured a look outside her bedchamber window, only to find a white world in which swirling snow hid all else, and resigned herself—with a lack of regret she knew she should find appalling—to an extended stay at the Hall.

It was still early morning when Cassandra left her room and, armed with directions from Sarah, found her way to the second-floor linen closet, where Mrs. Milton was at work sorting out pieces needing repair.

"Mrs. Milton, I am sorry to disturb you, but I just wanted to thank you for providing me with such a lovely and comfortable room."

Her sincere appreciation had the desired effect, and after no more than five minutes of casual conversation she was seated in a small parlor while the housekeeper poured out her woes to a willing and sympathetic ear. The situation was much as Cassandra had suspected; though Anatole had not, in fact, deliberately trespassed upon the housekeeper's territory, the rest of the staff recognized in him a stronger personality and a higher authority and had begun going to him for their orders. Mrs. Milton had done little to remedy the matter except to complain to some of the other staff members—which had served to lower her even more in their eyes.

Cassandra was careful to keep her suggestions thoughtful and tactful, basing them, she said, on a similar situation that had occurred in her uncle's house. By the time she was finished speaking, the housekeeper was nodding happily, convinced that only a minor adjustment or two would solve her problem.

Less than an hour after she had left her room, Cassandra found her way to the dining room where breakfast waited on the sideboard, kept warm in silver serving dishes. She helped herself, and when Anatole appeared to pour her coffee, she thanked him serenely and carried her plate to the table.

"His Lordship is doing his business accounts in his study, miss."

She hadn't asked—but she had wondered. Still composed, she merely said, "Thank you, Anatole. Pray do not disturb him on my behalf. I shall do quite well on my own. I believe I shall explore that splendid library I caught a glimpse of last night."

"An excellent idea, miss."

Cassandra was a little amused by his approval. Her first impression of him had not been good, but she was beginning to revise it—not so much because he was more polite to her now, but because she had the idea he was totally devoted to the earl—and she thought he would prove a valuable ally. . . .

Ridiculous thought. Why on earth would she need an ally in this house?

"I would like to speak to my coachman this morning," she told Anatole before he left the dining room.

He bowed. "I will bring him to the library when you have finished breakfast, miss."

He was as good as his word, delivering John Potter to the library some half an hour later and before Cassandra could do more than begin scanning the shelves. Her coachman came in, hat in hand, explaining that he was preparing to make his way to the stables where the coach had been taken.

She frowned. "It is still storming, John."

"Yes, Miss Cassie, but we've strung ropes down to the stables so nobody'll get blown away or lost—it's that bad, you can't see your hand in front of your face, I swear—an' His Lordship's man has a fire going in the stove, so we'll be snug enough. He says as how there's an old coach no longer useful, but the axle's stout enough to replace our broken one; we're going to change 'em over."

"With His Lordship's permission, I trust?"

"Oh, yes, miss."

"Excellent, John." She kept her voice cheerful. "Then we'll be able to start forward again once the storm is over and the roads are passable?"

"The coach should be repaired by the end of the day, miss. But as to the storm—I'm told it's expected to last at least another day or two, an' maybe longer. With the wind we'll have drifts as much as two or three feet deep in places."

"What are you saying, John?"

He turned his hat in his hands and sighed heavily. "I'm sorry, miss, but I wouldn't want to try pushing ahead for at least a few days after the snow stops."

"Then . . . we may be here a week?"

John Potter mistook her careful question for one of anxiety and hastened to reassure her. "As soon as the snow stops, I'll ride out an' check the roads, Miss Cassie. Maybe they'll be clearer than I expect—"

"It's all right, John, I quite understand. If we must remain here a week, then so be it." Cassandra smiled, hoping that he saw only resigned forbearance rather than the (really quite appalling) lighthearted pleasure she felt.

When she was alone once again in the library, which was a marvelous room with enough books to delight any reader, she took a more careful look around and was even more pleased by what she saw. The room was airy and more than spacious, yet as warm and snug as the rest of the house. The two tall windows were heavily curtained, effectively shutting out the sight of the storm and permitting very little of its wailing to be heard.

Cassandra, who had been raised to be self-reliant and independent and for whom reading was a particular pleasure, sighed happily and went to explore His Lordship's shelves. She quickly discovered a treasure: a recent novel she had not yet read by one of her favorite writers. Obviously, the earl also enjoyed adventurous fiction—or, at least, considered it worth adding to his library.

Ten minutes later she was comfortably seated in a chair by the fire and completely engrossed in the exciting activities of pirates sailing the high seas.

In the normal way, once Cassandra was involved in a book, it required either a loud noise or a shake to get her attention. But it appeared that she was peculiarly sensitive to the earl's presence, because even though the opening door made almost no sound at all, she looked up as if someone had shouted her name.

"Forgive me, ma'am—I didn't intend to disturb you." Back in his country buckskins, he looked unnervingly powerful as he stood in the doorway. His dark gaze was direct as ever and seemed to search her face.

"Not at all, my lord," she returned politely, using a finger to mark her place as she closed the book. "I hope you do not mind, but I took the liberty of exploring this wonderful library."

He came into the room rather slowly. "Of course I do not mind, ma'am—please feel free to explore any room you wish." His deep voice was a little abrupt.

Cassandra was oddly unwilling to allow a silence to develop between them. "My coachman tells me you have supplied an axle with which to repair my coach."

He shrugged, standing now near the fireplace and looking down on her with a very slight frown. "It is little enough, ma'am, and useless to me."

"Then why are you frowning, my lord?" She hadn't realized she was going to ask that until the question emerged.

"Was I?" His brows lifted, effectively altering his expression. "I beg your pardon. Business accounts are sometimes tiresome, ma'am."

"As are household accounts; I understand perfectly, my lord." She hesitated, then said diffidently, "Please don't feel yourself obliged to entertain me while I am here. I have no wish to disrupt the routine of the household—or your routine."

He smiled suddenly, crooked and slightly rueful. "Even if I wish it?"

Cassandra felt herself smiling back at him. It was doubtless the storm, she thought, making him feel restless and in need of companionship. That was all. But it was difficult to hide her own pleasure when she asked, "What did you have in mind, my lord?"

She felt the now-familiar fluttering sensation deep inside her for a moment, because there was something in his dark eyes she had never before seen in any man's gaze, something heated and hungry. She was suddenly conscious of her clothing touching her flesh, of the dim wail of the wind outside, and the nearer crackle and pop of the flames in the fireplace. She could feel her heart beating as if she had run a long way, and it seemed difficult to breathe all at once.

It was as if all her senses had . . . opened up. As if all her life she had seen and felt everything through a gauzy curtain until that moment when he looked at her.

There was a part of Cassandra, a rational, sensible part, which urged her to be on her guard. This, then, was his charm, it had to be—this ability to make a woman feel that no one else had ever looked at her, *seen* her. It was utterly compelling. This was the seductive power the men in his family were known to possess, the ability to enthrall a woman until she threw morals and scruples aside to do anything he wished her to do.

The sensible part of Cassandra offered that warning, but before she could make an effort to—to what? save herself?—his dark eyes were unreadable once again, and he was smiling in a perfectly polite and casual way.

"Do you play cards, ma'am?"

The written adventures of pirates held no appeal for her now, and Cassandra was barely aware of laying her book aside. "Yes," she heard herself say with astonishing calm. "Yes, my lord, I play cards."

THREE

HE TAUGHT HER a particularly intricate, often perplexing, and sometimes downright Byzantine card game which he had learned from a colorful ship's captain on a journey across the Mediterranean, and she astonished him by not only grasping the rules but soundly defeating him in only the third hand dealt.

"How on earth did you do that?" he demanded.

Briskly shuffling the cards, Cassandra showed him a mock frown and laughing eyes. "You should know, my lord. It was you who taught me the game."

"Yes, but it's the devil of a game to win," he told her frankly.

"Then we shall call it beginner's luck, sir. Did you say you learned it from a ship's captain?"

"I learned it from a rascally pirate who called himself one," the earl replied dryly. "And the bas— the ruffian emptied my pockets three nights running."

Cassandra picked up her hand and regarded him in amusement. "Does it have a name, this game?"

"None that I ever heard. In fact, I rather doubt it existed before Captain Bower invented it in order to fleece those of his passengers raw enough to sit down with him."

"I cannot imagine you being raw, my lord."

Ruefully he said, "Oh, I promise you I was. Hardly older than you are now, and not at all up to snuff. It was more than

ten years ago." He looked down at the cards he held, the
light of amusement in his eyes dimming and his mouth
hardening just a bit as his thoughts obviously turned painful
or bitter.

Before Cassandra could respond to what he had said,
Anatole came into the library where they were playing cards
and asked the earl if luncheon at twelve-thirty would be
satisfactory, and by the time he left the room, the earl's
abstraction had vanished and he was once more relaxed.
What might have been a brief opening through which she
could have learned more about his past was now firmly
closed once more.

The card game continued until lunchtime, with Cassandra
winning once more and then playing the earl to a draw.
Which meant, he said, that they were "evenly matched in
terms of possessing labyrinthine minds." Whether or not
that was true, it was obvious that each enjoyed the other's
company far beyond what was merely polite.

After luncheon they played chess in the earl's study, and
it proved another game in which they had like minds and
tendencies, both employing shrewd tactics and alert strat-
egy. And so they whiled away the stormy afternoon, pausing
from time to time in their conversation to listen to the wind
reach a crescendo and then fade away only to shriek once
again and send sleet rattling against the windowpanes.

"Nasty," Cassandra observed.

"Very. Check, ma'am."

"Now, how did you . . . Oh, I see. White must resign,
my lord, for I can see you mean to pursue my king across
the board."

"I would never be so unhandsome as that, I promise you.
Another game, ma'am?"

But the clock on the mantel chimed the hour just then,
and Cassandra excused herself in order to go upstairs to
change and freshen herself before supper. She had thor-

oughly enjoyed the day, and she returned to her room with a smile she didn't think about hiding until Sarah greeted her with anxious eyes.

"Sarah, he is a complete gentleman," she assured her apprehensive maid.

"Just be careful, Miss Cassie, that's all!"

But Cassandra only laughed, certain that her maid's fears were completely unfounded. Indeed, it seemed her own instincts were to be trusted, for the earl's behavior during the next two days was so exemplary that even Sarah seemed reassured (or, at least, she stopped issuing dire warnings). He was an entertaining and appreciative companion, forthright without being in any way offensive, and though she did not want to admit it to herself, Cassandra knew she was drawn to him in a way she had never known before.

That moment when he had looked at her with naked intensity was something she remembered far too often for her peace of mind, but it was not repeated during those days. He made more than one flattering observation, but since his comments tended to be quite casual and matter-of-fact, she could be sure of nothing except that he considered her attractive—and for all she knew he would have been just as appreciative of any personable young woman appearing on his doorstep.

It did not occur to Cassandra that the severe isolation of the storm had created a kind of refuge for both of them, and that the return of good weather might change that. All she knew was that the glittering but restrictive world of London society seemed very far away.

The storm raged outside, with a fierce wind blowing the existing snow about even when no fresh precipitation fell, and those inside the house became so accustomed to the sounds of fury that their cessation in the early evening of

Cassandra's third full day at the Hall was something of a shock.

She came downstairs after dressing for supper and found that she was early; the earl was not waiting for her. Restless, she wandered into a small salon near the earl's study, a room she had not so far explored except to note the presence of a pianoforte. There was a fire burning in the grate, though it had been allowed to die down a bit, and though the room was comfortable, it was not really warm. A candelabra set upon the pianoforte provided light that was only adequate, leaving the corners and much else of the room in shadows.

Cassandra sat down on the bench and sorted through several sheets of music until she found something familiar. She considered herself a fair musician without being in any way exceptional, and since she had had little opportunity to practice during recent weeks, her fingers felt a bit awkward on the keys. But it did not take many minutes for her to relax and find her touch, and the first tentative notes of a sonata soon became easier and more confident.

Nevertheless, due to her lack of practice, the piece required all her concentration, and she had no idea she was not alone in the room until the final notes faded into silence and he spoke.

"You play beautifully."

Startled, she half turned on the bench to find the earl standing only a few feet away. He was turned so that the light of the candelabra flickered in his eyes, making them glitter with a strange intensity.

Trying to collect herself, struggling with a curiously compelling awareness of him, she said, "Thank you, my lord." She wanted to go on, to make some innocuous comment about the excellent instrument or something equally as nonchalant, but she could not. Her throat seemed to close up, and she could feel her heart thudding.

Sheffield took a step toward her, then another, and quietly

said, "It is cool in here, ma'am, and your shawl has slipped. Permit me."

Cassandra did not move as he lifted the lacy edge of her shawl to cover her bare shoulders. The gesture was more than courtesy; his hands rested on her shoulders briefly, and she felt his fingers tighten just a little before they were removed. Then he offered his hand, silent, and she took it, turning toward him as she rose to her feet.

He didn't release her hand as he should have done, or tuck it into the crook of his arm casually. He held it and looked down at her with an expression she could not quite read in the shadows of the salon.

Cassandra did not know what was different, but she knew something was. In him or in her, or perhaps both, there was a change. The intensity of the moment lay heavily in the very air of the room, and she had the odd notion that if she moved too suddenly or spoke too hastily, something terribly rare and valuable could be destroyed.

Then Sheffield drew a quick breath, and when he spoke his voice was low and husky in a way that seemed almost a caress. "I think . . . I cannot go on calling you ma'am. Would it displease you very much if I called you Cassie?"

She shook her head just a little, unable to look away from his intent gaze. "No. No, of course it would not." Her own voice sounded so shaken she hardly recognized it.

His fingers tightened around hers, and he lifted her hand until his warm lips lightly brushed her knuckles. "Thank you, Cassie."

It wasn't the first time a man had kissed her hand, but it was the first time she had felt heat shimmer through her body in a shocking, exciting response. She knew he could feel her fingers trembling, and would not have been surprised if he could actually hear her heart beating like a drum. And the way he said her name, something in his voice, pulled at her.

Absurdly she murmured, "You're welcome, my lord."

His mouth curved in a slight smile. "My name is Stone, Cassie. A ridiculous name, I agree, but mine. If you could bring yourself to use it, I would be most pleased."

Almost imperceptibly, she nodded. "Stone."

He raised her hand to his lips again, the touch a lingering one this time as heavy lids veiled his eyes, and Cassandra felt another wave of heat when he whispered her name. Her name had never sounded like that before, tugging at all her senses and perhaps something even deeper and more basic inside her. And how odd it felt, the sensations he evoked. They seemed to spread all through her body, yet settled more heavily deep in her belly and in her breasts, until she ached.

She didn't know what, if anything, she would have said, but they heard the soft chimes of a clock in one of the nearby rooms proclaiming the hour just then, and the earl carried her hand to his arm.

"If we don't go to the dining room," he murmured, "Anatole will only come in search of us."

A bit dazed, she allowed herself to be guided toward the door, vaguely surprised that her unsteady legs could support her weight. And it was only then, as they reached the door, that she realized what was different, what had been different from the moment she had turned to find him in the room. It was a silence, a hush so absolute it seemed to have a physical presence.

"I—I don't hear the wind," she said.

He was holding her hand against his arm, and his fingers pressed hers. He looked down at her. "I know. I believe the storm is dying."

It was such a casual and ordinary thing to say, Cassandra thought, a perfectly reasonable thing to say—why did it sound so very ominous? So very disturbing? Why did she want to cry out a protest, or insist fiercely that he was wrong? Why did she suddenly feel almost frantic with anxiety?

She did not comprehend the answer to all those questions until she looked across the dining table at Sheffield some minutes later and remembered that once the storm was gone, the roads would soon be clear enough for travel . . . and she would have to leave the Hall. Her good name was already at risk because she had stayed here with him unchaperoned; if word of that should spread, the storm would probably be an acceptable justification—for now, at least, and for all the most suspicious and cynical members of the *ton*. But nothing would protect her if she remained here once the weather cleared.

She would have to leave very soon. And perhaps it should have horrified her to realize that she was more than willing to risk her reputation by remaining here—but it did not. It did not even surprise her very much.

Not after he had whispered her name.

Their conversation during supper was quieter than usual, desultory; she thought they were both very conscious of how quiet it had become outside as the storm died away. Cassandra could not seem to keep herself from stealing glances at his face, her gaze falling away swiftly whenever he chanced to look at her. He seemed somehow changed, she thought, his features not so harsh, the expression in his dark eyes direct as ever but warmer now and . . . tender?

Her imagination, most likely. She wanted to be sensible, to keep her head and not indulge in such foolish . . . imaginings. That was dangerous. She knew the pain of romantic flights of fancy brought cruelly to earth, knew that she had in the past more than once failed to judge a man accurately until his true character was revealed by his own actions. She had more than once seen her worth to a man

measured in the cold mathematical accounting of her
fortune.

But Sheffield—Stone—did not know who she really was.
Odd how she kept forgetting that. Or perhaps it was not so
odd, after all; she could not recall anyone in the house
addressing her by the name Sarah had offered since that first
evening. No one ever called her Miss Wells. She was "miss"
or "Miss Cassie," with nothing else added. And "ma'am" to
Stone, until now.

She had never discussed her background in anything but
the vaguest terms, and he had not questioned her even to ask
the name of the uncle she mentioned, so she had not been
forced to choose between the truth and more lies. But the
one great lie she had told was now weighing heavily on her.

It was when she was thinking of that during supper that
Cassandra almost confessed the truth. She even opened her
mouth to do so, but the words would not come. Not because
she feared that Stone was a fortune hunter, but because she
felt so guilty about lying.

When they left the table—earlier than usual—she had not
managed to confess and was unhappily aware of her
duplicity. She murmured an assent when the earl asked her
to play the pianoforte, but it was not until they went into the
salon serving the Hall as a music room that a flicker of
amusement lightened her mood. The room that had been so
dim and shadowed earlier was now much more inviting,
with several sconces and candelabras alight and the fire
burning briskly.

"Did Anatole know we would return here?" she asked the
earl, sitting down on the bench.

"He seems to know everything that goes on in this
house," Sheffield replied, then smiled as he leaned against
the side of the pianoforte. "I believe I have you to thank for
ending the feud between him and Mrs. Milton."

"I merely made some suggestions." Cassandra played a few notes idly, then began to pick out a soft tune from memory. "All she really needed was a sympathetic ear and someone to advise her to reclaim those areas in which she excels. After all, I doubt that Anatole *wants* to be responsible for the care of linen and the training of the housemaids—and so on."

"Very wise of you. And very much appreciated, Cassie."

She watched her fingers tremble over the keys but managed not to strike a sour note. What *was* the magic of his voice saying her name? Keeping her own voice casual, she said, "My pleasure. I must admit, I am most curious about Anatole."

"In what way?"

"He is not English, is he?"

"No, Greek." His attention caught by a smoldering log that had fallen half out onto the hearth, the earl went over to the fireplace to nudge it back into place. He remained there, leaning a forearm on the mantel and looking down at the flames. "I encountered him on that ship I told you about, the one with the rascally captain. He was the first mate."

"And you offered him a position?"

Sheffield smiled oddly as he looked across the room at her. "Nothing so ordinary, I'm afraid. Shortly after we docked in Italy, he saved my life."

Cassandra stopped playing abruptly. "He—?"

"Yes. I was set upon by thieves, and there were too many for me to handle. If not for Anatole, I would have been knifed in the back and left to bleed to death. It was the first time he saved my life—but not the last."

Obeying her instincts, Cassandra rose and went to him, halting so that they faced each other. "You must have been very young," she ventured, remembering that Anatole had been with the earl for a number of years.

"I was twenty-one." He gave her a twisted smile. "Wild

and bitter and bent on getting myself killed because I was convinced life had nothing more to offer me. God knows why Anatole chose to follow me across half the world, but he did. He kept me alive until I'd the sense to look out for myself, and after that he made himself useful—in fact, indispensable."

Cassandra studied his hard face curiously. "And you returned here—?"

"Four years ago. It took the next two years and more to get this place in some kind of order. The house had been closed up since I left England, and had been allowed to virtually fall into ruins, so I had my work cut out for me."

Which, she thought, was a fair explanation of why he had vanished so completely from the London social scene; he had been either out of England or else very much occupied here for the past ten years.

"I see," she said.

"Do you? I have not been what anyone of sense would call a suitable match for a young lady, Cassie." Matter-of-factly, Sheffield added, "I had succeeded to the title when I was nineteen, and found myself the possessor of a vanished fortune, useless properties, and a name painted black going back five generations. Naturally, it did not take long for me to add to the sins of my ancestors. I left England very much under a cloud and not quick enough to avoid the scandal I'd caused."

Cassandra had certainly been curious about his background and, in particular, the sin that had earned him the condemnation of society, but in that moment all she wanted to do was to ease the strain in his low voice.

"Stone—I heard all the rumors about you when I first came out."

He was obviously surprised, and not a little wary. "Good God, are they using the sins I committed more than ten years ago to frighten debutantes?"

She kept her voice solemn. "Oh, yes, and it's quite effective. They never explain what, exactly, you were guilty of, but then it never seems to be necessary. All those horrified whispers and sad shakes of the head are enough to cause any girl to think twice if she is contemplating some reckless act." Pondering the matter, she added thoughtfully, "I daresay you have saved any number of parents from the consequences of rash daughters. I shouldn't doubt it if they were not actually eager to welcome you back to society."

The earl smiled slightly, but his gaze was very intent on her. "I was not ostracized, you know. I can return if I choose to do so."

"I know."

"I suppose I should go back from time to time—if only to prove I lack horns and a tail."

Cassandra smiled. "Don't forget the cloven hooves."

"Has there been no other scandal in England since I sinned?" he demanded a bit ruefully.

"Not really. *I* believe it was because of the war."

"The war?"

"Yes. You see, so many of the young men were occupied with the war for so long that they simply had not the time or energy to get much tangled in scrapes and scandals."

In a grave tone he said, "I begin to see that the sin I was most guilty of was one of bad timing."

Sin. She wondered if he was fully conscious of his use of the word. "And you could hardly be blamed for that. After all, you were very young."

"Older than you are now," he retorted.

Cassandra laughed but said, "In any case, you should probably return to London society at least long enough to show that you have become perfectly respectable."

"For all you know, that might not be the case at all," the earl warned her in a voice that was not *quite* humorous. "They say some things are in the blood, and mine is certainly wicked enough to give any rational young lady pause—even without tales of my dissolute past. Perhaps I am only biding my time for my own amusement."

"Until?" she said, interested.

"Until I have . . . won your trust. It is the classic method of rakes, you know."

"Perhaps." She was smiling.

He looked into her big gray eyes and then shook his head a little in wonder. "You are not the least bit afraid of me, are you, Cassie?"

"Should I be?"

"Virtually alone with me in my house, cut off from the outside, no chaperon—"

"Should I be?" she repeated steadily.

He reached up and touched her face very gently, the very tips of his fingers tracing the delicate arch of her brow, the curve of her cheek, and the clean line of her jaw. "I would not harm you for the world."

Cassandra wondered if she was breathing, but it did not seem important. She felt feverish, yearning, vulnerable, and yet enthralled. His touch was like something she had felt in a dream, and if it was a dream, she did not want to awaken. She heard her voice and was not surprised that it was husky. "Then I have nothing to fear."

For a moment it seemed that he leaned toward her, but then his hand fell to his side and he smiled at her, only the intensity of his dark eyes hinting at something not nearly as calm as his voice when he said, "You promised to play for me."

"So I did." She turned and went back to the pianoforte, and when she began to play, she was not much surprised to realize that her fingers had selected a love song.

It was like a wonderland. Cassandra stood at the top of the front steps of Sheffield Hall and gazed around in utter delight. Snow had turned the bleak winter landscape into something so beautiful it made the heart ache. The brown grass had vanished beneath a blanket of pristine white, and the bare branches of trees seemed dressed now with their mantle of snow.

Already, the earl's servants had been at work, for the steps were swept clean of snow, and Cassandra had no fear of her footing as she closed the door behind her and set out. She was warmly dressed—and very glad of it when a sudden gust of wind snatched at her cloak as she was making her way cautiously through the uneven drifts of snow along the carriage drive toward the stables. Though the storm was apparently over, this was still winter and winter's name might have been caprice; the occasional wind was urgent in its warning that spring was far away.

Cassandra had awakened early and with the most amazing sense of energy. She had had her coffee in bed but had not yet breakfasted; Anatole had reported that the earl had gone down to the stables before his own meal, and she had instantly decided to go in search of him. She needed fresh air and the chance to get a bit of exercise, she told herself—and nearly laughed out loud at the absurdity of this attempt to delude herself.

If Sheffield had vanished into the depths of a dungeon or sallied forth to drive over a cliff, it was more than likely that she would have followed him without hesitation.

She saw her breath mist before her eyes as she did laugh out loud, and shook her head at this odd, bewitched creature she had become. It should have been appalling, she thought, or at the very least shocking, but she could not seem to summon those negative emotions. She was too happy. She wanted to smile all over, to laugh again and throw a snowball at someone.

Most of all, she wanted to see the earl.

She heard his voice only moments later when she reached

the stableyard and followed her ears to find him standing before a row of stables talking to a spare, middle-aged man who was no doubt the head groom or coachman.

"Watch his leg to make sure it doesn't swell, Flint, but if he's all right by afternoon, turn him out."

"Yes, my lord."

The earl turned then and saw Cassandra approaching, and his smile was instant as he stepped forward to meet her. "Cassie, I would have waited for you if I had known you wished to come down here."

She was only vaguely aware that the groom had gone away, all her attention focused on Sheffield. He was holding her hand, and she felt a flicker of annoyance that she was wearing gloves. "I had no notion where I would end up," she confessed. "Is it not beautiful out here? Who has hurt his leg?"

With a chuckle, the earl said, "Yes, it is beautiful—even more so now. And my favorite hack made a spirited attempt to kick down the door of his stable earlier; he dislikes storms *and* being confined for any length of time, and wants to kick up his heels in his paddock."

"Impatient as his master, I collect?"

"Now, when have I ever shown you impatience?" he demanded in a voice of mild surprise.

"That first evening," Cassandra replied promptly. "You looked at me in *such* a way, and spoke very brusquely."

"If I was brusque, I beg your pardon." He lifted her hand to his lips and kissed it. "As for how I looked at you, I can only say I was charmed and delighted to find a smoke-eyed beauty quite unexpectedly in my house."

Cassandra promised herself she was never going to wear gloves again, even if her fingers froze. She drew a breath and said rather uncertainly, "I—I see. Then I suppose I must forgive you."

"Thank you, ma'am."

"You are laughing at me," she said suspiciously.

He kissed her hand again, and there was a gleam in his dark eyes that was something more than laughter. "Never. Are you warm enough? May I show you my horses before we go back to the house?"

"I am quite warm enough, and I would love to see your horses." She smiled up at him.

He continued to hold her hand instead of tucking it into his arm, an arrangement Cassandra was delighted by. She did not even feel self-conscious when Sheffield introduced her to his head groom, Flint—but she was rather glad to be told that her coachman had borrowed a hack and ridden out first thing to check the condition of the roads just as he had said he would.

She was glad that John Potter was not confronted by the sight of her and the earl holding hands most improperly— but her coachman's eagerness to check the roads was an unwelcome reminder of time ticking away. The roads were not passable today, she knew, but what of tomorrow or the next day?

With that in her mind Cassandra's pleasure in being with the earl during the casual tour of his stables was even more precious to her than it would otherwise have been. She could not seem to get enough of hearing his deep voice or watching the changing expressions of his face (had she once thought it harsh?), and every time he said her name it was as if the sound of it touched something deep inside her.

Still, perhaps nothing irrevocable would have happened if Sheffield's favorite hack had not betrayed his native impatience by trying to ascertain if Cassandra had a lump of sugar hidden somewhere on her person. The big bay gelding nudged her so hard with his Roman nose that she stumbled back away from the stable door and would have fallen had not the earl caught her.

"Oh! My goodness, you—"

"Clumsy brute! Cassie, love, are you—"

They had spoken in the same moment, and she stared up at him as both their voices broke off. Had he said what she thought he had? He was holding her so close . . . even with his greatcoat and her cloak she could feel the hardness of his body, the warmth of him. Her hands had somehow landed on his chest, gloved fingers spread, touching him. Both his arms were around her, and then only one because he had lifted the other hand to push the hood of her cloak back and touch her face with his fingers the way he had last night in the music room.

"Cassie . . ."

It did not occur to her to push herself away, to make some attempt to stop this. It simply did not occur to her. Instead, she offered her lips in the most natural way imaginable, and when his mouth covered hers, she heard an unfamiliar little purr of pleasure in the back of her throat.

She had been kissed by boys—those eager young swains with whom she had shared country dances before her first Season—but never by a man, and the difference was shocking. His mouth was not awkward or wet and she felt absolutely no desire to burst out in giggles at the absurdity of lips pressed together; his mouth was skilled and sure, hard yet silken, and a shimmering heat ignited inside her at the first touch.

Cassandra thought she was melting. All the strength was flowing out of her legs, and the burning inside her intensified until it was a wild fever consuming her. She should have been shocked when the possessive invasion of his tongue turned the kiss into something more intimate than she had ever imagined was possible, but instead what she felt was pleasure and desire, and a dim wonder that he could make her feel this way. . . .

When Sheffield lifted his head at last, Cassandra opened her eyes dazedly, hardly aware that she had uttered a faint sound of disappointment. His eyes had a heavy, sensual look that made her pounding heart skip a beat, and she wished once again that her gloves were off so that she could touch his hard face.

He drew a slow breath, then said huskily, "I have wanted to do that since you walked toward me dressed in blue silk that first evening, so beautiful I could hardly bear it. Must I beg your pardon?"

She should have said yes, she knew, but propriety was beyond Cassandra. Far beyond her. She shook her head, unable to tear her gaze from him. "No." It was almost inaudible, and she cleared her throat to try again. "No, of course not."

His already black eyes seemed to darken even more, deepen somehow, until they were bottomless pools into which she knew she could lose herself. Into which she wanted to throw herself, body and soul. Then he bent his head again and rubbed his lips over hers in a brief, almost rough caress that was even more stirring to her senses than the prolonged kiss had been.

"For that?" he murmured.

Cassandra had the dazed notion that he was teasing her, but she was also aware that he was hardly unaffected; there was a tension in his body she could feel, and there was no disguising the hunger of his taut expression.

Her lips trembling and tingling, she whispered, "I am shameless, I know . . . but please don't beg my pardon, Stone."

Her tremulous words and guileless pleasure seemed to affect him most oddly. He moved slightly as if to kiss her again, but then his mouth firmed and he put his hands on her shoulders to ease her back away from him. A muscle flexed in his jaw, and there was a note of disbelief in his voice when he spoke.

"I must be out of my mind."

She blinked, the fingers clinging to his greatcoat beginning to slacken, but her sharp pang of hurt vanished when he continued grimly.

"A cold, drafty stable through which anyone might pass—and probably has—and I want nothing more than to find a pile of reasonably clean straw and make a bed for the two of us."

Burning color rose in her cheeks, but Cassandra was not nearly so shocked by his blunt desire as she should have been. Instead, she felt a hollow ache deep in her loins, a wild urge to cast aside every vestige of breeding and every principle of ladylike behavior by pleading with him to make that bed and carry her to it, and that shocked her more than anything.

He laughed, a low, raspy sound. "Have I shocked you?"

She caught her underlip between her teeth and felt the sensual tenderness left by his ardent kisses. "No—yes—I don't know. I cannot think."

His rather fierce expression softened, and his hands lifted to frame her hot face. "My poor darling—so bewildered." His thumb caught her bottom lip and pressed gently until it was free of her small white teeth, and the pad of his thumb rubbed back and forth slowly. "And so damnably young. I ought to be shot for taking advantage of you this way."

"Ought you?" She met his eyes steadily despite the virginal blush. "Even if—if it is what I want?"

He did not move for an instant, just looked down at her as if her honest response had stolen his breath or stopped his heart. Then, very slowly, he took his hands off her face, lifted her hood carefully to cover her raven curls, and then took one of her hands and tucked it into his arm. He was frowning slightly as he did all this, but it seemed to her a frown of concentration rather than anger, as if it required all his resolution.

"Come," he said. "We must return to the house."

"Must we?" she ventured regretfully.

"Yes," he said, his voice very rough, "we must. Before I forget you're a lady."

Stealing a glance up at his face as they walked, Cassandra wondered for the first time if being a lady might prove a definite stumbling block for a girl who wanted to become a woman.

FOUR

IT WAS NOT to be expected that their earlier relaxed companionship could remain unaffected by what had happened in the stables. Indeed, the awareness between them was so potent that Cassandra discovered only a glance from him had the power to stop her breathing, while his dark eyes instantly lit with the now familiar hot glow of desire when they met hers and his voice changed almost imperceptibly when he spoke to her.

She had the suspicion that the dusting of pink across her cheekbones that was all that remained of her blush in the stables had become a permanent thing; when she retired to her room late that evening, the face in her mirror wore it like a muted banner of sensual awakening. And her eyes seemed different, larger and more brilliant, she thought, gazing at her reflection as Sarah took down her hair and brushed it. *Smoke-eyed* he had said. A smoke-eyed beauty.

He *had* called her love. And his poor darling. And for the rest of the day, that note in his voice, husky and caressing, whenever he spoke to her.

Normally a young woman who was very sure of herself, Cassandra was both excited and bewildered by the earl and by her own feelings, and though she felt few doubts or hesitations when she was with him, alone in her bed that night she tossed and turned restlessly. Her body was feverish, her mind troubled.

They had gone for a walk in his snow-covered garden after breakfast, taking care in the drifts and attempting to guess what plants lay beneath odd-shaped humps of snow. He had held her hand, and once caught her when she would have slipped, but there were no more kisses or thrillingly blunt statements of desire.

John Potter found them there when he came to report the impassable condition of the surrounding roads, and though Cassandra tried hard, she was afraid her voice betrayed the relief she felt at knowing they could not leave just yet. Sheffield did not comment on the information other than to say calmly that it would likely be another day or two before travel was possible, and when they were alone together again he talked of other things.

The remainder of the day was much as the previous ones had been, with amusing card games and conversation and chess to occupy them—but when Cassandra went upstairs to change for the evening, he stood in the entrance hall and watched her go up; she could feel his eyes on her. And just before she retired to her room much later, she had accidentally (she assured herself) brushed against him as she rose from her chair; he had caught her in his arms and kissed her almost violently, and Cassandra had melted against him with a murmur of pleasure.

"This must stop," the earl told her fiercely, giving her bare shoulders a little shake and then kissing her again.

"Must it?" Her fingers clung to his lapels, but she wanted to burrow closer to his hard body, to slip her arms around him and press herself against him. The urge was shocking, and she did not care.

Sheffield half closed his eyes as he looked down at her, his face a hard mask. "Yes, dammit." But instead of shaking her once more, his fingers probed the delicate bones of her shoulders, then followed the graceful length of her neck upward until his hands cradled each side of her face and his thumbs gently smoothed the heated skin over her cheek-bones.

Without thought she moved her head a little so that she could feel the slightly rough texture of his palms. She was dizzy, excited, yearning, and half-frightened all at once, *wanting* without being able to put a name to what it was she craved so terribly.

"Cassie . . ." He bent his head to kiss her, his tongue sliding deeply into her mouth, stroking hers in a secret, erotic duel that made the fever inside her burn even hotter. Learning rapidly, she responded with a swift and total abandon, and his mouth was wild on hers for a moment before he jerked his head up and ground out a curse so savage it cut through the daze of her need.

She blinked at him uncertainly. "Stone?"

He gave her a fierce look that seemed to her to hold reluctance but something else as well. Anger? Bitterness? Whatever it was, she had little opportunity to try and understand it. He took his hands off her and stepped back until they were no longer touching. Then he drew a breath and said politely, "Good night, Cassie."

So she had left him, retreating to her room in some confusion, and now she tangled the bedclothes with her restless tossing and turning. Her body ached, and she could not stop thinking, suddenly worrying.

After all that had happened between them, Sheffield had not uttered a single word about the future. He had called her love, yes, and his poor darling—but did it signify anything? How could she be certain, after all, that what he said to her and the way he kissed and touched her was important to him? She had heard it said that, for a man, there could most certainly be passion without love. According to the discreet murmurs of older women, many men were held to make love with ease and without real meaning—what if Stone Westcott was such a man?

He certainly had the blood of rakes in his veins—as he had warned her himself—but did that automatically mean he could feel nothing but passion for her?

She did not know. But he had not so much as hinted there might be a future for them together, and Cassandra was very much afraid that *did* mean something.

He greeted her quietly but with shuttered eyes and an impassive expression at breakfast, and Sheffield spent that morning and much of the afternoon closeted in his study with his estate agent. That was neither unusual nor unexpected, since storms tended to cause problems on any large estate, and those would need to be reported to the earl and remedies planned. Cassandra did not resent the duties that occupied him—but she wished they could have been postponed a few days.

Even one day might have made a difference, because she was much afraid that was all the time she had left. The temperature had warmed during the afternoon so that the snow was already beginning to melt, and John Potter had offered his opinion that travel might be possible as early as the following day. The main roads were clearing rapidly; the mail had gone through, and the Bristol Light Post Coach as well, so that was strong evidence of improving conditions.

John had the coach repaired; the horses were rested; the weather was breaking. She would have to leave.

From the astonishing, dizzying pleasure and excitement of the previous day to the anxiety and fears of this day was such a plummeting drop Cassandra felt almost ill with reaction. She managed to keep herself occupied during the day but acknowledged to herself the uselessness of it when she realized she had read the entire pirate adventure and could not recall a single word of the story.

The earl was still shut in his study when she went disconsolately upstairs to change for the evening, and when the tall case clock on the landing chimed the hour cheerfully, she wanted to kick it. There were clocks *everywhere* in this dratted house, and all of them insisted on reminding her of the passage of time.

"Miss Cassie—will we be leaving soon?"

She thought that Sarah's voice was just a trifle too disinterested (considering her worries earlier), but Cassandra was putting tiny diamond drops in her earlobes and didn't look at her maid when she replied calmly, "I believe so. The roads are clearing, and so we should be on our way."

"To Bristol, miss?"

"Perhaps. Or back to London." She had lost her desire to continue on and felt the need to return to her uncle's cheerful house in Berkeley Square.

Sarah said no more, and Cassandra tried not to think of tomorrow as she went back downstairs. She had rather defiantly chosen to wear the blue silk dress again, her lace shawl draped across her shoulders, but when she went into the drawing room where they met before supper, he was not there.

Sighing, she went to stand before the fireplace, head bent as she gazed down at the flames, and when she heard his voice a few minutes later, it required every ounce of her control to keep from flinging herself into his arms.

"Good evening, Cassie." He closed the door behind him as he came in, then moved to stand at the fireplace so that they faced each other.

No one else had ever made her name sound that way, and she felt an absurd prickle of tears that she fiercely blinked away before meeting his gaze. "Good evening." Her voice was calm; what an actress she seemed to be! "I trust the storm did no lasting damage to your estate?"

"No, nothing that cannot be repaired." He was frowning

a bit, obviously preoccupied, and his eyes were still shuttered.

Cassandra wondered if he had even noticed the blue silk dress he had said made her look beautiful. She made her voice light and careless. "I believe I may be able to travel by tomorrow. John Potter reports that the main road is in quite good shape, so we shall only have to take care until we reach it."

"On to Bristol?" The earl spoke slowly, and his frown appeared to deepen.

"Oh—back to London, I think. I am promised to at least three balls after next week, and might as well return in time to attend them."

He nodded. "It is just as well you mean to go, Cassie," he said in a very deliberate tone. "These past days . . . shut off from outside contact and thrown together as we have been—"

However he might have finished what he meant to say, Cassandra was left with only painful conjecture when a sudden bustle of noise from the entrance hall caused Sheffield to break off abruptly and start toward the drawing room door.

"What the devil?"

Cassandra was feeling numb, hardly interested in visitors, but when the drawing room doors were thrust open before the earl could reach them and a woman swept in still speaking over her shoulder to Anatole, she could not help arriving at the forlorn conclusion that she was being punished.

"Oh, don't be absurd, Anatole—we hardly need announcing in my own brother's drawing room!" Lady Harleston, the wife of the vague but amiable Lord Harleston, sailed into the drawing room as if it were her own, with her much quieter husband following. She was a tall woman in her late thirties, quite handsome in a decided rather than pretty way, several years older than her brother, and it was immediately apparent that between them flourished a somewhat bristly tolerance rather than warm affection.

"Althea, what the devil are you doing here?" the earl demanded grimly.

"A fine welcome, I must say! When we took the time and trouble to get off the main road—on our way back to London, you know—only to make certain the storm left you and the Hall still standing!"

"As you can see, we stand," Sheffield retorted. "Hello, Jasper."

"Evening, Stone. Sorry to drop in on you like this, but Althea would have it you was frozen in a drift and needed to be dug out." Lord Harleston smiled, as good-natured as his wife was sharp-tongued.

"It would have suited me better," the earl said, "if she had waited until the spring thaw to look for me."

Lord Harleston's responsive chuckle broke off abruptly as he saw Cassandra—who had stood perfectly still and hoped she would pass unseen. His mild blue eyes widened, and he looked at the earl in some surprise, but before he could speak, Lady Harleston also took notice of her brother's guest.

"Why, is that you, Miss Eden?" she demanded, striding forward to shake hands briskly.

"How do you do, Lady Harleston," Cassandra murmured, hoping wistfully that all this would—somehow!—turn out right.

"How do *you* do is the question I want answered," Her Ladyship replied with all her brother's bluntness and none of his humor or charm. "Were you not supposed to be fixed at Bristol until next week? What on earth are you doing here at the Hall?"

It was the earl who replied, his voice unusually flat. "The lady's coach broke down, Althea."

"Today?" Her Ladyship demanded to know.

Deliberately he replied, "No. A few days ago at the beginning of the storm."

Cassandra had stolen one glance at Sheffield's face, and that had been enough. He had not missed his sister's use of the name Eden, and obviously realized he had been lied to; his expression matched his name, and his eyes were completely unreadable. Cassandra wished the floor would open up and swallow her, and be done with it.

Lady Harleston, shocked, exclaimed, "Days ago? And she has been here unchaperoned? Stone, what can you have been thinking of? A child of her age—with a man of your reputation! Do you for one moment think anyone would believe it innocent? When word of this reaches London—"

"Althea," her husband warned softly.

But Lady Harleston finished her warning defiantly: "—she will be ruined!"

There was an awful silence that seemed to Cassandra to last an eternity. Then she squared her shoulders and, without looking at the earl, said quietly, "If our society believes that a lady may not take shelter from a vicious storm in the home of a gentleman without sacrificing her reputation and marring his, then it is not a society of which I wish to be a part."

Lady Harleston glared at her brother. "Say something!"

The clock on the mantel chimed. Unemotionally the earl said, "Will you join us for supper, Althea? Jasper? I am sure Anatole has set two more places."

By the time Cassandra retired to her room several hours later, her nerves were so strained by the effort of preserving a composed front before the earl and his guests that all she wanted to do was crawl between the covers and indulge in a passionate bout of tears. *He* had seemed perfectly calm, of course, fielding his sister's insistent questions by simply refusing to discuss Cassandra's presence in his house, but Cassandra was exhausted.

Sheffield had made no effort to speak to her alone; in fact, he had hardly spoken to her at all. Whether he was furious over her using a false name, disturbed by the unexpected arrival of Lord and Lady Harleston, or simply impatient with the entire situation was not clear. He had retired behind a wall of remoteness, and what his thoughts were behind that impenetrable barrier was very much his own secret.

Now, in her bedroom, Cassandra changed from the blue silk dress into her nightgown and wrapper and allowed Sarah to take her hair down. But she did not want to be fussed over tonight and was about to dismiss her maid when there was a soft knock and Lady Harleston came in. She was not yet dressed for bed and seemed to take no notice of Cassandra's attire.

"May I speak to you, my dear?" she inquired briskly.

It was the last thing Cassandra wanted, but common courtesy forced her to dismiss Sarah with a nod and murmured, "Of course, Lady Harleston."

The earl's sister sat down on a chair near the dressing table and, as soon as the maid had gone, said, "I know we are barely acquainted, but this *is* my brother's house, and since you have no older female to advise you in this situation—"

"My lady, I thank you for your concern, but I assure you I require no advice." Cassandra kept her voice steady and met the other woman's eyes as directly as she could manage. "I took shelter here because there was no place else I could go under the circumstances, and I remained during the storm because I had no other choice. Lord Sheffield has been a most kind and hospitable host, for which I am most grateful."

Lady Harleston nodded but with an expression that said she had expected to hear such platitudes. "I have no doubt that *you* considered the circumstances innocent, Miss Eden, and I am perfectly aware you had little choice in the matter. However, the fact remains that you have spent several nights unchaperoned under my brother's roof."

Evenly Cassandra said, "During which time I had no need to lock my bedroom door, my lady. We may have been alone together upon occasion, but there were always servants about." Tactful servants. Not that she cared what they may have seen. She shut from her mind the aching memory of soul-wrenching kisses and forced herself to go on speaking what was nevertheless the literal truth. "I have not been compromised, and I refuse to behave as if I have. I cannot believe any right-thinking person could possibly condemn me, or blame the earl, for a situation which was not of our making."

Lady Harleston shook her head. "My dear, you've *been* in London this last year and more, and I've the suspicion you have more sense than most, so let us speak frankly."

Just the possibility of the earl's sister speaking more frankly than she already had was rather terrifying, and Cassandra tried to stem the flow. "My lady—"

She was ignored.

"It's never been forgotten that he ruined a girl more than ten years ago; I know you've heard the tales."

"Yes, but—"

"She was an heiress, did you hear that? And him with mortgaged estates and a borrowed coach he carried her off in, as well as the reputation of a rake, even though he was hardly more than a boy himself. Her brother was hours behind them, and when he caught up to them at an inn on the North Road, well . . . it was too late."

"Too late?" Cassandra assumed Lady Harleston meant that the couple had spent an unchaperoned night at the inn. "To travel together, even so far, and spend a night in the same inn—"

"In the same bed," the earl's sister said bluntly.

Cassandra stared at her for a moment, not as shocked as she should have been because she herself had learned firsthand just how effortlessly a Westcott man could seduce. She drew a breath and murmured, "And he refused to marry her."

"No."

"But—the tales—everyone believes—"

"I know what everyone believes." Lady Harleston's voice was matter-of-fact now. "My brother had too much pride and was too much a gentleman to set the wagging tongues aright, and I was already married with a household of my own and didn't find out the truth until much later."

"Then—what happened?" Cassandra was too curious not to ask.

"Stone was head over heels in love with that chit, didn't care a button for her fortune. He was wild then, quick-tempered and tempestuous like all the Westcott men when they're young, and I have no doubt the girl was carried away by all the high drama of being pursued by such a romantic figure. In any event, Stone offered for her, and though I don't know what precisely passed between them, I do know that her brother refused the suit harshly. It seemed he preferred something other than an impoverished earl for a brother-in-law. A likely guess is that he wished to control her fortune himself and had no intention of handing her over to a husband in need of money."

Lady Harleston sighed. "Naturally, Stone was enraged by the refusal. He managed to convince the girl to run away with him, and they set out for Gretna Green in a borrowed coach. Very bad, of course, but he *did* fancy himself in love and certainly would have married the chit, so if it had ended as planned the scandal wouldn't have been so bad. But it did not end as planned."

Obviously less prim than most ladies of the *ton*, the earl's sister added thoughtfully, "I suppose they were both of them carried away by the high drama of it all, and since they expected to be married right afterward, it must have seemed foolish to wait to have each other. Or perhaps he seduced her—though, to her credit, the girl never made that claim, at least not publicly."

Slowly Cassandra said, "Her brother found them—together?"

"No, for Stone had gone to a nearby livery stable to arrange for a better team of horses. What the brother found was his no-longer-innocent sister in a tumbled bed. She confessed quick enough, and tearfully I imagine—but what I can't be sure of is whether he took her away by force or she went willingly. When Stone followed them back to London—more high drama!—he was told the girl was betrothed to a nabob friend of the brother's twenty years her senior."

"How could she—?"

"I don't know. Nor do I know why the nabob overlooked her rather profound indiscretion—unless, of course, he had no idea she had actually given herself to Stone. I suppose the girl was swayed by her brother, or even forced by him, to turn Stone away, but he has always refused to talk about it, and only the two of them and the brother likely know the whole truth."

Cassandra swallowed hard. "I heard . . . there was a duel."

Lady Harleston nodded. "The brother would have preferred to avoid more doings sure to reach the ears of the *ton*, I'm sure, but Stone was past reason. I believe he offered what the gentlemen consider unpardonable offense, and they met a few days later. Both were wounded—Stone only slightly, but the brother nearly bled to death. Of course, gossip was rampant, and with the brother badly wounded and the girl sent off with telling speed to marry her nabob and go abroad to live, Stone was the only principal upon whom society could pile its condemnation. The brother left soon after to live abroad himself."

After a silent moment Cassandra said, "Stone—the earl left England after that?"

Lady Harleston did not appear to notice the slip. "Yes, that summer. I believe he has seen much of the world in his travels. He returned only a few years ago, and since then he has worked to restore the hall." She paused, then said, "He should have reappeared in society, of course, and quieted if not silenced the wagging tongues, but he did not. So the tales grew wilder, and in them he was painted blacker. You know as well as I that he is still seen as a rake at the very least."

Cassandra drew a breath. "Even so, I refuse to behave as if I have done something wrong."

"My dear, you know word of your stay here will reach London eventually. Jasper and I can be trusted to keep silent, you may be sure, but servants talk. Tradesmen come to the door, deliveries are made, gossip is exchanged—and before you can say scat, garbled bits of information take on a life of their own. What was, in fact, understandable and perfectly innocent will never be seen as such. If Stone cares a jot about his reputation I have never seen it, but you must care for yours. Your fortune and standing in society may protect you from open hostility, but you will be called upon to pay some price for this, my dear."

I already have. But Cassandra did not say those words, of course. Instead, she said steadily, "What would you have me do, my lady? Insist that your brother make me an offer so that we may forestall vulgar speculation?"

"Why not?"

Lifting her chin, Cassandra said, "Because it is very obviously not what he wishes to do, ma'am!"

"What about what you wish him to do?"

Cassandra felt heat sweep up her face but managed to keep her voice calm. "He has been very kind, but—"

"Oh, don't talk such nonsense! I believe it is said that love and a cough can't be hidden—and I am neither blind nor stupid. You watched him all evening, and if ever I saw her heart in a woman's eyes, I saw yours!"

Shaken, Cassandra could only murmur, "Whatever I may feel, my lady, I nevertheless refuse to force any man to marry me."

"He is not a fortune hunter," his sister declared, "so you need not worry about that. I don't understand how it came about, but Jasper says Stone turned his West Indian properties to the good after years of neglect, and so recouped much of the fortune our father ran through."

Cassandra was glad of that for his sake but shook her head slightly. "You have no need to tell me that, my lady. But I will not marry to protect my reputation. Tomorrow I will return to London, where I will tell my aunt and uncle the circumstances of my stay here."

"Sir Basil won't like it," Lady Harleston said shrewdly.

Conjuring a smile, Cassandra said, "Perhaps not, but I manage my own life. If there is talk, I will deal with it in my own way. And that way does not include marrying any man to suit society's notions of propriety."

The older woman eyed her for a moment, then rose with a gusty sigh. "It's a great pity, Miss Eden; I believe you and my brother would deal extremely well together."

Cassandra felt the sting of tears and blinked them away. Quietly she said, "Good night, Lady Harleston."

"Good night, Miss Eden."

When she was alone in her bedroom again, Cassandra sat there at her dressing table for a long time gazing at nothing. She thought she understood a few things now, the information supplied by Lady Harleston having drawn a clearer picture for her.

Sheffield must have loved that girl very much. Perhaps he still loved her; he certainly felt some bitterness or anger about that episode of his life. It hardly mattered. His attitude toward Cassandra today, as well as what he had said just before Lord and Lady Harleston had arrived, demonstrated his true feelings for her quite clearly.

"It is just as well you mean to go, Cassie. These past days . . . shut off from outside contact and thrown together as we have been—"

She really did not need to hear the rest. He did not want another chit of a girl losing her head and ruining his life a second time, obviously. And who could blame him for that? She had lied to him about her identity, had virtually thrown herself at him in the most wanton, unprincipled way . . . He had known how she felt, of course, even his *sister* had seen it, and this older earl, with his experience of flighty girls with fickle hearts, had decided to take no chances that Cassandra's foolishly romantic imaginings could cause him trouble.

Desire was one thing—love quite another.

Cassandra let herself cry a little, but not for long. She had too much to do, and very little time in which to do it. She dried her eyes and rang for Sarah, and when her maid appeared, said, "Sarah, can you contrive to get a message to John tonight without alerting the Hall staff?"

Bewildered, Sarah said, "Yes, Miss Cassie, but—"

"I want you to do so. Tell him we are leaving here at first light and returning to London. Ask him to bring the coach around to the front, as quietly as possible, and *not* to rap on the door if we are not already waiting. You and I will carry what baggage we can—the rest can be sent."

Sarah was staring at her.

Cassandra passed a hand across her brow and sighed. She was so very tired. "I am sorry to keep you working so late,

Sarah, but we shall have to pack tonight, and we must be ready before dawn."

"It's quite all right, miss," Sarah said mechanically.

"Thank you. Go and talk to John now, if you please—we have a great deal to do."

While her maid went to advise the coachman, Cassandra found paper and ink and concentrated fiercely on composing a suitable note for the earl.

The snow crunched softly but otherwise muffled the sounds of the coach and horses, and in the gray light of dawn Cassandra left Sheffield Hall. She looked out the coach window until the huge house was lost to sight, then settled back against the cushions with a weary sigh.

How strange it was to know that her life had been forever changed in less than a week. That *she* had been changed. A broken axle and a winter storm—fate's tools.

And now it was past. She had done the best thing possible by leaving this way. She would return to London, and if there should be talk about her stay at the Hall, she would hold her head up and reply calmly to any remarks addressed to her. And if, after the Season was done, she was unable to bear it any longer, she could retreat to either her uncle's country home or her own and have the satisfaction of knowing she had stood firm.

When Cassandra heard a miserable sniff, she thought at first it was her own. But then she turned her head to find Sarah trying to inconspicuously blot her damp cheeks with a square of equally damp linen.

"Sarah? Why, what is wrong?"

Her gray eyes red-rimmed, Sarah blinked several times, then blew her nose fiercely and very nearly wailed, "Anatole!"

Blankly Cassandra repeated, "Anatole?"

Sarah nodded.

"Oh, Sarah—do you mean to say that you and Anatole—"

With another watery sniff, the maid said, "I didn't mean for it to happen, Miss Cassie, but I just couldn't help it."

"But I thought you were afraid of him."

"Only at first, miss. But that scar isn't so bad once you get accustomed to it, and he has the *kindest* eyes. And such a deep, strong voice."

"I see."

The maid smiled somewhat mistily. "I was stiff with him at first, but he didn't let *that* go for long. With the Hall closed up against the storm and you and His Lordship spending so much time together, we just seemed to keep meeting each other here and there, and so we'd talk. He told me the most wonderful stories about places across the oceans. And it seemed so natural somehow, the way I felt . . . and the way he did . . ."

"Sarah, you haven't—you didn't—"

"Oh, *no,* miss! I'm a good girl—and he never treated me like anything else. Never. I think—I believe he would have asked me to marry him, but . . ."

"But I had to drag you away. I am sorry, Sarah, truly. I had no idea." She sighed, wondering why she was so surprised. If she could fall in love in less than a week, then why not Sarah?

"Miss Cassie? Do you think His Lordship might have a notion to come to London?"

Cassandra looked into that hopeful face and couldn't find it in her heart to say what she believed—that Sheffield would very likely avoid London at all costs. "I . . . don't know, Sarah. Perhaps."

But as the coach reached the main road and picked up speed, Cassandra gazed out the window and the passing landscape and wondered if it was only Sarah whose hopes she was so reluctant to dash. Did she—*could* she—still have hopes of her own? Could she possibly imagine that Stone would leave his restored estate and return to the society that had denounced him only because she was there?

Could she possibly be that foolish?

FIVE

"EXCUSE ME, MISS Cassie, but there is a gentleman to see you."

Cassie looked up from the stack of invitations and notes in her hand and frowned at her uncle's butler, Gargary. "I told you I am not at home—"

"Yes, miss, but the gentleman was most insistent," Gargary said with a slight bow, keeping to himself the knowledge of the very handsome sum bestowed on him by this insistent gentleman.

"Who is he?"

"He did not give his name, miss."

Cassandra felt her heartbeat quicken and wondered with despair if she would go on forever reacting this way to no more than the possibility of seeing Sheffield. Back in London for nearly two weeks now, she had tensed at the first step of every caller and searched every face she saw on the streets, but there had been no sign of him.

Now she realized she was rising and nodding mechanically to the butler. "Very well, then. I will—I will see him."

"In the front parlor, miss."

She paused to check her appearance in the mirror beside the door of her sitting room and was surprised to find that the dusting of pink across her cheekbones had returned. She had believed that she had left it at Sheffield Hall, that evidence of awakened sensuality, but now the delicate color bloomed, making her eyes sparkle and diminishing the wan look she had worn for so many days. She smoothed her hands down the bodice of her simple morning dress of dove gray, aware that she had lost a few pounds she could ill-afford to lose since returning to London.

Not that her visitor would notice, of course, because it would not be him. It was never him.

She went downstairs, her pace deliberate, and paused before the parlor door for an instant to gather herself. Then she opened the door and went in. "Good after—" Her voice broke off, and suddenly it seemed almost impossible to breathe.

He turned from the window, where he had been gazing out into the street, and something flared in the depths of his black eyes when he saw her. Immediately he came toward her, an unnervingly powerful man who seemed to fill the room with his presence. When he reached her, he held out a hand imperatively, and without a thought she put hers into it.

He bent slightly to brush his lips against her knuckles in a gesture far too intimate for a social greeting, but his voice was calm when he said, "Hello, Cassie."

Since it didn't seem he was going to release her hand, Cassandra pulled it gently away. She did not want to, and she felt bereft when the contact was broken, but she could not think when he touched her, and she needed to think. She eased past him and walked to a chair near the fireplace; she did not sit down, but rested her hands on the back as she looked at him. "I—am surprised to see you here, my lord," she said formally.

Sheffield closed the door she had left half open, then leaned back against it and met her gaze. Those dark, direct eyes were fixed on her face. "Are you? I came to deliver the baggage you left behind at the Hall," he said.

"Oh." She saw him smile at her deflated syllable, and

fought a sudden wild urge to throw something for the first time in her life. Apparently, her mother's half-French temperament was alive in her—and had needed only this utterly maddening man to bring it to the fore.

"And for a few answers," he added, pushing himself away from the door and coming to stand at the fireplace. He eyed the chair she had placed between them like a shield, and his mouth quirked again in that smile of amusement.

Cassandra lifted her chin. "Answers?"

"Well, I have a number of questions," he said casually.

"Oh?" She tried to make her voice haughty.

"Certainly. For instance, I would like to know why you had to carry off your maid just when Anatole was fixing his interest with her."

Cassandra blinked. "You knew?"

"Didn't you?"

"No. That is—"

Sheffield shook his head. "Well, never mind. Now that I plan to be settled here in town for a while, I depend upon you to allow Sarah to see Anatole. He was a confirmed bachelor, you see, and fell very hard for her. I believe that is usually so whenever one has . . . given up all hope for love."

Her throat seemed to close up, and Cassandra hardly knew what to say. "I—I would never stand in their way if—"

He bowed slightly. "Thank you, on behalf of Anatole."

She nodded. "Um . . . you said you had questions?"

"You left the Hall so abruptly we had no opportunity to talk," he reminded her. "In fact, you slipped away at dawn, without a word."

"My note—"

"Yes, your note—shall I tell you what it said? I have it memorized, you know." He leaned his powerful shoulders back against the mantel and crossed his arms over his chest, gazing at her unreadably. "It said: 'My Lord, thank you very much for your hospitality and your kindness in providing shelter from the storm. I am most grateful. I regret being unable to say goodbye to you in person, but I feel sure you agree that it is best I return to London immediately.' And it was signed: Cassandra Eden.''

He *had* memorized it. Cassandra cleared her throat. "Well, then? What questions could you possibly—"

"I think we can begin with your name. Why did you give me a false one?"

That was a question she had expected, and she answered it honestly. "Sarah gave it, because Anatole frightened her when he first opened the door and because she knew your reputation. I kept up the lie because . . . oh, at first because I was weary of—"

"Fortune hunters?"

She nodded. "The longer I kept up the lie, the more impossible it seemed to tell the truth, so I just put it out of my head."

It was impossible to tell if he believed or disbelieved her, or even if he felt anything at all about the matter; he merely nodded and said matter-of-factly, "Did you believe I was a fortune hunter?"

Cassandra hesitated. "No, not really—not after I got a good look at the Hall. It seemed to me you had no need to dangle after an heiress."

He nodded again. "I see. That seems reasonable enough. Now for the next question. Why, Cassie?"

"I beg your pardon?"

"Why?" His voice was infinitely patient. "Why did you feel it necessary to bolt for London at dawn?"

This was an answer that was more complicated. "The storm was past, the roads clear. I—I had told you I meant to go. There was—there was no reason for me to remain any longer."

"Was there not?"

Cassandra struggled silently for a moment, then blurted, "You did not discourage me when I said I meant to go! In fact, you said—"

"I know what I said," he interrupted. "And what you obviously do *not* know is why I said it. It is a pity we were interrupted before I could explain myself."

Back in control, she said stiffly, "I believe the reason is clear, sir, and required no further explanation. You as good as said that the—the attraction we felt for each other was due to the circumstances of our being thrown together by the storm."

"And did you believe that was true?" he asked politely.

Staring into his eyes, she saw a flicker of something she dared not try to define. But it roused a tiny spurt of hope in her, and it forced her to say hesitantly, "I—I thought you believed it."

In a very deliberate tone he said, "What I believed was that you should leave as soon as possible—for three reasons. Because you were unchaperoned. Because the storm *had* isolated us and quite possibly led you to believe you felt more for me than you actually did. And because I no longer trusted myself not to accept what you offered me so passionately with every look, every touch, and most especially every kiss."

She blinked at that last candid statement, knowing without a doubt that she was blushing furiously. But before she could either deny his words or somehow defend herself, she found herself caught by his intent gaze. The flicker in his night-black eyes had become the heated look that was achingly familiar to her, like the sensual curve of his lips and the faint rasp in his low voice. She felt her heart skip a beat and then begin to pound unevenly, and heat was rushing through her body even before he came to her and pulled her into his arms.

All the long days without him had only sharpened the need he had created in her, and Cassandra molded herself to him instantly, her mouth wild and eager under his, her arms slipping up around his neck in total surrender. He crushed her against his powerful length, his arms fierce and his mouth ruthless as it plundered hers. And when he jerked his head up at last, his eyes were brilliant with fire and ferocity.

"Do you understand now?" he demanded roughly. One of his hands slid down her back to her hips, and he pressed her lower body hard against his. "Do you?"

Cassandra caught her breath, dizzy from his kisses and the shockingly intimate awareness of his blatant arousal. Her body was trembling and she thought all her bones had melted. She could only stare up at him, mute, electrified, and enthralled.

His embrace gentled, his hands stroking up and down her back slowly, and his lips feathered over her flushed, heated face. "I wanted you so badly I knew it was only a matter of time before I lost my head," he muttered.

When he drew back just a bit to look down at her again, she touched his cheek with wondering fingers, and a tremulous smile curved her kiss-reddened lips. "That was why you were so—so distant that last day? Why you said I should go?"

"Yes." He turned his head to kiss her palm lingeringly. "Cassie, you were under my protection. I may spring from a long line of rakes, but only a monster would take advantage of a girl under such circumstances. And—"

"And?" she prompted.

He hesitated, then said, "At twenty-one I fancied myself in love, but what I discovered was that to one so young, powerful emotions are often something entirely different from what one supposes. I wanted to make certain you had the time to consider what you felt, Cassie, before anything irrevocable happened between us."

She frowned a little. "Is that why you waited all these days, leaving me to wonder if I would ever see you again?"

He bent his head and kissed her in apology, leisurely this time but with unmistakable hunger. When he raised his head, she was trembling again, and his voice was hoarse. "Can you forgive me for that? I promise you, it was the most difficult thing I have ever done in my life to stay away from you."

Cassandra drew a shaky breath. "I—I suppose I shall have to forgive you."

He chuckled, then gently drew her arms down and stepped back, holding her hands in his. Reluctance was clear in his eyes. "If I do not leave you now, I will not be able to."

"I suppose you . . . could not stay," she ventured.

Bluntly Sheffield said, "However willing your uncle is to allow you to manage your own life, my darling, I doubt very much that he would be sympathetic if he found me making love to you under his roof."

She found herself both smiling and blushing, pleased by his frank talk of his desire for her even as she was a little embarrassed—or thought she should be.

He smiled at her. "Do you attend the St. Valentine's Day Ball tomorrow night?"

"Yes."

"Good. Save all the dances for me."

She nodded without hesitation, but couldn't help saying, "I won't see you before then?"

Sheffield smiled but shook his head. "There are things I must attend to. Remember, it has been quite a few years since I've been in town during the Season."

Cassandra nodded reluctantly in understanding, and she managed not to throw herself back into his arms when he kissed each of her hands and then released them. She didn't object when he said goodbye, but when he reached the door, she said, "Stone?"

One hand on the knob, he turned to look at her.

Burning her bridges, Cassandra said steadily, "I am very sure of how I feel—I want you to know that. I fell in love with you that first night."

She had no idea what was in her eyes when she said it, what expression she wore, but whatever the earl saw caused him to release the doorknob and take a jerky step back toward her—and his face was taut with hunger.

He stopped, struggled visibly with his baser instincts, then muttered, "My God, Cassie—you'd tempt a saint," before jerking open the door and striding from the room.

Sir Basil, who had received the news of Cassandra's stormbound stay at Sheffield Hall philosophically, reacted to the news of the earl's return to London with characteristic perception. When Cassandra very casually mentioned after supper that evening that Sheffield had called upon her in the afternoon (since the earl had not stated his intentions in so many words, she was hesitant to inform her uncle that she was being courted), Sir Basil looked very hard across the dining table at his niece.

"I somehow doubt Sheffield's come to London to be measured for a new pair of boots, not when he's avoided the place for the better part of ten years. Should I expect a visit from him, Cassie?"

She hesitated, then replied, "I don't know."

His brows flew up. "You don't know if he means to offer for you?"

Candidly she said, "I don't know if he would ask your permission to offer for me."

Lady Weston, who sat opposite her husband, said, "Dear me," quite placidly and looked at Cassandra with interest. "You never seemed to wish to discuss it, dearest, but we gathered you had formed an attachment for the earl. You were so careful to barely mention him, you know, and that is always a dead giveaway. And then, naturally, we've noticed your low spirits since you came back to town."

Sir Basil, dryly, said, "Quite different from tonight, in fact. A blind man could see how you feel about the man, so I hope you don't intend to try keeping it a secret."

Cassandra smiled on them both, immensely grateful for their love and trust in her judgment. "People will probably talk," she said ruefully. "Even if there is no gossip about my stay at the Hall, I have a notion that Stone has no intention of being . . . circumspect in his attentions. And since he has been away from society for so long—"

"He will definitely be under observation," Sir Basil finished. "Some will call him a fortune hunter, you know; even a man with adequate funds risks that when he pays his addresses to an heiress."

"They may just as easily reproach me and say I wished only to be a countess," she commanded in a dry tone.

"Very true, I suppose. But more likely to go the other way. Will that disturb you, Cassie?"

Cassandra smiled faintly. "No, why should it? I know he is indifferent to my fortune."

Sir Basil eyed her thoughtfully. "You do, do you?"

"Oh, yes." There was something of her aunt's utter placidity in that response, and her uncle looked satisfied; when Eden women had at last made up their minds and were certain of something—of anything—they were invariably right.

It was a family trait that Sheffield would no doubt soon discover, Sir Basil mused. If he had not already.

It was an old English belief that birds chose their mates on February fourteenth, and out of that conviction had sprung up in London society the yearly event known as the St. Valentine's Day Ball, which was held on the evening of the thirteenth of February. It was a masquerade ball like any other, where the ladies wore costumes or dominoes with masks, and the gentlemen costumes or merely evening dress with masks. Dancing and conversation were exactly as usual, with the only difference being the Midnight Waltz.

At midnight the final waltz would be announced, and gentlemen were invited to choose their partners. Those gentlemen who did so were, by tradition and accepted practice, announcing publicly their choice of life mate.

Naturally, most of the couples who took the floor for the Midnight Waltz were either married or betrothed; for all its air of impulse and romance, the tradition offered few surprises because it was a rare gentleman who risked public rejection in the event his chosen lady refused him, and a rare lady willing to announce her engagement in such an impromptu manner.

In all honesty, Cassandra had forgotten the significance of the Midnight Waltz. She had certainly enjoyed the evening, not in the least because Sheffield had come to her within five minutes of her arrival and had not left her since.

To the astonished members of society, as yet still ignorant of Cassandra's stay at Sheffield Hall, it must have appeared the most startling and incredible romance of the Season— perhaps of many Seasons. The scandalous earl, after many years of travel and (it was said) adventure that had left him older and wiser and much more flush in the pocket (a pirate's treasure was alluded to, though no one seemed to know by whom) had returned to London society and, the very day after his arrival, become instantly smitten with the lovely but elusive heiress, Cassandra Eden.

While she was *masked,* for heaven's sake!

More than one former suitor of Miss Eden's, glumly watching the dangerous earl obviously delight and enchant her with apparently little effort, longed wistfully for the cachet of a mysterious and/or wicked past. And more than one scandalized debutante could nevertheless not help but think how thrillingly romantic it must be to know those black eyes followed one's every movement, and with a light in them that was really . . . quite extraordinarily amorous. . . .

"We are the talk of the ball," Cassandra informed the earl solemnly late in the evening. She had chosen to wear a blue domino rather than a costume, but her gray eyes, framed by the gleam of her black mask, seemed fittingly mysterious.

Sheffield, who had scorned a costume and early disposed of his mask (like many other gentlemen), could only agree with her. He knew most of their observers were scandalized—but in a relatively mild way. Not that he cared. Except where it concerned Cassandra—as when he had worried she might be wary of him because of the tales she had heard—he was indifferent to his reputation.

"I suppose they must talk of something," he allowed.

Rueful, she said, "Well, we have certainly given them something."

"Do you regret it?"

Cassandra smiled up at him. "Of course not."

Sheffield was about to speak again when the musicians struck up a flourish of drumrolls, and the dance floor began to clear of couples.

"The Midnight Waltz!" the lead musician announced.

Smiling, the earl reached up and untied the ribbons holding Cassandra's mask. "I believe this is my dance, ma'am," he said.

It took a moment for Cassandra to remember the significance of this particular dance. When she did, she murmured, "But, Stone—they think we have only met tonight, and that this is the first time you have seen me unmasked—"

"And now they will believe I fell in love with you at first sight—which is perfectly true."

Cassandra thought her heart would burst, it pounded so rapidly. "You—you did?"

"Certainly, I did." He tucked her mask carefully inside his long-tailed coat as one would a keepsake, then bowed low before her as the musicians struck up the Midnight Waltz. "May I have your hand in marriage, Miss Eden? Will you dance with me?"

Without hesitation she placed her hand in his and curtsied, her eyes glowing with happiness. "If you please, sir."

He kissed her hand and then led her out onto the dance floor, and it was only then that Cassandra realized they were the first couple to begin—because every other eye in the room had been fixed upon them in fascination.

"We have shocked them all," she murmured as, slowly, other couples joined them on the floor.

He was smiling down at her, his mouth both tender and sensual, and his black eyes heated. "We will shock them still further if I am able to persuade you to marry me quickly, my love."

"How quickly?" she asked, solemn.

"By the end of the week—if I am able to wait that long. A special license, a private ceremony—and a very long honeymoon."

Still solemn, she said, "I believe I would like that of all things, my lord."

And her lord, inflamed by the love and desire shining in her gray eyes, waltzed her out of the ballroom and onto a dark and private terrace, under the shocked, scandalized, and wholly envious eyes of society.

BETRAYED HEARTS

by

Kathleen Kane

Dear Readers,

As in my other stories, members of my family are making an appearance.

In this year's Valentine story, you'll meet my Aunt Margie and Uncle Dom. Though Uncle Dom passed away a few years ago, his gardening skills remain legendary. He was truly the only person I've ever known who could grow a six-course meal on one tomato plant.

And Aunt Margie's cooking is *just* as legendary. The chocolate cake you'll read about is one that I personally tasted. Quite an experience. I still can't understand how my brother not only managed to finish his slice, but asked for more!

But to give her her due, usually her cooking is enough to make me gain weight just by walking in her door.

When my aunt read the story in manuscript form, she told my mother, "Thank God she never found out about the cayenne pepper in the apple pie!" Well, "Ain't" Marge, *nothing* is safe!

Happy Valentine's Day, everybody!

Kathleen Kane

ONE

"DILLIGENCE!" DALLAS SNORTED inelegantly as she passed the sign at the edge of town. The tiny collection of woodframe buildings hardly merited such a name. Small wonder the residents had long since privately referred to the town as Slipshod.

She yanked at the reins and pulled her swaybacked horse to a stop in the middle of the narrow dirt road. Even from a distance Slipshod wasn't a pretty sight, but close up the place looked even worse.

Actually, she told herself as she stared at the livery stable and adjoining corral, the rest of Slipshod didn't look too bad. It was that *one* structure that made everything else seem so awful.

Paint peeling, the building itself tilted precariously to one side as if wanting desperately to lie down for a while and recover before standing up straight again. The corral posts, the ones still upright, shuddered in the slightest breeze and toppled over completely whenever one of the horses rubbed up against them. Dallas wrinkled her nose at the smell floating out of the empty stalls and told herself that it was a disgrace how Jedediah had let the place fall to ruin.

But ever since his wife, Temperance, died, Jedediah'd managed to avoid work of any kind. In fact, he put more effort into "resting" than anyone she'd ever known.

Dallas shook her head, tapped her heels against her

horse's flanks, and continued the short ride to the general store. When she passed Margie Fontenot's restaurant, she nodded to the small group of men clustered on the front steps, but kept riding.

"Would you just *look* at her?" Jedediah Ludden spoke out of the corner of his mouth. Jerking his head at the young woman passing them, he added, "She's gotten downright scrawny here lately!"

"I must admit," Henry Duncan said, "I like a little more meat on my women."

"Hah! *Your* women!" Jed's bushy gray eyebrows wiggled. "Like you got more'n one. Hell, you don't hardly know how to handle the one you got!"

Henry frowned and started to speak, but Webb Caldwell asked quickly, "You figure she's all right? Dallas, I mean?"

Jed stared at Dallas Baker as she swung down off that piece of crow meat she called a horse. She was wearing an old shirt of her husband's stuffed into a faded, patched skirt that dragged in the dirt as she walked. The nasty, floppy-brimmed hat she wore looked as though she'd dug it up out of a hole, and it covered up what Jed knew to be a real pretty fall of long brown hair. He shook his head and watched her untie her basket from the saddle horn and climb the steps to the Caldwells' store. Seemed a shame that Dallas Hale Baker would come to such a pass. She used to be such a smilin', pretty little thing.

"Jed?"

The older man turned to look at Webb.

"I said, do you reckon she's all right?"

"Couldn't say." He ran one hand over his shiny bald head, then smoothed the gray fringe of hair that lay just above his ears. "Ever since her husband passed on, she's about worked herself to death on that ol' place of hers."

"Yeah," Henry agreed. "My wife, Mary, says Dallas ain't been in her dress shop for more'n a year now."

Jed snorted. "That ain't hard to believe." He closed his eyes in thought and tilted his head back. "I don't remember seein' her in anything pretty and female like since before Bill crossed over." He opened his eyes wide and cackled. "Sure do miss ol' Bill. He could tell a tale like nobody else."

"Yessir," Henry agreed fondly. "Bill *did* have a way with him all right. Reckon we *all* miss Bill."

Behind them the restaurant door flew open, crashing into the wall. A tall woman with rich auburn hair and snapping blue eyes stepped out onto the porch, swinging a broom like it was a scythe at harvest time. "I don't miss him any! It's one less lazy no-good clutterin' up my steps!" The business end of the broom connected with the back of Jed's head, and the older man leapt up nimbly. Margie never stopped, she just turned her attention on the other two.

As his friends jumped clear of the angry woman, Jed turned on her, shouting, "I'll remind you, woman, that *I* am the founding father of this here town and—"

"Yes, yes, I know." She cut him off and shook her broom at him. "But you ain't *my* pa! And if you're so durned proud of this town of yours, why don't you get yourself off and clean up that mess of a livery?"

Jed tugged at his suspenders.

Margie nodded knowingly at him. "I thought not. Why, if Temperance, God rest her, could see you now, I swear she'd be after you with a bullwhip." She took a small satisfaction at seeing Jed shudder at the mere suggestion of his wife's reappearance. "But at the very least," she continued, still shaking her broom at him, "you and your *loafer* friends"— she glared at the other two—"can take your worthless bones to somebody else's steps for a change! I'm tired of lookin' at you!"

Jed straightened up, deeply offended. He looked around quickly for support but saw that Henry and Webb had already scuttled off. Muttering under his breath about

ill-tempered females, Jed started for the livery. It was time
for a nap.

Margie stared at Caldwell's Mercantile across the street.
She turned slightly at the footsteps directly behind her and
watched as the man came up to stand beside her. Her sharp
blue eyes went over him quickly, and though she'd spent the
better part of the last hour talking to him, she could hardly
credit the change in him since last she'd seen him. Tall,
standing well over six feet, he wore a beautifully tailored
gray suit with a crisp white shirt and black string tie. His
new black boots held a mirror shine, and there wasn't even
a speck of dust on the flat-brimmed black hat he held in one
hand. Blond hair was smoothed back from his forehead, and
his blue eyes were focused on the storefront across from
them.

"She's changed some," he finally said softly.

"You been gone a long time."

There was no accusation in her tone, but the man
explained anyway. "It took a bit longer than I'd planned, but
I thought she *knew* I'd be back for her."

Men! Never mind writin' a letter now and then. Lettin' a
body *know* that you care and that you're comin' back . . .
Never mind proposin'. Or sayin' I love you.

Why, even her own husband, Dominic, a good man if
ever there was one, wasn't much for speaking his thoughts.

No. Men figure a woman should just *know*. And they
never plan on some slick-talkin' fella to move in and
romance their woman right out from under them.

Margie shook her head, then turned to follow his gaze.
Inside Caldwell's store, Dallas Baker was wandering
around, making her purchases just like always. And she had
no idea at all that the hard, lonely little life she'd built for
herself had just come tumblin' down.

TWO

DALLAS'S MOTHER USED to say that Elva Caldwell would find a way to talk at her own funeral. Now, listening to the woman rattle on and on, Dallas had to admit that her mother'd been right.

Just as she had been about Bill.

Now, without warning, her mother's words echoed through Dallas's mind. *"Oh, he's a nice fella all right. And he's got all the soft talk and ready laugh that rests easy on a girl's ears. But he's the kind who'll forever be bringin' you flowers and such and not worry about gettin' food on the table."* Dallas shook her head to dislodge the memory, but still she heard her mother's last warning. "Mark my words, Dallas Hale. You marry Bill Baker and you'll spend the rest of your life workin' like a mule. You'll end up doin' your share of the work *and* his."

No. Dallas pulled in a deep breath and pushed the past aside. There was no point in thinking about it. What was done was done, and it didn't make sense going over it time and again. At least, she told herself, since her parents had moved back to Kentucky soon after her wedding, she hadn't had to face her mother's knowing eyes every day.

Giving herself a mental shake, Dallas turned away as Elva Caldwell filled her small order of supplies. Deliberately the younger woman let her gaze wander over the well-stocked shelves of Caldwell's Mercantile.

Though wistfully acknowledging that she couldn't buy much, Dallas still enjoyed looking. She walked slowly around the store with Elva's cheerful voice as accompaniment. Her fingers trailed regretfully across the spines of a dozen books, then slipped down to the cold glass top of the jewelry case. She averted her eyes from the row of wedding rings and kept walking until she came to the bolts of dress goods. Stored neatly in shelves that stretched from floor to ceiling, the tempting array of fabrics struck her like nothing else in the store.

Cottons, wools, and silks in every color imaginable called out to Dallas, stirring a long-denied thirst for pretty things. She found herself reaching for a particularly lovely piece of green wool before she stopped suddenly and let her hand drop to her side.

There was no extra money for that sort of thing. Deliberately she smoothed her palm over the threadbare fabric of her skirt and told herself that it wouldn't always be like this. Someday she'd be able to walk into Caldwell's and buy whatever she needed. Or wanted.

Resolutely Dallas turned her back on the pretty material and continued her walk around the store. At the counter she stood quietly waiting while Elva measured out the half pound of white sugar Dallas had ordered.

"My, my," the woman chuckled softly, "I'm about out of sugar myself!" She tilted the metal scoop and let the sugar slide into a small paper bag. "What with Margie's restaurant and Mary Duncan startin' in on her baking already . . ."

"Hmmm?" Dallas forced herself to pay attention. She didn't want to hurt Elva's feelings by being caught not listening. "Baking?"

"Sure, honey!" Elva reached across the counter and patted Dallas's hand. "It's almost Valentine's Day. Only two weeks to go now. And you know how folks around here look forward to Mary Duncan's Valentine sweets."

Somehow Dallas managed to smile, though inwardly, she was screaming. Valentine's Day. Romance. Hearts and flowers, pretty cards with even prettier words on them . . . and it all meant *nothing*.

Who should know better than *she* just how many lies could be covered up with empty promises and smiling sweet talk? How visions of romance and lacy Valentines could blind a person to what was real? Hadn't Bill made an occasion of Valentine's Day? Didn't *he* know all the right words to say? And because she'd been fool enough to listen to him, she'd married him. It wasn't until after the wedding that she'd discovered Bill was never as interested in work as he was in talking and laughing. It hadn't bothered him a bit to let his wife slave all day every day from dawn to dusk just to keep food on the table!

She hadn't discovered until too late that her mother'd been right. It was *romance* he was good at. Not the day-to-day living and loving.

Dallas never wanted to *see* another Valentine.

The door behind her swung open, and the overhead bell jumped and clanged out a welcome. A heartbeat later Elva Caldwell gasped in stunned surprise.

Frowning, Dallas watched the other woman and noticed the furtive glance Elva shot at her. A hard, cold knot of apprehension settled in the pit of her stomach and grew when she noticed Elva chewing at her lip nervously.

It could be anyone, Dallas told herself. And yet . . . one look at Elva's frozen expression was enough to tell her that whoever'd just entered the store was someone completely unexpected. Breath held, spine rigid, Dallas slowly, hesitantly turned around. Her eyes widened. Her jaw dropped. Her heartbeat staggered.

Jefferson Page.

An unwelcome flush of pleasure shot through her as her eyes met his. Somewhere in the back of her mind, Dallas noted his fine clothes and his confident stance. He looked different.

Five years older, surely. And more prosperous. But his sharp, clean features were still as familiar to her as her own. As always, his blond hair needed a trim, and she curled her fingers into fists to keep from acting on the urge to push a stray lock of hair off his forehead. His blue eyes, she noted, still held the shine of suppressed laughter that had always been able to make her smile.

Lord, she thought with a passing groan at her own appearance, why had he come back? And why did he have to look so *wonderful*? Nervously she turned away from him. Her left hand swept across the counter and accidentally knocked a display of hand-painted Valentines to the floor.

She stared down at the bits of lace and ribbon lying scattered across Elva's gleaming pine floorboards. Then her eyes fixed on one card. A fat Cupid lying in a field of dainty yellow tea roses laughed up at her. Dallas gratefully felt a cold calm seep back into her soul. All she had to do was remember that it was *that* sort of nonsense that had gotten her in the mess she was in!

As Jefferson bent to pick up the cards, she closed her heart to the memories threatening to swamp her. As clearly as if it had been the night before, she saw the two of them nestled close on her parents' porch swing. Dallas could almost feel his lips against her throat. In memory she heard his husky voice outlining where they would build their house. She saw his eyes twinkle wickedly as he teased her about needing a big bed so they'd have plenty of room to romp.

Inhaling sharply, Dallas gave her head a good shake. He'd been gone five long years. And just because he'd finally come home, didn't mean that he'd come back to *her*. Besides, even if he *had*, she wasn't interested. Not any more.

*   *   *

Jefferson straightened up slowly and set the stack of cards down on the counter. Absently he heard Elva rattling on, but he paid her no mind. He'd only been back in town a couple of hours, he told himself, and already it was as if he'd never left.

From the men on Margie's steps to Elva Caldwell's happy chattering, nothing had changed at all. Nothing and no one, except Dallas.

He glanced at her covertly. She looks *tired*, he thought sadly. Tired and thin and still so beautiful, it hurt to look at her. His gaze swept over her quickly, thoroughly. Her small hands were sun-browned, the palms calloused. He wanted to reach out and pull that godawful hat off so he could see the hair he'd dreamed of running his fingers through. He wanted to wrap his arms around her too-thin frame and hold her to him so tightly, they'd never be separated again. But he couldn't.

As soon as he looked deeply into the pale blue-gray depths of her eyes, he was lost. Here were the most disturbing changes.

The tender, loving eyes that had haunted him for five years were gone. Now they were bruised, hurt. Filled with shadows despite the brief spark of excitement that had flared at first sight of him.

What the hell had happened to her while he was gone?

"Jefferson!" Elva nearly shouted at him.

"Hmmm?" His head snapped around to look at the woman. "Yes, ma'am?"

She shook her head as if to say it was plain he hadn't changed much. "I was askin', how long you plannin' on stayin' in Slipshod?"

A long, breathless moment passed. He turned back to face Dallas before answering, "I'm home to stay, Elva. I'm not goin' anywhere."

"You bring a wife with ya?" Elva asked quietly.

"Nope." Jefferson's eyes never left Dallas. "Not married yet. But who knows? Maybe I will be. Real soon."

Dallas swallowed heavily, and Jefferson was pleased. She wasn't indifferent to him anyway, despite the "Keep Away" warning evident in her rigid posture.

"Dallas," he said softly, trying to ignore Elva's presence, "it's good to see you again."

She gave him a stiff smile and the briefest of nods.

"I was sort of hopin' you and me could . . . talk?" He held his breath. Somehow, he'd never planned their first meeting to go like his.

He saw the hesitation in her eyes momentarily, then she said, "There's nothing to say, Jefferson." She turned to Elva. "Is my order ready?"

The woman looked uneasily from Dallas to Jefferson. He shook his head slightly but wasn't sure she'd seen him until he heard her say, "Not quite, Dallas honey. Got to go into the storeroom for that flour you wanted."

"That's all right. I'll pick it up next time." Dallas reached for her basket, but Elva was quicker.

As she marched toward the storeroom, carrying Dallas's supplies, she called back, "Shouldn't take more'n a half hour or so, dear."

Silence lay thick and heavy between the two people left alone in the store. It was all Jefferson could do to stand beside her and not touch her. Hold her. Kiss her. He'd waited so long, worked so hard. And now she wouldn't even look at him.

Well, he told himself firmly as he stepped up close behind her, she damn well *would* look. They were going to get married, just like they'd always planned. And they were going to be *happy*, dammit!

With an effort he kept his frustrated anger out of his voice as he asked, "Since you have to wait anyhow, why don't we go over to Margie's for some coffee?"

"Thank you, no." She lifted her chin and straightened her shoulders, managing to look like a princess despite her ragged clothing. "I'll wait here."

Despite his regrets over how their reunion had gone so far, Jefferson grinned. No matter what else had happened to her in the last five years—it was plain to see Dallas hadn't lost any of her stubbornness. He cocked his head to one side, bent down slightly to get right in her line of vision, and grinned even wider. "What's the matter, Dallas? Scared? Of *me*?"

Her gaze shot to him, and it was a look filled with the fire he remembered.

"I am *not* scared of you, Jefferson Page."

"Prove it."

Her lips twitched mutinously, and Jefferson held his breath and waited. He could almost *see* her thinking. He only wished he knew what she was thinking *about*. Gently he laid his left hand on her shoulder and let it slide down the length of her arm. When he reached her hand, his fingers wrapped around hers in a firm grip. Changing his tactics, he whispered, "Come on, Dallas. For old times' sake? One cup of coffee with an old . . . *friend*?"

She trembled from head to foot, then pulled her hand free. He jammed his hands into his pants pockets so she wouldn't notice that her trembling had transferred itself to him.

Jefferson held his breath. He was more than prepared to toss her over his shoulder and carry her to Margie's, but he knew their little talk would go a lot better if she was to come of her own accord. After all, it was pretty hard to tell a woman how much you love her when you're totin' her around town like a sack of grain.

Several long moments passed before she finally said, "All

right, Jefferson. *One* cup of coffee. But only because I think there's something you should know."

Without another word she turned and marched to the door. Puzzled, Jefferson stared after her. This was supposed to be *his* little talk.

THREE

DALLAS KEPT HER gaze fixed on the tabletop as Margie poured out two steaming cups of coffee. As if from far away, she heard Jefferson and the older woman chatting easily and wished she could think of something to say. But she couldn't.

God, why did he come back? Why hadn't he just stayed away? She'd finally gotten used to his absence. Finally come to believe that he was either dead or long married to someone else. Finally convinced herself that she hadn't *really* loved him anyway.

Damn him! What right did he have showing up after five years? If he thought he could shatter her world again, he had another think coming. The sharp sting of tears filled her eyes, and she blinked them back. She wouldn't cry over him. Not again. Five years ago she'd cried enough tears to float the town of Slipshod right out of California. And it hadn't changed a thing.

She sucked in a deep gulp of air and raised her gaze to his slowly, hesitantly. His shining blue eyes stared into hers, and Dallas battled down the bubble of excitement rising in her chest. In spite of *everything*, all she had to do was look at Jefferson Page and her better judgment dissolved like sugar in lemonade.

In a heartbeat, images of the two of them filled her mind. All the quiet nights they'd spent together on her parents' front porch swing, talking about the future. They'd made so many plans . . . where they would live, how many children they'd have, how they'd love each other until they were too old to move.

She remembered the touch of his hand, his warm breath on her cheek, the kisses that fueled a fire so bright it was frightening. She remembered it all.

Jefferson smiled and reached across the table for her hand, and suddenly Dallas remembered standing in the road calling after him, begging him not to leave without her.

Cold, hard resolution filled her. She lifted her chin, straightened her spine, and pulled her hands back out of his reach. She wasn't a girl to be taken in by soft words and breathless kisses any longer.

And it was time Jefferson knew that.

"It's so good to be home," he said quietly, leaning his forearms on the table, "and so good to be with you again."

Dallas lifted her coffee cup and took a small sip. "You're not *with* me, Jefferson. Not any longer."

He frowned, but she went right on. "Before I say what I have to, I want to know one thing."

"What's that?"

His voice was deep and seemed to echo through her soul. Dallas's fingers tightened around the hot china cup. "Where have you been all this time?"

"It's a long story, Dallas."

"I expect so, Jefferson. You've been gone *five years*."

He winced and pushed one hand through his straw-blond hair. She watched the furrow between his eyebrows and knew he was upset. She'd known him so long and so well, Dallas read the turmoil and hurt in his eyes but didn't allow herself to be sorry.

She'd been hurt, too.

"First I went to Chicago," he said softly. "Worked in the

slaughterhouses for a while. But I couldn't stand that for long and went on to New York."

"New York?"

"Yeah." He looked at her curiously. His long fingers toyed with the handle of his coffee cup. "I told you when I left that I wanted to make some money for us." He caught her eyes with his and held them. "That's the only reason I left at all, Dallas. I wanted to make things *easier* for us."

She shifted her gaze away and heard him sigh gently at the broken contact.

"Anyway, I drove a carriage for hire for a couple of years. A lot of my customers were bankers and such. The men working in the stock markets?"

She nodded, though she wasn't quite sure she knew what he was talking about.

"Dallas"—he grinned—"it was amazing, listening to those men talk about *mountains* of money like it was nothing. And you know, those rich folks talked about everything right in front of me. It was almost like they didn't know I was there. Or maybe they just figured I wasn't important enough to worry about." He shook his head slowly, remembering. "But if you pay attention, you can learn a lot from folks' conversations. And I paid attention."

"To what?"

He looked at her, pleased at her interest. "To *everything*. What they bought and why and what they sold and why. Every spare nickel I could round up I saved and bought what stock I could. When it got up high enough, I sold and bought others."

"So you stopped driving rigs?"

He laughed and shook his head. "No, I just paid another driver to let me take over his route, too. That way I heard more, made more, and bought more."

In spite of herself, Dallas was fascinated. "Jefferson, when did you sleep?"

"In between hires. Just slept in the carriage most of the time."

"But that's crazy."

"No. I didn't plan on doing it forever." He leaned toward her, glanced toward the restaurant door to reassure himself that Margie was still in the kitchen, then added, "I figured the harder I worked, the quicker I could get back home to you."

Quick? He thought five years was *quick*?

"Then, a couple of years ago, I went in with some other men on a cattle venture in Guatemala."

"Guatemala?"

He nodded, smiling. "They needed fresh beef down there in the worst way. Took us forever, what with buying the cattle, then driving them down there and arranging for buyers and the like. . . ." Suddenly he stopped and stared at her. "Now I want to ask *you* something," he said.

"Hmmm? What?"

He cocked his head to one side. "Why the hell didn't you wait for me? The minute I got back in town, folks were lined up waitin' to tell how Dallas is now the Widow Baker. Dammit, Dallas! How the hell could you marry somebody else?"

"I waited *two years* for you, Jefferson Page."

"Two years!" he snorted.

"That's right. Two years. Two years without a word from you. No letter, no telegram, *nothing*. For all I knew you were dead!"

His jaw dropped and he stared at her in disbelief. "What do you mean, *no word*? I wrote to you!"

"Hmmph!"

"I *did*! I sent you two postcards. One from Chicago and one from New York." He shook one finger at her. "And a little over two years ago, I wrote you a real long letter."

"A letter?"

"Yeah. I told you all about the cattle trip and how I prob'ly wouldn't be able to write to you again 'cause we'd be out in the back of nowhere, but that as soon as I was finished I'd be comin' right back here. To you."

Brow furrowed, Dallas said thoughtfully, "I didn't get any letters or cards from you, Jefferson."

"Maybe somebody forgot to give 'em to you."

She shook her head.

"Maybe they got lost."

Still shaking her head, Dallas told him, "Nope. Bill was the postmaster here then. If there'd been word from you, he'd have spotted it and given it to me."

"Bill." Jefferson nodded shrewdly and leaned back in his chair. "The same Bill that wanted to marry you?"

"Yes."

"Uh-huh. Dallas, what makes you so sure that this Bill would have given you my letters if he wanted you for himself?"

"Well . . ." Flustered, she bit at her lip and tried to think. Finally she burst out, "Of course he would have. It was his *job*."

"Uh-huh."

"I figured," Dallas went on, her voice shaking despite her best efforts, "that you just plain forgot about me. That you found somebody else."

"How could you think that?"

"What was I supposed to think?" She glared at him and was pleased to see him shift position uneasily. "I never thought you'd leave me at all, but you did, didn't you?"

"That was different. That was for us."

"No, Jefferson. That was for you." She shook her head slowly, her eyes filled with regret for the time lost. "I never cared about having money. All I wanted was you and a place of our own. I didn't care if it was a shack. Just as long as you were in it." Her voice was shaking badly now, and she knew she should stop talking, but now that she'd started, there was no turning back. And whether Bill *had* stolen Jefferson's letters or not didn't really matter. Jeff never should have left in the first place. If he'd stayed in Slipshod, none of this would have happened. "*You* were the one who wanted money. *You* were the one who wasn't happy. *You* were the one who left. Not me. And when you didn't come back . . ." Dallas dragged air into her heaving lungs. "I made the biggest mistake of my life."

Jefferson reached for her hand again, but she pulled back and grabbed her coffee cup. He watched her gulp at the hot liquid as if for strength, and he cursed himself for a damn fool for ever leaving her.

But he couldn't change the past. It was gone. Done. The future, however, was wide open and brand-new. And he intended to make it a damn good one. For both of them. All she needed was a little convincing.

"Dallas, I'm sorry you were so unhappy. Hell, I'm sorry for everything." He was talking fast and he knew it. But Jefferson sensed that she was about to run out. He had to make his case quick. "But I'm back home to stay now. And I *love* you."

Her eyes met his, then slid away.

"I *love* you, dammit. And I want us to get married." He ignored her sudden gasp and pushed on. "I figure Valentine's Day would be a nice, romantic day for a wedding. What do you think?"

Dallas jumped up so abruptly, her chair clattered to the floor. She stood staring down at him, and Jefferson hadn't felt the cold so much since that last winter in New York.

"What do *I* think?" she said, her voice rising. "*I* think you're out of your head! And I think you didn't listen to a damn thing I told you!" Without another word, Dallas ran across the room and out the front door.

"Dallas!" Jefferson hurried after her, shouting her name.

It was as if she were deaf. She didn't stop. She didn't even slow down.

He finally caught her just as she was about to climb aboard the ridiculous animal she called a horse. Jefferson grabbed her elbow and swung her around to face him. At the same time her "mount" dipped its head toward Jefferson, curled its lips back, and snapped its yellowed teeth at him.

Warily Jeff took a step back and pulled Dallas with him.

"Why the hell did you run away?" he shouted, heedless of the crowd beginning to gather.

"*I* didn't run away," she accused. "*You* did. Five years ago."

"That's over, dammit. I'm back! I love you!"

Dallas held up both hands, palms facing him as if warding off a blow. "Don't. Don't even start with all the sweet talk. I'm not interested!"

"Dallas!" Jefferson tried to hold onto his patience. He'd just become aware of the people surrounding them, and though he didn't relish the idea of hangin' out their dirty laundry in public . . . he'd do whatever he had to do. "I want to *marry* you!"

She yanked her arm free of his grip, shook her head, and backed up to her waiting horse. "No, thanks. I'm not interested in a husband, either." Her lips curved in a bitter smile. "The last one near killed me with work!"

"True, true," someone in the crowd muttered, and Jefferson's insides twisted.

She turned her back on him for a moment, swung aboard her horse, then looked down at him. Eyes weary, her face grim, she said flatly, "Look at me, Jefferson. *Really* look. I'm not the girl I was. It's been five long years, and every day of them lasted a lifetime."

Jefferson's gaze locked with hers as he took the few steps separating them. In a motion so fast Dallas didn't have time to resist him, Jefferson pulled her down from her horse, wrapped his arms around her, and kissed her.

And when his mouth touched hers, Jefferson offered her the long years of loneliness and longing. He poured his soul into the kiss and silently demanded that she accept it. After only a moment's hesitation Dallas's arms tightened around his waist, and her soft sigh told him that she'd forgotten nothing. That despite her words, she still loved him.

Regretfully then, Jefferson broke away and in one smooth movement lifted her and set her back in the saddle. As if from far away, he heard the delighted mutterings of the interested crowd, but his attention was focused only on Dallas.

"Say what you will, Dallas," he whispered huskily as he leaned against her, "what's between us isn't finished. Not by half."

She swallowed heavily, tugged on the reins, and turned her horse for home.

She hadn't gone more than ten feet when Jefferson shouted, "I swear to you, woman! Come Valentine's Day—we *will* be married!"

Dallas stuck her nose in the air. Jefferson smiled.

FOUR

THE NEXT DAY Dallas brought her horse to a stop at the edge of town. If she'd had any sense at all, she told herself angrily, she'd have remembered to get her supplies the day before. Then she wouldn't have had to come back to town for at least a week.

She snorted derisively. Remember her supplies indeed! Why, after Jefferson kissed her, she'd been lucky to remember the way home. Dallas clutched the reins tightly in one hand, her thumb and forefinger rubbing the torn, cracked leather. Even twenty-four hours later her body still reeled from the impact of that kiss.

Oh, Lord, why had he come back? Why couldn't he have just stayed away? She'd finally gotten used to living without him. She'd finally convinced herself to stop listening for the sound of his voice at town meetings. And until last night, she'd even stopped dreaming about him.

Dallas shifted position in the saddle as the memory of her too-vivid dream flashed through her mind. It had been so real. She would have sworn that Jefferson's hands really *were* moving over her flesh. That she could feel the warmth of his breath on her throat.

But when she woke, she was alone in her tiny cabin. Her breasts ached for his touch, and her insides trembled with unfulfilled desire.

Her breathing ragged, Dallas forced herself to push the

dream away into the darkest corner of her mind. No matter what she longed for in the middle of the night, she wasn't willing to trust *any* man *that* much again.

Straightening her spine, Dallas told herself that maybe she'd get lucky. Maybe it was too early in the morning for Jefferson to be about. Maybe she could get in and out of town before he knew she'd been there. She gave her horse a gentle kick in the ribs and held her breath as she entered Slipshod.

As she neared the restaurant, she kept her gaze fixed straight ahead, on the general store. She knew full well that the town loafers would be on Margie's steps, and she was in no mood for idle chat.

Only a few feet from her goal, though, Dallas heard Jed shout, "Jefferson! Your woman's back!"

She gritted her teeth to keep from yelling at the old coot and tried to hurry her stubborn horse. It was no use. From behind her she heard someone running, and without even looking, Dallas knew it was Jefferson.

Deliberately she climbed down, tossed the reins over the hitching rail, and started for the steps. She didn't make it.

He snatched that mangy hat off her head and grinned when a thick, brown braid fell to her waist. "You ought not to cover up such pretty hair, Dallas."

"Give me that hat, Jefferson," she snapped and grabbed at it.

Smiling and shaking his head, he held it out of reach. "I don't think so, sweetheart. I'd much rather look at your hair than this ol' thing." He leaned toward her, one hand moving for her braid. "And why don't we just get rid of this bit of rawhide and undo that braid, too, huh? You know I always liked your hair best long and free."

Dallas jumped back. "I thought I told you yesterday that I don't much care what you like anymore."

He crossed his arms over his dirty, bare chest and smiled. "Sure you did, honey. But I know you didn't mean it."

"Don't call me honey!"

"Sure thing, sweetheart."

Dallas glared at him, and he could see she was havin' a fine time trying to hold on to her temper. And that suited him just right. He figured that it had been so long since she'd felt anything at all that even makin' her mad was better than nothing.

"Dammit, Jefferson." She shook one finger at him. "I told you and told you, I'm not interested in hearing any more compliments or fine talk. Fancy, empty words don't mean a blasted thing to me!"

He took one step closer to her. "*My* words aren't empty, Dallas. You best get used to that right now."

She backed up and he took another step, closing the gap between them. "*And* you'd best get used to hearing all the pretty words and compliments, because I'm gonna keep right on saying them."

"But—"

"No *buts.*" Jefferson leaned down toward her. Her nose wrinkled, and she drew her head back. For a moment he couldn't understand what was wrong. Then he remembered. Grinning sheepishly, he glanced down at his bare, dirty chest, then back to her. "Guess I don't exactly smell like roses, huh?"

She shook her head, reached up, and pinched her nostrils shut.

"Well, it's just sweat and a little horse 'perfume' from the livery."

"What? Why?" she mumbled around her hand.

"I'll explain in a minute." He stared into her blue-gray eyes and wished again that he had Bill Baker in front of him for just five minutes. Five minutes was all he'd need to make that damn fool sorry for ever hurting Dallas. But, he reminded himself, if Bill Baker were around again, then Dallas wouldn't be free to marry him, Jefferson.

He reached out and slowly ran the tip of his index finger down the length of her jaw. Wisps of brown hair blew about her face, and even though she was still dressed in rags, Jefferson thought she was the most beautiful woman he'd ever seen. And if it took him the rest of his life, he would make her believe in his love. Gently he said, "I know about Bill."

She stiffened and moved away, but he grabbed her shoulders and held her still. She *would* listen.

"I know what a hard time you've had of it, Dallas. And God help me, if I could change it, I would." He saw the tears fill her eyes and wished there was an easier way of reaching her. One thing he didn't ever want to do again was cause her pain. He breathed deeply and went on. "I know he let you down. Hell, *I* let you down, too. I know that."

She bit her lip and blinked furiously.

"But, dammit, Dallas. Don't mistake me for the same kind of man as Bill Baker. Just because I want to tell you how beautiful you are and how much I love you, that doesn't make me a shiftless, lazy liar."

"Doesn't it?" She lifted her chin and stared him down. Her eyes seemed to accuse him of all manner of things, and it was all Jefferson could do not to look away. "Didn't *you* lie to me, too? Didn't you propose marriage to me? Didn't you say as soon as you came back we'd be married?" She pulled away from him so forcefully, she lost her balance and plopped down onto the wooden steps behind her. From her sitting position, she added, "At least Bill Baker *married* me when he said he was going to."

A flash of anger swept through Jefferson, but just as quickly it died away. Even though *he'd* spent every moment of the last five years thinking about her, she couldn't know that. To her way of thinking, he'd forgotten about her. And now he had to prove himself all over again.

Well, so be it. In fact, he'd already started.

"So Bill married you when he said he would."

She nodded.

"Well, I'm here to do just that, myself." He dropped to a squat right in front of her. "And I'm here to give you all the pretty words I've been savin' up for the last five years, too."

"Jefferson . . ."

He ignored her, half turned, and pointed at the livery. "You wanted to know why I smell so bad?" His lips quirked into a lopsided grin. "Why, I'm so godawful dirty? It's because I bought that tumbledown collection of firewood from Jed."

Her jaw dropped. Gently he pushed it shut with his finger.

"That's right, darlin'. I bought the livery. Now I grant you, it's no prize right now . . . but you give me a few days . . ." He paused and shrugged. "All right, maybe a few weeks. And I'll have that place turned into the best damn livery in the state of California." He brushed one hand down his chest and smiled ruefully. "If the dirt and stink don't kill me first."

"But why?" She shook her head slowly, confusion etched on her features.

"For you. For us." He leaned close and glanced a quick kiss against her mouth. "I've tried to tell you, Dallas. I'm not afraid of hard work. I'm home to stay. And if I have to prove it to you, I will."

"Jefferson . . . I—"

"The livery's just the start. As soon as we're married, we'll build us a decent-size house for all those kids we used to talk of having. We can live in town or out on your land. Whatever you like." He cupped her cheek with the palm of his hand. "You'll see, Dallas. It'll be just as we dreamed it so long ago."

For the briefest of moments she rubbed her face against his hand, then pushed herself to her feet and climbed the steps to the general store. At the door she paused and looked back at him, a world of sadness in her eyes. "Can't you understand, Jeff? I don't believe in dreams anymore."

Two days later Jefferson shook his head and stared openmouthed at Dallas's house. It hadn't been easy, staying away from her, but he knew she had to have time. She had to think about all the things he'd stirred up. But he also didn't want her to think too much. That's why he'd ridden out to her farm. It would be much better for him if he could keep her just a little off-balance.

Now he stepped down from his horse and shook his head slowly. It was a wonder she wasn't in town daily, just to get away from this place, he told himself. His gaze moved over the tiny cabin quickly. Old gray paint bubbling and peeling, the hinges on the window shutters broken, two planks missing from the porch steps, even the hitch rail leaned to one side like a Saturday night drunk.

He rubbed his jaw thoughtfully and turned in a slow circle. Cursing under his breath, he noted the weeds and brush left to grow much too close to the house. The water trough leaked enough to cause a small lake at its base, and the barn door was hanging loosely at an impossible angle.

If he hadn't seen it, he never would have believed it. And where, he asked himself silently, was Dallas? Then, as if thinking her name had conjured her up, Jefferson saw her in the distance. She was out in the field with that foul-tempered, swaybacked excuse for a horse, trying to plow.

Angrily he started to mount his horse and ride out there. For God's sake, why did he have to love such a *stubborn* woman? Suddenly, though, he stopped. Glancing quickly around him one more time, Jefferson smiled.

Whistling under his breath, he led his horse to the dilapidated barn.

By late afternoon Dallas was so tired, she could hardly walk. She should have known better than to try and plow this early in the year. The ground was too hard. And by rights, she ought to have the plow blade sharpened.

Cursing herself for a liar, Dallas silently admitted that it had nothing to do with the plow or the ground or the season. She turned her head and glared at her one and only horse.

"It's *your* fault, Eli! And so help me, if you don't start earnin' your keep around here, I'll . . ." Hell. She didn't know *what* she'd do. Eli snorted at her and tugged her toward the barn. "Don't know why you're hungry, you miserable bag of bones. You didn't do a lick of work all day!"

She stopped dead in her tracks. The barn door was fixed. Someone had been by here and rehung it. Uneasily Dallas looked around the empty yard. She dropped Eli's reins and ignored his hungry protest.

Slowly Dallas walked to the cabin. It only took a moment to see that the front steps had been mended and even the hinges on her shutters had been nailed back into place. She laid one hand on the hitching rail and somehow wasn't surprised when it didn't wobble.

Jefferson!

It *had* to be Jefferson. No one else would have come out here and taken it upon themselves to fix up her house! Dallas pulled in a deep breath as she tried to think what she should do.

Bacon. She sniffed again. Bacon and fresh coffee. It smelled wonderful. Her stomach growled noisily as she let herself enjoy the aromas drifting out of her cabin. *Usually*, after working outside all day, she was too tired to even think about cooking something to eat. Most times she made do with some jerky or apples if she had them. It was just too much trouble going to the fuss of cooking only for herself. She closed her eyes briefly and smiled at the thought of fresh, hot food.

The front door creaked as it opened, and Dallas looked up. Jefferson stood in the doorway, wearing her old, faded blue apron over his jeans and plaid shirt. He held her battered coffeepot high and grinned. "Afternoon, darlin'. You ready for supper?"

FIVE

SHE COULDN'T MOVE. Her eyes raked over him quickly, thoroughly. He looked so pleased with himself. Dallas swallowed nervously. Jefferson was probably the only man alive who could wear a woman's apron without looking completely ridiculous.

He reached over and pulled up the limp-ruffled shoulder strap, then waved his spoon again. "You comin'? I don't want it to get cold, now!"

"Uh-huh," she mumbled and forced her feet to move.

Inside the cabin her lopsided little table was set with her mismatched plates, and there was even a tiny bouquet of scraggly wildflowers in a water glass in the center. Fresh coffee bubbled on the stove, and the scent of frying potatoes had her stomach growling in response.

Jefferson grinned. "I heard that. Everything's about ready." He stepped up behind her and gave her a gentle shove toward her bedroom. "Why don't you go wash up, and I'll put the food on the table."

She nodded and walked slowly across the room, trying to make sense of all that was happening. She knew she should toss him out, tell him he had no business being in her kitchen. Her house. But, Lord, she sighed, that food just smelled too good! As she closed her bedroom door, Dallas heard him whistling under his breath.

*   *   *

He refilled her coffee cup for the third time, and she reached for one last biscuit. As she broke it open, Dallas told herself that whatever else was said about Jefferson Page, he was a fine cook!

She tossed a quick glance at him covertly. He was enjoying himself. Acting the part of host even though they were in *her* house. Not for the first time since she'd entered the cabin that afternoon, a niggling thought tugged at the edges of her mind.

No matter how much she enjoyed coming in and finding supper on the table and a smiling Jefferson to greet her, she didn't want him feeling as though he *belonged* there. And it was clear that he did. He sat across from her, arms crossed over his chest, tilted onto the back legs of his chair like a king on a throne.

She lowered her gaze back to her nearly empty plate. Not only had he taken over her cabin, he'd done more work around the outside in one afternoon than she'd been able to get done in a year and a half! Well, Dallas told herself, she didn't need his charity! She hadn't *asked* for his help. She hadn't asked for *anyone's* help.

Maybe her place and her clothes didn't look like much— but they were *hers*! She'd worked long and hard keeping her little piece of land together, and she didn't need anyone coming in and taking over. *Least* of all, Jefferson Page!

His voice broke into her jumbled up thoughts and her uneasiness grew as she listened to him.

". . . and then I figured we could plow up that back section of yours and plant it in winter wheat. Give us a good crop just when we'd need it most." He nodded at her graciously. "'Course, if you had somethin' else in mind, we could talk about it."

"No."

"No?" His brow furrowed, then his expression cleared

and he smiled at her. "Good. Then it's settled. Winter wheat it is!"

"No, Jefferson."

"No, Jefferson, what? The wheat?" He lowered his chair softly and reached across the table for her hand. She drew back. "Dallas, whatever you want, that's all right with me. You know that."

Trying to avoid looking into those blue eyes of his, Dallas shook her head. Her insides twisting, her mouth dry, she struggled for words. "What I want is for you to leave."

"What?"

"Leave, Jefferson. Go back to town. Or better still, go back to New York." She swallowed heavily and pushed herself up from the table. Turning quickly, she lifted the edge of the curtains and stared out the now clean window. "You don't belong here anymore, Jeff. That's over. And this isn't *your* home. It's mine."

"Dallas—"

"Don't. Thank you for what work you did today, though. I'll . . . uh, find a way to pay you for your troubles as soon as I can."

Before she could blink, he was out of his chair and behind her, spinning her around to face him. His blue eyes stormy, his features thunderous, he growled out, "I don't want to be *paid*, dammit!"

"Well"—she refused to look at him; instead she stared at his boot tops—"I can't give you what you *do* want, Jeff."

"Yes, you can, Dallas." His voice was softer now, and it settled over her like a warm quilt in winter. One finger tilted her chin up, forcing her to meet his gaze. "*You're* what I want. You always were. God, Dallas, don't you *feel* it when I hold you?"

His arms closed around her, drawing her up against him. She *did* feel it. That same giddy magic she remembered and had dreamed about so many nights. Her flesh tingled and her heart skipped erratically. But it was no good. It was too late.

Deliberately she pushed away from him. Her voice husky with unshed tears, she said, "No, Jeff. I'm not that girl anymore. I don't even *remember* her!"

"*I* do." He reached for her and held her face between his hands.

Bending down, he pressed his mouth to hers and teased her lips open with his tongue. Dallas's breath caught as he swept the inside of her mouth. Instinctively she pressed closer to him, snaked her arms up around his neck, and answered his passion with her own. It had been too many years since she'd felt such an overwhelming desire to touch and be touched.

Jefferson. Always Jefferson. Fire raced through her blood, and she felt his hands move knowingly over her back and the rounded curve of her behind. He held her tightly, and when he broke away to let his lips trail down the length of her neck, Dallas shuddered under the onslaught of feelings crashing over her.

Her need for him was almost painful in its strength, and her fingers clutched at his shoulders as if afraid to let him go even for an instant.

Then suddenly it was over. He stepped back, leaving her to grab a chair back to steady herself. She watched him drag air into his heaving chest and knew she was doing the same. He rubbed one hand across his jaw, then pushed it through his hair.

Dallas gulped in a breath and reached up to draw the edges of her shirt together. She didn't even remember him undoing the buttons.

"That's all for now, Dallas," he finally said on a ragged breath. "If I stay any longer, I'll have you down on the floor before either of us knows what happened."

"Jefferson—"

"No!" He shouted and held up one hand to silence her. "You had your say; now it's my turn. I'm sorrier than you can know for the time we've lost. And for what you went through with that husband of yours." Shaking his head, he struggled for control, then went on quickly. "But that's over now, Dallas. And the only thing that matters is *us*. Now, don't you even bother tryin' to tell me that you don't care. I believe we just found out that you *do*."

He had to understand that just because he had the power to turn her into a quivering mess, it didn't mean that she would marry him. "That doesn't mean—"

"Stop it!" He stalked over to the hooks on the wall and took down his coat and hat. Shoving his arms through the sleeves, he said, "What it means is that when we tumble down on this floor or, preferably, in a bed"—he jammed his hat on—"we'll be good and *married*. Valentine's Day isn't even two weeks away now, so we don't have long to wait. You get yourself ready, Dallas. I'll take care of the rest."

"I am *not* going to marry you, Jefferson." Strange. Her voice wasn't shaking even though she was trembling from head to toe.

One quick step took him to her side. He grabbed her, dragged her up against him one more time, and slanted his lips across hers, as if to burn himself into her heart. When he pulled back, he dropped a quick kiss on the tip of her nose.

He marched to the front door, paused, and looked back over his shoulder. "Oh, yes, you are."

"Jefferson! Your woman's here!" Jed's voice boomed into the still afternoon air. "And you best watch out, son! She's wearin' her courtin' clothes!"

Dallas glared at Jed, but he was too busy laughing with his two cohorts to notice. Good Lord, she thought disgustedly, *courting clothes*? Maybe Jefferson hadn't heard, she told herself with a sudden burst of hope. Just as quickly she realized that the only people who *wouldn't* hear Jed's voice were lying up in the cemetery.

Why on earth did Jed have to take such an interest in *her*? She already felt self-conscious enough. She surely didn't need that nosy old buzzard shouting out an announcement every time she rode into town!

Oh, forget about him, she told herself firmly. There's nothing to be done about him, anyway. Folks had been trying to find a way to shut Jed up for years and hadn't once managed it. Besides, she had more than enough on her mind already.

Uneasily she ran one hand down the front of her best dress. Four years old and pretty much faded from too many hours spent drying in the sun, the yellow calico gown with tiny green flowers was soft and hugged her body like a lover. It had been so long, though, since she'd even *tried* to look nice, just *wearing* the dress made her jumpier than a flea on a near-bald dog.

Even as she dismounted in front of the restaurant, Dallas couldn't help wondering if she'd done the right thing by coming to town. A gentle breeze lifted the ends of her shining clean hair, and she told herself she should have braided it.

But she knew why she hadn't. Jefferson liked it better hanging free. She inhaled sharply and blew it out in a rush. For heaven's sake. What on earth was she doing?

It had only been three days since he'd fixed her supper at the cabin, and here she was, pining away like some lost calf! Of course, she reminded herself, it *had* been the longest three days of her life!

Somehow, she'd kept expecting him to come back to her place. She'd been on edge constantly, never knowing when he might pop up. And when he *didn't*, her disappointment was greater than she'd admit, even to herself. Of course, it didn't help matters that she relived that soul-shattering moment in his arms, over and over.

Until he'd kissed her, she'd almost forgotten how wonderful it was to be held by him. How being with Jefferson made her feel more alive. How his lips caressed hers in a motion that was at once gentle and demanding.

She shook her head, disgusted with her traitorous feelings. *Stop it!* what was left of her rational mind screamed. Kisses and pretty words was what got you into trouble the last time! Yes, she silently argued, but though she'd been fond of Billy in the beginning, she'd never felt for him anything *close* to what she felt for Jefferson. What she'd *always* felt for Jefferson.

All the more reason to be careful. Go easy. Don't let your heart run your head again.

I won't, she swore silently.

Then why are you in town? her brain countered.

I need supplies, that's all. Grumbling under her breath, Dallas climbed the steps to the restaurant, ignoring the comments from Jed and his friends. When she reached the porch, Margie came bustling through the door, swinging her broom.

"Go on, you bunch, git!" She took a swipe at Jed, but he was too quick for her. "Make way for a *paying* customer!"

Managing to look both deeply offended and angry at the same time, Jed and the two other men shambled off down the street.

"You come on in with me now, Dallas. I'm gonna give you a nice piece of cake, and we can chat awhile."

"Oh, no, Margie. Really. I just came to town to pick up a couple of things at the store. I only wanted to stop and say hello for a minute."

Auburn eyebrows arched over Margie's knowing blue eyes. "Is that right?" She looked past Dallas's shoulder for a moment and smiled. "Then you wouldn't be interested in knowing that Jeff Page is on his way over here right now?"

Dallas's heart skipped and her stomach churned. Though she'd come to town with the hope of seeing him, now that the moment was upon her, she wanted to pick up her skirts and run.

"Afternoon, Jefferson!" Margie grinned and waved. "I was just gettin' ready to cut Dallas a piece of cake. Why don't you come in and have some, too?"

"Margie . . ." Dallas groaned softly.

"Now, now. No arguin'." Margie wagged a finger at the couple. "I'm tryin' out a new recipe. And I need some volunteers to sample it. You know Dom doesn't care for sweets any."

Dallas rolled her eyes. Everyone in town knew that the way Margie loved to bake, if her husband Dom *did* eat sweets, the poor man would weigh five hundred pounds by now.

"After you, Dallas." Jeff held the door open for her and grinned.

There was no getting out of this now, she told herself. Taking a deep breath and lifting her chin, Dallas stepped into the darkened restaurant.

SIX

DALLAS TRIED TO keep her gaze from straying to Jefferson's broad, nearly bare chest. He was still tugging the edges of a clean shirt together, trying to button it up as they took their seats by a table near the front window.

"Kinda caught me off-balance, Dallas," he said, smiling. "Showin' up like you did."

She looked down at the tabletop and idly toyed with the knife and fork in front of her. "You, uh . . . didn't have to stop what you were doing, Jefferson. . . ."

"I'm glad for the chance to sit and rest a bit, believe me." He grinned and leaned his elbows on the table. "That livery was in such a state, I've been workin' like a crazy man all day, every day." Shaking his head, he added, "You know, I'll bet ol' Jed hasn't done a lick of work on that place since Temperance died."

Well, she told herself wryly, at least she knew now why she hadn't seen him for a few days. He'd been too busy mucking out stables.

"So," he asked with a knowing wink, "what brings you to town, Dallas?"

"I, uh, only came to town to pick up a couple of things from the store."

"Didn't you just get supplies a few days ago?"

She clenched her teeth. Wouldn't you know he'd remember that? "Yes, but I forgot"—frantically, she tried to think of *something*—"tea!" she nearly shouted.

"Oh, well . . ." Disappointment flashed across his features before he smiled again. "Whatever the reason, I'm glad to see you. I want to—"

Dom Fontenot's voice cut in to whatever Jeff might have said.

"Before you leave," the older man called out as he entered the room from the kitchen. "I want you to take some of these vegetables with you, Dallas."

She looked over at Margie's husband and smiled. Almost the same height, the couple were as different as night and day. Margie's smiling, always cheerful demeanor contrasted sharply with Dominic's leathered, deeply tanned features. But behind the growling front he showed the world, Dallas knew that Dom Fontenot was as soft as a brand-new feather pillow.

And the man could grow *anything*. Some folks swore that if Dom stuck a twig in the ground, by the following week it'd be bearing fruit. Whether that was true or not, he surely kept the restaurant and many others homes in town filled to bursting with vegetables and even, on occasion, one or two of his prize roses.

Before she could thank him for the basket he'd left on the corner table, Dom had turned and walked back out to his garden.

Alone again, Jeff said softly, "You look real nice, Dallas."

She felt the heat rising in her cheeks and cursed herself for a fool. *Why* had she come? Why was she putting herself through all this?

"Here we are," Margie called out and carried in a tray laden with two thick pieces of cake, a coffeepot, and two cups. She set the tray down in the center of the table and announced happily, "You be sure and tell me what you think, now. Valentine's Day is comin', and I can't let Mary Duncan get the best of me this year like she did last!"

Margie was gone as suddenly as she'd appeared. But her interruption had served to give Dallas time to control her reeling emotions.

Confused, Jeff reached for a piece of cake and asked, "What's she talking about? What did Mary beat her at?"

Glad for something to speak about, Dallas offered, "Last Valentine's Day, some fool had the bright idea of having a contest between Margie and Mary Duncan. See whose cake was best. Well, Mary's cake won, and Margie was fit to be tied. For two weeks after that contest, I don't think her oven ever cooled off. She had more cakes, pies, cookies, and such flying out of this place, nobody in town could *look* at sugar for months."

Jeff grinned and shook his head. "Wish I'd been here to see it."

"Yes, but you weren't."

"Dallas . . ."

"Let's just have our cake, Jefferson. Please?"

He nodded and took a bite of the chocolate-frosted white cake. After a moment or two, though, Dallas noticed a strange expression cross his face. When she took a bite of cake, she understood why.

"What do you think she did to it?" he whispered and took a big gulp of coffee.

Dallas shook her head and swallowed. "I'm not sure. But it's . . ."

Jefferson poked at the offending cake with his fork. "It's not *bad*, but . . ."

"I know. I think it's the frosting." Dallas dipped her finger into the thick, smooth chocolate. Licking her finger, she grimaced. "It's not sweet at all."

"It's not *anything*."

She smothered a laugh. "We have to eat it, Jefferson."

"What?"

"We *have* to. She'd be so hurt if we didn't. *And* she'd probably go into another baking dither and drown us all in goodies."

His eyes widened just at the thought of it.

Margie poked her head in. "Well? Do you like it?"

"Delicious, Margie," Jeff called immediately and took another bite.

A bubble of laughter escaped Dallas at the look on Jeff's face, and she about choked trying to hold it back. It only got worse when the older woman's pleased voice answered, "Just give a yell if you want more!"

Like wicked children, they ducked their heads and grinned at each other. And staring into Jefferson's laughing eyes, Dallas felt like a girl again.

"It doesn't look like much right now," he said and tugged on her hand. "But back here, I figure I can set up a small saddle shop." He looked down at her and grinned. "You know, repairing saddles, bridles, and the like. . . ."

Dallas turned in a slow circle, letting her gaze sweep over the amazing changes he'd made in the livery. Fresh straw was piled on the floor in each of the newly repaired stalls, gaping holes in the roof had been patched, he'd even *painted* the inside of the old place. Now the wooden walls were a clean, fresh white.

She shook her head slowly and pulled in a deep breath. It even *smelled* clean! Sneaking a glance at Jefferson's pleased-as-punch expression, she had to admit that he *was* a wonder. She'd never have believed that *anyone* could make such a difference in a place in such a short time.

But then, she told herself, Jefferson Page wasn't like anyone else she'd ever known.

"And in the back room, there"—he pointed to the far

corner—"I've got a nice little bedroom all set up. You want to see it?"

She shook her head. She didn't want to go *near* a bedroom with Jefferson. After all, there was no point in throwing temptation in her own path.

"Oh," he said softly, a little disappointed. "Well, that's all right. It's not for me, anyway."

"What?"

"Yeah." Jefferson grabbed both of her hands. "That's one of the things I wanted to tell you. The room's for Webb Caldwell's boy, Scott. I hired him to manage this place for me."

"You mean, you're not planning on running the livery yourself?" Her voice was tight, but she couldn't help it. Visions of Bill swam before her eyes. All she could remember was the many ways Bill had found to avoid work.

"No, I mean . . ." He leaned down and planted a kiss on her forehead. "To run this place, I'd have to live in town, and I figured you'd rather we lived on your place. . . ."

She stiffened slightly and tried to pull her hands free, but his grip was tight.

"You'll see, Dallas," he went on, his voice mounting in excitement, "this little place will grow. It's bound to. Hell, there's people moving in all over the country. *Everybody'll* need a place to stable their horses or hire rigs, or . . ." He shrugged, threw his hands wide, and grinned happily. "Who knows? This is just the beginning, Dallas. You'll see. . . ."

It was Jefferson's voice, but in her mind it was Bill's face smiling down at her. Filled with his own big talk and elaborate plans that always came to nothing.

No! she shouted inwardly. Not again. She'd heard enough plans and dreams to last a lifetime. Dallas had learned the hard way that the only way to survive was to work. Not dream. Not talk. Work.

"Dallas?" Jeff stared at her. She hadn't said anything, but

he suddenly knew she wasn't listening anymore, either. He stifled a groan and tried to rein in his impatience. It had been going so well.

The easy talk and laughter at Margie's, and then her enthusiasm for the improvements he'd made at the livery had about convinced him that he was getting through to her. What in the hell had happened to make her close up and draw away from him? What had he said?

"It's all very nice, Jefferson."

He almost shivered at the icy tone of her voice. Instead, he reached for her hand again, but she stepped back.

"I wish you well. You and Scott, I mean."

"Dallas—"

"I have to be getting along now. There's work waiting for me at home." She turned and walked quickly to the door.

As she stepped outside into the afternoon sunlight, he heard her whisper, "Goodbye, Jefferson."

Waiting at the counter for Elva to bring her tea, Dallas told herself she should have gone straight home. But she didn't want Jefferson thinking she'd come to town only to see him. So, whether she wanted the tea or not, she *would* buy it.

Muted whispers from two young girls at the back of the store floated up to Dallas, but she ignored them. She had too much on her mind to give in to idle curiosity.

How could she have been so stupid? Hadn't she learned anything from her brief marriage? Hadn't she spent the last two years vowing that she would never again put her trust in a man?

And yet, here she stood. She glanced down at her faded yellow calico and frowned. Dressed in her best, she'd come to town looking for the very man who'd deserted her five years before. He hadn't changed a bit. He'd left Slipshod because of his own big plans, and now he was building *more* plans. How long would it be, she wondered, before Jefferson Page decided Slipshod wasn't grand enough to hold his dreams? How long before he left town *again*?

The bell over the front door jumped and clanged, announcing another customer's arrival. Dallas straightened up and forced a smile when she heard Mary Duncan call out, "Dallas, dear! Why, you look *lovely*!"

"Thank you, Mary."

"It's been too long since I've seen you looking all done up good and proper!" The smaller woman staggered under the weight of a tray she carried until she lowered it gently to the countertop. Flicking off the white towel covering, she displayed row after row of heart-shaped cookies, a heart-shaped cake with white frosting, and a cherry pie. "Don't you just *love* Valentine's Day?"

Mary smiled down at her creations and didn't notice that Dallas said nothing in response.

"You know, dear"—Mary turned and let her gaze wander up and down Dallas's too-thin frame—"if you want to have all of your nice things ready in time, you really should stop by the store and let me take your exact measurements."

"You mean you haven't done that yet?"

Dallas spun about to stare at Elva's horrified expression. What on earth?

"No, Elva," Mary continued, "she hasn't. Now, I still have your old dress form in the back of the shop, but"—she walked a slow circle around the younger woman—"I do believe there's been some changes in your shape, dear."

Dallas gaped at her and wondered wildly what was going on! Cocking her head, she asked quietly, "Take my measurements?"

"Oh, my, yes," Elva said to Mary, totally ignoring Dallas's question. "Her bosoms haven't changed much, but everything else seems to have shrunk some!"

Mary pinched in the fabric at Dallas's waist. "Yes, indeed. At *least* a couple of inches."

Dallas swatted at Mary's hand and turned an indignant eye on Elva. She fought down the urge to hide her unchanging bosom under crossed arms and instead glared at the women she'd known her whole life as if they were strangers. "*What* are you two talking about?" Her gaze flicked quickly to the two sighing girls now staring at her in wistful admiration, and away again.

"Well, for heaven's sake, Dallas!" Mary straightened up, looked from Elva to the girls, then back to Dallas. "We're talking about your trousseau!"

"My *what*?"

"Trousseau, dear." Elva reached across the counter and patted Dallas's arm. "Are you feelin' all right?"

"I'm fine." Dallas stepped back from the counter, keeping a good distance between herself and the others. "And I don't need a trousseau!"

"Oh, honey"—Mary waved one hand at her as if dismissing her objections—"of course you wouldn't think so. I admit that having the groom pay for the bride's things is a *bit* unusual . . ."

"The *groom*?"

"Yes, dear. But Jefferson always was a hardheaded man. Dead set on having his own way. And, truth to tell, most folks around here think it's mighty *romantic* the way he's taking charge of all the details!"

One of the young girls sighed heavily, and Dallas frowned at her. Romantic? Taking charge? Jefferson.

"What details?" Dallas congratulated herself silently for keeping her voice even.

"Why, *everything*!" Elva grinned delightedly. "He's got the church set, arranged for flowers, got old Mrs. Murphy to play the organ . . . he's even sent to San Diego for the weddin' dress!"

Mary sniffed. "No need. I *told* him I could do it in plenty of time. . . ."

"Now, Mary, there's plenty for all of us to do between now and Valentine's Day. . . ."

"No, there isn't."

"Hmmm?" Mary said.

"What'd you say, dear?" Elva asked.

"I *said* there's nothing to do." Dallas pulled herself up, lifted her chin, and looked from one to the other of the women in front of her. "There's nothing to do because there isn't going to *be* any wedding!"

"Now, Dallas . . ."

"Tsk . . . tsk . . . tsk." Mary shook her head. "I *told* Jeff that you wouldn't like not picking out your own things. But we can take care of that." She turned to Elva, and the two of them trotted to the back of the store, still discussing the upcoming wedding day and all the work that had to be done.

The two girls giggled and hurried off.

Dallas wanted to scream.

No one was listening to her!

They hadn't heard a thing she'd said.

Her heartbeat sped up, and her breathing was ragged. Everyone in town was going ahead planning a wedding, and it didn't seem to bother them a bit that they weren't going to have a *bride*!

Stunned, trapped, furious, Dallas spun on her heel and marched out of the store. By thunder, they'd see who had the last laugh! *Let* them make all the plans they wanted. It would be a cold day in hell before she walked down that church aisle again!

SEVEN

DALLAS APPROACHED HER house cautiously. Her gaze moved over every inch of the familiar ranch yard, searching for the latest "gift" from Jefferson.

In the four days since her last trip to town, she'd found everything from a love poem tacked to her door to a bright red ribbon tied around Eli's bridle. A reluctant smile teased at her lips as she remembered the huge red heart she'd found painted on the inside of the barn doors just the day before.

Annoying or not, Jefferson was certainly determined. And how he managed to leave all of his little surprises without her catching him in the act was just short of amazing. But he'd done it. She hadn't seen a glimpse of him since she'd left him standing alone in the livery.

Of course, she hadn't seen *anyone*. She couldn't bring herself to go back to town. Not with everyone in Slipshod planning a wedding! *Her* wedding!

She tugged uncomfortably at her sodden shirt, pulling it away from her skin. *Wedding!* Dallas turned in a slow circle, looking for any indication that Jefferson had been there. She *still* couldn't believe it. That damn . . . *man* had convinced an entire town to throw a wedding party for a woman who had already turned him down!

Then, instead of facing her with what he'd done, he'd spent every spare minute riding out to her ranch leaving romantic poetry and wilted flowers. She shook her head. How was a body supposed to argue with a man like that?

"Nothing," she muttered to the empty yard. "Not a trace of him. He didn't come today."

Everything looked exactly as it had when she'd left for the waterhole early that morning. A surge of disappointment hit her. Maybe he'd gotten tired of trying. Maybe he'd finally given up on her.

Dallas stood completely still and listened to the silence. Not even the wind was moving. She swallowed heavily and tried not to mind the suddenly *too* quiet ranch yard. She should be pleased. Jefferson was probably convinced at last that she'd meant what she said. That she *wouldn't* be marrying him.

The harsh sound of her own sigh only served to emphasize how *alone* she suddenly felt.

A long, wet strand of hair slipped down over her eyes, and she gingerly pushed it aside. Grimacing slightly at the green slime her action left on her already filthy hand, Dallas shook her fingers hard, hoping to dislodge most of the scum.

It was no use. A simple sponge bath wouldn't do tonight. After a day of cleaning out the waterhole, she desperately needed a sit-down *tub* bath.

Pushing thoughts of Jefferson aside, she wearily turned for the barn. She'd better drag that tub inside now, while she still had the energy.

With the old copper tub in the middle of the room and water heating on the stove, Dallas took the time to look at the plate of heart-shaped cookies on the table. Right beside the offering, a sad-looking bouquet of daisies had been stuffed into a water glass.

A wistful smile curved her lips, and she touched one of the flowers gently. Jefferson. He'd been here after all, she thought. He *hadn't* given up.

She snorted a laugh suddenly and glanced down at herself. Soaking wet and covered with green pond scum, she was hardly the picture of a soon-to-be bride! Glancing up into a small, square mirror, she said aloud, "It's almost too bad Jefferson didn't stay around today. One good look at you, and he'd be scared off for sure!" She grinned at her reflection, then began unbuttoning her shirt. No reason to dirty up the rest of the house.

Jefferson smiled. He hadn't *meant* to fall asleep on Dallas's bed. It was just that between all the work at the livery and running to and from her place . . . hell, he was worn out. Of course, she'd waked him up when she dragged that tub inside.

Then he was caught. He knew he should let her know he was there. It was the only right thing to do. And yet . . . when she began undressing, it occurred to Jefferson that he was in the middle of a *very* interesting situation.

He hadn't had much luck talking her into marrying him. Maybe if he could *compromise* her, she'd give in.

His breath stopped when she pulled her shirt off and dropped it to the floor. She didn't have a damn stitch on under that ugly plaid shirt! Hungrily his gaze moved over her high, full breasts. She shivered with cold and her nipples hardened. Jefferson ran his tongue over suddenly dry lips and forced himself to breathe.

He couldn't look away. Not if it meant his life. It had been so long. He hadn't touched her breasts since one soft summer night too many years ago as they cuddled on her parents' front porch. And even then, her chemise had stood between him and the warmth of her flesh.

A gnawing pain chewed at his middle when he allowed himself to remember that another man had touched her in his stead. That because of his own stubborn pride, he'd once lost her. He wouldn't let that happen again.

He shook his head and rubbed one hand across his jaw. She was completely undressed now. His gaze locked on the curve of her behind as she leaned over, pouring pans full of first hot, then cold water into the old tub. When she reached for the bar of soap and stepped into her bath with a contented sigh, Jefferson stifled a groan. His whole body ached with the need to touch her. To love her. To bury himself inside her warmth forever.

Her back to him, she began to hum softly as she lathered up the soap and rubbed it into her soaking wet hair. Quietly he eased the bedroom door open, then shrugged out of his shirt, letting it drop to the floor.

Water slapped against the side of the tub. He heard his own heartbeat thundering in his ears. He took a step. She lowered her arms tiredly, and Jefferson came up behind her. Quietly he knelt down and whispered, "Dallas?"

She gasped and turned quickly, sloshing water over the side of the tub to the floor. "Jefferson! Good Lord! What? Why? . . ."

"I, uh, fell asleep on your bed," he offered lamely. "You woke me up."

Her eyes wide, Jefferson read a mixture of excitement and desire in their shining depths.

One arm folded over her breasts, she ordered, "Well, you're awake now. Get out."

"Dallas," he said, his fingers threading through her hair again, "I know you're tired. Why don't you let me help you wash your hair?"

"No," she argued, then shut her eyes against the pleasure of his touch. "You have to leave, Jefferson."

"Just relax, darlin'," he urged. "Let me wash your hair, and then if you still want me to go, I'll go." He held his breath for what seemed a lifetime, and then she slowly settled back into the water.

Smiling, Jefferson leaned in closer, his fingers moving

leisurely over her scalp. She sighed and he let his hands move down to her nape. He slid his fingers over the length of her neck and onto her shoulders. A few minutes later he rose and picked up the bucket of warm rinse water by the stove. Dallas sat up straight and tilted her head back as he poured the water over her hair and ran his fingers through the long locks until no soap remained. Sighing, she leaned back and gently, soothingly, he rubbed her tired muscles, gliding over her wet skin with a sure touch.

Head back against the rim of the tub, Dallas's eyes were closed, and Jefferson moved his attentions to her arms. His big hands moved easily down her arms, and once under the water, he traced his fingers over her waist and up her rib cage to stop just under her breasts. Her rosy, erect nipples peeked through the bathwater, begging for his touch. Shifting position slightly, Jefferson leaned over her and gently captured her breasts with his hands. His thumbs moved lazily over the hardened buds, and when she arched her back, he dipped his head and took one of them into his mouth.

Dallas moaned and bit at her bottom lip when Jefferson's tongue traced a warm circle over her nipple. Deep inside her, long-denied desire flickered into life. Unconsciously her body writhed under his touch and successfully hushed the small part of her brain that clamored for reason.

She gasped aloud when his mouth closed over her nipple and he began to suckle at her.

Her eyes flew open. She looked down and watched him through slitted eyes as he drew on her breast. His mouth worked at her nipple, and with every warm tug of his tongue, knife blades of desire cut at her. Her breathing ragged, Dallas reached up to cup her hand against the back of his head, holding him to her, silently demanding more.

His right hand slipped from her other breast, trailed down through the water, over her abdomen to the warm center of her. She held her breath, knowing that nothing else in the world mattered at that moment. Only Jefferson. And then his fingers slipped inside her, and Dallas forgot everything but the wonder of his touch and the hunger growing and building inside her.

"Oh, God," she whispered and moved her hips against his hand. Warm water splashed against her core and added its own delightful caress. Jefferson's thumb stroked the hard bud of her sex while his long fingers dipped in and out of her body, teasing her, tormenting her with her own desire.

He lifted his head and looked down into her eyes, a soft, knowing smile on his lips. "Do you want me to go, Dallas?"

She licked her lips and shook her head wildly.

He kissed her mouth, running his tongue over her lips before adding softly, "You have to *say* it, Dallas. Do you want me to leave?" His fingers plunged into her body and Dallas's hips ground against his hand.

"No!" Her whispered shout was breathless. "No, damn you, Jefferson. Don't leave. Stay with me."

"Always, darlin'. Always." He quickly lifted her from the tub and carried her to the bedroom.

It seemed to take a lifetime for him to pull his clothes off and join her on the mattress. And then he was there, everywhere. His hands moved over her body with a sure, gentle touch, leaving a trail of fire behind him. She moved against him, stretching herself out along the length of him, rubbing her breasts against his hard, muscled chest. Eagerly, then, Dallas let her fingertips slide down his back to the curve of his hip. Running the flat of her hand over his thigh, she kept on until she felt the hard proof of his need and closed her fingers gently over him.

A low groan came from deep in his throat, and Dallas smiled. She'd waited for this moment for so many years. And now that it was finally upon her, she wanted all of him.

She wanted to feel his warmth stretched out on top of her, pressing her into the bed. She wanted to wrap her legs around him and hold him inside her until he had no strength to leave her.

His fingers once more laid claim to the damp center of her, and she released him to deliberately cup his hand with her own. He smiled down at her, clearly delighted with her forwardness. Then slowly, their hands joined, he stroked the tender flesh between her thighs.

Her head tilted back, she licked dry lips and swiveled her hips instinctively. When his other hand slipped behind her to cup her behind, she lifted herself off the bed slightly to accommodate him.

Heart pounding, Dallas felt as through every inch of her flesh was on fire. She couldn't seem to catch her breath, and she was stunned to realize that she didn't care. She wasn't an inexperienced virgin anymore. She'd been married. Shared her bed with a man.

And yet . . . she groaned softly and lifted her hips again to meet Jefferson's questing fingers. *Never* had she felt anything like this! It wasn't merely her body burning with his touch. It was her mind. Her soul.

She opened her eyes, stared up into his, and felt herself drowning in the love shining there.

"Dallas," he whispered, "oh, God, Dallas."

She pulled his head down to hers and kissed him as he shifted to lay atop her. Her lips parted, his tongue darted into her mouth and then his body slipped inside hers. In an ancient rhythm, they moved together, each pushing the other toward the precipice that waited just out of reach.

Her fingernails dug into his shoulders, and she lifted her hips for the final plunge that tore a scream from her throat as her world exploded around her. Vaguely, as if from a distance, Dallas heard Jefferson cry out her name.

*   *   *

"Sweet *Jesus*!" He rolled carefully to one side of her and lay staring up at the ceiling. If he'd only known what bedding Dallas would be like, Jefferson swore he'd have married her when they were both still kids! He glanced at her and was pleased to see that she looked every bit as shattered as he felt. Leaning up on one elbow, he smiled down at her.

"Are you . . . all right?" he asked and could have kicked himself for asking such a stupid question.

But she reached up and laid her hand against his cheek. In a shaky voice she answered, "I . . . think so. Jefferson, I . . ." She stopped suddenly and cocked her head to one side, listening.

Then he heard it, too. A buckboard. The noise stopped and Jefferson heard the unknown driver push the heavy brake on. Someone was here.

Dallas shot out of bed like she was on fire. "Get up," she whispered frantically. "Get dressed. Get out." When he didn't move, she snapped, *"Hurry!"*

She turned and began to paw through her dresser looking for clothes. With her back to him, Jefferson grinned. This was *one* sure way to make certain that she couldn't pretend their lovemaking had never happened. Rolling off the bed, he snatched his jeans off the floor and pulled them on.

Someone pounded on the front door, and Dallas gasped. Horrified, she looked at him as he buttoned up the fly of his pants.

"Dallas?" Mary Duncan's voice seemed to echo through the small cabin. "Dallas, honey? You in there? I brought out your trousseau so's we could fit it to you! Dallas?"

Jefferson grinned and Dallas held a finger to her lips, shaking her head. Totally ignoring her, he yelled, "Be right there, Mary!"

"What are you doing?" Dallas's eyes grew wider every

second. She held a chemise up in front of her body like a suit of armor and took one step toward him. "For the love of heaven, Jefferson! Hush before I'm completely ruined in this town!"

He shook his head. "For the love of *you*, Dallas . . . I won't hush." Hair mussed, barefoot, his jeans buttoned only high enough to be decent, and his chest still damp from their heated lovemaking, he started for the front door.

"Jefferson, *no!*"

He glanced back at her. "We're not children, Dallas. And we're gettin' *married* in four days." He deliberately emphasized the word *married*. "Mary'll understand."

Dallas ducked back into her bedroom as he pulled the front door open.

"Afternoon, Mary!" He smiled and pulled the small woman into the cabin. "Sorry it took so long to open up, but . . . well . . ." He winked and finished buttoning up his jeans.

Mary's cheeks flushed a deep rose. Looking everywhere but at Jefferson, she muttered, "Quite all right, Jeff, dear." Her voice was strained. "I only wanted to see Dallas for a moment. Perhaps I'll just leave her things and come back another time."

"She'll be right out, Mary. Soon as she's decent."

A heavy thud from the bedroom caused both people to turn and stare at the closed door. He could be wrong, but Jefferson was pretty sure that noise was Dallas hitting the floor.

Beet-red now, Mary hurried to the door and raced to her buckboard. Before Jefferson could stop her, she unloaded her packages and climbed onto the high seat.

Dallas came up behind him, buttoning her shirt, in time to see Mary wheel the horses around and race toward town.

After a long, silent moment Jefferson said, "Well!"

Dallas looked up at him and wasn't surprised to see a satisfied smile on his face.

"Looks like you'll have to marry me now for sure, Dallas. Widow or not, folks in town aren't gonna let us get away with *this* kind of behavior."

She looked back at the road leading to town and saw only a dust cloud, moving fast. She was trapped and she knew it.

There *would* be a wedding after all.

EIGHT

SHE'D HARDLY GOTTEN a wink of sleep all night. Tired, disgusted, Dallas picked up her coffee cup and walked to the front window. Despite her every effort and her best intentions, she was going to be married in only three days.

There was no way out. Jefferson had seen to that. Although, she admitted silently, if she hadn't been so eager to lay with him, he never could have forced her hand.

She took a big gulp of coffee and tried to think logically about her situation. Her fingers toyed idly with the thread-bare curtains as her mind wandered. She remembered the pleased look on Jefferson's face when Mary'd shown up. If she didn't know better, she'd have sworn he'd arranged the whole embarrassing incident.

But, she told herself, poor Mary'd been shocked half to death. There was no denying that. Maybe it was fate. Maybe it was all *supposed* to happen the way it did. Maybe someone, somewhere *knew* what it would take to get her to agree to a wedding!

A soft, reluctant smile curved her lips. Poor Jefferson. He'd worked so hard at wooing her only to win her hand because of an accident of fate. She let herself recall all the little things he'd done for her in the last two weeks. All the small surprises and gifts. The work he'd done. His cooking.

She swallowed heavily. His lovemaking.

Maybe, she thought hopefully, maybe he's right. Maybe this time things'll work out fine. A spark of anticipation started in her stomach and began to spread. And *maybe*, she added silently, it was time to admit that she loved Jefferson Page. Always had. Always would.

As if a weight had been lifted off her shoulders, Dallas grinned, set her cup on the table, and headed for her bedroom. She'd go right into town to see him. To tell him she loved him. She believed in him. And this time she wanted to look her best.

Sitting astride Eli, Dallas tossed her head, setting her wavy hair dancing over her shoulders. Jed, Henry, and Webb were sitting on the steps of the restaurant, as usual. And for the first time she was looking forward to hearing Jed's voice announcing her arrival.

But the old coot didn't even open his mouth.

She rode straight to the livery, eager to see Jeff and get everything settled between them at last. Sliding down off Eli's back, she called out, "Jefferson? It's me!"

Scott Caldwell stepped from the shadowy building, a quizzical expression on his face.

"Good morning, Scott." Dallas grinned and looked past him. "Is Jeff inside or is he at the restaurant?"

Scott kicked at a rock, screwed up his face, and jammed his hands in his pockets. "Uh, Dallas—Jeff ain't here."

"Oh." She swallowed back her disappointment and forced a smile. "Well, where is he?"

"He, uh . . . hell, Dallas, he rode out this morning."

"Rode out?" Her voice was flat.

"Yeah. Didn't say where he was goin'."

"I see." She pulled in a shaky breath. "Well, I expect it's business for the livery is all."

The young man shook his head. "Don't think so. He sold the place to me late last night."

"What?"

"My pa put up the money for it, but the livery's all mine now."

His mouth kept moving, so Dallas knew Scott was talking. But she couldn't hear him. Curious. All she heard was a rushing sound. Finally she realized it was her own blood boiling.

Gone.

Rode out.

Sold the livery.

In a rage beyond words she climbed aboard Eli and turned him for home.

The day before Valentine's Day and her supposed wedding, Dallas was finally finished. She'd hunted down everything Jefferson had given her and stuffed it into an old crate. Satisfied at last, she glared down at the collection.

Heart-shaped cookies, lace and ribbons for her hair, a hand-painted card with Cupid smiling like a simpleton. Suddenly she reached down and turned the card over. She didn't even want to *look* at another Valentine as long as she lived. Then she snatched up the withered bouquet of daisies from the table and tossed them into the box, too. Now she was ready.

Since Scott's visit at the break of dawn, announcing that Jefferson was back and wanted her to come to town, Dallas had been in a frenzy of motion.

He hadn't even had the *decency* to come out to her place himself! No, he'd sent *Scott* out to fetch her. Like she was some stray hound looking for a home.

Eyes narrowed dangerously, her jaw clenched, Dallas lifted the unwieldy box and walked outside. She had quite a few things she wanted to say to Jefferson Page.

"Jefferson! Your woman's here!"

Dallas glared at Jed. "Jed Ludden, hush your mouth this damn minute!"

The older man's jaw dropped, and he blinked in stunned silence.

Jefferson stepped out of the livery's open doors and came up to her, a smile on his face and a big white package under his arm.

As he reached her side, Dallas dumped the box of gifts at his feet. He jumped back just in time to avoid crushed toes and stared up at her in astonishment. "What the hell?"

"I don't want 'em." She lifted her chin and looked down her nose at him. "I don't want a damn thing from you, Jefferson. *Least* of all a Valentine!"

"What's goin' on here, Dallas?"

A crowd was beginning to gather, and Dallas was pleased. There wasn't a thing she'd like more than to tell him just what she thought of him in front of God and everybody!

"Why don't we go have some cake and coffee?" He smiled tentatively. "Y'know Margie figured out what was wrong with that cake the other day . . . by mistake, she used cornstarch instead of sugar for the frosting and—"

"I don't give a good damn about cake frosting!"

A gasp from someone in the crowd, and Dallas heard some woman mumble, "Shameless!"

Jefferson pulled in a deep breath, obviously trying to keep a grip on his rising temper. "They why don't you tell me what's got you so het up?"

"Be happy to!" She slid down off Eli's back, planted herself in front of Jefferson, and poked his chest with her index finger for good measure. "You never intended to stay in Slipshod, did you?"

"What?"

"You heard me! I already know that you sold the livery! Why'd you come back at all? Want to make sure I missed you? Was pinin' for you? Well, you'll be disappointed, mister. *Nobody's* going to make me cry again! Nobody!" She shoved him, hard, and he staggered back a pace. "So why don't you just pick up your money from Webb and leave us all in peace?"

"You about done?"

"About."

"Good!" Jefferson shouted and started toward her, backing her up until she was crowded against her horse. "Now it's my turn!"

She crossed her arms negligently, ignored the muttering crowd, and waited for his explanation. *If* he had one.

"I *did* sell the livery."

"Hah!"

"Because I only *bought* the damn place to convince you that I was staying! Besides, I *thought* we'd live at your place!" His voice roared out over her, drowning the crowd's interested comments.

"Oh, so *I* could do all the work for you? No, thanks! I've had that kind of *help* before!"

"Damn you, Dallas!" He grabbed her with one hand while holding the package tightly with the other. "How many times do I have to tell you, I'm not *Bill*!"

"What'd he say?" old Mrs. Murphy called out.

"Said he ain't Bill," someone answered.

"Course he ain't," Mrs. Murphy snorted. "Bill's dead."

"Now I'm gonna tell you where I've been," Jefferson growled out.

"Not interested."

"Too bad," he thundered. "I've been in San Diego. I bought up that parcel of land adjoining yours!"

She flicked a glance at him.

"That's right. *And* I bought a new plow and a work team to replace Eli. . . ."

Dallas's eyes shifted uneasily.

"*And* I hired a couple of hands, too."

She looked up at him directly. He wasn't lying. He was too mad to be making these things up as he went along.

"I don't *need* to work, Dallas. I tried to tell you that before. I made enough money in New York and on the cattle drive to take care of both of us!"

"What'd he say?" Mrs. Murphy asked.

"Hush, Eileen," Margie said. "I'll tell you later."

"But, Dallas"—Jefferson's voice was softer now. His rage spent, he only looked disappointed—"having money and land . . . that isn't gonna be enough." He hooked one finger under her chin. "You've got to have a little faith, too."

So confused she couldn't think straight, Dallas said nothing.

"Now," he said, suddenly brusque again, "tomorrow's Valentine's Day. And I believe we have a date at the church." He handed the package to Dom, lifted Dallas, and slammed her back into the saddle. Then, taking back the box, he thrust it into her arms. "You be at that damn church on time, Dallas. And I expect to see you wearing *this*!

The big white box sat unopened on the table all night. After a fitful sleep Dallas got up and wandered into the main room, her eyes going unerringly to the package.

Was Jefferson right? Was it all a matter of faith? And did she have the right to keep judging him by what Bill had done?

She just didn't know what to do. What was right. Her glance flicked over the mantel clock. Only a half hour until her "wedding."

Would Jefferson be there?

Yes. From deep inside her came the sure knowledge that Jefferson *would* be waiting right where he said he would. After all, it had taken him five years to come home . . . but come home he *had*.

She smiled and walked the few steps separating her from

the box on the table. Her fingers slid along the lid's edge before hesitantly lifting it off.

Tears filled her eyes and she bit down hard on her bottom lip. A wedding dress.

Carefully, reverently, she lifted it free of its wrappings. Yards and yards of white satin trimmed in ivory lace and pearl buttons, it was a gown worthy of a princess. Or a woman in love.

Dallas glanced at the clock again. She would have to hurry.

Riding into the silent town, Dallas clutched Eli's reins in one hand and Jefferson's most recent gift in the other.

Smiling down at it, she realized that he must have been out at her place before dawn. Just to leave a Valentine on her porch for her to find.

Fragile and delicate, the pale pink card held a painting of a single, soft yellow rosebud, surrounded by bits of spidery lace. Inside were just four little words: *I love you, Jefferson*.

She wanted to believe. She wanted to be happy again.

All around her the quiet screamed at her. Taunted her. Plucked at her failing confidence. She breathed deeply, tightened her grip on the Valentine, and kept riding. No one was on the street. Curtains were drawn across blank windows, and doors were closed. It was as if overnight, an unseen hand spirited everyone away.

But she went on. She had to trust him. She *loved* him.

Even the doors to the church were shut tight. And still Dallas dismounted carefully, adjusted the hang of her gown, and tied Eli's reins to the hitching post. Lifting the hem of her dress, she slowly climbed the six steps to the church doors. With every beat of her heart, she told herself, *Believe, trust him.*

When she reached the top of the stairs, her fingers curled around the shining brass doorknob and slowly, hesitantly, she turned it. The heavy door swung open, and waiting for her on the other side was Jefferson, grinning from ear to ear.

He took two long strides, swept her up in his arms, and kissed her soundly. His mouth moved over hers in a tender promise of more to come. And when he finally broke away, he smiled down at her. "I told you, Dallas honey. All you needed was a little faith."

"I know," she whispered and ran one finger down the length of his jaw.

He pointed at the frilly Valentine still clasped in her hand. "I see you found my gift. . . ."

She nodded. "Thank you."

"Happy Valentine's Day, darlin'."

Dallas grinned. Valentine's Day. Romance. Love.

Jefferson.

"Are you ready to get married?" He jerked his head toward the filled church behind him. "Everybody's getting a little antsy, sittin' in there being quiet for so long."

"Oh, I'm ready, Jefferson." She wrapped her arms around his neck and squeezed. "I'm more than ready!"

PERFECT MATES

by

Karen Lockwood

Dear Readers,

I'm an incurable romantic. Confession: For twenty-three years, I've saved the Valentine ski hat I knit my then future husband. It was dark red, of course, and had a box of candy hearts hidden inside. Knitting long ago went out the window in favor of writing, but not the notion that men, as much as women, enjoy love tokens on Valentine's Day.

Each February, through the years, I've played an eager Cupid, giving my three sons stuffed animals, funny cards, and their personal favorite, heart-shaped boxes of chocolates with wisecracking animals on the lids. When two of the boys went off to college the goodies followed via mail. I've asked if they want the custom abolished, but twenty-year-old boys on a budget are amazingly indulgent where food is involved. Ah, the fun involved in teaching sons to be romantic! But the older they've gotten, the harder it has become shopping amongst the rosebuds and frilly candy boxes. I need some new, less mushy Valentine surprises to please my guys' tender hearts.

So when I set out to write this story, I first went on a search through the library for Valentine ideas I might have overlooked. A lovely book led me to an intriguing custom that's fallen by the wayside. . . . Once upon a time (before the postage stamp popularized greeting cards), *gloves* were a favorite gift. Everything from plain to extravagantly bejeweled gloves.

Gentlemen wishing to propose on Valentine's Day might give gloves to literally ask for a lady's hand in marriage. If the lady accepted she could signify by wearing the gloves in public. Enchanted, I knew at once I wanted to write a variation on the Cinderella story. My hero, Max, has but one desire for St. Valentine's Day: to find the mate to a lost glove—and of course the lady to whom both gloves belong. I set my story during a time when love and romance seemed especially precarious—the late 18th century. The resulting story, like the mysterious foil-wrapped bon-bon in the center of a candy box, took even me by surprise.

This February 14, if I give out gloves, it'll be my way of reviving a quaint custom. But I won't expect my sons to accept handwarmers in place of sentimental chocolates. They'll want both.

I hope my story warms your heart. I know I'll never again slip on a pair of gloves without looking over my shoulder for Cupid.

Heartfelt Wishes,

Karen Lockwood
P. O. Box 3411
Idaho Falls, ID 83403

London, 1794

CUPID, MAXIMILIAN DECIDED, had no mercy and gave no quarter.

Why, the Christmas greens were barely down, the New Year scarcely rung in, yet for at least a week now, the house had been cluttered with tradesmen showing samples of everything from cloth of gold hearts to out-of-season roses to paper cupids. . . .

"Don't you think," Maximilian said calmly to the ladies of the house, "that we ought to cancel the masquerade ball again this year?"

Outside the library, raindrops batted valiantly against the mullioned glass, the wind howled mightily down the chimney, but neither was sufficient to block out the sudden storm of feminine protest.

"Cancel the ball?" His stepmother dropped an armful of paper cupids and sank into the nearest chair, staring at him as if he'd gone mad.

Her goddaughter Caroline Cordell quickly joined the attack. "Max, why would you suggest such a thing?" She knelt to pick up the cupids. "Naturally, if you were still on your deathbed, then your stepmother might have to consider the notion, but you're recovered." After depositing cupids in Lady Shelburne's lap, she eyed him skeptically. "Aren't you?"

At last his stepmother recovered a measure of composure. "You're not going to start in having those dreams and delusions again—not when there's a houseful of guests coming?"

Caro bent to pat her godmother's hand and stared in disapproval at the heir to Shelburne House. "Why, Max, last February you were gone, endangering your life, and now all London has a chance at the ball to see that the heir to the house is recovered, that you're well. Shelburne House *has* to hold the masquerade."

Max looked up, frowning fiercely. Since her arrival a year ago last fall, Miss Caroline Cordell had insinuated herself into the household in grand style. But while the orphaned minx might have his stepmother wrapped about her little finger, working her wiles on a world-weary and jaded viscount like himself would be far more difficult.

"I'm completely recovered, dear Caro, but you look suddenly pale. I only made the suggestion because I believe it's unseemly to be celebrating when across the Channel people are suffering—"

"Really, Maximilian," his stepmother scoffed, "if you must relive your French adventure a thousand times, then why don't you use it as inspiration for your costume? Masquerade as a smuggler dealing in contraband—gloves or brandy. And Caro can come dressed as a French émigré, just like the one you're always having delusions about in your sleep."

"How do you know what I say in my sleep, *maman*?"

"Servants, Max."

"I have dreams and talk in my sleep, but not delusions."

"Max," Caro said, "your stepmother only wants you to be happy and well."

Dubious, he considered the suggestion and the young lady both. Caro's hair—fair and once longer than his, was newly cropped *à la mode* in France; her gown—high-waisted and diaphanous—succeeded in camouflaging her plumpness. To Caro, *revolution* was an abstract word, signifying nothing more than new and daring freedom in fashion, and her goal was to outshine—outshock—everyone.

"Caro," he reminded her, "I have friends in France enduring the chaos." Unlike her, he'd witnessed firsthand the terror, the families torn asunder. Trials were mockeries. Suspicion sufficient for death. It seemed a sacrilege, when in Paris the gutters reeked of blood and fear, to celebrate Cupid. "I care," he finished simply. "And if London should be so besieged, I would hope someone would care about us."

Caro stamped her foot. "Oh, what does all that matter here in London? *We* have no guillotine, and Shelburne House should have its St. Valentine's Day Ball the same as always." At a warning glance from Lady Shelburne, she softened her tone. "Oh, please Max, don't spoil your stepmother's plans."

But he wearied of arguing, wearied of trying to reason with them about how his "grand adventure" to the Continent had gone awry. Smuggling émigrés had occupied him for longer than his family intended . . . and nearly cost his life. And his sanity.

She was black-haired and very young, and for three days he guided her through the back roads of France, and no one touched her, not even Max, himself, who had the most temptation. . . .

Even now the memories made his blood run faster. Too many images haunted him: The dark of the moon. An escape boat. The rabble. Fanatic and idealistic. But always it came back to Yolanda . . . the dark-haired waif. No delusion, she'd been as real as the knife to his ribs . . . and her memory an obsession. Still.

"Yolanda—"

"Max, you're *talking* to yourself again." His stepmother was standing, shaking a finger at him as if he were still the thoughtless schoolboy who'd slid down the grand staircase during tea. Lady Shelburne. Wife of the eighth Earl of Shelburne. She'd go to her death in a trumbel, he suspected, rather than give up this house and her aristocratic position.

Music began to drift from another room; afternoon callers had arrived for Caro, and someone was plunking out a melody on the pianoforte.

His stepmother paused in front of Max before going to greet her callers. "You must remember, Max . . . your father has approved this Valentine masquerade entirely. He's expecting a full account in writing mailed to America, and he expects to hear news of Caro's happiness and your good health. So there's to be no more talk of canceling our ball. . . ."

"Since I can hardly override my father's wishes, then the ball goes on," he said, adding ominously, "but I may not attend."

Caro, who'd been sashaying out, whirled, mouth open. "Not come? But you *have* to—"

"Why?"

Caro stammered. "Well, because . . . else your friends won't come. . . ."

His friends! The only reason Caro needed his friends there was to make him jealous. Oh, he knew how the two ladies schemed. The earl—his own father—goaded on by his stepmother, had offered to sponsor Caroline Cordell's debut into society. That coming out had, because of Max's health, already been postponed a year, and the ladies were most anxious to get on with it. So perhaps the sooner she was bid on in the marriage mart, the better off the household would be. Which is why, he realized, he'd have to give in and let the ball go on as scheduled—to surround Caro with as many other marriage prospects as possible.

With unaccustomed humility Caro knelt in front of him. "Oh, *please*, Max, please, forget whatever happened in France. Please. Just for St. Valentine's Day. It's your duty."

"Duty?" That was a strange word to hear falling from the lips of Caroline Cordell. His St. Valentine's Day duty! Max must be more sentimental than he realized. If courtship became a duty, he'd resolve then and there to remain a bachelor.

"Max," she pleaded, "I need you to . . . to rescue me from unwelcome suitors." Her voice trembled. Why, had the young lady been less well born, she'd have had a future on the stage.

"Please?"

Desperation indeed. "I'll try," he said simply, and satisfied, Caro swirled out, followed a moment later by his chattering stepmother.

"Caro, postpone the glovemaker till after our callers are gone. You simply must meet the Davenports; years ago at a St. Valentine's Day Ball, they made every guest draw names for dance partners. Two liaisons resulted . . . well, it was quite the talk of London. I want our ball this year to outdo theirs. . . ."

Levering himself out of his chair, Max called for his greatcoat. If he didn't get out of this house and its talk of cupids and memories of St. Valentine's Days past, he'd go mad for certain. So while everyone gathered around the parlor pianoforte, he snuck down to the servants' hall, barely making his escape before the strains of Mozart—shamefully out of tune—followed him.

But when it came to that, no one was more out of tune with London Society than Max. And he cursed the Revolution, Cupid, and the temptation of women in general, especially the black-haired waif, who, like a perfect melody, haunted his mind.

*   *   *

Standing in the tradesman's room of Shelburne House—waiting for the lady of the house to come and sample her wares—Violet felt a keen nostalgia and a longing to turn back time. Once she, too, had been a fine lady, young and full of dreams and eager to dance.

Now Violet's sole duty, besides earning her keep, was to learn through the newspapers if her brother had escaped the guillotine. Searching lists of names and praying. The papers, in their lack of news, had shown mercy. More mercy than the scraps of gossip in London streets. Recent émigrés whispered it about that somewhere in France, Armand Sangueille had met his end, a swift and certain end. Other émigrés, especially those who had begun to patronize the glovemaker's shop, counseled caution. In France rumor ruled. In Violet's heart confusion, guilt. She tried to let life go on.

After all, before she and Armand had gone their separate ways, she'd promised him not to dwell on what was, only on survival. "We two, brother and sister, have a duty now to the Sangueille name," her brother had told her. "A duty to our family to get safely to London, no matter what. I will rendezvous with you on the coast, if all goes well, if no one betrays us. Trust no one, not even the people who claim to help. We can't know in these dangerous times who is enemy and who is friend. Treat everyone as contraband."

Armand, her daring brother, had never rendezvoused with her, and she blamed herself, no, blamed her fatal indiscretion. Acting like a common wench while her brother needed her. If she lost her brother, she would never, ever forgive herself. Even now, nearly a year later, she made the trek daily from the glove shop to the modest church in Covent Garden, praying for forgiveness, for mercy to her brother. The church was always, it seemed, covered with noisy pecking pigeons and beggars, and like most of London, it was too preoccupied to worry about what befell strangers across the Channel. Life went on.

And now, once again, another St. Valentine's Day approached—her first in London, and the closer St. Valentine's Day came, the more requests for gloves poured into the Gilded Glove, until the shop was virtually overwhelmed. Violet had jumped at the chance to help make calls on customers with simple demands. It would be a respite from the tedious hours spent in the shop learning to decorate gloves. A chance to escape the back room where she lived—where she hid. Surely steady customers would be understanding if just this once a substitute came in Simon's place.

"Especially since I'm only going to the houses where ladies desire samples of ribbon and beads," she'd reassured Simon. "It'd be different if I had to measure."

Simon and Fanny Doublet had together taught her much, but measuring a hand for the precise fit of a fine glove took practice.

"Her Ladyship's glove measurements are already at the shop," Simon's wife reminded him, "as are those of the young lady, Miss Cordell, and the other customers. Oh, let her go, Simon. She's worked too hard in here for too long."

At the last minute, pressed with calls, Simon relented. Violet, with her air of quality, was the only one in the shop who could stand in for Simon. Indeed, her French accent would reassure the most discriminating customers that they would indeed receive the finest finished gloves. And so it happened. Her earlier two customers had been charmed with her samples. The morning flew by . . . until she reached Shelburne House, where she'd been kept waiting for nigh on to an hour now. Tapping her foot. Rearranging her basket of wares. Staring longingly at her own white kid gloves, then pocketing them. Then pulling them out again. And tapping her foot again.

For the longest time the melody of a pianoforte had drifted from the parlor far upstairs. The candlelight flickered against the ceiling, the walls, almost in time to the music. Entranced, Violet put down her valise of measure tapes and ribbon samples, and picking up her skirt, began to move in time to the music. Her feet would not stand still, no matter how she tried to ignore the music. She was so young and had been alone so long. Could duty not spare another twirl, one more pirouette? Her feet would not stand still, and wasn't that an irony considering her circumstances a year ago this time?

She was done in. Her feet wouldn't take her another step. Out of breath, she knelt beside a fence, the wind stinging her face. Her family was gone, her guardian an Englishman disguised as a French Republican—right down to the green cockade in his hat. They'd arrived at the end of the road from Paris, she and Max, and now he took her hand and tugged her toward the edge of the windblown cliff, where, behind the shelter of rocks, they could await the rescue boat. Overhead, stars flickered, the one constant in her world. Like the smuggling of contraband goods, the rescue of émigrés was all done at night by the dark of the moon, but tonight the moon was full, and they would have to wait for it to wane. Wait and hope her brother would find them. Sitting so close, she had nothing to do but cast surreptitious glances at her handsome guardian, his profile highlighted by the moon. A dark stubble of a beard shadowed his jaw, underlining his masculinity and at the same time adding to his dangerous aura.

Even in the face of danger, desire beckoned. Oh, to have met this man in another time, another place . . . Such thoughts were sacrilege.

"Armand is late for our rendezvous." Her voice trembled, and she dropped her gloves.

"He will find his way," the Englishman said.

*Without warning, the horses galloped out of the night,
and the Englishman clamped a hand to her mouth. "Say
nothing, and if we're lucky they'll not be fanatics. . . ."
His skin tasted half of salt, half of smoke. His touch was
surprisingly gentle. Strong but gentle. His words vibrated
through her, and for the first time she felt a calm, as if she
were not alone in the center of the storm. He tugged her
toward a haystack then, gathered her against his taut frame.
It was the first time in three days he had been anything but
the aloof stranger, giving orders, the first time Violet had
admitted that she—proud, headstrong daughter of a
comte—might actually need the handsome Englishman to
save her life. Worse, she forgot her brother's admonition.
Trust no one. How could she not trust Max when she melted
inside, turned liquid in his embrace? She went as dizzy as if
he had twirled her about a ballroom.*

"He will find his way," Max repeated.

"And if he doesn't . . . ?"

Again, she had to reprimand herself. No dancing . . .
No, Violet, you are masquerading as an apprentice to a
glovemaker in London and lucky to have your life, and
shopgirls, Violet, do not dance at noon in the homes of
English noblemen.

Sighing, she stared at the ceiling of Shelburne House,
where shadows flickered. She was a long, long way from
the coast of France, even farther from Paris, and further yet
from the innocence of girlhood. She forced her feet to stand
still, hugged her arms about her waist. Remember, Violet,
she cautioned herself, you have come a long way from your
father's chateau.

Still, the music of Shelburne House drifted up and made
her feet dance again. Her hands—well, they begged for her
to try on her gloves—the only memento with which she'd

escaped. Like lucky charms, they were with her always, and now she pulled them on, just for a few minutes, so she could admire again the embroidery in thread of gold and silver. An indulgence, but she was oh, so young, and so torn between her duty to family and her longings for love. After all that had happened in France during her escape, could another moment's indiscretion hurt? She twirled in place.

The dance of a long-ago ball at home was still fresh in her memory, and to stand there in a darkened room moving in time to Mozart was balm. It was to this melody that she had danced with her father—her brother, too—on her eighteenth birthday, elegant in her new white gloves. It was to this melody that in her imagination she danced with her mysterious guardian, Max. His hand would gently hold hers, and he would guide her through the steps with masterful ease. For now a shadow would suffice.

Without warning, a figure filled the doorway. Violet stopped in midstep, heart pounding.

"Dance," a man's voice said. "Keep dancing."

The little room on the lower floor was dim, lit only by a few tallow candles, and Max stood in the open doorway, waiting for his eyes to adjust to the light.

Shadows moved on the opposite wall, and he stood there longer than he needed to, watching those shadows dance. Intrigued, he moved closer. When the dancer stopped, again he commanded her to dance on.

It occurred to Max that once again his stepmother, overcome by whimsy, had forgotten a loyal tradesman. It wasn't Max's job to dismiss tradesmen; some would call it a breech of protocol, but given the anarchy across the Channel, household rules left him impatient lately. Not so impatient, of course, that he couldn't admire a shopgirl's movements.

The young lady, dressed in a simple gown of dark wool,

danced in time to the Mozart. How, he wondered, ever more intrigued, could a mere shopgirl have learned such intricate steps, a dance of the aristocracy? But more than her exquisite grace held him transfixed. Her hair was black, inky black and cropped, her figure slight, her profile wistful in expression. Most of all, she looked familiar. Disturbingly familiar.

He pushed the door open wider, and as she turned, the candlelight illuminated her face.

He stood stock-still, the blood draining from his face, his pulse throbbing heavily. Yolanda? Here in his very own house? In the tradesman's room? In all of London she'd made her way to him? For the first time in months he believed in miracles, in dreams come to life, in the kindness of fate. . . .

His throat was tense; perhaps he was hallucinating. "Yolanda?" he whispered. If it was her, it would be a dream come to life.

Violet froze in place. The voice was so familiar, but out of place. She looked toward the door, hand pressed to her heart, and just managed to stifle a gasp.

It was a dream come to life . . . Max?

Max. She just managed not to say his name out loud.

Her brother was still missing, in danger, and his life depended on her discretion. *She was Violet, incognito, and had best remember that. Trust no one, not even people who try to help you.*

She bent to her valise, and trying to keep her trembling hands busy, picked through the shop samples, sorting golden braid from silver ribbon. Her mind whirled. A quirk of fate had led her here to the very house where Max lived.

Incredulous at his good fortune, Max took a step toward her, then another. Her hair was cropped, her gamine face thinner, but her eyes were the same—pansy dark and calling

out to him. . . . And the closer he got the more he
trembled, attraction alive and tangible. This could be no one
but her, the woman who haunted his dreams.

"Yolanda?" he asked, shaking. "Is it you?"

She shook her head.

"I am Violet." She could not lie, only give the English
version of her name. Her real name. If she was lucky, he
would have forgotten his French. "My name is Violet."

Confusion swept across his face and, like a wave, quickly
receded to leave nothing but bleakness. "You look so like
her . . . Yolanda, daughter of the Comte de Sangueille."
His voice seared her, tugged at her heart.

She averted her face, tugged away from him. "There is no
such person. They neither one exist. May I help you in some
other way, milord?"

Oh, yes, Max thought, that soft voice was the one that
haunted his dreams. She was lying, and he advanced on her.
"You fear me. After trembling in my arms, you deny you
ever knew me. . . . I know it's you. Where have you come
from?"

She stood straight and proud, chin high. "You have
mistaken me with someone else, milord. I am Violet and I
have come from the Gilded Glove, the shop of Simon
Doublet." She lifted up her valise and began to pull out
ribbon. "I have come to show samples of decorative trim to
Miss Caroline Cordell. It is for her order of Valentine's
gloves."

"For her costume?" Caro's costume interested him not a
whit. He asked only to keep this black-haired angel in
conversation.

She looked down, rummaged through her basket, coiled a
measure tape around and around her hand. "I know nothing
of her costume. Near St. Valentine's Day many ladies order
gloves or leave us a list of their favorite gloves and their size
and their preferred decorative work."

"Do they? Why?" A half smile tugged at his mouth.

"Why?" She blushed beneath his steady gaze. "Why, milord, it is the custom, surely you know. . . ."

"What custom?" He pretended ignorance.

"To give gloves on St. Valentine's Day as a way of asking for a lady's hand in marriage."

"Indeed?" Max gazed down at the tiny gloves she wore. "And some ladies are so confident of a proposal they order their gloves in advance?"

"Well, at least the gentleman can be confident, if not of a favorable reply, that the glove will fit and please the lady."

"How well planned betrothals have become."

She looked up into his eyes, gaze steady. "Naturally, at this time of year, the shop is very busy," she said softly. She looked away, and it was then her tone grew businesslike. "Did you wish to order gloves?"

Max smiled. She might have changed her name and cropped her hair, but this was Yolanda, and he'd get her to admit it yet, take her in his arms, and kiss her till he wore down her defenses.

"Since Miss Cordell . . ." He cleared the huskiness from his voice. "Since Miss Cordell has obviously forgotten her appointment, I will look at your samples. Perhaps I'll find something that will please a young lady. Sometimes the gentleman likes to choose for himself, does he not?"

"Yes, milord," she said briskly, still playing her masquerade for all it was worth. "I have fringe, and I have samples of beadwork, and I have thread of gold and silver."

"I think," Max said, "that I'll start with a pair of gloves for myself—unadorned. Can you make them in time for St. Valentine's Day?"

She paused, uncertain. "Mr. Doublet will do his best, but he'll need your measure." She rummaged in her basket for a paper. Fanny might not have taught her how to custom-measure gloves, but Violet had watched the Doublets often enough to know a trick. Sometimes when the measure was in doubt, Simon, to be safe, traced the hand. That she could do.

She could draw Max's face in the dark for that matter. Tawny hair tumbling over his forehead. Prominent cheekbones. Aquiline nose. Sensuous mouth. And midnight blue eyes. Inscrutable eyes. Dangerous Max. Dangerous and oh, so tender.

"Do you need me to remove my coat? Turn up the ruffs at my wrist?" he asked.

"Milord, you shock me. I am only measuring your hand."

"You shock *me*."

"Dancing in your house?"

With his thumb he tilted her chin. "I thought you were a lady who'd lost her way, yet you would have me believe you a common wench."

"Milord, I don't know who you mean." She averted her face.

"Admit you know me."

She rummaged in her valise, pretending to look for something. "Milord, please . . ."

"Max. My name is Max. You know me. Admit it."

She turned her back to him, willing him to leave. How could this be happening to her?

He came up behind her, and she held her breath, half afraid he'd touch her, half afraid he would not. Too late, she looked down at the gloves she'd pulled on. The white gloves with her family crest. The only thing that could give her away to this man.

She hesitated, face flushing. "You taunt me, milord, talking so. How could I be a lost lady in so humble a dress?"

"Rubbish. That humble dress saved your life. It's a costume."

She tugged from his grip. Her masquerade would not fail,

not now. Not with the man who'd taught her how to hide in the first place.

He reached for her hands, turned her around to face him. Too late, she tried to draw back, but he held fast, staring at the elegant white gloves.

"These are not the gloves of a shopgirl."

"I told you—samples."

"Yours. These gloves prove you're a lady."

"These gloves give you away as a lady. Hide them. Down your bodice." He handed them to her.

"Max, you shock me."

But he was right, and she knew it. The gloves could give her away as nobility. Incriminating gloves—white gloves embroidered in thread of gold and silver. Her sole memento of the past, they were at once her greatest treasure or her ticket to the guillotine.

"Hide them," he ordered in a whisper that seared. Modesty was gone. Under his watchful eye, she stuffed them down her bodice and then curtsied for his approval.

He stared at her long and hard. "Don't let them hear you talk," he reminded her. "It's too refined . . . giggle, like an infatuated wench. . . ."

"I—I don't know how." How did one learn the deportment of a wench?

Inside she turned to liquid fire beneath his touch as he pulled back her cape to show off her costume. Wench clothes. From the peasantry he'd stolen an old mobcap, and swiftly he tucked her hair up in it. Just as quickly his hands moved down to crisscross a kerchief, and finally he spanned her waist, reached behind her back to tie an apron. Roaming hands. Each brush of his fingers left her throbbing, yearning, frightened of him as much as the enemy. "I can't go on . . . I can't."

She'd no sooner spoken the words than the horsemen

*appeared, and in their hats they too wore a green cockade,
in their hands they carried torches and knives. . . .*

*The gang—fanatics, one and all—was there then leering
down at them. "Hand us your traveling papers, Citizens!"*

*It was time to begin her charade. How did wenches
behave? And she shut her eyes and turned into her guardian's shoulder. He tensed and then his arms, strong and
reassuring, gathered her scandalously close, so close she
could feel his muscled contours, listen to his wild heartbeat,
feel her own slam against her breast in answer. She had a
peasant costume, but no papers. It was over. She had no
papers. She was caught. . . .*

But it would not happen a second time. Not after a year
of hiding in London . . . nor could he possibly remember
the gloves—not after nearly a year. She turned, feigning
calmness.

"We need to measure your hand."

Without missing a beat, she flattened the plain brown
paper on a little table, then turned back to Max. "Place your
hand on the paper."

He spread his fingers and waited while she rummaged for
something with which to trace. "Every hand is different, and
Mr. Doublet has not fully trained me in the proper way to
measure—"

"Yolanda?"

At his voice she looked up, realized her error, and turned
away. "It is Violet."

"Very well. I'll try to remember . . . Violet," he said
softly, "I only wanted to lend you this."

He was holding out a pencil. She snatched it, avoiding the
gleam in his eyes. The current between them pulsed.

In order to trace, she had to place her left hand over his.
Even through the fine white kid of her gloves, she could feel

his strength, his warmth. After a moment's hesitation, she began to move the pencil beside his hand.

While not work-roughened, his hand was not effete, either. It was a man's hand, a hand that could touch with both gentleness and intimacy, with reassurance and protection. "Your little finger curves in—like mine," she noted.

"Don't all little fingers curve?"

"Oh, no, some are straight. It's a family trait."

"Indeed. What do you think? Shall I be easy to fit, despite my crooked little finger?"

"Mr. Doublet, I predict, will say it is an unusual hand."

"It is a steady hand, though, Violet," he said tenderly, "unlike yours, which trembles over mine."

Snatching the pencil, suddenly he reversed their hands and pinned hers under his. Gently he covered it and traced the swan design on her glove with his finger.

Feigning bravery, she looked up. "What color of glove did you prefer, sir? Dyed leather or natural?"

"Violet—Yolanda—Violet, I don't care what color of gloves your shop makes for me or what your name is now. I only care that you remember me." The anguish in his voice was palpable.

She slid her hand out from his. "That is impossible."

"Why?" he said, voice hoarse, pain-filled. "Why are you playing this masquerade? Pretending not to know me? Why, Violet? You're not in France anymore."

Reaching for her again, he caught her face in his hands and stared down into dark eyes. "Violet," he pleaded, "you're safe. Stop playacting. Now that I've found you, there's no need for masquerades. . . ."

Every sensory point throbbed with her own pain. But an émigré from France was in too much danger; in France the leadership changed too fast for people to remain loyal to anything save their heads. She couldn't risk giving out any information that might hurt her brother, not a second time.

"This is no pretense, milord." She shook her head and tried to back away. "I am an honest shopgirl who earns my keep."

"You're French."

"And a shopgirl. You are mistaking me, sir, for another." She would lie. Make him doubt himself. "You are imagining I am someone else, don't you see?"

Max went cold. No, he didn't see why everyone was out to prove him mad. Even the woman who had caused it all. "You deceive yourself, Violet—and me. Why?"

She backed up, and he followed her around the table.

In two strides he was beside her again, this time his hands on her waist and turning her so that she had to look into his eyes. "But it's me . . . Max. The masquerade is over. Don't you see? It's over, and there's nothing to fear."

Violet looked up into his eyes. Yes, that was the whole problem. The masquerade they'd shared in France *was* over. Everything between them was over. At least, for her it was. Max could be anything—a spy, a double agent, an informer, the man who'd turned in her brother.

"Milord, if you won't let me trace your hand, then please, would you tell the ladies I am here to take their ribbon orders for the trim on their gloves? Else I must leave and attend my next customer."

"No."

One option remained: to reach for her cloak, to leave. It would have worked if only she hadn't looked up at him, so handsome in the coat and breeches of a gentleman. His tawny hair was pulled back with a black ribbon. Oh, she'd known that out of rough garb, he'd look this elegant, this desirable.

Once again he reached for her hand and studied the fine white gloves she wore, rubbed his finger across the intertwined swans, tracing the golden threads, and then the silver, anything to keep her tiny hand in his.

"Please, milord. These gloves are merely sample merchandise."

"They remind me of gloves I've seen. Could I buy them?"

"Not exactly," she stammered and chanced a glance up at intense blue eyes. "The gloves at Mr. Doublet's shop are unique. Every pair is different."

While she spoke, slowly, ever so slowly, he peeled off one glove, one of her precious white gloves, raised her hand to his lips, and without removing his gaze from hers kissed her hand. She couldn't speak, couldn't breathe. "I nearly died after you sailed off," he said.

Oh, Max. Her heart ached, but pity would not draw her out. She snatched up the glove he'd removed and fumbled to stuff it in the pocket of her cloak, her throat tight. "I'm sorry to hear of your misfortune, sir," she whispered. She chanced a glance up. "You are fully recovered now?"

He hadn't recovered, and it had little to do with the gash from a knife. *Only get her to England. Do whatever you must do to keep her safe and alive. That's all we ask is her life.* Max scarcely knew her family, but accepted the trust. And *this* was his gratitude?

She ducked around him, determined to escape, but he stole up behind her and pulled her close against him, so close she shut her eyes to hide her longing.

Silence. Except for the familiar thrill of his heartbeat against her back. Stillness. Except for the strength pulsing in his arms.

"Why?" he asked for the third time, as if the third time might hold a different answer. "Why are you pretending to be a shopgirl to a glovemaker?"

Should she answer? She had to put her family first. Max was of the past, the past she wanted to forget. But if she didn't leave this room, this house, now, more than gloves would betray her. She'd be caught by her own longing, betrayed by her pounding heart.

The music, though distant, made its own spell. . . . In the little tradesman's room, cluttered with chairs and mannequins, he held her in his arms, and she was immobile, liquid with desire. Old longings slipped over her like a warm cloak, and it had been such a long lonely year surviving with only her own wits.

Before she could move, he pulled away the brown paper outline of his hand and wadded it up. "Yolanda . . . Violet, whatever name you want . . . admit it. You know me and know me well."

He buried his face in her hair, and she shut her eyes in ecstasy.

"Sir, you take more liberties than the rabble who stormed the Bastille, you realize that?"

Max, determined to wear her down, turned her in his arms and touched his lips to her skin, starting with a kiss to her temple, the crown of her head, her forehead. She stood still as stone, willing herself not to tremble.

"Violet, now you cannot pretend. In my arms you give yourself away. . . ." Closing what little space remained between them, he tilted her chin up and touched her lips, ever so softly.

And then, against her will, she was kissing him back, her lips telling the truth, turning back time. Maximilian. Max. Within a minute the same current pulsed between them, poised them on the brink, threatened to make her forget what she was about.

The door squeaked on its hinges. Breathless with longing, Violet broke away, guilty, and stared in terror at the door. There, outlined in the faint candlelight, stood a rather plump young lady with fair cropped hair.

Who was this? His wife? A fiancée?

"Caro," he said on a half smile, "you forgot to come for

the glovemaker." He spoke as casually as if the kiss had been a nobleman's stolen sweet. *Trust no one. Especially those who claim to help. They may be contraband.*

The woman named Caro flicked a disapproving glance over Violet's tattered gown, her severe hairstyle, her flushed face. "Maximilian," the woman said, voice cool, dangerous. "What are you doing?"

"Giving some business to the glovemaker you forgot."

"This is no glovemaker."

"She is no shopgirl, either," Max said. "This is Yolanda . . . a young lady from—"

"If she's a lady, my name is not Caro."

Caro. A cold name. As cold as the rabble in France, who would have guillotined her had Max not helped her . . . Caro. A name to match the fury in her face as she circled Violet.

Caro turned a narrowed gaze on Violet. "What are you doing here instead of the Gilded Glove's owner? I summoned Mr. Doublet here. He always measures and cuts our gloves. Mr. Doublet and no one else."

"I beg your pardon, miss, but the glovemaker has so many calls today. Valentine gloves to measure, so they'll be ready for the gentlemen to give as a—a proposal. I offered to make the calls for the ribbons and decorations."

"Excuses. Has he found a richer client? Someone he prefers to spend his time with?"

"You are his favorite."

"Then the old man?"

Violet backed closer to the door.

"He's ill, I fear." Gaspard was her guardian now, and his precarious health was no lie.

"How do I know you even work for Simon?" She glanced at Max.

Maximilian, face taut, took a step toward the woman.

"Caro, you're interrogating her. She's been through enough questions, more than you could ever endure."

"Then she should find another occupation."

"Caro, apologize at once."

"To a shopgirl you've had in your arms? If your father hears of this, he'll make you apologize to *me*."

"She is no shopgirl."

Caro laughed, as if she'd heard the most amusing joke. "But, Max, that's only too clear from her behavior. She's less than a shopgirl."

"She's a lady. If you let me explain—"

"No, *monsieur*, please." Violet stepped between them. "She is right. Don't say anything to make matters worse. It's of no consequence who I am—"

"It is of consequence. You're the daughter of—"

"Just the humble employee of a glovemaker."

"A vulgar charlatan," Caro said.

"No! No!"

As Max reached for her, she picked up her skirts and ran. Once again, escape. Escape. In her haste, the glove fell from her cloak pocket, but she could not stop for sentiment. Escape. Escape. When, oh, when would it end?

Max stared after her, as if unable to believe what was happening. He was still warm from holding her in his arms.

One heartbeat passed, and then he came to his senses and gave chase.

Caro shrieked. "No, Max. You're having delusions again. Do you hear? Delusions!"

He ran all the faster. "Wait!" Max twisted through the dimly lit servants' quarters. Ahead of him—footsteps, the swish of Violet's petticoats. This couldn't be. Violet fleeing from him over and over again.

He stumbled over a washbasin, turned a corridor, and tripped on a bucket. Servants ducked their heads out of doorways everywhere to see what the clatter was about, but he kept on running down the hall until it straightened out, and he caught a fleeting glimpse of her black hair ruffling, her skirts flying.

"Violet, wait. Don't go—"

With a swift tug at the outer door, she slid outside, and the door slammed tight behind her. Just seconds behind he pushed it open and burst out into the street, smack into a chestnut vendor. Backing up he dusted the fellow off, then circled in place, people and wagons surrounding him. Gone. Violet was already swallowed up in the streets of London, swallowed up amidst the chimney sweeps and hansom cabs, the clouds of soot, the mud puddles, the winter outlines of trees, reaching for the drizzling skies.

He screwed up his face and yelled to the sky. "Violet! Vi—!" He sank down, slumped against the house.

Dear Violet. She was still living a charade. Still living with the terror, and only he could explain that it had not all been charade.

But she was gone, thanks to Caro's interrogation. Gone.

* * *

As the interrogation began, bayonets and knives teased at Violet's cloak—a challenge to the masquerade of her peasant dress. One knife aimed at Max's ribs. He pulled out a piece of paper and thrust it at them, then spoke rapidly in the patois to distract them from the girl.

"Does the Revolution require permission for me to bed a wench?"

She gasped, and he tightened his hold, a reminder to keep silent, to play along, no matter what he said, no matter how he bluffed.

"She led me a merry chase, and now I'll have her. For my Valentine. Go and find your own wenches if you're of like mind."

"She has no papers?" They turned a cold eye on the white-skinned beauty, the pampered daughter of a comte.

Dirt smudged her face, her nails were torn, hands scratched. Max held them up as if to prove she was a hardworking wench. "Why would a farm wench need papers? Especially on St. Valentine's Day?"

"If she's a wench, then show us more than her hands to prove it, Citizen. Prove it with deeds." They guffawed.

He proved it all right. He bent to her lips, not as one would bend to a lady in public, but as he'd grab a tavern wench. His kiss was wild and sensual and so thorough that he hoped it would block out the raucous guffaws and the terror of the knife tip at their ribs. When he was done, all she could feel were his arms, his lips.

What else could any man have done? Except carry out the masquerade and hope a kiss would be enough. A kiss between a Citizen and a wench. A Valentine masquerade in exchange for her life. . . .

"Violet!" Max stood on the Mayfair street and called her name into the sky. "Violet!"

"You wish a posy, milord?" A passing violet seller displayed a toothless smile as she thrust toward him a posy of winter violets, dripping with rain. Knees weak, voice too hoarse to talk, he thrust a few coins at her as he waved her away.

Teeming London life swirled around him, as the darkness of despair threatened to overwhelm him. He'd found her, a needle in a haystack, only to lose her. Shoppers and tradesmen passed him by. At a nearby windowbox a gardener, hands coated in dirt, planted the first primroses of the season. Max stared at his own empty hands, wondering how she'd slipped away, back into the vast haystack that was London. . . .

And that was when he remembered the glove that she'd dropped.

The glittering white glove!

He yanked open the door and hurried back to the servants' hall, backtracking the route she'd fled. There it was, gleaming white against the wooden floor. Proof that she'd been here. Here and in his arms.

Snatching it up, he pressed it to his face, to his lips, to his cheek. One clue. One glove, white and soft as down and embroidered all over in thread of gold and silver. He stared at the intertwined swans. This was not at all a homely glove like shopgirls wore. This was the glove of a fine lady.

No, he was not suffering delusions. She was indeed Yolanda—now Violet. By any name, she was indeed the aristocratic girl he'd rescued. Questions flew through his mind. Where did she live? How soon could he find her again? For the first time in months, he felt invigorated, shaken of his lethargy. Somehow he'd find her. He had to, had to tell her how she haunted him, how he'd never forgotten her . . . to ask her why she'd pretended not to know him. Why? Had the tenderness of that night never overcome the terror? Why?

Until he found her, there would be no answers, but this he did know. Thanks to Caro's preference in glovemakers, his luck had finally turned. Oh, yes. He slapped the glove against his palm. The glovemaker's shop. That's how he'd find her and explain away her fears.

Outside the tradesman's room, Caro was already regaling her godmother with the mysterious shopgirl's indiscretion.

"She's a kitchen wench, as I live and breathe. Naturally, it's not my place to suggest, but for Max's sake, to spare him a relapse, I'd pressure the glovemaker to dismiss her. . . . Why, she deliberately lured Maximilian into her arms. Doubtless she visits grand homes where the most wealthy, eligible men are her prey and makes them her conquest. Many helpless girls could do worse than obtain the position of mistress to a titled gentleman."

"Let's not be hasty, Caroline. She's gone. Maximilian is safe."

"Max has lost his head over her." Gingerly Caro picked up the valise and quickly handed it to a servant hovering near the door, then she dusted off her hands, as if they'd been soiled.

At his footsteps they both whirled. He knew what was going on. The household plot again. Convince Max to wed Caroline, the goddaughter of his stepmother, and then, even after Lord Shelburne died and Max inherited the title, his stepmother's access to this elegant life would be secure. Her goddaughter would be safely wed to the new Lord Shelburne. An ally in the house would stall off exile to a dower house. Oh, yes, both ladies had much to gain.

His stepmother managed a look of concern. "Are you quite all right now, Max?" she asked, her voice solicitous. "No relapse?"

"No relapse. That was the young lady of whom I've spoken. The French refugee. The household can call me mad, but now I've found her, and that's proof I wasn't making up tales. She's real, and Caro is my witness."

Caro and his stepmother raised their eyebrows and exchanged patronizing looks. Dear Max, out of his head with delusions again. "Oh, Max," his stepmother said while blowing out the candles in the little room. "Don't say things like that so close to the servants' quarters. Your station as your father's heir. You know how they talk, and if you don't care about your own duty in the marriage arena, there's Caro to think about. You may know that female, but I wouldn't boast about it." She swirled out, calling over her shoulder, "Come along upstairs and tell us about your costume for the St. Valentine's Day masquerade. . . ."

He stood looking after them. They'd never believe the truth, none of them. All he wanted was the mate to this delicate glove. And he would find Violet again, if he had to turn London inside out.

"Caro," he asked as casually as possible, following her upstairs, "where is this glovemaker? Tell me the location of the shop."

She turned and gave a scathing glance at the tiny embroidered glove Max held. "You're not going to chase after her?" she asked with incredulity in her voice. "Really, Maximilian, haven't you been listening? You don't expect me to lead you to her?"

"She took the measure of my hand. I thought I might order a few pairs of gloves."

"But you haven't worn gloves in years," his stepmother said in confusion.

"Pray, tell me why I cannot change my mind."

"And even then you lose every pair you've ever purchased. . . . Look at you there, holding one glove yet again."

"This is *her* glove—"

Caro reached over as if to snatch it, but Max held it up out of reach.

"Oh, fie, no shopgirl wears a glove that exquisite. She doubtless pilfered it from the shop supply."

Before either could snatch it away again, Max tucked the glove into his coat pocket. "She's not who you think, and contrary to what else you believe, I have not lost my head."

They were no sooner in the parlor than his stepmother clicked the door shut and, free from prying servants, turned on him. "Never mention this glove girl again. You sound positively obsessed, and your father is counting on you, his son and heir, to behave in a respectable manner at the St. Valentine's Day Ball. We mustn't scare off Caro's marriage prospects."

Caro preened in front of the fireplace mirror. "Yes, Max, and that—that girl even smells of leather . . . doubtless spends her spare time tramping egg yolks into the leather like those Italian peasants who squash grapes. Didn't you notice her hands? And her accent? Dreadful.''

"She had fine hands." Warm and soft and gentle when she traced about a man's hand. And she'd smelled of fresh soap and innocence. "As for her accent, she's French." And more endearing than he'd remembered.

"Tell me the address of the shop."

Caro tossed her head and reached for a fashion periodical. "There are perfectly good glove shops everywhere in London, especially for ordinary men's gloves." She looked down and examined a fashion plate.

Max snatched the periodical from her hands. "I want to go to *her* glove shop."

"Why?"

Miss Caroline Cordell was more spoiled than an ale gone sour.

"Why not? The glovemaker comes highly recommended . . . by you—"

"I lied."

"Then if you don't want to be helpful, I'll simply find my own way. It's the Gilded Glove, isn't it?"

Caro's face reddened in frustration. "Even if you succeed in finding the shop, you'll never find your strumpet. She'll be dismissed before you can get there." Caro turned to her godmother. "That's what she deserves, isn't it? To be sacked for behavior unbecoming a tradesman."

Wide-eyed, Lady Shelburne nodded her agreement.

But Max, incensed, advanced on them both, circled them in disgust. "Her behavior is none of your affair, and I'll find her, Caro. If I don't, I'll turn the St. Valentine's Day Ball into a grand gambling party, and all the eligible males will leave you on the sidelines."

Caroline's eyes narrowed. "You're obsessed. You're mad.

The mad heir to the Shelburne title. You should be locked in Bedlam!"

His stepmother clapped her hands. "Stop this bickering at once, both of you, or I *will* cancel the ball."

Picking up her skirts, Caroline tore out of the room.

Max followed. "I intend to find her, and no Valentine's Ball will stop me. Cupid be damned."

And with that, he stalked out to the mews. A startled stableboy and groom jumped up from a game of dice.

"Can either of you find the Gilded Glove?"

The groom stared at the single glove Max pulled out of his pocket.

"A lost glove, sir?"

"Yes! No. The shop. My stepmother's favorite glove shop."

The groom's face lit up in comprehension. "Ah, only a few blocks over, sir."

Excellent. He tossed them each a guinea and climbed into a still horseless carriage.

"Hitch up the team and take me there now," he ordered, "and bring every carriage."

The groom and stableboy exchanged looks. The mad heir to Shelburne House was at it again, determined to ruin another St. Valentine's Day Ball.

"Make haste," he bellowed. "Every carriage shall follow me." Caro would not sabotage him. The groomsmen and coachmen were still staring at him, sitting in a horseless carriage. They looked at him as if he were out of his head again, like the rumors from the house had it. Well, let them gossip. Max was mad—mad with desire. Violet was his perfect mate. Only how could she know if he didn't tell her? If he didn't find her?

"Did you hear me?" he repeated. "Get the horses! Every carriage is to follow me to the Gilded Glove. And let no passengers in—least of all my meddling stepmother or Miss Cordell!''

Violet sat again at a table in the workroom of the Gilded Glove, concentrating on threading her needle, hoping no one noticed her shaking hands.

The Gilded Glove was a popular shop with both ladies and gentlemen of fashionable London, and Violet counted her blessings that in the dark dawn when she'd made her escape with the other émigrés, who should have befriended her on the boat, inquired after her tears, but the old glovemaker named Gaspard. It was the grandfatherly Gaspard, an acquaintance of Simon's since his journeyman days, who'd brought her here to Simon's shop and insisted Simon hide her.

And as soon as it became known about London that a master glovemaker from France was working there, the bell over the shop door jangled more and more often, for gloves of the French style and workmanship were much in demand and hard to come by in these Revolutionary days. The shop became a beehive of work and gossip from customers.

It was a solution made in heaven; in her girlhood Violet had always been skilled with a needle and with a paintbrush. Her eye for design had always been praised by her tutors. Violet naturally took on the embroidery work, dazzling plain Fanny with the elegant designs remembered from past gowns. Fanny, in turn, tried to teach her how to fold over and sew the seams on gloves, but it was new and frustrating work. Because of the long apprenticeship in glovemaking, all Violet could hope for in mere months was to sew a respectable thumb into the thumb hole—the first piece stitched together in the making of gloves. Gaspard, always concerned and proud of her progress, often examined her work; she had become the grandchild he never had, he her new guardian.

Fanny arrived at the table. "Violet, are you ready for our lesson?"

"Lesson?" She dropped the glove she'd been embroidering, bewildered, her mind filled with Max. Fanny placed two carefully cut pieces of leather in front of her. The outline of a glove. Four fingers flat and a hole where the thumb waited to be stitched in.

Of course. Thumbs. Another lesson in thumbs. The task required dexterity, even more dexterity than she'd needed to evade Max today. It was only practice on the least expensive leather, but it served its purpose—to take her mind off Max for a while.

Eventually, Gaspard finished cutting out several pairs of women's gloves and came over to see how "his little apprentice" as he teasingly called her, was doing with her thumbs.

"I see progress, little apprentice. The stitches are more even." He tactfully smoothed out a few wrinkles around the stitches. "But your great talent, you realize, lies in embroidering. Your work is much admired by customers. Before I know it, you will be more renowned in the Glovers Guild than I."

Dear man. "Impossible. No one, *no* one knows the work is mine." And now that Max had seen her, it was even more important to remain anonymous, hidden. No more visits to the church even. And she bent to the piece of leather and poked at the leather with her needle.

She dropped the glove and bent to lick the sudden drop of blood that swelled on her finger.

"You are all thumbs, little apprentice." There was concern in his voice.

"The needle slipped," she apologized.

Gaspard kept looking at Violet, as if puzzled by how quietly she worked.

"What happened at Lord Shelburne's house today?" he asked, returning to his cutting table.

She was silent.

Though he was old, Gaspard was wise. "What happened?" he repeated.

"The lady preferred doing business with Simon."

"That's all?" Simon chimed in. "Silly female. I should be flattered, but I find such attitudes boorish."

"I did discredit to the shop."

"Never."

Violet held her silence, setting aside the wrinkled thumb and pretending to concentrate on her embroidery.

"You are frightened, little one," Gaspard said. "More frightened than the night I met you on the boat on the Channel."

Oh, but Gaspard could pick up on emotions as easily as he once could cut the tiniest little fourchettes for the fingers.

"I am merely nervous for Armand."

"You met someone who made you nervous—someone from France."

"Yes," she conceded. "Someone from France."

"A gentleman."

"The son. The heir, I believe, to Lord Shelburne." She was still tingling from his touch. Her heart beat faster, even now.

She gazed up into her guardian's face. "Gaspard, please, if someone comes looking for me, tell them you have never seen me." She looked over to Simon and begged for his silence as well.

"You wish Gaspard and me to lie? What did this man do to you?"

Her entire tray of beads spilled onto the floor then.

"Oh, Violet," Fanny scolded, kneeling down to help her pick up the tiny ornaments. "You're behaving like a girl who's just received her first kiss."

And blushing, Violet knelt and chased the tiny silver beads. Did they think a first kiss was an easy thing?

Max spoke in a whisper against her lips. "Say nothing, it's only pretend. Kiss me back, Violet. Kiss me, 'wench.' " A desperate command.

Violet knew nothing of kissing, except for the time she'd stumbled upon the groom and the kitchen maid tangled together under the apple tree.

All around them torches flared, and one of the ruffians rustled Max's papers. No one could move in France without papers. Documents. Max lifted his head long enough to growl at them. "What takes you so long? Or are you all in need of lessons in how to handle a wench?"

"Give me my papers. Go find your own wenches."

"Who says you know what to do with a wench?"

They guffawed. And then Violet, remembering the kitchen maid, flung her arms around his neck and kissed him back. His body tightened in surprise, then relaxed as in turn he laughed a triumphant laugh and, grabbing her by the waist, bent her back into a deeper kiss. A masquerade for Louis, Etienne, Jean, and Jacques. For fanatics.

But an instant later she forgot where she was and who watched even. Max teased her mouth open and seared her mouth with his tongue. His hands slid up beneath her breasts. Their tongues touched, she melted in the core of her, and all around her, a haze. A dizzy haze.

"Enough," the leader bellowed. "Louis, Etienne . . . I'm for the tavern. I want some wine and another look at the wench who warms the door. I've a craving for one of my own."

Someone threw Max's paper down into the dirt. "Safe journey, Citizen."

And they rode off. She was free. But she could not seem to let go of Max.

Nor did he untangle her. They clung amidst the salt spray

*and wind off the Channel. She had forgotten every lesson
she'd learned about how ladies behaved around gentlemen.
And to her utter shock, she kept on kissing him.*

Violet stood up, the tray of beads clasped tight to her
stomach.

"What did he do?" Simon asked again, looking concerned
at her silence, at the ways her eyes must show red. He took
the tray of beads and handed them off to Fanny. "The man
you saw today. What did he do?"

"He helped me escape."

"And now you want this man to think you do not exist?
He has seen you. You might as well try to erase St.
Valentine's Day from the calendar."

"As long as Armand remains in France, I can trust no
one."

"Why?"

She paused. "He may have . . . delayed me, hid Armand,
so we could not rendezvous . . ."

"Caused Armand to instead meet the enemy?"

She nodded. "Would you not do anything to keep your
family alive?"

Simon scratched his bald spot and considered the question. He nodded. "I would kill for my family."

And Violet had merely acted the wench for hers. . . .

"Then believe me, so would I." By now, she'd regained
her composure and was sewing one last bead onto a kid
glove. "Men have sworn to avenge my escape by taking
Armand."

Simon had come in to stretch a treated hide, the last step
before the leather was ready to smooth out in readiness for
the glove patterns.

Gaspard looked up from his shears. "Do you hear that,
Simon? She asks us to lie for her. Should gentlemen do that
to protect a lady?"

"In times like this, many things are justified—even a lie to a handsome gentleman."

Violet looked up sharply. "How did you know he was handsome?"

"A guess, little one. You cannot have left France without breaking some man's heart. Handsome men have hearts, too."

Max was best left in the past. "Armand, my brother, is the only man I have time to love. No one else." And she broke off the thread and turned the glove right side out. It was finished.

Not just the glove, but Max. He had done his duty, she was alive, and that was that.

Simon clucked in disapproval. "Revolution is all good and well," he said on a weary sigh as he stood up to stretch. "But why, I ask, do these young bloods who start chaos go about in so disorderly a fashion? Look at the lives they've upset," he grumbled, declaring it was a fine mess when a man Gaspard's age had to be uprooted.

Gaspard shrugged in resignation. "The world is peeling off the old for the new. And without any apprenticeship—doing it like a young glovemaker without any instruction. . . ." Again, he bent over his shears. "*Eh, bien.* So be it."

The shop bell jangled, and Violet, startled, leapt to her feet and moved well away from the flimsy door that separated her from view.

Simon stared at her a moment. At last he went to wait on his customer, who was no one remarkable. Moments later Violet returned to her worktable, still trembling. She had, she realized, been slightly disappointed it had not been Max, and that thought shocked her more than anything.

"You're certain this is it?" From his coach Max stared at the windows of the little shop, sandwiched in between a long row of other shops—stationers, booksellers, tea merchants. From all along the street tradesmen shoved their heads out their doors or upstairs windows, all open-mouthed and hopeful at the great parade of coaches with matching livery that slowed and—merciful heavens—stopped. A collective sigh of regret went up when Max ignored them and entered the Gilded Glove.

"The glove shop's cornered all the business this season," they grumbled in turn and one by one shut their windows.

Before the last coach in Max's caravan had reined to a stop, he was already inside the Glided Glove, striding to the balding proprietor who stood at the counter, arranging gloves for display. Unadorned. Simple stitchery. Less costly leathers. Sheepskin instead of lamb.

"A thousand pardons, milord," the proprietor said in answer to his query, "but the girl in question has not been employed long. She is still learning, but too slowly for this busy Valentine's season. I had to sack her."

"Where did she go?"

"Well, I don't ask my former employees what they do. Free to embark on an emigrant ship, if they so desire."

The rage that had been building up in Max exploded. He leaned over the counter and grabbed Simon's shirt. "I know she's hiding. You're hiding her."

"Milord!"

Max let go and watched, as Simon, white-faced, smoothed his shirt.

"A thousand pardons." He shut his eyes momentarily as if praying for strength. "Only confirm for me that her name is Violet."

The proprietor looked toward the piece of cloth that separated the shop from the back room. "Milord, I have many females who stitch gloves for me. They come and receive a bundle, take them home to sew, and then return them. I don't always know them by their Christian names."

"But this girl you'd remember . . . inky hair, pearl complexion, eyes of pansy black, soft, full lips."

"Milord, I am a married man."

Max flushed. "My point is—you don't need a name to remember her."

The proprietor of the Gilded Glove shrugged. "I'm sorry I cannot be more help." With a sweep of his hand Simon indicated the display on his counter. "Would you be interested in gloves? In the French style?"

Violet, mesmerized by the nearness of Max, edged close to the curtained doorway. Through a crack between the wall and the muslin, she had a perfect view of Max, and the sight took her breath away. He'd come for her. In her imagination it was because he loved her and would turn heaven and earth to find her. In reality, it was probably as the lady named Caro said—he wanted her for the selfish reasons of men. So he deserved a lie.

From behind the curtain Violet flattened herself against the wall. Max had tricked her, played a perfect charade. She could never trust him. Never.

While she secretly watched, he pulled from his coat the white kid glove she'd lost at his house. It had broken her heart when she'd had to leave it.

But Max had found it, had that little piece of her past. What irony. Each of them had half of a pair.

He held it out, gently smoothed it. "This . . . see . . . it is hers. It belongs to the girl you sent to my house. . . . You know her. You have to. Someone has to. . . ."

Simon took it and politely examined it. "I regret the indiscretion, but I don't know that glove, milord. I suggest you search some other shops." And as he handed back the glove, Violet held her breath, afraid she'd run into Max's arms and give herself away.

She couldn't trust herself to look up at him. Still clinging, her breath rose and fell with his. Finally the pounding horse hooves receded, and they were left alone in the moonlight,

*listening to nothing more than waves lap against the rocks
below. Waves and her pounding heart. Hours remained until
the moon would wane.*

"I had to kiss you, Violet," he said apologetically.

"It's all right." She stared up at him, mesmerized.

"My duty is to protect you, no matter what."

Even if it meant forcing himself to kiss her. "I understand," she said shyly. "It was a game, an adventure, a
dangerous charade outwitting the rabble, but we did it."

"Yes."

*She trembled from the cold, and then he took her by the
hand and tugged her up the shore.*

"We should wait for Armand." She stared at his lips, still
trembling from the magic they'd aroused in her. There was
so much she wanted to ask about the way he'd kissed her.
"Max—"

"Don't talk about it. It's over."

*He stared down at her lips, too, eyes burning, hands
framing her face, then toying with a windblown curl.*

"What of Armand?"

He seemed to shake himself, as if trying to concentrate.
"Until he comes we can do nothing."

"Nothing?" *Emotion shook her voice.*

*Max pulled her close then, and whispered against her
lips,* "Nothing."

*His kiss stalled her tears and consumed all talk of her
missing brother. It consumed all sound, except for the echo
of despair in her heart. . . .*

When the bell over the shop door jangled, and Max was
gone, only then did she allow the tears to roll down her
cheeks. If only they'd met during some other time in the
world. How might their meeting have been different? But
such thoughts were luxuries.

Simon came into the back and stared at her. "I lied for

you, Violet. It's what you wanted?" Even as he spoke the question, he pulled out a handkerchief and handed it to her. "Revolution makes a poor Cupid. I'm sorry."

She sniffled. "Simon?"

He looked down fondly.

"Thank you."

"Not necessary. Fanny and I will give you shelter forever. As long as you want, I will lie. May God forgive me."

"May God forgive *me*," she whispered and, to hide her red eyes, moved to check on Gaspard, who was napping. "There are times when lies help more than hurt, don't you agree, Simon?" She was thinking of the moonlit coast of France, not Simon's shop.

"If there is a greater truth to cherish, little one, then yes," he agreed and returned to working the leather.

In less than an hour the shop bell jangled again, and Simon went to greet a customer. This time Violet recognized the voice of Max's houseguest, angry because she'd had to hire a hansom cab to transport her here. And she wasted no time in stating her business.

"My godmother was most displeased today."

"The young lady did not bring the ribbon?" Simon asked in wicked innocence.

"I never saw her ribbons, but I saw her behavior with the heir to the house. Why, she was so bold as to make improper advances right under the Shelburne roof. I hope, my good man, that you have her sacked; otherwise, my godmother shall be forced out of principle to give our business elsewhere. She would have come herself, but due to the delicacy of this conversation, I offered to come for her."

Simon was silent a minute, and Violet pressed a finger to her lips, reliving Max's kiss. Sweet. And oh, so dangerous.

"A shocking thing."

"You mock me?"

"I value your patronage, Miss Cordell, too much to mock you."

"It was an improper situation." She lowered her voice. "I must inform you the girl had a pair of exquisite gloves in her possession, and you'd best look to your inventory as well in case she took them. They're very fine, too fine for her kind."

Simon pretended to be shocked. "I'm grateful to you," he replied smoothly, lying yet again. "Is there anything else with which I may assist you?" He gazed hopefully at his shop door.

An hour later a visibly worn Simon appeared around the curtained doorway.

"Her name is Miss Cordell."

"Caroline Cordell," Violet said.

"She wasted no time following the handsome gentleman here."

Again Violet shrugged. "Miss Cordell jumped too easily to false conclusions, and it's because of her I ran away so fast and lost one of my gloves." Ashamed of all the commotion she'd caused, Violet bent over her embroidery, hoping this was the end of it.

"What happened in France?" Simon asked. "Between you and the gentleman?"

"I told you. I'm just another émigré he helped direct to a boat for England."

"He was your friend?"

"You cannot be sure these days who is friend and who is not. You've said so yourself."

"Are you in love with him? The gentleman?"

She looked up, blushing. "What does it matter? Cupid has no business lounging about glove shops while across the water the world is in turmoil."

"Cupid, I suspect, does as he pleases. Does Cupid carry a watch, a map, align with armies?"

Slowly she shook her head. Oh, but Cupid could steal up on the heart at the most unexpected times. "I don't believe in Cupid," she lied.

"Violet," Simon asked, "what are you going to do?"

"Do, Simon?" she echoed. "I shall stay here seven years and be your apprentice."

"And become my competition? I'd prefer it," he joked, "if you helped me through this frantic Valentine's season with your embroidery. You are giving my shop a reputation for elegance, and for that I owe you much."

"Only a place to stay." She forced a smile. "And endless thumbs to practice sewing into gloves. I'll learn how to be a proper shopgirl yet—a glovemaker if I put my mind to it."

Her hair was black, and her profile elfin; her dress was that of a shopgirl. If Max took her in his arms, she'd melt against him and warm his blood with her kiss.

"Stop! Stop, I say," Max called out to the black-haired girl across the street from the church in Covent Garden. "I want to see your gloves. The white gloves." After a furtive, frightened glance over her shoulder, the girl picked up her skirts and ran.

"Violet, no!"

He stopped her in her tracks, grabbing her hands, inspecting her gloves for the swan design. They were plain, unadorned. His gaze moved upward into startled hazel eyes. It was a stranger, and she looked at Max as if he were out of his head.

"Take my gloves, milord," she said, "but you get not a stitch more off me. Are you thinkin' I'm a common doxy? You're wrong, you know. I belong to a fine lord, and when he hears of this, he'll want satisfaction."

Abashed, he let go of her hands and let his arms fall to his side. "I beg your pardon." He backed away three steps and bumped into a lamppost. "I—I mistook you for someone else." He turned on his heel and strode off before she could threaten more.

Back at Shelburne House, Max slammed the door and yelled at his butler. Immediately he apologized. "Bring me a sherry." He headed to the library where he could warm his hands over the fire. In three short weeks he'd become the talk of London. Now the word had spread to all the great homes of Mayfair, and gossip had it that Lord Shelburne's son, the daring viscount, had had a relapse and was obsessed more than ever, this time with a glove. A lady's glove. Lord Sherlburne's son and heir was searching for a lady who possessed the mate to a tiny embroidered glove. Ladies clucked over tea; maids tittered over their scrubboards.

Gossip be damned. Yolanda—Violet—was here and alive in London and still too terrified to drop her masquerade, even for him. Why? Why? He laid a fist on the mantel, frustrated. How could he have found her only to let her slip through his fingers? He relived their last touch, their last words, as if each concealed a clue. Longing, swift and sweet, returned to haunt him. Where was she?

So far every glovemaker denied knowing anyone resembling Violet. It was as if a conspiracy of silence existed amongst the members of the Glovers Guild. Tit for tat. He gave no clues, kept the lone glove hidden in his pocket, and only when he was alone in the library did he pull it out, like now. With one finger he caressed the leather, savoring its smooth-as-silk softness. It didn't matter what Caro and his stepmother or all London wore to the St. Valentine's Day masquerade. All that mattered was that he touch Violet again. Hold her, kiss her, make her his . . .

He was staring with longing at that tiny white glove when a footstep sounded behind him. He turned.

Caro stood poised on the threshold. "Max, may I see the glove?"

He dropped it back down his coat pocket. "It belongs to another lady, Caro."

Caroline Cordell tilted her chin in a haughty gesture.

"Everyone, even impoverished fathers and wastrel brothers, are helping their sisters search for glittery white gloves to match the one you're hiding. And gossip has it they're all bringing them to the Shelburne St. Valentine's Day Ball." She sounded amused. "Every lady in want of a beau will come wearing a single glove. You've set a new fashion trend, I do believe."

"I'm flattered that so many people care what I do. I'm not used to setting the fashion."

"Well, like it or not, you have, and the ladies are less concerned this year with their Valentine costumes than with their gloves." After a well-timed pause, she added slyly, "A great debate also rages as to whether the missing glove is for a right or a left hand."

Actually, he'd never noticed. "I'm not telling, Caro."

"No matter. The entire city thinks you obsessed, Max. They'll bring left and right gloves, both." And with that she handed him the newspaper, folded to an advertisement. Then she swirled out to chatter with his stepmother, talk about where precisely to hang the paper cupids and whether they'd have to supplement the meager winter roses with flowers of silk.

He studied the advertisement, first in dismay, then amusement.

"The Golden Palm, Fine Glovers and Leather Breeches. For ladies in need of single gloves to accommodate the latest fashion. The Golden Palm can accommodate special orders for the St. Valentine's Day Ball at Shelburne House. Single gloves sold for those ladies hoping to have their hand claimed by the gentleman who is looking for his lost mate. French designs, of course, and reasonable rates. If a lady wins the viscount's hand with a Golden Palm glove, the purchase price will be refunded!"

After wadding the newspaper, he threw it into the fire.

Caro had not exaggerated. There was no escaping the talk. The newspaper gossip. The eccentric viscount chasing after an elusive shopgirl he barely knew. Ah, but there they were so wrong. So wrong . . . All he needed was a miracle.

And then, just two days before St. Valentine's Day, when he'd almost begun to believe the household gossip that he was mad again, a stranger came to call. A gentleman whose handsomeness was marred only by a scar at one temple.

The butler showed him into the library, and as greetings were exchanged, the young man's distinctive French accent at once captured Max's attention. Violet's brother? But émigrés all whispered Armand Sangueille was dead.

"*Pardon,* monsieur," said his visitor, "but I've heard of a man who is searching London high and low for a beautiful young lady, and it came to my attention this is the same man who helped émigrés escape the terror. I too am looking for a beautiful and—much beloved—woman who escaped a year ago. . . . I have reason to believe you are the very same gentleman who helped her."

Max felt dazed. A *beloved* young lady? So . . . Violet had a suitor, perhaps a fiancé. Is that why she'd run from him? She was not wed, of that he was certain, but could this be a long-lost fiancé finally escaped to claim her?

"Are you the one who helped her escape?"

Max looked at the man, wondering what else he knew. "I helped her."

"Then I owe you much."

Max was wary. "How do you know of me?"

"In France, among those who fear, you are legend."

"Here in England I am legend, also—as a madman."

"I don't listen to gossip, only fact. And émigrés tell me Yolanda is here in London and that you know her."

"She belongs to me, you know." Max threw out the challenge the way a man tossed down a glove. A dare.

His guest blinked, then smiled. "You know her, then? Where is she?"

Max stared down at the mantel, then turned abruptly and stared at this stranger. "Do you love her?"

"Of course," his guest answered easily.

Max paced the room, finally decided, and turned back. It was all or nothing. If he couldn't have Violet, he'd sooner die. "If I tell you, you shall, I believe, understand why I cannot live without her . . . or else you will call me out in duel."

"Will I?"

"I take that risk . . . but when I am done, you will give up all claim to her."

"No, I won't."

Max gave a wry smile. "Will you give me a fair hearing? Hear all before you judge?"

"That depends on your tale." The man tossed his hat on the chair and stood at the window, silhouetted by the light, listening.

"That last night, after many nights traveling alone in the underground roads from Paris to the coast, we thought the worst was over. We were wrong. . . ." He told it swiftly, revealing only the necessary parts, omitting cherished details. "It was a charade, a dangerous game, but it worked. . . ."

His guest turned, unsmiling, and looked Max in the eye. "Where is she now?"

"I came upon her by accident—in this very house. She is in London, hiding somewhere, and I will never rest until I find her." He held out the glove. "This is all I have left of her. This is my proof that she is somewhere in this city."

His visitor's eyes gleamed. "I am glad to learn she has

such a staunch champion. Perhaps even more devoted than I. . . ."

Max's heart sank. "You are her fiancé?" The remote possibility did exist of a marriage. Not consummated, but legal. A proxy wedding in the midst of turmoil. "Her husband?"

"Her brother," the man said easily with a smile and reached out his hand. "And I came first to tell you of my gratitude in trying to find Yolanda."

"Her brother?" He looked the man up and down, searching for resemblance to Violet, trying not to contain the raw hope that washed through him. Her brother? Please, let it be. "In France they say he is dead." Max was naturally on his guard. "The Comte de Sangueille?"

"Our father was the Comte. If they could capture me in France, now they would call me Citizen Sangueille." He thrust out his hand. And with it, a glove bearing the crest of intertwined swans. Swans damp with raindrops.

She wept and wept for her missing brother, wept until finally she pulled out of her bodice a glove to wipe away the tears.

"Here, then," Max said gruffly, taking it from her. He finished blotting her tears with his handkerchief and smoothed out the glove, staring at the swan design. "You're drowning the poor swans. You don't want to ruin the only fine thing remaining to you, do you?"

She smiled then and took the glove back. "The swans don't matter anymore. The Sangueille family crest is no more." She sniffled, and he folded her close to him. Her tears were still warm against his cheeks; the waters of the icy Channel lapped against his ankles, and he carried her up the rocky path. He'd no sooner wrenched her from his arms and hid her behind a stone wall than another gang of horsemen descended from the dark. At the rendezvous point. Five minutes sooner and his black-haired waif would have been caught.

"Armand Sangueille?"

"The Sangueilles have no business with you."

If he could stall them, Violet's brother would see them from a distance and stay away, and so he walked with them.

"You are hiding him?" *The leader grew suspicious.*

"No."

"You lie."

"No."

The ruffian suddenly brandished a knife. "You are his agent?"

"I am a friend." *And he started to pull out his papers.*

The leader wadded them and fed them to his torch. "Who cares what his papers say? This man shall be Armand Sangueille. Who's to know the difference? A jury? Tomorrow morning we spread the news—Armand Sangueille, traitor and friend to émigrés, died on this cliff this night, and no one will ever know the difference. We collect the price on his head and retire to Switzerland."

As Max doubled over from the thrust of the knife, he cried out. Yolanda, the black-haired waif, had not seen the knife. Thank God. But she was waiting, calling . . . "Come back for me, Max. Where are you? Come back!"

As he stanched the blood with his cloak, the moon was lowering.

"Many thought I was dead," Max's visitor confirmed. "Rumor in France says Armand Sangueille was stabbed and left to die in the sand last winter."

Still cautious, Max was silent. Only Violet could confirm or deny the man was her brother. "She expected me to save both her and her brother." He clenched his fist and leaned into the mantel. "It was impossible. I was forced to choose. And lost her while I was at it."

"You have no idea where?"

"I had one brief encounter. . . . She is posing, I believe, as a glovemaker's apprentice." Turning, Max pulled out the glove and displayed it for Armand. "As I said, this is my only clue."

Armand briefly examined the glove, his gaze lingering on the swans. He looked up. "It is hers."

Max shrugged. "Unfortunately a hundred shaking heads know nothing of a dark-haired waif from France with one embroidered glove."

"Or choose not to tell," Armand offered. "Surely, there is some way we can draw her out."

"Only if she'll accept an invitation to the Shelburne St. Valentine's Day Ball," he said in jest, "and unless she knows you'll be there, that's highly unlikely."

"While my only hope is the grapevine of émigré news."

Max nodded, and at that moment Caroline Cordell appeared in the doorway, obviously curious. He dared to open the door on hope even wider.

"*Pardon,* monsieur," he said quietly, "but I believe I have a more reliable source of information for you than the émigrés."

Quickly he called out, "Come in, Caro, and meet my visitor. He has promised to come to our St. Valentine's Day Ball two nights hence." With a nod of his head he signaled for Armand to play along. An idea was forming. A hope.

Armand waited with twinkling eyes for the introductions.

He bowed low over her hand. "*Enchanté,* mademoiselle."

"My pleasure, monsieur," Caro said, eyes narrowing as she sized up this handsome newcomer, her gaze lingering in fascination on the scar that added drama to Armand's otherwise ordinary face.

"It is a masquerade ball," she informed him, batting her eyes coyly.

Armand smiled easily. "Perhaps you can recommend a costumer. . . ." He turned to Max. "*Pardon*, do I have your permission to take the lady for a turn about the Park in my carriage? Chaperoned of course."

When they were gone, Max stared out the window at the passing coaches, children chasing a tomcat through the mud puddles, the drooping flower boxes, the February rain dripping down the window.

He hoped Cupid was a gambler. That's all he and the mischievous cherub had to work with now. A gamble that Caro would be unable to contain her own obsession—for gossip.

Heart pounding, Violet positioned herself by the curtained doorway so she could watch Simon—and her glove. Simon had borrowed her glove to measure against the smallest glove in his shop. Unfortunate timing. Miss Caroline Cordell had arrived a moment later.

"You've quite outdone yourself, Mr. Doublet." Miss Cordell ran a finger along the golden thread of a particularly fine pair of kid gloves. She examined them closer, looking in particular at the construction. Then her gaze fell on the glove Simon held, and she reached for it.

"Mmm, yes, very nice." She looked up as her godmother, Lady Shelburne, joined her in the shop. "Come and see this one, Godmama. A treasure." Miss Cordell set the glove back down on the counter, the better to admire it.

Simon turned around, as if to look for another sample on a shelf, caught Violet's eye through a narrow slit in the curtain, and flashed her a reassuring smile. If only the fine Miss Cordell knew that the glove she admired the most—with swans embroidered in thread of gold and silver—was Violet's own glove, the mate to the glove the viscount guarded closely.

"Now, this is a glove I'd like to receive from a gentleman.

Especially the Frenchman. *He*, I believe, has the power to make Max jealous, and his scar is so intriguing. I finally worked up the courage to ask about it."

"And what did he say?"

"I thought he might have been a pirate, but no, it's from some childhood fall off a pony. Still, it suits him, I think. I do like a man with a dangerous aura."

Violet clamped a hand to her mouth to keep from gasping out loud. A Frenchman? With a scar—from a pony fall? After weeks of listening to inane gossip about gloves, at last Violet heard something hopeful. She slid closer to the curtained doorway.

Miss Cordell picked through the gloves on display. "Why, with that scar on his temple, he's so dashing and certainly handsome."

Violet's hopes soared. Only one man she knew had a childhood scar on his temple, and that was her brother. Armand. Could it be? Her heart beat faster with hope.

And Simon, attuned to Violet's quest, tried to help. "Would the ladies like to leave a list of favorite gloves for the . . . uh, French gentleman, as well as his name?"

"I'd never stoop to the level of other ladies with such plotting," she said airily and turned to Lady Shelburne, who was picking through the glove samples. "He's so recently over from France that he has Max consumed with news of politics, you know. I can't wait to get them out of that library and into the ballroom. He's invited for Valentine's night, isn't he?"

"Indeed," Lady Shelburne said, her glance darting around the shop, curious. "I've already made certain. Perhaps a dose of jealousy will make Max see you in the right light."

"Exactly." Miss Cordell held up a particularly lovely pair of gloves, embroidered in silver, like a snowflake. Violet's latest work. "Oh, exquisite. Charming. I'll take these." She spied another pair. "And these . . . and these . . ."

She rummaged through the shelves for the most expensive gloves—all white, some perfumed, and all decorated with intricate stitching. Pair by pair she began to lay them out on the counter. She added one last pair to the pile.

"Bundle them all up," her godmother ordered. "And let us pray one of the pairs will be right. . . ."

Violet stood open-mouthed, awestruck at Lady Shelburne's generous order.

"And we wish them delivered."

"Of course," Simon said, elation in his voice at this enormous sale. Violet could understand his happiness. Why, Simon's family could all buy new shoes, attend a balcony performance of the opera, even the children. Perhaps even splurge on imported oranges from Covent Garden.

"On Valentine's night," Caro added, "deliver them all to Shelburne House. Even this one." She plucked the odd one she'd admired earlier from the counter and added it to the stack.

"Oh, no, that one is not for sale," Simon protested.

"Nonsense. Everything is for sale. Deliver it."

Violet had to swallow hard at that. It bore her family crest; it was the mate for which Max searched. Still, what did it matter if Caroline Cordell wanted to trap Max. It was Armand, her brother, she needed to find.

As soon as Simon came into the workroom, Violet snatched her precious glove from his outstretched hand. Such a close call.

"I presume you overheard?" Simon was tying on an apron and heading for the latest batch of leather, newly treated and ready to be stretched and softened.

Violet followed him about the workroom. "Let me make the delivery."

"It's for the St. Valentine's Day Ball, Violet. I thought you wanted to avoid Shelburne House at all costs."

"That Frenchman she gushed over might be my brother. I have to see him."

"Even if it means bumping into the gentleman of the house?"

"I can't run forever. Someday I have to face him. Besides, it's a masquerade ball, and he'll be busy with many ladies . . . vying for his hand. I'll never be noticed."

Fanny looked up from the thumb she was stitching into a kid glove. "I can borrow a domino for her to wear—in exchange for a pair of our gloves. From the seamstress across the street."

But it took more than a mere costume to convince her guardian, Gaspard. "I thought you blamed the gentleman of the house for your brother's mysterious vanishing?"

"I do. All the more reason to go to that house and try to find Armand. He may not be safe, even in an English house."

"Miss Cordell may take exception to your presence."

But Violet was as determined as a needle struggling through the most difficult of leathers.

"Trust me, Gaspard. I'll know Armand the second I see him, and if I do find him, it matters little to me what Miss Cordell thinks of me. Please . . ."

Gaspard pursed his lips in displeasure, and Simon started to shake his head, when Fanny's voice came from behind. "Let her go, Simon. Her brother is her only family. No matter the consequences, as she says. She needs to go."

Simon shrugged and gave a rueful smile. "My wife's father willed me this shop," he said at last. "And I think softening so much leather over the years has softened my heart too much, too. Go then. Yes, Gaspard?"

Reluctantly the old man nodded.

Briefly Violet shut her eyes. "Oh, thank you, Simon— Gaspard, thank you."

"Just be careful." This from Fanny.

After Violet's escape from France, the warning seemed tame. "The worst that can happen is I'll be shown the door."

"And the best?"

"Armand." She tried to say her brother's name with conviction, as if finding him were the extent of her heart's desire. But the name of another man echoed back from her heart. Max . . . Max . . . Max . . . She whirled away to hide her shimmering eyes. "Finding Armand," she finally said. "Armand is the best I could ever hope for."

On the night of the masquerade ball, with the hood of a borrowed domino pulled low over her face, Violet braved a London drizzle to walk to Shelburne House. In the black cloak she blended in with the shadows. Only what she carried in her hands might have called attention to her— under one arm, the telltale package, the package of embroidered gloves. In the other hand the half mask on a wand, the signature accessory of a domino. She clung to it so tightly her knuckles stung; that mask was her courage, as on this second St. Valentine's Day in a row she played an unwilling masquerade.

At Shelburne House coaches lined the street for blocks, and fine ladies and gentlemen, costumed and bewigged in bygone styles, arrived in a steady stream at the front door. Violet watched for a while from the doorway across the street, until, during a lull in the arrivals, she darted toward the house dodging puddles, and headed for the servants' door.

A harried maid answered, impatience on her face.

Violet stammered, "A delivery for one of the guests— Miss Caroline Cordell."

"And what is it?" The young maid had reason to be dubious. Few, if any, tradesmen came garbed in a domino.

"Gloves of course," Violet said calmly. "Valentine gloves. Miss Cordell is expecting them."

There wasn't a servant within miles of London who hadn't heard of the search by Lord Shelburne's heir for the mate to a lost glove. And the rumor now had it whichever lady could produce the perfect mate would win his hand in marriage this St. Valentine's night.

Sure enough, from behind came the gruff tones of a male servant. "Let 'er in, Sally. Don't you know 'ow many ladies are waitin' on gloves? Enough to fill a contraband ship, I wager."

The maid smiled in amusement and then opened the door to admit Violet. "Follow me, then. Miss Cordell is still dressing, but we'll take them up to her private anteroom."

"She's not there, is she?"

"Ain't you the impertinent one?" the maid said, still eyeing the elegant black cloak.

"She's not fond of me. So I came in costume myself."

The maid chuckled. "Well, is there any of us lowly ones she's fond of? That miss cares for only two people in this world—herself and the heir to the house, in that order." She pushed open the door to a small room on the same floor as the ballroom. "Here we are. Her private retiring room."

Cautiously Violet entered and shook off her cloak, which was dripping rain all over the parquet floor. Violet untied her package on a side table and under the maid's watchful eye began to spread gloves across the table, pair by pair by pair until they glittered prettily in the candlelight.

"Behavin' like a Covent Garden sideshow, if you ask me, all this fuss the gentry are makin' over gloves," the maid gossiped, thinking Violet just another servant. "Shall I find Miss Cordell and tell her you're expectin' payment?"

Violet shook her head. "It's on the Shelburne account. . . . Tell me, is there a man named Armand here?" she asked. "A Frenchman?"

The maid looked surprised. "Blimy, and I can't gossip about the guests. They'd sack me, they would, especially if they caught me talking about 'em by their Christian names—"

The door suddenly opened, and they whirled. The maid bobbed a curtsy as a haughty lady garbed in red silk came toward them—Miss Caroline Cordell herself—resplendent in the silk gown and elaborate black wig of Spanish royalty—Catherine of Aragon, no doubt.

"Lady Shelburne does not pay you to gossip."

Violet gulped. Oh, dear, but her plan had not accounted for this. Thankfully, the room was dim, and Miss Cordell headed right to the display of gloves. "It's about time Simon sent them. I was beginning to think a rival lady had waylaid my gloves." She quickly destroyed Violet's careful arrangement, searching . . . searching . . .

Violet edged toward the door.

"Stop."

Violet turned.

Miss Cordell was staring at Violet.

"Come here and stand by the candlelight." To the maid, she gave swift instructions. "Take that dripping cloak from her before water ruins the floor. Bring it here. Quickly!"

Stripped down to her simple dress, Violet moved toward the candelabra and waited, heart in her throat while Miss Caroline Cordell examined her.

"You're the girl, the shopgirl Max is chasing after, aren't you?"

"He's mistaken me for another."

"I had you sacked."

What could she do but nod? "The Valentine season is a very busy time for gloves, miss. I had to help Simon."

"No matter," she said as if to herself and draped Violet's cloak over a chair. Suddenly she looked up again. "As long as you're here, make yourself useful. Where's the single glove, the one embroidered in gold and silver? The swans."

"Many of the gloves use both threads," Violet pointed out.

"I can see that, but I want the one with the swans intertwined. I want it. I paid for it."

"There was only the one. . . . I didn't think you'd want a single . . . without a mate."

Miss Cordell's face turned livid. "Incompetent fool. Get out."

Violet fled. Behind her Miss Cordell's voice drifted out, yelling at the maid. "Take this cloak out of here, too. Out."

It was some minutes later before the hapless maid found her staring into the ballroom and thrust the damp domino at her. "I knew you'd bring me trouble. 'Leave,' the lady commands. 'Leave at once.'" On that bitter note, she herself fled.

Violet should have obeyed at once, but Shelburne House was all abustle, everyone in costume, and, she reminded herself, Armand might be somewhere out there. No one else bothered her. The few who glanced her way smiled as if her simple dress were part of a costume, and so, feeling safe in the crowd, she lingered.

Everywhere above her paper cupids perched on arches of roses, and beneath swarmed a sea of eager ladies, each wearing a single glove. With so many gloves embroidered in thread of gold and silver, the ballroom dazzled her, but she ignored the frivolity. She was only lingering to search for signs of Armand. And, her heart admitted, she couldn't help scanning the ballroom for just a glimpse of Max. Just one last glance. If she saw him, heaven help her, for she wasn't sure what she'd do.

"How many ladies did you say have come wearing a single glove?" Max asked his valet in his bedchamber as they adjusted the last of his formal dress.

At the answer he winced. "Embroidered?"

"Gold and silver on every one," the valet confirmed. "Not even a pair. Just single gloves. Most unusual. At past Valentine masquerades, the ladies have fought to be unique rather than copy each other, but then there's no explaining fashion to a simple man like me."

"Nor me, Giles. A pity they all went to so much trouble for so little chance. Still," Max said with practicality, "in the end the glovemakers ought to be grateful for the business."

With that he sighed and allowed his valet to assist him into his coat. It was cut from blue velvet. Fichu and ruffs of pristine white highlighted his neck and wrists. Silver-gray breeches fit snugly. And buckled shoes were polished to a high shine. His hair was pulled back with a simple black ribbon. No out-of-fashion wigs. No costume at all for Max, who'd had his fill of pretending. The night of his charade with Violet on the French coast was the last masquerade he ever wanted in his life. He was going to the ball as himself.

"Very handsome, milord," his valet said, tugging at the lace ruff of first one sleeve, then the other.

Downstairs awaited dozens of London ladies, all marriageable and all with mamas hoping for a St. Valentine's Day marriage offer. Max wondered if Cupid had arrows strong enough to penetrate his armor of cynicism.

"I feel like a prisoner about to be led to trial. The mamas tonight are fiercer than the Frenchwomen who marched for bread."

"You look resplendent, sir. The ladies will be impressed. The mamas will behave."

"The ladies," he said wearily, "will be too busy showing off their gloves to care what I look like." Oh, that he'd never found the glove. It had only increased the frenzy amongst the ladies, and an invitation to the Shelburne St. Valentine Day Ball had become the most sought-after invitation in London. Other hostesses had canceled their Valentine's Balls due to all the regrets. Shelburne House, on the other hand, received not a single regret, and Max's stepmother, savoring her success as a hostess, had gleefully doubled the volume of punch.

"Milord?"

Max's valet held out the glove. Violet's glove. For the past three weeks Max had not considered himself fully dressed until that tiny white glove was tucked into his coat pocket. It had become habit for his valet to hand it to him last of all. This time, though, Max debated whether or not he should leave it here. A single memento of unrequited desire. Perhaps this lone glove was symbolic, an omen that they were never meant to be together, meant to always be apart.

"You'll need this tonight."

"Will I?"

"Certainly, if only to prove to many ladies that their glove is not the perfect match."

A wry smile touched Max's mouth, and he glanced gratefully at his valet. "Indeed. So I shall at that." Inside, though, he felt defeat. Even if Violet had heard gossip of Armand, that did not mean she could gain entrée to the ball.

From her vantage point Violet was able to scan the entire ballroom to look for signs of her brother. But from the instant she laid eyes on Max, she was unable to tear her gaze from him.

He stood beneath a dangling lace heart on a dais at one end of the ballroom, and as he stared at the mate to her glove, her heart ached for him, for them. As each lady was presented, Max continued to examine each gloved hand, politely showed the tiny white glove for comparison, and each time shook his head in regret. Their mamas' faces fell with disappointment.

To her dismay, he handed her glove to a ruffed and powdered "Queen Elizabeth," who tugged and pulled in an attempt to make it fit. She couldn't budge the little glove past her knuckles, though, and, clearly disappointed, handed it back to Max, who bowed and kissed her hand. Oh, but Violet yearned to show off her glove, the mate, and claim Max for her own Valentine. She yearned so much that it was natural to reach down into her domino pocket and feel for it, to touch the embroidery, trace the swan outline of her family crest for reassurance. Deeper and deeper she reached.

Her glove was gone!

She turned the pocket inside out, and then her heart fell to her heels. The pocket of her cloak was empty. No, no . . . not after all she'd been through. That glove, that single white glove was all she had left of her former life, of her family, of youth, of . . . of Max. She groped about in her other pocket, then looked about the floor, backtracked a few steps, and returned to her secluded lookout. Had she dropped it in the anteroom? Dare she go back to look and risk Miss Cordell's wrath? Oh, Max.

She glanced back over her shoulder at him. Even now he was staring at the other glove, lost in thought. The line of young ladies—all wearing one embroidered glove, the other hand bare—stretched serpentine fashion around the ballroom. No one danced; they'd only come to try on her glove. And Miss Caroline Cordell, resplendent as the red-gowned Queen of Spain, was making her grand entrance, ignoring the line of hopeful ladies and heading straight for Max, as if to cut into line.

Max looked up, his expression inscrutable, and Violet turned and headed for the anteroom. There wasn't a gentleman in sight who resembled Armand. She couldn't bear to wait around and watch anymore.

As Caro sailed over, like an overloaded spice ship about to dock at his feet, Max vowed this was the last masquerade ball he'd ever attend. Cupid, he realized, had the right idea wearing no clothes at all. Costumes had nothing to do with the heart. Nothing.

At once on his guard at Caro's smug expression, Max frowned.

"Aren't you going to wait your turn?" he asked, indicating the long queue of ladies behind her.

Caro smiled. "Now, why do that when I can save all these other ladies from standing in line for nothing?"

"What do you mean?"

"I have the perfect mate to your lonely glove."

For a moment he just stared at her, speechless. She couldn't. "I don't believe you."

"Don't you want to compare our gloves?"

Max cast a skeptical eye on Caro, who held out a white-gloved hand, palm up so he couldn't see the design. So coy.

Oh, the lengths the marriageable ladies and their mamas would go to snare an eligible gentleman, the things they'd contrive. Especially his own family.

With a sigh he pulled out the tiny glove for the hundredth time that evening and displayed it.

At once Caro turned over her left hand, close to the glove Max held.

Max went as ice cold as if his opponent in cards had flipped over the winning trump. Like the glove he held, Caro's glove was white. Tiny. Embroidered in a design of intertwining swans. Caro was wearing the match. The perfect match.

Max stared in shocked silence. "How did you come by this?"

"Does it matter?" Actually, Caroline had gone to wicked lengths to obtain the matching glove. Snatched it from the pocket of Violet's cloak when she was pretending to have a tirade.

But clearly, the cut of the glove was at fault or else the leather had no stretch. For tug as they would, pull as they might, the leather had not stretched to accommodate Caro's hand, and, desperate, she had handed her maid a pair of scissors and ordered her to snip the leather in strategic places. It was a shame to ruin a perfectly good glove, but in the end worth it, for here she was, victorious and ready to claim her prize—a St. Valentine's Day proposal from Max. Oh, yes, the end did justify the means, she thought, and smiled at Max.

Despair. Violet, who had escaped near death without giving up hope, sank onto a settee and let tears scald her face. She'd failed: Armand was not here, and she'd lost the last precious memento of her former life, her glove. Worse, she felt incredibly jealous of all the ladies out there hoping to make a perfect match. Had one of them found her glove? Did it matter?

After all, what was Max to her? Someone who'd taught her passion and then betrayed her own brother. Cupid could be incredibly fickle, she decided as she began to match up the rejected gloves and lay them pair by pair upon the wrapping paper. An emigrant from France could do worse these days than spend the rest of her life sewing beads on gloves. Far worse.

Cupid, Max decided, staring at that glove, had a wicked sense of humor. And an unexpectedly merciful soul. For if Caro had that glove, then Violet was somewhere at this ball. He'd wager the last boat out of Calais on it.

But first he could not deny himself the pleasure of disappointing Caro. As she lifted up her gloved hand for his closer inspection, all the ladies crowded so close he could scarcely breathe. And the entire roomful of guests oohed and aahed, expecting a romantic Valentine proposal.

Caro smiled in triumph, then glanced sideways at Max. "No need to look so terror-stricken, Max. St. Valentine's

Day is a natural time for announcing betrothals. Don't forget, your *maman* is watching," she prompted.

The little minx had gone too far this time. Grabbing Caro's hand, he turned it over and saw the knife slash. "Where did you get this glove?"

"It's mine."

"It doesn't fit."

"It does."

"You've cut it."

"I didn't touch it. You're imagining things again. Really, Max, try to keep your head in front of your guests."

"Then who cut it?" He was tugging it off.

"Max, are you insane? What are you doing?"

"I have," he said, voice impassioned, "never been saner, and this is not your glove." It was sacrilege to see this glove stretched over Caro's conniving hand.

"It *is* mine."

"Then be so good as to give me your other hand. You must try on the mate."

At once Caro stuck her left hand behind her back.

A man costumed as a simple monk, face hidden in the folds of his hood, pressed close to her to see, and she shoved him away. "Simpleton, look who you bump into."

"Caro!" Max stepped off the dais and faced her. "If you truly have the perfect mate, you'll show everyone how well *both* gloves fit."

Reluctantly she presented her bare hand, and Max gallantly allowed her to squeeze into the tiny glove of Violet's. But try as Caro might to shove in her fingers, the glove would not move past her knuckles. Already the seams were strained, the fine stitching threatening to give.

"Where is the young woman from whom you obtained this glove?" demanded Max. He wasted no time in peeling off its mate, and then he clutched both gloves. Gloveless,

Caro stood there, face flushed, trying to ignore the growing whispers from the guests.

"The shopgirl?" Caro said in defeat. "That shrinking violet? Doubtless where I left her." Her gaze automatically went to the anteroom.

Max pushed past her, past all the eager ladies in the crowd. One man followed him, the guest costumed as a medieval monk. Together they shouldered their way past all the costumes—past the simple shepherdesses and milk-maids and King Arthur's own Guinevere and dozens of women costumed in the simple domino, the better to highlight their gloves.

Like Moses parting the Red Sea, Max strode past every one, past every outstretched glove, till he reached the door to Caro's private receiving room. With precious little ceremony he shoved open the door and gazed upon the bent head of a tiny figure in humble dress. A black cape and half mask were abandoned at her feet.

And all around her—gloves! Stacks of white gloves.

"Violet," he whispered, afraid if he startled her she'd run off again. "What are you doing here?"

Slowly Violet turned. She knew at once it was Max, come for her; she knew, too, that she wouldn't be able to deny knowing him. Her London masquerade was over, and there was no running this time. He filled the doorway and then moved in to allow another man to join him—a man in the hooded costume of a medieval friar. But it was Max—Max, curse her traitorous heart—who held her in his spell.

He stood out, of course, because he was the only one at the entire ball not in costume. Max wore the most splendid coat of blue with snow-white stock and looked more magnificent than all the costumed guests put together. Her gaze moved up to his face—the lean handsome jaw, the intense blue eyes, the tawny hair—and her heart turned over.

"Rumor has it you've lost a brother," he said softly.

She looked up, utterly vulnerable, definitely wary. If he weren't afraid of scaring her, he'd have stridden right over and taken her in his arms that moment. But one revelation at a time. . . . He turned to someone at his side.

"Armand, go in and tell me if you know that young lady."

As Max moved aside, the friar filled the doorway and captured her attention. What a strange costume.

"Yolanda," the "monk" said softly. "Is it you?"

"Remember, she calls herself Violet now," Max cautioned.

At the sound of a too familiar voice, Violet took a step closer and held her breath. The months fled away and there was the young man with whom she'd shared life in a chateau far away in another world. Gently she reached up to trace the scar that marked him as nothing else could. The old familiar scar from a youthful pony fall.

"Armand . . . oh, Armand." She whispered the name and touched her brother on the cheek, the mouth, as if afraid to believe he was real.

He slid back the friar's hood and revealed his face fully, and in one moment of certainty, all the fears and doubts fell away.

"Armand," she squealed and threw herself into her brother's arms.

After a few moments she pulled away, looking up into his dear face, laughing, weeping, overcome by her joy. "What are you doing here? Masquerading as a friar while I read the lists of condemned and worry?"

"In France I masqueraded as many different men before I could escape. Everything from blacksmiths to fishmongers."

"Oh, Armand." She hugged him tight. "I prayed so for you. I feared we'd never meet again. I feared you dead."

"I was, little sister. Because of another man who let a group of fanatics believe he was Armand Sangueille, I got away, and because I was 'dead,' I had an easier time making my way to safety."

"Another man did that for you?"

"And for you." He turned with a meaningful gaze at Max. "It was you, wasn't it?" Armand asked. "You who took the knife."

Max inclined his head. "They were not particular that night whether they found the right man or not. A fisherman reeled me in and hauled me back to England, half dead. Violet—" He turned to give her a tender look. "Violet was on the last boat of émigrés I helped." He was silent then, staring at Violet.

Armand cleared his throat. "And so not only she but I owe you my life. You have our family's gratitude, for what that's worth. . . ." He turned to Violet. "I wager you did not know what he risked for us both, did you, sister?"

She stared at Max. "You said you nearly died after you got me on the boat. . . ."

"The rabble mistook me for him," Max confirmed.

"So you see, because of Max," her brother said, "we *both* escaped that night."

Oh, Max. He was standing there, rather pale, watching Violet's reunion with Armand, as if not quite sure he liked her in another's arms, brother or not. All this time she'd assumed he might be in league with the rabble, be guilty of leading them to her brother. She moved closer.

Violet looked from one man to the other, overjoyed and yet so relieved. Ashamed, too. She reached out for Max's hand. Max had played the ultimate masquerade a year ago on that rocky beach in France, had nearly died himself to save her brother. "I—I misunderstood." Emotions washed over her so fast. So much had suddenly come clear. It was like moving from a storm to sudden still waters; she needed time to take it all in.

Like an unexpected anchor, Max's fingers closed around

hers, their grip warm and sure. "There was no way to tell you, until now." His solemn gaze never left her face.

Her throat tightened with gratitude . . . and more.

"I wanted to explain, Violet, but how could I? Tell you more ruffians had come? I was trying to protect you. And then—you were gone on that boat for England, and when fate brought you to me here in London, you clung to your new masquerade."

"Life became one masquerade after another." But not the longing in her heart. That was real.

Max reached into his coat pocket and pulled out two pieces of white kid, glittering with gold and silver thread. "You've also, mademoiselle, lost both your gloves." He was holding them out, a Valentine offering.

"So I have." Smiling, she made a tentative move to take them, but he moved his hand out of reach.

"Not yet . . . Violet, there was more I wanted to say to you."

"About why I'm here," she guessed.

"No, about *last* St. Valentine's Day." With his free hand he ran a finger along her cheek, looked down into her eyes.

Armand cleared his throat, and they sprang apart.

"Armand," Max said, "I want a formal introduction to your sister."

"But—"

"We're going to pretend we've never met. We're going to start over—the proper way with a formal introduction at the ball."

He turned to Armand, who broke into a smile. "Gladly. But as Max the smuggler and Violet the glovemaker's apprentice—?"

"A formal introduction," Max repeated, loudly enough for all the ladies who'd pressed behind in the hallway to hear.

Armand's face lit up. "Milord, I present the former Marie

Yolanda Antoine Rochelle de Sangueille, now, like me, Citizen Sangueille. . . ." He motioned to his sister. "You need to decide on your name, little sister. Is it Yolanda or—"

"Yolanda is from another time, another place. I am Violet. Miss Violet Sangueille." What did a title mean when compared to her desire? As for the object of that desire, she thought of him, not as a viscount with a string of titles, but as Max. Beloved Max.

"Everyone out," her brother said so softly she could barely hear him. "Violet," he said with a meaningful look at Max, "I believe that you and I shall postpone our reunion a while."

"You'll stay at the ball?" she asked.

"I shall be at the ball, waiting to see my sister dance again," he reassured her.

Then her brother wisely retreated from the room and herded the curious ladies back to the ballroom. Only she and Max remained.

There she stood unadorned in her simple woolen gown. Max reached out to graze her cheek with the back of his hand, as if reassuring himself she was real, and with a little moan she shut her eyes, lost in his touch. It had been like that from the beginning—he had only to touch her, and she forgot where she was. . . .

"Are they gone?" she asked, not looking away from him.

He looked down into her eyes, his gaze burning with shared memories, with the fever of a man who would toss away kingdoms for one woman. The door clicked shut. "All gone. We're quite alone."

All alone. She'd known when the last ruffian's pistol clicked empty and he tossed it at her feet before riding off.

"They're gone."

"We're safe then? They won't come back?" The gallop-

ing horses still echoed faintly in the distance. Louis, Etienne, whatever their names were . . . their leering faces taunted her, terrified her.

"Please hold me."

Max obliged, for longer than she expected. She clung in return, and then they stumbled to a nearby shed, the hiding place they'd been heading toward when the fanatics found Max.

Inside, she collapsed on the hay. It was a farmer's storage shed, and in the darkness there were only shapes and scents—hay and the scrape of metal tools Max pushed away before he sat beside her. From the doorway they watched the moon through a crack in the door.

"Hold me again, Max."

"You do not know what you ask, little one."

"Max, we neither of us know if we'll live to see the dawn, and you worry about the rules of stuffy matrons? Hold me. Don't you want to?"

For days Max had wanted too much to hold her. That charade with the rabble had set his blood to roiling, left his pulse intoxicated. It was only because there were spectators that he'd maintained a shred of control. Here in this shed with nothing to stop him . . . well, she asked too much. As he began to stroke her back, kiss her hair to reassure her, reason fled in the temptation.

She slid her hands inside her open shirt.

"You're bleeding."

"Shh. It's water, and a scratch. Nothing serious."

She laid the palm of her hand against his cheek, and he forgot where he was, lost his head.

Holding her gently by the arms, his lips brushed her face, potent, coaxing her response. Trembling with an unfamiliar need, her arms came up around him, and as he teased her lips, the yearning deepened, pulled her into him, like a tide beckoned by the moon. Desire ebbed and flowed, in and out, around and within till she was dizzy.

He peeled away the bodice of her dress with the expertise of a man who knew exactly what to do with wenches.

Her breath rose and fell, and she was raining kisses on his neck. He kissed her lips, the hollow of her throat, her breasts, one at a time until she writhed beneath his touch. Their touching grew frantic, took on an urgency akin to their flight together. They were racing again, to some intoxicating destination. Fevered, urgent, she was half, yearning for Max to make her whole.

His tongue slid in to tease her mouth. His hand shadowed his tongue in the most secret recesses of her body. Wench. If this was a charade, she never wanted it to end. The moon waned low; moonbeams touched his face, highlighted the stark longing in his eyes. She gasped and again he kissed her, fell with her against the haystack, desire taut. The core of her was aching, arching for him. The next few minutes were fervent, full of whispered words, intimate exchange of caresses, as desire—no longer willing to be banked—burst into flame. His entrance was a wild thrust, a burst of pain, then aching tenderness, intoxicating oneness. She lay there luxuriating in their oneness. Perfect mates. Their desire was ebbing and flowing like the eternal tide that crashed against the shore far beneath them . . . ebbing and flowing . . . until she like Max abandoned caution and let ecstasy take them where it would. It was a sinful way to die and a foretaste of heaven.

A bell clanged once far out in the bay. It was a signal to go. He held her fast. "Stay with me, my darling wench . . . I have to explain what just happened, what it meant . . . I'll protect you till the next boat . . ."

There might not be a next boat. Trust no one. She grabbed her gloves and pushed out of his embrace.

*"I know what this meant, Max. We played out the
masquerade—me as the wench, you as—"*

"No."

*Wench. Trust no one. And she ran from him then. From
the rabble hiding, waiting to snatch her. Faster, she ran. She
had nothing left, not even virtue. She had to escape. Now.*

Violet stared up at Max, still torn between her desire and
the months of terror. Dare she believe the tender gleam in
his eye now or trust the way her heart reached out to him?
Just one question; that's all she needed to hear the answer to,
a question requiring all her courage.

"Do you think me a wench?"

His answer didn't need words. Just the remorse that
flashed across his face, the deepening sadness in those blue
eyes. And then he pulled her into his arms, cradled her face
against his heart.

"When we were hiding alone and waiting for the moon to
wane, it ceased to be adventure . . . or charade. And you
were never my wench."

"Not even now?" she murmured against his chest.

"Gentlemen don't love wenches . . . except those in
costume." He took her by the arms and gently shook her. "It
was you I loved, my lady, not your masquerade."

She looked at him, wanting to believe, terrified to give up
her charade.

"Violet," he pleaded, "when you walked into my house
masquerading as a glovemaker's apprentice, it was like a
miracle. I nearly went insane when you vanished again.
Everyone in London thinks me mad, and they're right. I'm
mad with love, and I've loved you since I met you, since I
guided you across France. Did you hear what I said,
Violet?" His voice was intense. "It was no masquerade.
When I kissed you . . . and after, that was not a charade,
that was real. If you'd not run off, if the boat had been

delayed two minutes . . . I would have told you my feelings. It was no masquerade, just as now I speak to you devoid of masquerade."

He stood still then, like a man condemned, waiting for her to pronounce sentence. She could condemn him to a life without love, or grant mercy.

"I love you, too," she said at last.

He reached for her hand and kissed the palm.

"Will you be mine?" he asked tenderly.

Violet took the gloves he proffered and began to pull them on. Never mind what Caro's scissors had done to them. Gaspard could make her more. Gaspard could make her all the gloves she needed.

Max right now was all she wanted. No more masquerades, just Max.

He escorted her out to the ballroom, where he led her to the place of honor. The musicians struck up a tune, and as everyone gazed in wonder, Lord Shelburne's heir and his Violet, the glovemaker's apprentice, the woman for whom the son of an earl had turned London inside out, began to dance.

And she was wearing a gift of gloves.

Except for a few knowing smiles when Caro flounced out in a huff, no one seemed to mind that the search for the glove was over. The rage for single gloves would soon be forgotten, replaced by another fashion. A winged cherub, Cupid, hovered in the shadows, exhausted, sighing over a pile of discarded Valentine hopes. The spoils of love.

Lady Shelburne, Max noticed ever so briefly, recovered her poise quickly, though, and soon was at the center of a great debate whispering its way around the ballroom.

"They met in the tradesman's room right here in Shelburne House!" said a young lord. "A formal introduction just this evening."

"No, no," argued a bewigged matron, "she dropped a

glove one day, and he never gave up searching for the owner. Isn't that romantic?"

"That's not how it happened," said one of the mamas. "He met her at the glovemaker's shop."

Another mama turned in her tracks. "You're mistaken. It was on an émigré ship. He helped her escape from France."

"You're all wrong," Lady Shelburne said. "It was love at first sight, right here at my ball. At my very *own* ball."

"I do believe everyone in the ballroom is arguing about how we met." Violet smiled up into the eyes of Max.

"I think," Max said calmly, "that next year we ought to cancel the masquerade ball. . . ."

Alarmed, Cupid sat up. Cancel the ball?

"Cancel the ball?" Violet said. "But Caro has not yet found her mate—"

Max leaned down to kiss the crown of her head, and her heart paused. "Since by then you'll be Lady Shelburne, you decide. But I've found my mate, and so if there is another ball, *we* may not linger, dear heart."

"Then we'd best dance our fill now."

Long into the night they danced—long after the fine ladies had taken their gloves and their mamas and driven off in their carriages.

Oh, yes, for Cupid's sake, there would be another ball at Shelburne House—come what may in the world. Cupid needed balls . . . for these modern lovers, they gave no quarter anymore. Oh, mercy, yes, next year there *had* to be a ball.

Masquerades optional.

HEART OF ERIN

by

Bonnie K. Winn

Dear Readers,

Being a true romantic, I was thrilled when my editor, Judith Stern, asked me to write an historical valentine story. As most of us are wont to do, my thoughts centered on the most famous symbol of the holiday, valentine cards. Despite the beauty and fame of the handmade cards of that era, I wondered about the people who produced manufactured cards—the tycoons, the entrepreneurs, and the immigrant laborers they employed. Cutting across those social and economic lines, one thing continues to persevere: love.

To celebrate that love and the spirit of our immigrant ancestors, I present "Heart of Erin," dedicated to those incredible forefathers who carved the difficult path we now trod with ease, and to my own true love, my husband, Howard.

I hope you enjoy meeting Brianna McBride, an unusual sort of Irish immigrant, and Michael Donovan, an enterprising publisher of valentines, as they walk their own special path to love.

May all of your romantic moments shine with the excitement of Valentine's Day and your life be filled with love. Happiest valentine wishes to you all.

Bonnie K. Winn

I enjoy hearing from you. Write to me c/o the Publicity Dept., The Berkley Publishing Group, 200 Madison Avenue, New York, NY 10016.

ONE

New York City, 1860

BRIANNA MCBRIDE CLUTCHED the creased newspaper in one hand as she raised the other to knock. The words of the advertisement rang in her head:

> Wanted: An artist to design lithograph pictures for Griffith Publishing. A grave, sedate personage of at least thirty years. IRISH PEOPLE need not apply, as the wages are sure.

The only qualification she possessed of all those listed was artistic ability. She was neither thirty nor particularly grave or sedate. And with a stiffening of her spine she acknowledged that she was most assuredly Irish, a fact that had kept her from obtaining any other position in the city. Luckily her English nanny had helped her remove all traces of a brogue, but she could not disguise her common Irish surname.

Looking at the run-down red brick building housing Griffith Publishing, she doubted this employer could afford to pay the wages other artists might demand, which was the only factor in her favor. Her knock rang clearly in the chilly, early morning air.

The sound of clattering boots came closer, and with a rush

the door flew open. Brianna stared at the young man of perhaps nineteen years. Obligingly he stared back, apparently pleased with what he saw. Recovering her composure, Brianna smiled. "I'm here about the artist's position."

The lad scratched his head in confusion, then opened the door wider. The inside of the place looked nearly as dismal as the exterior. The vast space echoed with emptiness. Vacant, scarred desks lined walls that were barely covered by crumbling paint. The scuffed wooden floor was in great need of polishing, and the threadbare rugs covering the pathway needed to be either cleaned or burned. Situated to one side a huge black stove attempted to warm the drafty interior.

Leading Brianna past the dim offices, the young man took her down the stairs and past the loading dock to the factory area. The huge warehouse was in the same decaying condition as the offices. A much older, silver-headed man tinkered with an ancient printing press, stopping when he caught sight of her. A large apron covered the man's clothing, protecting him from the dirt and ink surrounding them. Behind him, about a dozen other men labored on the assembly line and at various machines, ignoring her presence.

"She's here about the drawin'," the young one who'd answered the door explained in a loud voice, battling the noise of the running presses.

"Well, close the door, Jimmy, 'fore every scrap of heat escapes!" the older man ordered. Moving from the sad-looking piece of machinery, he wiped his hands on a rag before sizing her up. "You'll be needin' to talk to the boss."

"Thank you, that would be fine," Brianna answered, trying to force some enthusiasm into her voice. Had she not spent nearly all of her time seeking work since her arrival in America, she would be tempted to leave without speaking to the person in charge.

"Come with me," the silver-haired man ordered. She started to follow him when he stopped abruptly. "I'm Finnigan."

"I'm pleased to make your acquaintance, Mr. Finnigan." Brianna smiled tentatively as he seemed to take her measure.

"Just Finnigan." He turned back and led the way to a small cove of an office that was just outside the view of the main office area she'd walked through. "In there."

Swallowing her trepidation, Brianna knocked on the dusty glass portion of the door.

"Come!"

Since the voice was a barked order, she complied.

"Yes?" he asked, without raising his head.

Brianna focused on the man behind the desk, who had yet to look at her. His head was bent forward, allowing well-trimmed mahogany hair to cover his forehead. She appraised his immaculately tailored waistcoat and stiffly starched pleated shirt, and then moved her gaze to his clean-shaven face. But before she could analyze the intriguing planes and hollows of his face, he tipped his head back quickly, pinning her with striking deep blue eyes. Swallowing, Brianna wished suddenly that she fit more than just one of the job requirements.

"You wanted something?" he asked again, a trace of impatience coloring his tone.

Collecting her thoughts rapidly, Brianna inched forward. "Yes, I'm here about the artist's position."

"But you're a woman." He frowned as though wondering why she hadn't realized such an obvious fact.

It occurred to her that she wouldn't have been surprised if she'd sprouted a second head at that point. It was the only liability Brianna didn't possess. "I'm also an artist," she replied, remembering the portfolio she carried.

His dark eyebrows drew together in an even deeper

frown. "I distinctly remember specifying a person of at least thirty years of age."

She flushed under his scrutiny, but pushed her portfolio forward nonetheless. After a long stare which Brianna was sure had revealed all her inadequacies, he took the proffered sketches. Rather than flipping carelessly through them as she expected, he carefully deliberated over each one, lingering on the final sketch of cupids and flowers. It was a rather silly thing, but she'd impulsively piled it in with the others that morning while talking herself into following up on the only job left in the newspaper for which she could qualify.

"Do you have more of these?" he asked abruptly.

Brianna thought of all the sketches left at her home across the sea. What she had with her now were the sketches she'd prepared for her aunt and uncle since her arrival. Apparently it wasn't much of a representation. Heart sinking, she shook her head in denial.

"How long would it take you to make up a few more like this?" he asked, holding up the cupid and flower drawing.

Calculating quickly, she blurted out, "No time at all."

He rose from behind the massive desk, an impressive sight as his tall body unfolded from the chair. "Let's see."

Barely having time to blink in surprise, Brianna found herself installed at one of the battered desks in the vacant office area, pencils, paints, and drawing pad in hand. She looked up into those deep blue eyes expectantly.

"I'm planning to print a new line of valentines," he began. Brianna digested this information, realizing immediately why he'd been attracted to the one sketch. She remained silent as he paused for a moment. "Draw me a valentine no one can resist buying."

Brianna kept her mouth from sagging with considerable effort. Saying no more, he turned on his heel and left her to the drawing. Glancing up, she met Finnigan's eyes and thought she saw a sparkle of encouragement before he turned and headed back to the printing press area. Young Jimmy clasped both hands together over his head in a sign of victory, scampering after Finnigan when the older man barked an order. She pulled off her gloves and put them with her tiny drawstring purse, then, taking heart, concentrated on the blank page.

Two hours later she stared at the results. At the top of the valentine was a robin's-egg-blue disk with a scalloped edge mounted against a larger red one at the back of the cherub's head. Gold and white medallions beneath it relied on vivid azure disks as background. Tiny stars seemed to float beneath the words "Forget me not."

A flush of success was accompanied by a rush of nervousness. What if this wasn't what he wanted? The shadow darkening her desk told her it was time to find out. Reluctantly she tipped her head to meet his gaze, but found it centered on the drawing.

Her gaze followed the direction of his hands as he picked up the sketch. Long powerful fingers rested against the delicate paper.

"This is acceptable," he finally uttered, still staring at the drawing. Brianna's breath released in a whoosh. His frown returned, however. "I hadn't planned on hiring a woman."

She straightened up in the chair. "But you like the drawing."

He stared at the sketch again. "Yes," he admitted.

Brianna rose from the chair, deciding it was time to be bold. Her ingrained politeness had only served to have her turned away from other prospective employment. "Then perhaps we should discuss wages."

Jolted in surprise, his heavy dark brows drew together. Only an employer should broach the subject of wages, and Brianna knew it. But it was also time for her to get past the fact that she was a woman of only twenty-two years.

"If I were to offer you the position, it pays twelve dollars a month." His words were flat, uncompromising. She sensed he was a seasoned negotiator.

Brianna listened to the amount in surprise. It was just a few dollars more than a domestic earned. "I don't suppose you've had many artists responding to such a low offer."

"That's not your concern," he reminded her sternly.

Deciding diplomacy might be a good course, Brianna nodded in agreement. "You're right. However, I would need fifteen dollars a month."

A small twitch near the corner of his lips told her that her boldness had both intrigued and amused him. "Perhaps we could settle on thirteen and a half."

Deciding not to quibble further, Brianna offered her hand. He seemed to hesitate for a moment before taking it. Business handshakes with women were no doubt a novelty for him.

"When can you start, Miss . . . ?"

She took a deep breath. "McBride. Brianna McBride. I can start today. Or when—"

"I specifically advertised for no Irish, Miss *McBride.*" Anger darkened his face, and she involuntarily took a step back.

"I realize that, Mr. Griffith. However, I believe you can see that I have talent, and if you'll give me the opportunity, I can prove what a hard worker I am."

Finnigan had rounded the corner from the machinery area and paused, holding a well-greased rag which he used to wipe his hands. "His name's not Griffith, Miss. It's Donovan. Michael Donovan."

Brianna and Michael both looked at Finnigan with an array of emotions. Brianna looked surprised, and Donovan gave him a glare of anger and exasperation.

"Mr. Donovan?" Brianna questioned sweetly, wondering

why the man chose to discriminate against his own. Still, she was willing to press the advantage.

"Don't think that makes any difference, Miss McBride. I specifically do not wish to hire Irish." His face flushed in a renewal of controlled anger.

"Your loyalty is touching," she couldn't help saying before rushing on. "Nonetheless, we just shook hands on the deal." She threw out the challenge, instinctively guessing he was a man of pride who took his honor seriously.

The silence was deafening as Finnigan and Brianna waited for Michael Donovan's reaction. "But that was before you told me your name," he accused, obviously not happy to be the unwitting pawn of her maneuvering manner.

"Are you accustomed to welshing on a deal, Mr. Donovan?" she asked calmly. She needed this job. It would have been preferable to have been accepted at face value. If it couldn't be that way, a bit of manipulation seemed in order.

"I don't go back on my word," he gritted out as she smiled. But her expression drooped a bit as he continued. "There are certain terms to the employment, however. I'll give you sixty days of probation. If you don't meet my specifications in that time, you'll be out. Is that understood?"

Swallowing, Brianna nodded her agreement. The emotional toil of the morning was beginning to wear on her. She'd channeled all of her energy into the unaccustomed bargaining, and now she lost some of her stamina.

"Good. Now I'd like to see some more sketches."

She started to sink into the chair, when he turned around abruptly. "You will have a ten-minute break for lunch at noon. Don't linger overlong. I'll expect you here in the morning at seven o'clock sharp." Her eyes widened as she nodded in understanding. As though an afterthought, he flung the last words over his shoulder. "You may put your hat and wrap in the cupboard."

The door to his office closed, and Brianna stared at the empty space. Jimmy came around the desk and grinned much like a puppy hoping for a new master. "The cupboard's over here, miss. And you needn't worry. Mr. Donovan lets us have a cup of tea now and then, too."

Brianna was certain her answering smile was weak as she put her things away. Smoothing a hand over her hair, she wondered if she'd undertaken more than she was capable of. As she gazed around the broken-down, disheartening place, she thought perhaps she'd been rash in accepting the position. Then, remembering her purpose in obtaining the job, she stiffened her resolve. Sorting through the unfamiliar materials, she found pencils and flipped the drawing pad open.

The hours passed quickly as she penned sketches. Only when Jimmy lit the lamps did she realize that dusk had approached. Finnigan's sharp but kindly gaze settled on her as he came out from the press area. "About quittin' time, miss."

As she rose, her body protested from being forced into such a cramped position for so long. Still, she looked with pride at what she'd accomplished.

"Right nice pictures, miss." Finnigan studied the drawings with her. "You plannin' to come back tomorrow?"

She glanced up in surprise. "Of course. Why shouldn't I?"

"Some folks don't take to Michael's ways," he replied bluntly, his eyes unreadable.

"I'm here for employment, not socializing." Despite her fatigue, a spark of resistance crept into her voice.

The lines in Finnigan's face deepened. "That's for the best, miss."

Examining his animated face beneath a shock of silvery-white hair, Brianna could see a combination of wisdom and regret. She was quite aware that Finnigan, too, was Irish.

She couldn't understand the oddest set of contradictions she'd ever encountered. Too tired to wonder further, she bid him good night and left for home.

In less than an hour she spotted the large house and the welcoming oil lamps lighting it. She hastened the last few steps. When a shadow approached from beside her, she nearly jumped in fright.

"I'm sorry, Miss McBride." The man doffed his hat, holding it in his hands. "I didn't mean to startle you. I was comin' to deliver the bill."

"Oh. And you're . . . ?" He looked vaguely familiar, but she couldn't place him.

"Rafferty, ma'am. The butcher. I don't mean to be of trouble, but if you could see that your uncle gets this, I'd be grateful." The man handed her a paper. "He must've misplaced the others."

"Others?"

Rafferty shuffled his feet a bit, his head bowed. "It's been close to six months now since he's paid the bill. But I know Mr. Lynch. He's a decent sort—wouldn't run out on a bill."

"Of course not. I'll see that you're paid immediately." Brianna thought of her paycheck at the end of the month. Somehow she guessed it wouldn't be nearly enough for their needs.

"Thank you, ma'am. Give my best to the mister and missus."

"Certainly." Her steps slowed as she approached the front door. Glad to be out of the cold, Brianna shook her cape to rid it of snowflakes before hanging the garment on the peg of the clothes tree in the front hall. Mary's concerned face peered around the corner of the great hall.

"There you be. I worried myself to death all day. Come along now, and we'll fetch you a cup of hot tea." The older woman clucked as she hustled Brianna down the hall and around the corner toward the warmth of the kitchen hearth.

Unable to get rid of the incriminating bill, Brianna clenched it in her hand. Taking the comfortable rocker in the kitchen, she hid the paper in the folds of her skirt.

"How's Uncle Robert?" Brianna questioned as she took the cup from Mary, warming her hands for a moment against the delicate porcelain.

Mary's face wreathed into wrinkles of concern as she shook her head. "The doctor was by again. Left more medicine. Your poor aunt was beside herself."

Brianna sighed as she stared at the flames in the hearth. Her uncle's health was precarious at best. Always hearty, no one had expected Robert Lynch to fall ill. Knowing her aunt was alone with him in America, Brianna had chosen to travel from Ireland to be with them. But after her arrival, she'd sensed that her uncle's finances were another matter of concern. One day, while looking for stationery, she'd come across a drawer full of unpaid bills. The butcher was only one of the many creditors her uncle owed.

A solicitor of notable reputation, Uncle Robert was the sole source of their income. Months of not being able to work coupled with expensive medical treatments must have taken their toll. He spoke constantly of needing to return to work, and Brianna realized quickly that she was yet another mouth to feed.

"How about a biscuit to go with that tea?" Mary asked, offering a plate of fresh shortbread.

"Thank you." Brianna accepted the cookie and laid it on her saucer. Taking another sip of the warming tea, she gazed at the flames leaping in the hearth, examining her alternatives once again. She didn't want to ask her parents for money, since they'd advised her against traveling to America. It had seemed a simple matter to locate employment as a governess to ease the burden. She hadn't expected the vicious lack of tolerance for the Irish, which was especially harsh in New York City. Despite her breeding and background, her inquiries were always returned once they heard her name. Today had been her first breakthrough, one she didn't intend to lose.

Brianna heard the whispery flutter she had come to recognize as Aunt Virginia's new method of entering a room. Always fearful of wakening her sick husband, Virginia Lynch had adopted a waiflike movement. Brianna smiled at her aunt, whose impish personality had only slightly dimmed because of her husband's illness.

Red hair traced with barely a sprinkle of gray topped a gamin face dominated by huge eyes of emerald green. Always close to the aunt who had never had children of her own, Brianna was gratified to see the resilience Virginia never seemed to lose.

"So, moppet, where have you been all the day?" Virginia asked as she drew an affectionate hand across Brianna's hair.

"I had an exciting offer today."

Virginia's smile turned into an expression of concern. "What sort of offer, child?"

"To be an artist." Brianna stretched the truth a bit. "You know how I've always wanted that."

"I've told you that you needn't seek employment, Brianna. I've been thrifty through the years, and we've saved our money well. You seem to have the wrong notion—"

Brianna could see the pride puffing up in her aunt and knew she had to dissuade her. "It's not the money, Aunt Virginia. I'm to design valentines. It's so exciting."

"Valentines?"

Relieved to see that her aunt was slightly intrigued, Brianna launched into a fanciful description of the job. When she finished, Virginia still wasn't completely convinced. Starting to rise, her aunt patted Brianna's knee and chanced on the wadded-up piece of paper.

"Whatever do you have there?" Virginia asked, unfolding the wrinkled scrap of paper. "Oh, the butcher's bill. I simply have no head for business. Your uncle always took care of all the creditors, and I don't even know how to pen a cheque. But it looks as if I'll have to discover how."

Brianna tried to smile at her aunt's obvious deception. She wondered if Virginia's charade was for her benefit or if she just couldn't face the reversal in their monetary situation.

"More tea?" Mary asked.

"Thank you, yes," Brianna replied.

Virginia slipped the bill in her pocket. "I want you to meet some nice young men while you're here, child. A working woman will not attract the sort of man you'd be interested in."

A sudden picture of Michael Donovan's chiseled face and striking blue eyes flashed through Brianna's thoughts. While he hadn't cracked a smile, he had intrigued her in a way no man before ever had.

Mary refilled her cup of tea, and Brianna rearranged her features into a pleasing smile as she turned to her aunt. "I believe I can promise you that I'll meet a young man while I'm here."

Virginia relaxed, and Brianna sipped the fragrant, warm tea as she thought of the man in question. What lurked behind the stern countenance and distinctive surname remained a mystery, one that beckoned even as the bells of warning rang.

TWO

MICHAEL DONOVAN ABANDONED the ledger and rose to stare out the grimy window that overlooked the bustling city street. Hackney cabs and omnibuses roared over the boulevard, battling with the sea of pedestrians. But his attention wasn't on any of the people outside.

He knew he should be meeting with distributors, finding outlets for the valentines and stationery he hoped to sell. Still, he'd allowed the morning to pass as he caught up on orders and stared through the tiny pane of glass in his office door at Griffith Publishing's new employee.

This was Brianna's third day, and he'd been absent on the first two days of her employment while dealing with booksellers. Expecting her to be tardy, he'd paced the floor expectantly, surprised when she arrived half an hour early prepared to work. In the hours since, she'd bent over the old accountant's desk as she tackled the folder of size specifications and then started preliminary sketches. She had refused Jimmy's offer of tea to remain at her task, only taking time to speak with Finnigan.

A knock at the door interrupted his musing. Finnigan poked his head around the doorway. "We got that last stationery order finished."

"Good. Will you get it out right away?"

Finnigan's expression told him the remainder was unnecessary. "Just like I always do."

Michael smiled at Finnigan's brashness. He'd worked here since Michael had been a boy. He knew his job and did it without direction. Michael's expression grew thoughtful. Finnigan had been with them during the good times and the bad.

In a flight of unexpected memory Michael saw the offices and factory as they'd once been under his grandfather's competent hand. At that time, now many years past, the machinery had been both well oiled and fine tuned, running with uncanny precision. A score of salesmen, bookkeepers, and workers filled the spots that he and the only remaining employees now occupied.

Michael's grandfather, Ambrose Griffith, had been a stern but caring taskmaster, expecting the best and receiving it. As a small boy, Michael had watched the burgeoning empire, dreaming of the time he would take his place there. He had never imagined that such a dynasty would be crippled under his own father's direction.

After his grandfather's death, his father had taken control of the thriving business. At first the publishing firm ran under its own steam, but gradually it disintegrated, much like a rudderless ship. For Timothy Donovan had never learned from his father-in-law the intricacies of business and had no real desire to do so. His passions ran to drink and gambling.

Although Michael admitted that his late father had indeed possessed a heart of gold, he hadn't a bit of ambition to accompany his kindness. Slowly the empire vanished, to be replaced by a nearly bankrupt, broken-down publishing business.

Michael's mother, a fine English gentlewoman, accepted her husband's shortcomings and loved him until the day he died. But Michael found it more difficult to be forgiving and had tried to erase every bit of his Irish heritage. Now only his name stood between him and success. He knew that potential clients shuddered at the impulsiveness and propensity for strong drink associated with the people of Erin. The prejudice had haunted his youth and threatened his future.

Michael turned and stared at the dark-haired beauty in the outer room. Now he'd hired another Irish. His gaze settled on the pale blue of her eyes—as light as his own were dark. Skin of fairest ivory porcelain was relieved by a faint blush in her cheeks and lips of deepest rose. As he watched, her dark eyebrows drew together while she gazed critically at the drawing in her hand. He couldn't hire a sculptor to mold a more beautiful profile.

Knowing his own deadline to meet payments was scarcely more than the probationary period he'd granted Brianna, he cursed his impulsiveness. Struck both by her beauty and the sketches in her portfolio, he'd not asked the most rudimentary questions about her working ability. Refusing to allow history to repeat itself, he'd set goals for himself, determinedly closing his heart to love. None of those goals included a young Irish beauty who could circumvent all his carefully laid plans.

As he watched, she rose, stretching her petite frame from its cramped position. He tried to ignore the press of her curves as they strained against the serviceable dress she wore, but still he stared as she gathered her materials and approached his office. Turning from the tiny pane of glass, he was but a foot from the door when the rap sounded upon it.

Adopting a stern expression, he opened the door. "Yes?"

"Do you have a moment, Mr. Donovan?" she asked. It seemed to him that she was trying to hide a touch of nervousness. He motioned her to a chair and paused beside her as she settled in. When she glanced up, he felt his midsection tighten as her pale eyes fringed by dark lashes settled on him.

He made his attitude purposely brusque. "What is it?"

"May I speak with you?"

"Very well, Miss McBride." Despite his intentions, his voice lingered overlong when he said her name. The slip strengthened his resolve. "I've a busy morning scheduled."

"Yes," she answered, gradually losing some of her temerity. "I have some initial sketches I'd like you to see."

Michael glanced at the drawings that she held crushed against her breasts. Clearing his throat, he tore his gaze from her body and tried to focus on what she was pointing to. Not certain what to expect, nonetheless he frowned at the simplicity of the sketch.

"It looks as though you've lumped the whole design in the middle," he observed, wondering why she'd done so.

Brianna's eyes sparkled as she spoke. "I'm so glad you noticed that. If the design were to be placed on embossed letter sheets, the scalloping would surround it."

Despite her enthusiasm, he was not pleased. Embossed sheets would be expensive. Apparently she'd wasted an entire morning on a fool's errand. "There's been a misunderstanding. We have the machinery for lithography, which is what I intend to use. Your job is to design drawings that can be printed on standard paper. I have no intention to manufacture handmade valentines."

She leaned forward eagerly, and Michael felt the press of her knee. The warmth took his concentration away momentarily. "But I know. I spoke to Finnigan. We could give the illusion of handmade valentines by using either scalloped or embossed paper, while keeping the cost of production down."

So she'd spoken to Finnigan. Michael wondered what else the man had told her.

But Brianna wasn't finished. "Most of the publishing companies can provide hand-colored lithographs, but no one is supplying embossed valentines, unless they're handmade, and those are too dear for most people to afford."

"We can sell lithographs for sixty cents a dozen," Michael reminded her. "I can't even begin to imagine how much embossed cards would cost."

"Approximately seven dollars and twenty cents per dozen," she replied with an intelligent gleam in her eyes. "While they would cost more than lithographs, they would still be far less than a single handmade card that cost as much as ten dollars. You'd have a much larger market."

"I didn't realize you were a shrewd businesswoman as well as an artist," he commented dryly, determinedly trying to ignore the flush of beauty that accompanied her enthusiasm. The folly of pursuing such an attraction was apparent.

Her head straightened as she met his gaze. "I come by it naturally, sir."

The reference to her heritage didn't pass him by.

"Miss McBride, I hired you to draw valentine designs, not to reorganize my business." He paused as he watched her gaze around the crumbling office. Her meaning was clear—the business had the look of one in dire need of help. She waited silently, but he refused to explain how the firm had come to such a state. The memories were both painful and private. "I will consider the sketches and the idea, but I need new designs for the lithographs already ordered."

Brianna drew more sketches forward. "I worked on these, also."

Michael accepted the drawings, pleased by the fanciful renderings. He was forced to admit her talent was far greater than any of the other applicants who had demanded higher wages while looking down their noses at the work conditions. Remarkably, although the sketches all represented the holiday of love, no two were alike. While Brianna's presence disturbed him, he knew he couldn't afford to dismiss her.

"These are acceptable," he finally uttered. He wondered if he imagined the brief look of relief on her face before she gathered the materials together. When she stood, they were but a foot apart, and he realized too late that he could span the distance between them with an outstretched hand. Abruptly he moved back, striding behind the desk. "I have a full schedule," he reminded her brusquely.

A smile tinged with mischievous humor emerged at the unnecessary reminder. "Yes, sir. You already told me."

Shutting the door to his office behind her, she disappeared. He let out his own indrawn breath. It was a trifle late to realize that Miss McBride was far more than he'd bargained for.

THREE

"BUT, FINNIGAN, THAT part of the design must be blue for the effect to work," Brianna argued.

"Means I'll have to run the machine on three colors," he warned.

Brianna smiled sweetly. "I know."

Mutterings filled the press area as Finnigan prepared the process. In the weeks since she'd been hired, she and Finnigan had formed an unusual alliance. Discovering that he was the employee with the longest tenure, Brianna had pestered him into telling her how the business had come to be in such sad repair. Once Finnigan had told her the whole story, including why Michael was so bitter, Brianna knew there was far more to her employer than appeared on the surface. Realizing that Michael Donovan was fighting for his life, she decided immediately that she would be in his corner whether he so desired or not.

In those same weeks she had pressed friends of her aunt and uncle to order the embossed valentines, and the sales had poured in. Despite Michael's reluctance for the plan, she was certain the more elaborate cards would bring in a higher profit.

She knew Michael purposely distanced himself from her, and based on Finnigan's information, she could guess why. After badgering Finnigan for more insight into their employer's brusque ways, Finnigan had finally revealed that

Michael hadn't allowed time in his carefully calculated plans for anything other than business. Brianna had guessed the rest. Michael certainly had no time for romance. And he certainly wouldn't pursue a romance with someone of the Irish persuasion.

Still she stubbornly championed his cause. It was a weakness she'd had from birth. She'd driven her parents to distraction taking in every lame creature in her path. She sensed Michael Donovan could use her help.

Despite his seeming arrogance and well-concealed emotions, she believed his need was far greater than any she'd ever encountered. Trying to dismiss the effect of his gaze upon her, she concentrated solely on the mission of making the business and her position profitable. Staring out the window at the busy street below, she imagined restoring Griffith Publishing to its former glory, the smile that would soften Michael's often harsh features, and the change in how he would look at her.

"Daydreaming, Miss McBride?"

Brianna flew around with a gasp. Indeed she had been occupied in just such fancy. Michael Donovan's body was far too close to her own for comfort, she realized as she moved casually away. "I was considering a new design," she improvised.

The knowing look in his eye caused her to flush. Lines of tension remained etched around his mouth, and she longed to brush them away. Wondering what those same lips upon her own would feel like, she dropped the pad in her hand.

Together they bent to retrieve it, their faces scarcely inches apart. Brianna saw the blood rise in his neck even as her own heartbeat accelerated. He recovered first, picking up the errant sketchpad and offering his hand to help her rise.

The touch was unexpected and unnerving. Seeking composure, she hoped her pale skin wasn't as flushed as it felt. "Thank you. I'm afraid I was quite clumsy."

She waited what seemed to be ages before he replied, his voice a trifle huskier than usual. "Not at all."

He still held her hand, and the realization seemed to strike him even as she mirrored the thought. Abruptly he withdrew his hand, and she immediately regretted the loss of contact. Shaken by the thought, Brianna clutched the pad to her chest, unable to think of a sensible reply.

"Would you like to show me the new design?" Michael asked, jarring her already scattered sensibilities.

She stared at him stupidly. "What design?"

"The one you were considering," he reminded her.

Collecting her whirling thoughts, Brianna turned toward her desk, grateful that she'd spent time the previous night sketching. But before she could reach for the designs, he stopped her. "How about a cup of tea first?"

Surprised, she nodded her agreement. Usually he was strictly business, scarcely taking time from his own work to catch a bite of lunch.

She watched the strength in his long, slim fingers as he poured the tea and arranged a plate of biscuits. His mother's English heritage had apparently been deeply ingrained in him, judging from his speech and habits to his very cautiously guarded emotions. She wondered if any of his father's legacy still existed.

Accepting a cup of tea, she was pleased to see that her hands didn't tremble. She only hoped her face held a fraction of the same composure. As she bent to take a sip of tea, Finnigan approached.

He unrolled the colorful new lithograph, and Brianna cautiously watched Michael's face for a reaction. She hadn't spoken to him about the new method that would allow them to produce the cards without hand-coloring. "What do you think?" Finnigan asked.

Michael reached out to touch the paper. "This wasn't done by hand."

Brianna held her breath, wondering how long it would take him to realize he'd stated the obvious. Apparently not long at all.

"Who decided to run the press for each color?"

Finnigan and Brianna exchanged glances, but Finnigan spoke first. "Well, Michael, do you like it or not?" Never standing on ceremony with the boss he'd known since Michael had been in short pants, Finnigan obviously didn't intend to start now.

They launched into a discussion of the time involved in running the press three times as opposed to hand coloring. Brianna started to excuse herself, but Michael waved her back into the chair. Her stomach clenched nervously, certain he was aware of her participation in the new idea.

"What about the last order of sheet music?" Michael asked Finnigan. Before the man could answer, Michael turned to Brianna. "That is, if it's all right with you. Sheet music *is* one of our principal means of revenue."

She smiled weakly, wondering if she was about to be dismissed. While she wanted to help him, she also knew how important it was to be earning her own keep. Despite her aunt's assurances, she didn't want to be a burden to her relatives.

The tea forgotten, Brianna rushed to her desk as Michael walked over to the machinery area with Finnigan. She reached for her drawing materials, hoping to immerse herself behind a wall of work before Michael returned.

"Don't worry, miss." Jimmy's cheery brown eyes peered over the roll of paper he carried. Always ready with a smile, today was no exception. "The place needed a bit of new life. Mr. Donovan will thank you eventually." Seeing Michael approach, Jimmy shifted his load and hastened on his way. Brianna took a deep breath, preparing for the worst.

"Why wasn't I consulted about the new technique?" Michael questioned without preamble, his fingers drumming the desktop.

"I thought if you could see how it worked, you might be more receptive," Brianna explained, wishing she hadn't been so impulsive.

"Despite what you seem to perceive, I am not an ogre, Miss McBride. If an idea warrants attention, I will see that it gets such. I do not like being manipulated within my own firm, however." Brianna's chin sank a bit closer to her chest, anticipating his next move, realizing she should have used some restraint. The idea wasn't worth losing her job over.

"The new process merits a second look," he continued. So she wasn't to get the sack. Raising her head, she met the steady regard in his eyes. He seemed on the verge of adding more, but instead turned and entered his office, closing the door behind him. Slowly laying the pad on her desk, Brianna stared at the space he'd vacated, long after the sound of his shutting door stilled. Despite the stern tone he'd adopted, she could see the appreciation in his eyes for her ingenuity. He might not be able to acknowledge it yet, but the realization was there. She hoped it wasn't only her wishing that had made it seem so, but it appeared that a flicker of attraction had hovered in his expression as well. Her own thoughts rang clearly in her head. *More than the idea deserves a second look, Mr. Donovan. So do you.*

FOUR

MICHAEL CLENCHED THE invitation in his hand, having read it several times already. To have garnered the invitation was a coup, the culmination of months of preparation on his part. It would be his opportunity to enter a society that seldom acknowledged the son of Timothy Donovan.

The innocent lettering that mocked him was unexpected, however. He was required to bring an escort, which should be an easy task. But he'd always turned his back on romance, deciding he had no time for such pursuits. A derisive voice reminded him that he might make the same poor choice his mother had.

Spending all his time working to rebuild the business, he'd never missed what had been so easy to ignore. Now he wasn't acquainted with any young woman he could ask on such short notice. Turning his head toward the open office door, Michael looked at Brianna, knowing it would be a breach of etiquette to offer her a social invitation.

As always, her appearance was neat and serviceable. Dismissing the effect of her considerable beauty, he wondered how she would look attired in a ball gown. The thought was preposterous. He doubted she even owned such a dress.

Still, his gaze lingered on her fine features. In the time since she'd joined the firm, laughter was once again heard in the gloomy offices. Despite his pessimistic attitude, secretly Michael welcomed the gaiety. It had been far too long since hope had echoed through the halls of Griffith Publishing.

Brianna's perceptive ideas were both intelligent and highly credible. It was a rare combination in a woman— beauty, humor, and intelligence. As though sensing his thoughts, she raised her head and smiled in his direction.

Thinking no further, he approached her desk. She waited expectantly, her smile still firmly in place. "I have a request to make of you," he began. Again she waited. He cleared his throat. "It is one that is not required of your employment." At her look of confusion, he rapidly outlined the invitation. "And, of course, should you accept, I will open an account at a dressmaker's for the purpose of obtaining a suitable gown."

Her expression was difficult to ascertain as she seemed to ponder the request. "I would be happy to accompany you, Mr. Donovan." His breath released in relief. "But there will be no need to provide my apparel." He wanted to protest that it was important how she was clothed, but knew he couldn't extend such an insult. Swallowing, he nodded. There were but four days until the event—days he was sure would pass as slowly and uneasily as the early morning fog shrouding the building.

Michael glanced through the delicate side window of the doorway, glad that the huge circular fanlight above the structure allowed the light to stream through. He could see Randolph's ancient form bent over the entry table. The butler had been part of the home even before Michael had been born. Rapping lightly, Michael opened the door. Randolph's dour expression of disapproval turned into a reserved smile of greeting.

"Good day, sir."

"Randolph." Michael laid his hat on the Chippendale piecrust candlestand. His eyes skipped over the drawing room, seeing the familiar walnut furniture that had always stood there. "Is my mother home?"

"Yes, sir." Randolph spared Michael another glance before turning his wizened body toward the staircase. "Good to see you, sir."

"You, too, Randolph." Shoving his hands in his pockets, Michael's gaze roamed the room. Finely molded plaster cornice boards were topped by gilt eagles. A portrait of his grandfather stared at him above the fireplace on the paneling of the chimney breast. The upper hall was a tour de force of Ionic detailing, but all he saw was the sameness that had always been there. A warm rush of the strength and security he had always felt in this house shot through him. His grandfather still dominated here. It had been one of his primary residences, the one his mother had taken over when Michael's father died and she'd sold the home that was haunted with memories, both good and bad.

"Michael." The soft voice floated down the stairs, and he jerked his attention upward. At fifty, Elizabeth Griffith Donovan was still a beautiful woman. Not handsome, as most people were wont to be labeled after the flush of youth had faded. No, her chestnut hair had yet to succumb to gray, and the blue of her eyes was still brilliant. She moved forward with a rush, embracing her much taller son.

He relaxed for a moment under the comfort of her touch. Her concern flowed through, and he sensed it immediately. "You look good, Mother."

Her laugh tinkled through the air that was scented with the fresh flowers she arranged in each of the downstairs rooms. "You say that as though you think I should be in my dotage."

Michael's eyes of an even deeper blue than hers now

sparkled with unexpected amusement. "I had thought of bringing you a cane . . ."

Tapping his arm playfully, Elizabeth gazed into his face, every maternal instinct alerted. Something was wrong. She didn't know what, but he was troubled.

Randolph shuffled in with a tray holding a pot of fragrant tea and an assortment of biscuits. After he deposited it on the table with an effort, he straightened up as far as his arthritic body would allow. "Will there be anything else, madam?"

"No, Randolph. Thank you." She poured the tea, watching her son's face, hoping for a clue as to what was bothering him.

Michael accepted the tea, took a sip, and then returned the cup to the table. "Mother, have you ever wondered . . ." He paused, and she waited. "What would it have been like had you married someone closer to your own background?"

It was an old subject, but one that she knew her son had never resolved. "I suppose I would have led a very different life. No doubt the business would be in better condition." She let the words sink in before continuing. "But I'm not certain that would be a fair exchange for love."

The anguish that always accompanied Michael's struggle when discussing his father was evident. "I loved him, too. But it didn't change the way he was." A note of bitterness had crept into his voice, uninvited but not unexpected.

Elizabeth laid a smooth hand on her son's arm. "I know you don't understand, but I never wanted him to change. He had no business sense, that's for certain, and not much more ambition. At times he drank a bit more than he should, but . . ." Her thoughts were far away now, caught up in memories of her late husband. "He possessed such a great passion for life, for love . . . and for me." Unashamedly she met her son's gaze. "I wouldn't have traded that for all the solid ambition in the world."

Michael wouldn't give up. "You had other opportunities."

"But no other love. When you have that kind of love, common sense disappears. I don't want to pry, but I sense you're a bit torn right now. I can only tell you that if I had a thousand other chances, I would still choose your father."

Rays of winter sunlight speared the magnificent Aubusson rug which covered the highly polished wooden floor. "When Father first courted you, did you expect it to lead to marriage?" Michael asked.

"I'm not certain in that first rush of infatuation if anyone ever knows what the outcome will be. But if you don't allow yourself to get close to someone, you'll never know for certain." Elizabeth was aware that Michael refused to become entangled in any emotional relationships. She wondered if there was a special girl who now disturbed him.

"I see."

"Can I be presumptuous enough to ask if there's someone you're drawn to?"

Michael thought of Brianna and the inordinate amount of time he spent wondering about her. "Not in the way you think, Mother. When I meet a suitable young woman, you'll be the first to know."

Elizabeth disguised her flinch. *Suitable.* What a distressing notion. No mention of love, just suitability. She wished Michael could have focused on his father's many good qualities instead of his shortcomings. But her son had always admired his grandfather, emulating him in every possible way. She ached for the pain she sensed her son would experience. If he refused to follow his heart, he would live a loveless existence. And if he found love, he wouldn't trust himself to take it.

Michael stared again at the address on the scrap of paper in his hand. Looking at the prominent house of distinction located far above Bleecker Street, he was sure a mistake had been made. This was the area of the smart set, society patrons who kept carriages, subscribed to the opera, attended Grace Church, and gave balls on a regular basis. While relieved that Brianna didn't reside in the Irish squatter settlement on Dutch Hill, he knew she couldn't belong here, either.

He thought rapidly. Perhaps Brianna was related to one of the domestics employed in the household. Deciding that must be the answer, he strode around to the servants' entrance, pulled the bell cord, and stepped back. In a short time an older woman with ordinary features and graying hair beneath her service cap opened the door.

"May I be of assistance, sir?" Mary asked.

Michael removed his top hat. "Does Miss McBride reside here?"

"Yes," Mary answered, a look of confusion covering her face.

"Could you tell her that Mr. Donovan is here?"

Mary glanced back at the kitchen behind her, obviously uncertain whether to ask the gentleman to step in. "Yes, I'll be but a moment, sir."

Leaving the door ajar, Mary disappeared, and Michael walked the length of the service porch while he waited for Brianna. Several minutes passed before she heard approaching footsteps. These were not like the ones of the older domestic. Instead light, fluttery sounds seemed to sweep from the door. He turned, prepared to speak. But as he gazed at Brianna, he forgot what he wanted to say.

She was a vision. The vaporous evening dress of white tulle and Malines lace was a perfect foil for her dark hair and incredibly pale skin and eyes. The trained skirt, puffed to the waist, was trimmed with a deep flounce and caught up with zinnias as though to form diamond puffs. A coronet of matching flowers encircled her head, emphasizing the dark, shining curls that were caught up to cascade down her back.

A velvet cape protected her from the cold but didn't disturb the picture of perfection. She held out a hand encased in a white kid glove, and he moved forward to accept it as though in a trance.

Michael couldn't even begin to wonder how she'd come by such a dress. Instead he escorted her to the waiting carriage, ensconced in silence as he assisted her. Once settled, the driver started forward, and the quiet seemed to ring in the closed quarters of the cab.

Darkness cloaked the carriage, relieved only by the weak rays of the quarter moon. The small space seemed even more intimate because of the blanket of night. The spark of Brianna's eyes and the moistness of her lips seemed to stand out in the waning moonlight. Feeling robbed of speech, Michael strived for normal conversation, but it failed to come to him. As though a streak of madness possessed him, he longed instead to tell her how beautiful she was, how her presence moved him.

"You look quite handsome, Mr. Donovan." Her voice broke both the silence and the insanity.

"I haven't failed to note your own appearance, Miss McBride." Feeling much like a pompous ass, Michael tried to loosen the grip on his formality. "We might certainly drop our titles for the evening," he added.

Her eyes gleamed again in the darkness. "Whatever you say." She paused, then added in a huskier voice, "Michael."

It was the first time she'd addressed him by his given name. Spoken by Brianna his name sounded lyrical, driving away the taunts of "Mick" that had chased him through his childhood and adolescence.

Jolted by the sudden halting of the carriage, he was flung precariously close to her. Putting out both hands to stop himself from landing upon her, he succeeded but now was a scarce few inches away from her. It seemed he could almost taste the delicate breath that was deliciously close to his own. The moistness of her lips beckoned, and he started to bend his head toward them when reason intervened. He felt as much as heard her sigh when he bolted back to his own half of the cab. The brisk chill of the night disappeared as the heat seemed to envelop the closed space.

When the carriage stopped for a second time, Michael didn't know whether to pray that they had arrived or had miles yet to travel. Looking out the small window, he saw that they had indeed reached the Giles house.

Unlatching the carriage door, he stepped out first, gulping draughts of the cold air before turning to assist Brianna. Feeling his head clear, they moved forward together to be ushered in by a footman who stood beside the huge double doors leading to the entrance of the huge mansion. The red brick building faced with marble was made unique by the steep mansard roof, extremely tall windows, and double porches of exquisite ironwork. Michael took a deep breath. It had been a lifelong dream to be accepted by this set, and now all of his old memories rose to torment him. He was surprised to feel a comforting hand on his arm. Looking down, he met Brianna's reassuring gaze.

Together they moved inside, and Michael removed Brianna's cape and handed it to the butler along with his own greatcoat and hat. Music from the orchestra floated into the hall. Michael turned to Brianna to offer his arm, and he noticed the slight flush in her cheeks. Wondering if her reaction to their closeness in the carriage was similar to his own, he led them forward as they merged with the growing crowd in the ballroom.

Seeing his host approaching, Michael drew a deep breath as he prepared to introduce Brianna. "Miss Brianna McBride, allow me to introduce Etienne Giles."

Bent over her hand, Etienne murmured, "*Enchanté*, mademoiselle."

"Mais c'est moi qui est enchantée," she replied in impeccable French.

Michael stared in burgeoning amazement as a surprised but delighted Etienne captured her arm and chattered with her in his native tongue. Finally Etienne released her arm with regret, his dark eyes sparkling with attention. "I will not presume to ask for the first dance of the evening." Etienne spoke in English for Michael's benefit. "But you must save me a waltz on your card, Mademoiselle McBride." With a bow Etienne left them, and Brianna smiled saucily at Michael, which knocked the wind from him.

Hoping to recapture his equilibrium, Michael requested a dance. Once she was in his arms, he wasn't certain this was the most prudent course of action. The touch of her hands singed him as he guided them around the room. The heated feeling intensified when she tipped her head back, fastening her gaze on his, tilting her lips upward in a smile. He could scarcely believe this lithesome creature was the same one who slaved tediously hour after hour, preparing drawings in his worn offices. The importance of the evening was beginning to fade in comparison to the discovery he held in his arms.

The dance ended, and he could see Etienne Giles making his way forward to claim his waltz. His reaction to Brianna was far better than any Michael could have hoped for—she had totally charmed the people he wished to impress. Yet he felt an unreasonable stirring of anger when Etienne whisked her away. Michael watched from the sidelines, ignoring the important contacts with whom he had intended to mingle. When the dance ended, he kept his distance as Etienne introduced Brianna to the select group of people Michael so desired to know. He could hear laughter and snatches of French from the congenial group. When Brianna turned and caught sight of him, he remained in place as she swept toward him.

"Michael, these people are anxious to make your acquaintance!" she exclaimed, pulling him forward. "Here he is," she announced as they approached.

"Miss McBride has told us all about your innovative business," one gentleman offered. "With such a champion as she, you must in fact be the talk of Wall Street."

Michael exchanged a glance with Brianna, seeing the encouragement in those intriguing eyes. "We are just now establishing ourselves," he demurred.

"Spoken like a true gentleman," Etienne announced. "I can see why your lovely Miss McBride places you in such high regard."

Michael wondered just what Brianna had told the group. "It is a mutual regard." He watched her surprise turn into a becoming blush. Enchanted, the group about them laughed in appreciation.

"I see we've kept her away from you far too long." Etienne bowed formally. "Perhaps lunch next week at the club, Michael?"

Scarcely daring to breathe lest he test his good fortune, Michael nodded in agreement. Lunch at the club meant an exclusive introduction to the very businessmen he'd toiled to meet. The glow of success stirred him as the group moved away, and Michael met Brianna's steady gaze. This was a night of triumph and confusion. At the moment he didn't dare examine which was foremost in his mind.

FIVE

BRIANNA HUGGED HERSELF as she rose from the postered bed. The night before was a memory to be savored like a fine wine or an exquisite sweet imported from the finest European confectioners. Throwing back the drapes at the window, she stared into the gray fog of early morning, not seeing the bleak cold, but instead feeling the warmth of strong arms as she danced the night away.

A crash of wood in the fireplace made her turn with a start, but she smiled happily at Mary as the older woman bent to light the kindling. "Like to freeze to death in this weather," Mary grumbled.

"Oh, but it's a glorious day!" Brianna exclaimed.

Mary straightened up to stare out at the gloomy weather. Shaking her head at Brianna, she *tsked* in disapproval. "You haven't been right since the gentleman rang the service door."

Brianna laughed. Mary, in her way, was correct.

"Why *did* he come to the back door?" Mary questioned in her forthright fashion.

Brianna started to shrug off the question, then realized she needed a listening ear. She didn't dare confide in her aunt or even allow her to know she had accompanied Michael the previous evening. Fortunately Virginia's time was so filled with caring for her husband, she didn't question Brianna's comings and goings. Taking a deep breath, she eased out the words. "I believe he's under the impression that I must be connected with the domestics in the household rather than the master and mistress."

Mary's face drew into a frown. "How'd he get such an idea?"

Brianna swallowed, knowing how important it was that Michael not discover her true station in life. If he did, he might feel she couldn't be counted on, that she'd taken the job on a lark and could leave any moment in a flight of fancy. Fear of losing her job made it essential that she keep the knowledge secret. Mary continued to stare, and Brianna finally answered her. "Perhaps because he's my employer."

Scandalized, Mary stared at her. "You know better'n to socialize with an employer. And whatever would your aunt think, knowing the man believes you to be a servant?"

"But she can't know, Mary. She has so much to worry about with Uncle Robert. The reason I sought this job was to relieve her burden, not add to it."

"You've got your mind set all wrong. Your aunt and uncle can more'n provide for all of us." Mary's scowl punctuated the words.

"Then why did Grace and William leave?" Brianna asked, referring to the couple who had been in her uncle's employ for over two decades.

"Because William couldn't take the work anymore." Mary glared at Brianna in exasperation. "They were getting on in years, you know. They stayed more than a year longer than they wanted to 'cause of your uncle getting sick and all. Your aunt's waitin' for another couple from the old country to hire."

Brianna patiently heard Mary's words, thinking they sounded more like an excuse than a reason. But then she doubted Aunt Virginia had taken the housekeeper into her confidence, fearing to worry the woman. Mary and the cook were the only servants left, and Brianna wondered how long they would remain in her uncle's employ, considering the stack of unpaid bills that lay in the study. Deciding that she should keep her own counsel, Brianna smiled at Mary. "I didn't mean to worry you. I guess I couldn't keep my thoughts to myself this morning. I'd best get dressed so I can get to work on time."

Mary left, muttering and shaking her head. Bounding to the wardrobe, Brianna pulled open the doors, gazing at the selection of day dresses. Her hand rested on a street dress of blue foulard, and immediately she thought of Michael's expression the night before, his eyes of an identical shade of blue darkening till they were almost black as he bid her good night, their faces scant inches apart. A shiver ran through her body as she thought of the magical evening. An equal shaft of apprehension gripped her when she thought of the day ahead. How was she to act unaffected at work when she'd spent the night dreaming of how the touch of his lips would have felt? Dressing hastily, she paused only to survey her reflection in the cheval glass. Satisfied, she rushed down the stairs, ignoring Mary's offer of breakfast. Her stomach was in far too much turmoil for her to consider eating anything.

Her journey to the publishing firm was a blur, Brianna realized as she stared up at the crumbling red brick of Griffith Publishing. Hesitantly she approached the door and entered, glancing shyly toward Michael's office. Seeing that the lamp remained unlit, she released her breath in a disappointed rush. Usually he was the first one to arrive, toiling long before and after the others in his employ.

Deflated, she took her position at her desk, glancing down at the sketches she'd made the day before. Putting them aside, she reached for her drawing materials. Hours passed, and still Michael didn't arrive.

"Now, those are different," Finnigan commented as he stared over her shoulder at the new designs.

Brianna blushed unexpectedly. Far more intricate in design, these cupids were interwoven amidst a pair of golden wedding bands. Feeling absurdly transparent, Brianna withheld a reply.

"I expect they'll look good on the embossed letter sheets," Finnigan continued.

"Have they arrived?" she asked, glad of the diversion.

"About an hour ago. Got Jimmy unpackin' 'em now."

Genuinely delighted, Brianna followed Finnigan into the loading area. Clumps of packing straw littered the floor, and she gazed into the crate alongside the men. Jimmy handed her a packet. Reverently she opened it, gasping at the elaborately scalloped stationery. "This is wonderful!"

Finnigan shook his thick mane of silvery hair. "Didn't expect it to be so fancy."

Jimmy caught Brianna's infectious enthusiasm. "I think it's right lovely."

"As though you'd know a wart from a petunia," Finnigan scoffed. They all burst into laughter at his unlikely choice of words.

"Is anyone minding the store?" Michael's voice overrode their laughter, and all three turned to stare at him. It was hardly the meeting Brianna had envisioned.

"Got that shipment in, sir," Jimmy spoke up. "We was admirin' it."

"It's right unusual, Michael," Finnigan added.

Michael's glance rested on Brianna, and she simply couldn't speak. It seemed hard to reconcile the man of the night before with the one who gazed at her now in crisp inquiry. Had he simply shut off the feelings that had flowed between them last night?

Michael walked closer, glancing at the paper Brianna still held. "You are right, it is quite exceptional." Following his gaze upward from the paper, she couldn't compel her eyes to leave his.

"Late mornin' for you, Michael," Finnigan commented.

"I had an inquiry to follow up on. The Landry Orphanage benefactors have granted us a contract to produce valentines. The children will sell them and collect a few pennies from each."

Brianna's voice heightened as it came out in a rush. "But that's wonderful. Both a contract and an opportunity to help the children."

"It's a business deal, pure and simple." Michael's voice was flat. "I expect to make a profit on the publishing. This is not a charity, Miss McBride."

Brianna's enthusiasm drained away along with her smile.

Michael started to walk toward his office, then turned back momentarily. "These will all be lithographed valentines. The embossed and scalloped ones will be for special orders only." The distinctive thud of his door galvanized the trio into movement.

"I'd best be seein' to our supplies." Finnigan spoke first.

Brianna moved as though in a trance to her own desk. Had she only imagined the magic of the previous night? Staring at Michael's closed door, she willed it to open, to have him smile and acknowledge their changed relationship. But the seconds turned into minutes and passed without the slightest movement. Gradually she averted her gaze, realizing she had designs to prepare.

"It's all right, miss. Sometimes Mr. Donovan gets a bit short. He don't mean it, though." Jimmy's perpetual grin was in place, but try as she might, Brianna couldn't force one of her own in response. Knowing that Jimmy wasn't aware of the cause of her distress, she tried to close her mind to the man on the other side of the door.

"I believe I shall have my lunch," she said, deciding she

needed some fresh air, some time to rethink the changes in Michael.

"I'll get you a cup of tea," Jimmy offered.

"Thank you, Jimmy, but I'm going to take a stroll instead."

"But won't you get hungry?" Jimmy looked at her in concern.

Brianna glanced briefly at the firmly closed door. "I don't think so."

The afternoon passed in agonizing slowness. Forcing herself not to glance toward Michael's office, Brianna tried to concentrate on designs for the new order. But each heart and flower brought another round of dismay. Only as dusk descended did she lay her pencil down.

"'Tis 'bout closin' time, miss." Finnigan stood in the growing darkness, silhouetted by the flare of an oil lamp.

Regretfully Brianna realized he was right. With dragging steps she collected her cloak and reticule. With one final backward glance, she left and walked down the steps of the building. Despite the people crowding about her, the street seemed even dimmer as she traced her way home. Did Michael think that since she was a working girl, he could trifle with her affections and then treat her as though nothing had happened?

Thoughts of the previous night tortured her as she tried to understand what had truly transpired. Had she only imagined the attraction she'd glimpsed in his eyes? Warmth stole over her despite the chill of the weather. No, in spite of the heavy weight settling in her chest, she was certain that glint in his eyes had been no trick. She knew she had to find out why he'd slammed the door on what they'd shared.

Michael eased the drape back in place as he stood by the window. The shadow of Brianna's figure had finally disappeared. Watching each step, each movement was slowly calculated torture. He passed a hand over his forehead, trying to ease the pressure that lurked beneath his brow.

Finnigan opened the door and stood just inside the office. "You got somethin' on your mind, Michael?"

Turning away from the window, Michael tried to dismiss Brianna's image. "Why do you ask?"

Finnigan released a grunt of exasperation. "You, the little miss. I ain't blind, son."

Michael fingered the cording on the back of his chair. "You still got two sets of eyes, Finnigan?"

A hint of a smile crept into the older man's expression. "Aye, and you're still runnin' into brick walls instead of climbin' over them."

Considering his behavior, Michael had to agree. Now he'd created an impossible situation. He had been addled to think he could socialize with Brianna and then continue working with her as though nothing had changed. He never expected the shift in his feelings when she'd stepped out the door—a fantasy creature destined to transform each neat plan, each well-controlled thought.

And now what? Question her as to where she'd obtained such a dress while living in the domestic quarters of one of the city's finest homes? Not to mention her fluency in a Continental language. Where had she obtained such an education?

"Won't help to take it out on the girl," Finnigan commented, breaking into Michael's wandering thoughts.

The furrows beside Michael's mouth deepened. "You're right."

"We need her, Michael." Finnigan's expression was grim. "We won't be fillin' orders without designs."

We need her. What an understatement. It had taken all of Michael's restraint not to rip open the door and apologize for his gruff behavior, to tell her how beautiful she looked in the day dress. As beautiful as she'd been the night before.

Meeting Finnigan's steady regard, Michael knew he had created an impossible situation. One he wasn't certain he could mend.

SIX

BRIANNA PERCHED ON the edge of her chair, smoothing the linen napkin in her lap. Self-consciously she adjusted the material of her skirt. The dress was appropriate for the evening—a gown of lilac silk trimmed with point lace and black thread lace leaves. The unexpected dinner invitation had taken her by surprise, especially when she hadn't seen Michael for several days. Intending to clear up the misunderstanding between them, she was disappointed to find that he would be out of the office following up on sales while she and the others prepared for the orphanage's large order. The invitation to tonight's dinner had been delivered by courier, handwritten by Michael, and she took it as the overture she'd hoped for.

Staring at the assemblage, Brianna eased into the conversation, relieved to find Etienne seated at her side. His sister, Aimé, faced her across the table, and Brianna couldn't miss the sidelong glances the woman sent in Michael's direction. To his credit, he seemed determined to pursue the conversation with the gentleman to his right. Unfortunately he ignored not only Aimé, but Brianna as well.

Distracted by Etienne's attention, Brianna found that the first few courses passed comfortably. Obviously pleased to have someone to converse with, Etienne had tactfully seated himself next to her while placing Michael near the businessmen he wanted to meet.

As the dinner progressed, Michael's concentration continued to be centered only on the businessmen at the table. Feeling much like a wallflower, Brianna chafed silently when he seemed to have forgotten her presence completely. Despite a few overtures on her part designed to recapture his interest, his responses were merely polite, his attention returning immediately to his other dining companions.

Picking up her wineglass, Brianna tasted the selection provided for the fourth course of the meal. Glancing up, she caught Michael's frown. Obviously believing she would become intoxicated as her heritage warranted, he seemed to be sending her silent signals to ignore the wine. It was hardly the attention from him that she was hoping for.

She didn't know whether she wished to rail at him for his ignorance or accept that he was as unchangeable as the other prejudiced people she'd met since her arrival in the city. Her heart sank. No wonder her parents had discouraged her from coming here. They must have known that although her uncle was a respected solicitor, New York wasn't an easy place for the Irish to be. Now Michael was making it equally unbearable in yet another way.

Disregarding the now unappealing wine, Brianna turned her attention to Etienne and her back toward Michael.

"Would you care for another selection, mademoiselle?" Etienne asked, referring to her untouched wine.

"I believe I've had my fill," she replied evenly. Brianna angled her head further away, purposely avoiding Michael's censorious gaze. Clearly Michael's invitation had been borne of necessity, rather than a heartfelt desire to spend time with her. Once again he'd needed an escort, and she'd made herself available.

"The music is quite diverting this evening," Etienne commented as a waiter approached to clear the table. "May I have the pleasure of the first dance of the evening?"

Relieved to see the last course of the meal whisked away,

Brianna accepted Etienne's invitation to dance in the adjoining music room. Keeping her back to Michael, she didn't wait to see his reaction as she departed. Since he apparently considered her little more than a temporary escort, Brianna doubted he even noticed she was gone.

Despite Etienne's grace and expertise, she didn't feel the same thrill in his arms that she had in Michael's. The comparison rose up unwanted, unrelenting. Moving about the floor, Brianna smiled at the appropriate times, laughed in unison with Etienne, but only her unshakable breeding allowed her to do so. She wondered why Michael couldn't see her in the same light.

Pausing between dances, Etienne went in search of some punch, and Brianna pulled out her fan, hoping to stir some fresh air. A tantalizingly familiar touch on her arm caused her flush to deepen.

"Are you having a pleasant time?" Michael's voice was tight, controlled.

Brianna forced a wide smile and willed her eyes not to reveal what was in her heart. "Yes, delightful, thank you."

"I've been wanting to talk to you," he began. Looking up expectantly, she waited for his next words. "It's about this last week. I've been rather brusque, and I would like that to end."

Brianna felt the hope clutching her heart. "I agree," she murmured.

"I realize that you've brought laughter to the firm for the first time in far too long. I'd like that to continue. In fact, I would like our relationship to return to what it was."

Feeling her smile start to waver, Brianna tried to keep the brilliance in her eyes. That wasn't difficult since a sheen of threatening moisture was already in place.

"As for these social occasions . . ." He paused as though searching for the right words. "I greatly appreciate your presence. You have enhanced my entry into this circle."

Holding a firm grip on the crushing sensations, Brianna held her silence as he continued. "But I don't want you to think that your employment depends on accompanying me."

Keeping her head stiffly upright, she managed a smile despite the pain of his words. "I've been happy to do so."

Relief seemed to color his face, and she realized with a stab of dismay that she was willing to accept his leftover crumbs rather than have nothing at all.

The music started again, and Michael opened his mouth to speak. Etienne arrived at just the same time, however, offering Brianna a glass of sparkling punch. "Will you be ready for another dance after your refreshment, mademoiselle?" Etienne asked.

Bending to sip the drink, she saw a flash of resentment cross Michael's face before he carefully schooled his features. Heartened, she quickly finished the tiny cup of punch. "Yes, I would like that very much." Smiling at Michael, she deposited the cup in his hand. "You don't mind, do you?"

Etienne shrugged in Michael's direction as he gave his own cup to a passing waiter and then pursued Brianna onto the dance floor.

Purposely leaning close in Etienne's arms, she sensed his surprise before he tightened his grasp a bit. Whirling away, she was pleased to see Michael gripping her discarded glass as though wishing to break it. He might believe he wanted their relationship to remain strictly professional, but his actions disproved his words.

A genuine smile lit her lips as she tilted her head back to speak with Etienne. She sensed that Michael was in for the surprise of his life.

Brianna smiled and waved through the tiny pane of glass in Michael's office door. His return greeting was stiff. It pleased her enormously. Humming as she gathered her materials, Brianna made a point of stopping to chat with Jimmy. Predictably, he was ready with a grin, and soon his laughter rang out across the room. With some persuasion, she managed to get several of the laborers to join in as well.

Making an inordinate amount of trips across the space in front of Michael's office, Brianna hummed a little louder. Seeking out Finnigan, she consulted him about the new batch of designs, prodding until he, too, issued a gruff laugh. If Michael wanted laughter in his offices, she would provide it. She hoped she would drive him to distraction.

Lunchtime arrived, and she cajoled Finnigan into joining her at her desk. Jimmy was, as always, a willing participant. Their combined chatter eased through Michael's still open door. Only as the lunch break ended and they were rising to replace the tea things did Michael appear.

"Would you care for a cup of tea?" Brianna asked brightly. "We've all finished ours, but it would take but a moment to prepare another cup."

Michael's gaze swept over them, but there wasn't anything to find fault with. They'd kept to their allotted time for lunch and were preparing to return to work. He stared at the three expectant faces, lingering a moment longer on Brianna's. She was pleased by his reaction to her answering grin.

"No, I haven't time," he announced gruffly. When he retreated back into his office, she almost smirked in victory. Escape was a better description for his rapid departure.

Satisfied, Brianna replaced the teacups and returned to her work. She dug through the cubbyholes of the desk until she found her chalks. Starting to close the opening, she paused when she saw a bit of paper stuck inside. She had to yank to pull it loose, but it finally gave way, and the paper slid into her hands. Studying it for a moment, her exuberance dimmed. The paper was an invoice for last year's valentines for the Landry Orphanage. Penned across the sheet in Michael's bold handwriting were the words *No monies to be collected on this account.*

Swallowing, Brianna realized that Michael had indeed provided the service he'd dismissed as charity. It was as though he couldn't acknowledge the charity that could be misread as weakness. She'd initially sensed his need to both share and reach out to others. Finding the note proved that intuition. This was a man with a wealth of emotion to give, yet he locked his compassion carefully behind a well-constructed façade designed to keep intruders out. The contrived laughter forgotten, Brianna raised sober eyes to the open door.

After concealing the paper in the cubbyhole, she rose and placed a pot of water on the boiler top. She rinsed a cup clean and prepared a fragrant blend of tea she'd brought from home. Knocking softly on his door, she walked inside and set the cup on his desk. Before he could speak, she began. "No one should be too busy to have a spot of tea."

He looked confused as she gave him her first genuine smile of the morning. It was a gentle smile, designed to soothe, and she was glad to see it had some of that effect.

Quietly she retraced her steps toward her desk. Just as she reached her chair she heard his words float through the still air. "Thank you." He paused. "Brianna."

The rest of the afternoon passed uneventfully as she concentrated on the new order. When evening approached, she laid her pen down with regret and gathered her papers into an orderly stack.

She took her hat and cloak from the cupboard, preparing to leave. Glancing up, she saw Michael approach.

"Going home?" he asked.

She gestured to the gathering darkness. "It's difficult to draw by lamplight."

"I wasn't suggesting you should." Offering her reticule,

he took up his own derby and coat. Together they moved to the door.

Reaching the bottom of the front steps, she paused, her breath causing a white cloud in the cold air. "I'll bid you good night, then."

She couldn't read his expression in the dim light as he spoke. "May I walk you home?"

Trying to diffuse the sudden warmth that filled her, Brianna nodded in agreement. "That would be nice, thank you."

They walked together, passing under the halo of over-hanging gaslights. Other pedestrians filled the sidewalks fighting for space, while hackney coaches and omnibuses rumbled over the cobbled stones of the street. The chill of the January air pressed about them, but Brianna dismissed its discomfort. As darkness descended, the soot-stained snowbanks no longer looked like dreary reminders of the last storm, instead glinting in the moonlight as though sprinkled with diamond dust.

Approaching Nassau Street, they turned, and she sensed Michael's hesitation as they passed the store windows of T. W. Strong, one of the most prolific publishers in the city.

"Why don't we look?" she suggested. Together they read the advertisements: "Valentines! Valentines! All varieties, imported and domestic, sentimental, comic, witty—lace paper and gold, the most superb style without regard to expense!"

"He's quite successful, isn't he?" Brianna commented, impressed by the huge assortment displayed in the window. The exhibit partially proved her argument about the em-bossed cards. Mr. Strong's elaborate valentines obviously sold well. Deciding it wasn't a prudent time to point out that she was right, Brianna gazed at the presentation without further comment.

As though just remembering to answer, Michael tore his

attention from the prominent display and turned toward her. "He's the most successful valentine maker in the city."

"So far," she added softly.

Michael searched her eyes for a moment before starting to walk again. Joining the other people who crowded the sidewalks, they walked companionably, ignoring offers of food, drink, and flowers from passing vendors. The bright gaslights of bars and hotels threw a glare over the main thoroughfare nearby. Continuing down the quieter street, Michael glanced at the sign for Gosling's, a popular-priced restaurant that served over a thousand patrons a day.

"Would you care for a bite of supper?" he asked.

Surprised, Brianna agreed. "I am hungry."

"Would you prefer the dining room in the Astor or Delmonico's?" he asked, obviously deciding he wanted a quieter setting than Gosling's could provide.

"The Astor would be very nice," she replied, disregarding his offer of Delmonico's, a restaurant located on South William Street that was patronized only by the wealthy. Entry was restricted to the socially elite by its fastidious proprietors, and Brianna had no wish to see how far they could push the boundaries.

Their conversation flowed easily as they strolled toward the Astor House. Stepping inside, Brianna allowed Michael to take her cloak while the chill of the evening fell away in the warm interior. Fortunately the newer hotels in the city had eclipsed the Astor's popularity. The lobbies of the St. Nicholas and Metropolitan resembled human beehives just before the dinner hour, and Brianna was comforted by the relative serenity of the Astor.

Seating them, the proprietor apologized for the small, out-of-the-way table. But its location pleased Brianna. The area was quiet, softly lit, and surprisingly intimate in a restaurant that served a great number of patrons each day.

"You're certain you wouldn't prefer the sky parlor at the

Metropolitan?" Michael asked, referring to the fashionable feature where couples could sit high above Broadway and watch the promenade.

"Very certain," she replied with a smile. "I'm not quite up to their evening ball." Polkas and magnums of champagne dominated the evening balls at the Metropolitan, requiring a frenzy of energy from the patrons. It was far more preferable to sit across from Michael in quiet seclusion.

Allowing him to select their entrées, Brianna concentrated instead on trying to guess what had again changed his mood. The waiter left, and Michael toyed with the cutlery. "Thank you for accompanying me tonight."

Impulsively she laid her hand over his. "I'm here because I want to be."

Only a few moments passed before he took her hand, placing it within his own. A sudden rush of heat skimmed through her body. The waiter's reappearance with bowls of clam soup was both untimely and unwanted.

Brianna picked up her spoon and dipped it into her soup, not tasting it as her mind tried to maintain balance. She noticed that Michael seemed equally reluctant to break their contact.

"The business is very important to you, isn't it?" she asked.

This wasn't a trivial subject, and it couldn't be passed by with a casual answer.

"You can't imagine what the firm was like with my grandfather at the helm when I was young," he mused. "I made myself a promise that I would make it even more profitable again."

Brianna leaned forward, her food forgotten as she saw the yearning in his eyes. "You'll succeed, Michael." She chose her next words carefully, knowing she trod a precarious path. "It took awhile for the success of the business to diminish. But hard work and time can rebuild your firm."

"But I want it now," he said vehemently, then paused to stare into the candlelight flickering on the table. "But not just for the money."

Brianna knew he sought to recover his pride more than monetary wealth. "I think you've made quite an impression on the circle of businessmen in the city."

Michael held her gaze. "Largely because of you." She started to shake her head in dismissal, but he ignored her protests, knowing the truth. Without her he would have still been standing outside, looking in. "You charmed them until they could scarcely refuse me entry."

He watched as the beginning of a blush suffused her face, then he picked up her hand. "I didn't intend to embarrass you." Seeing the pale pink dust her cheeks, he felt a tenderness he didn't know existed. Somehow this charming, magical creature had opened a pathway to his closed heart. Stroking the soft, delicate skin of her hand, he brought her fingers to his lips. For the first time in more years than he wanted to remember, he could feel the stirrings of hope. Brianna's belief in him had ignited that hope.

She finally lifted her head and met his eyes. Embarrassment fled as she continued to hold his gaze. The tiny table seemed to grow even smaller as only the diminutive bit of wood separated them. Words proved impossible to grasp as she watched him trace the length of each finger of her hand. The sensuous motions created sensations she didn't know existed. The warmth in her stomach grew and spread until it reached her shaking knees. Grateful for the solid chair beneath her, she didn't withdraw her hand or remind him of propriety. Instead she savored the new unexpected feelings.

When the waiter interrupted this time, Michael was even more reluctant to withdraw his hand. The next courses were delivered, but Brianna and Michael stared at each other rather than at what was served. Between spontaneous bursts of conversation, the waiter brought a forequarter of lamb with mint sauce, followed by salmon with peas, and then asparagus. The superb food was partially consumed, yet if pressed Brianna couldn't have recalled its nature. With regret she saw the dessert whisked away. But Michael seemed equally hesitant to depart, and they lingered over coffee, talking more than they had since they'd met. Reluctantly they finally left.

"Are you tired?" Michael asked suddenly as they paused on the street.

All traces of the day's weariness had vanished the moment he had asked to accompany her home. Truthfully she replied, "Not at all."

"Are you up for some adventure?"

Laughing, she raised her face to his. "Very much so."

After hailing a hackney coach, Michael handed her up into the vehicle. "Forty-second Street, Driver. The Crystal Palace." Intrigued, Brianna watched in fascination as they approached a tower.

"Latting's Observatory," Michael explained after the cab departed. The curious, hastily constructed observation tower was built by an enterprising businessman during the World's Fair of 1853. Located directly across from the fairgrounds, it was visited as frequently as the exhibits. Latting's Observatory and Ice Cream Parlor allowed visitors to dine on ice cream before going to the outside deck at the top of the tower for a spectacular view that included the Croton Reservoir, whose high walls gave it the look of a vast Egyptian Temple.

Bypassing the ice cream parlor on the ground floor, Michael led them directly to the new experimental steam elevator. Brianna stared at it in mild trepidation.

The operator grinned at her. "It's a bit balky at times, miss, but we haven't lost a body yet."

Hardly reassured, she glanced at Michael.

"If you're frightened . . ." he began.

Resolve stiffened her backbone. "Not at all. I said I was ready for adventure." She swallowed an unexpected gulp. "Let's go."

The lift lurched and jerked as they made their ascent. Brianna clung to the precarious metal railing of the cage-like conveyance. When the elevator shuddered to a stop, she was ready to leap through the opening to solid ground. The operator pulled open the door, and she was surprised to see that Michael held her shaking hand firmly in his grasp. Together they escaped the lift and stood at the top of the tower.

"Oh, Michael, it's magnificent!" Awed, Brianna stared at the spectacular view of the city. Rising higher than the nearby Crystal Palace, which had been built as a replica of the London original for the World's Fair, the tower provided a glimpse of the bustling mainstream that seemed far removed from the quiet, star-filled sky.

"Was it worth taking your life in your hands to get here?" he asked, amused.

"Absolutely," she declared, still entranced by the wealth of the view spread out beneath her. Finally turning back to face him, she regained some of her own humor. "But I do think the establishment could have installed a stairwell instead."

"But then you wouldn't have jumped into my arms in fear," he teased.

Her gaze softened, and her eyes glistened. Gusts of wind teased her hair. "It wouldn't have required fear."

The seconds ticked by agonizingly as she watched him bend his head toward hers. The shock of his lips against hers was as welcome as his earlier touch. The cold of the January evening was forgotten. Brianna felt a heat build inside her greater than any she could have ever imagined. Michael's hand cupped the back of her neck, his fingers sending additional waves of desire down her back, rippling toward her already weakening legs.

The kiss began chastely enough, but Brianna moved closer into his embrace, accepting the deepening pressure of his lips. Savoring his unique and fresh taste, she shuddered when his lips moved down her neck, tantalizing the tender skin. Issuing a sound between a sigh and a moan as his lips connected with her flesh, Brianna began to lose sight of reason. Placing her hands tentatively in the thick mahogany hair that fell just above his collar, she twined her fingers through the well-groomed mane, allowing her hands to travel over his shoulders.

He sucked in his breath quickly, an immediate response to her touch. Gratified by her effect on him, Brianna offered her lips once again. Mere warmth could not describe the heat building between them. When they finally broke apart, their breathing sounded ragged, their eyes dark with anticipation and desire.

Brianna opened her mouth to speak, but Michael's fingers rested on her lips, stilling the words. He lifted that same hand to tenderly stroke her cheek. They clung together as they watched the city beneath them continue its frantic activity. Isolated above the frenzy, they stared into the dark, star-dotted sky, allowing their questions to remain unanswered. For this moment, this time all else was forgotten.

SEVEN

BRIANNA AND FINNIGAN stared at the broken piece of machinery.

"Are you sure it can't be repaired?" she asked, gazing at the silent pile of ancient metal. If the press didn't function, what was left of Griffith Publishing would be finished.

"Yes, miss. I'm afraid the old thing's given its last." Finnigan was as abject as Brianna.

"What are we goin' to do?" Jimmy asked. His normal good cheer had been replaced by fear.

"Mr. Donovan will take care of it," Brianna replied confidently. Catching Finnigan's look of skepticism, she turned to Jimmy. "Perhaps we could all do with a tea break if you'd put the pot on the boil."

After he left, Brianna questioned Finnigan. "Michael will be able to replace the machine, won't he?"

"I don't see how." Finnigan stared at the disabled machine in disgust and resignation.

"But surely there's a line of credit at the bank?"

"It's all gone. Michael's countin' on the money from the orders he's sellin' now to pull through." The older man's wrinkles seemed to multiply as his frown deepened. "The other machines won't carry the load. I don't know how we're goin' to tell him when he gets back."

She thought of Michael on his trip outside the city, trying to sell more orders. Orders they couldn't deliver without the press. Beginning to feel a bubble of panic, she knew he couldn't come this close to realizing his dream only to be thwarted by the death of an ancient machine.

Suddenly resolving that such a catastrophe could not happen, Brianna came to a decision. After patting Finnigan's arm in reassurance, she hurried to the cupboard to fetch her cloak.

"But your tea!" Jimmy protested, holding an empty cup in one hand and a box of tea in the other.

"I'll only be gone for a short time. Perhaps I can pick up a pastry to go with the tea." Ignoring his look of distress, Brianna bolted down the steps and out to the street. Dodging the onslaught of people filling the avenue, she searched for a cab. Hailing a hackney, she knotted her handkerchief into an unrecognizable mass as the buggy stalled in the Broadway traffic. Finally she arrived at her uncle's bank and, after paying the driver, rushed inside.

Immediately asking for her uncle's banker, she paced the tapestry rug until the man arrived. Seeing her anxiety, he drew her into his office and smiled in a grandfatherly fashion.

"What may I help you with, Miss McBride?"

Launching into the tale, she paused, her hopes rising when she saw signs of encouragement on the banker's face. "Then you can help me?"

"Certainly, Miss McBride. I'll draw up the papers and send them over to you later this afternoon." She let out a sigh of relief. "Simply have your uncle sign for the loan, and the money will be ready in the morning."

Dismay filled her. She couldn't ask Uncle Robert such a stressful thing, not now. "Isn't there any other way?"

"What do you mean?" The banker's generous expression turned into an inquiring frown.

"Must I have my uncle's signature on the papers?"

He smiled in a condescending fashion that had always

annoyed her. "I'm afraid so, my dear. He is the customer, after all."

After thanking him for his time, Brianna dragged her feet as she exited the bank building and walked down the street. Dodging people bent on racing down the busy sidewalk, she thought about all of Michael's hopes and dreams wrapped up into a sinking business. It simply didn't seem fair. It wasn't only all the hard work he'd poured into the firm, it was his last chance at proving himself. Even though she knew his heritage was of little consequence, apparently nothing but success would convince him differently.

Dejected, she gazed about at the bustle of people filling the streets. Surely with all this mass of humanity, she could find someone with the money she needed to purchase a new machine. Of course!

Not bothering with a cab, she hurried down the street, her destination firmly in mind. She thought briefly of Michael's reaction to what she was considering and just as quickly dismissed it. Knowing how important the business was to him, Brianna was certain she was doing the right thing.

Etienne's face lit with surprise as he greeted her. Outlining the problem, she found his reaction difficult to gauge. His fingers were held together in a steepled fashion when he finally spoke. "Does Michael know you're here?"

"Well, no." She leaned forward in a rush. "But I've told you how important rebuilding the business is to him. I know if he were in the city, he'd be here himself."

"When do you expect his return?"

"Not for over two weeks." Michael had only been gone a short time, since just after their evening together.

"Have you considered how long it would take to have a new machine shipped to you?" Etienne asked, his face still carefully noncommittal.

Brianna felt her hope start to wither. She hadn't even

considered that aspect. Raising saddened eyes, she shook her head negatively.

"Then perhaps you should think of purchasing a used machine," Etienne suggested.

"From whom?" It occurred to her suddenly that she was way beyond her limitations in business dealings.

"One of the larger publishers in the city. You could offer to subcontract some of their work as an incentive," Etienne suggested.

Brianna's mind whirled. How she wished Michael or even Finnigan were here to decide. Hesitantly she pressed her most vital question. "You still haven't told me whether you would finance the purchase."

Etienne stood and walked around the desk, taking up one of her hands. Seeing regret in his eyes, she was surprised by his words. "Of course. Make the arrangements for the purchase, and I will contact my bank."

"Oh, thank you." Jumping to her feet, she impulsively kissed his cheek, missing the shaft of pain that flashed across his face. "I'm sure Michael will want to thank you himself as soon as he returns."

Leaving his office, her mind humming with the possibilities, she didn't hear Etienne's sad, quiet murmur. "We shall see."

EIGHT

THE NEW PRESS hummed from the machinery area. Brianna felt like singing herself. Michael was due back soon, and the impossible had been accomplished. Following Etienne's suggestion, she had found a publisher willing to part with a machine they intended to replace within a short time. In exchange for selling the press before they were ready, Brianna had agreed to the subcontract work. While the agreement would require more labor and longer hours to fill both their own orders and the subcontracting, the purchase was the salvation of Griffith Publishing.

Although Finnigan was pleased, he didn't exhibit the same enthusiasm she did. He muttered more than ever and watched the slick operation of the far newer press with a combination of admiration and misgiving.

Brianna couldn't understand his concerns. Certain that Michael would agree with her, she'd taken more orders for the special embossed valentines. All that was missing was Michael and the gratitude she knew he would share with them.

It was a week of encouraging news. Uncle Robert had made some progress, enough for the doctor to give a cautious report of improvement. Hearing the door open, she looked up in surprise. Mary stood timidly in the doorway, and Brianna felt her heart stop for a moment.

"Uncle Robert?"

"He's fine, but you left your purse to home," Mary exclaimed breathlessly. "You'll be wantin' to take a cab home tonight, and you won't have the fare."

Caught up in her thoughts of Michael, Brianna had little memory of the morning's actions. She was lucky to have arrived fully clothed, she realized with a flush of awareness. "You were thoughtful to have brought it to me." Taking the purse, Brianna looked up just as Michael walked in. His eyes sought hers immediately, and she felt the warmth in them.

"Hello," he greeted her.

"Hello." She continued to stare at him for a moment, realized Mary still stood expectantly, and fumbled for introductions. "Michael, let me present Miss Mary O'Toole. Mary, Mr. Michael Donovan."

Recognizing each other from the night of the ball when he came to the servants' entrance for Brianna, Michael and Mary looked awkwardly at each other until he walked forward. "I'm pleased to meet you, Miss O'Toole."

"'Tis my pleasure, sir." Mary practically curtsied when he took her hand.

Glancing between them, Brianna quickly bid Mary goodbye, not wanting the woman to inopportunely reveal anything about her true status in the Lynch household. After Mary left, Brianna waited in anticipation while Michael surveyed the offices and, more important, her. "I'm glad you're back," she murmured.

"I am, too," he answered, not taking his gaze from her.

"Humph." Finnigan stood behind Brianna, and she spun toward him, a blush covering her face.

Feeling foolishly transparent, she searched for something to seize upon. "I'll put the pot on the boil," she announced, moving toward the tea things.

Finnigan stayed in the office area, keeping his back

firmly toward the machinery. "Thought you'd want to know the orders were all shipped on time."

Michael clapped Finnigan on the shoulder, including him in his goodwill. "I knew I could count on you." Casting one more glance in Brianna's direction, Michael entered his office to unload the filled portmanteau.

Humming, Brianna watched Finnigan approach. "Why didn't you tell him about the machine?" she asked.

Finnigan wiped his hands on a rag. "He'll be learnin' about it soon enough." Some of her brightness dimmed at the mournful sound of his words.

Mindful of his dire warning, her sketches kept her occupied for the rest of the day as Michael organized the orders he'd brought back with him. As evening descended, she approached his office, knocking lightly before entering. "I believe I'll close my desk for the day."

He stood up, glanced at the mountain of work yet to be gone through, and uncharacteristically decided to ignore it. "My thought exactly. Would you possibly be free for supper tonight, Miss McBride?"

She answered with an equal touch of wry humor. "I believe I might be, Mr. Donovan."

"Good." There was no mistaking the message the single word conveyed.

Finding her own breath a bit short in coming, she turned to fetch her wrap. She felt both disturbed and gratified to find his hands covering hers as she draped the cloak expertly over her shoulders.

Together they emerged from the building to the bustling street below. Avoiding the rush of people, they blended into the crowd, moving with the flow of humanity. The avenue seemed to take on a magical radiance as the gaslights threw their glow into the incessant torrent of traffic, amidst the roar of the city's burgeoning population.

Tucking her hand at his side, Michael moved forward

with purpose, then stopped suddenly. "Are you terribly hungry?"

Wondering what form of adventure he would dream up, she shook her head in denial.

"We could see if there are any seats left at Wallack's Theater or the Academy of Music," he suggested. "Then we could go for a late dinner."

Delighted with the prospect of a midnight supper with him, she agreed readily. "I would like that." She thought of her aunt and uncle's enforced isolation. "It's been some time since I've been to the theater or opera."

"Should we let someone know that you'll be out late?"

Pleased by his thoughtfulness, she agreed. Hailing a hackney cab, he gave the driver Brianna's address after assisting her inside.

"You remembered," she noticed.

"It was hard not to," he admitted.

Afraid to breathe lest she disturb this discovery, she smiled tentatively, willing her lips not to tremble in obvious anticipation. He took her hand, and she slipped it in his willingly. As the cab rattled over the rough streets, Michael told her about his trip, the orders placed, the success he felt was within his grasp. Transfixed by the passion she saw in his expression, she kept her counsel about the new machine.

Despite the traffic, in short time they arrived at her home. When the driver started to pull toward the front, Michael ordered him around the back. She felt guilty about her continued deception but wasn't sure he was ready to hear the truth. Instead she dashed inside, spoke quickly to Mary, and then ran upstairs to find a proper gown for the evening. With Mary's assistance, she changed in an incredibly short amount of time, well aware that Michael waited outside.

Panting with exertion, she ran down the stairs that led into the kitchen and then out the door. Slowing as she reached the carriage, she was pleased to see admiration lighting his eyes.

"You are quicksilver, Brianna McBride. Like the leprechauns and fairy nymphs."

Surprised, she stared at him. It was the first time he'd ever exhibited a trace of the Irish blood that flowed in his veins. "And you are like the islands rising from the sea," she replied. A vision of the great craggy shores of her homeland struck her as she stared into the planes and hollows of his face. Much like the noblemen of Ireland, Michael was tall, proud, and rugged.

One hand reached out to stroke her cheek tenderly, and she felt the rush of growing hope within and a realization she'd yet to acknowledge. She loved him, this man of impossible contradictions and rigid beliefs. The need she'd first sensed was there, but an endless set of other qualities pushed forward—tenderness, humor, adventure, and hope. He'd shared them all with her. The need to spill out her feelings was stilled as he gave the driver instructions, closed the door, and then drew her forward.

Words weren't necessary as he captured her lips, plundering the softness, inciting the sensations she'd just begun to discover. The world outside the small confines of the hackney cab was quickly forgotten. Knowing this was the man she was destined to spend her life with, Brianna lost some of her usual caution. Exploring timidly, she reveled in his caresses so unlike the few chaste kisses she'd received from other suitors. When he drew back, she felt an overwhelming disappointment.

The driver knocked again at the door, and she blushed in the darkness. "Wallack's, sir."

Brianna stared at the city's premier theater, the nation's leading playhouse. Known as the home of high comedy, both classic and modern, the theater had introduced the plays of T. W. Robertson to New York. Situated on

Broadway and Thirteenth Street, it was one of the largest playhouses in the city, and Brianna was pleased that Michael had thought to bring her here. Once inside, he purchased orchestra stalls at the outrageous price of one dollar each. Fortunately it was not an opening night, and seats were available. Entering the handsome lobby, Brianna could see why it was acclaimed as the last word in elegance. The interior was a rococo masterpiece. The ceiling was a dazzling display of plaster's art and the intricate carvings continued down the columns where marble then took forecourt. Exquisite tapestries and oil paintings covered the recessed cherrywood walls. Proud to be on the arm of the man she considered the most handsome one there, she settled in the seat beside him with excitement.

Despite the refined but delightfully natural play *Society,* Brianna found her interest dwelling on her escort rather than on the performances of the best actors and actresses in the country. When her knee accidentally bumped his, she felt the heat seem to sear through all the layers of petticoats and skirts. Never before feeling this way about a man, she wondered at her own sense of recklessness but easily accepted his hand when he slid it over hers. Pleased that the dim interior masked her perpetual blush, Brianna nonetheless enjoyed the torturous pleasure.

When the play was over, she stood next to him as the crowd emptied into the street. The aristocracy of fashion and wealth made up the distinguished audience along with the most beautiful *demimondaines*, celebrated stage and opera stars, artists, and journalists. But Brianna didn't notice any of them. The most important person there held her arm as though it were made of the most fragile, irreplaceable porcelain. When they paused near the line of waiting hackney cabs, Michael seemed to be wresting with a decision.

"The restaurants will be quite crowded," he said as their

cab pulled up. "We could have a cold supper in my home."

Knowing the impropriety of his suggestion, Brianna was certain she should have hesitated and certainly refused. "I would like that," she answered instead.

Once inside the cab, a sense of heightened anticipation struck them both. The ride seemed both interminably long and frighteningly short. When the hackney pulled up in front of the house, Brianna drew a deep breath of courage. The cab departed, and Michael unlocked the door. Darkness greeted them, and Brianna realized how lonely his life was. How dreadful to come home to a cold, dank house, she thought, remembering the warmth and cheery greetings she always received at home.

"Your mother doesn't live here?" she asked as he lit the lamps, relieving the awful stillness. He added logs to the dwindling fire, sending flames of warmth into the room, before removing her cloak.

"No. This was one of my grandfather's smaller homes. It's close to the office and convenient. She prefers to stay in the house that was his primary residence." Michael turned to her, the glow of the lamps warming his silhouette.

"It's a lovely home." She saw that it really was. Somehow she could envision the grandfather she'd heard so much about in these surroundings. Conservative yet comfortable furnishings merged with tasteful artwork and shelves of well-used books. The home reminded her of English country estates that she'd been privileged to visit. It didn't surprise her that Michael felt at ease here.

"I should see to our supper. The charwoman usually lays it out on the table when she leaves."

Together they walked toward the kitchen. Brianna's heart wrenched when she saw the solitary plate covered with a spotless linen napkin. He lifted the cloth. "There's always enough for two people. The woman can't seem to realize that."

Together they gazed at the food and then at each other. It wasn't the food that either wanted to taste. Barely a moment passed before they greedily devoured each other's lips. Gentleness gave way to growing seeds of passion. Brianna questioned her willingness, but with a surge of belief knew that this was the one man she wanted by her side forever.

Pulling her along with him, Michael escaped the cold kitchen to the now warming parlor. The fire sputtered in the hearth as they stood in front of the settee. Gazing into her face, he wondered at his intentions. The sweetness of her inexperienced responses convinced him that she was an innocent. Why then had he brought her to his home? Her hair rustled under his touch, and he grappled with his conscience. Knowing what he was proposing was unfair to her, he started to turn away, but she laid a tentative hand on his shoulder. When the fingers of her other hand slid over his face to rest on his lips, he knew he was lost.

Amazed at her own boldness, she gasped as Michael kissed her hands and then trailed his lips over the tender flesh of her arms. Shuddering under his touch, her head arched back in delight as Michael's hands roamed over her, pausing near her breast, then enveloping it within his hand. Her nipples hardened despite the layers of protecting material. Bypassing the settee, they sank to the thick wool rug covering the shiny hardwood floor.

Shocked by the overwhelming feeling of his body so close to her own, she scarcely realized that Michael had loosened the bodice of her gown. One hand flew behind her to touch the gaping material, and though he paused to give her time to resist, she didn't protest. Instead she murmured loving words into his ear.

The air nipped her skin as it was slowly exposed. The fastenings fell away beneath his capable fingers. She gasped as her dress dipped forward and she caught the lavender silk briefly in her hands before he gently loosened her grasp, allowing the dress to fall free. Seeing desire darken his eyes, she reveled in the passion as his gaze raked her exposed shoulders. He shed his own coat and then pressed her hand to his chest. Despite the cloth barrier of his shirt, she could feel the beat of his heart, the ragged rhythm matching her own.

In little time they had shed their clothes, and she gasped when his naked body touched hers. Skin like tightened wire beneath velvet stroked hers, and she heard her own cries of pleasure. His kisses trailed a path from the tender flesh of her neck over her breasts, nipping the globes and then traveling the length of her stomach. Knowing the inevitable destination she and Michael traveled, she wondered if she should stop him. But, remembering his need, the loneliness she'd witnessed, she doubted she could choose a different path. He needed her as much as she loved him.

Her cry of pain was smothered beneath the caress of his lips, and her discomfort gave way to pleasure. Following his lead, she matched his movements, discovering the joy of his fullness, the extent of his strength. Not sure what to expect, she was stunned by her own response and overwhelmed by his.

Lying in his embrace, she savored his touch as he reverently stroked her cheek and then gently kissed her. His voice was still husky when he spoke. "Regrets?"

Seeing the sincerity in his eyes, she answered from her heart. "None. I love you, Michael."

Crushing her so close she thought her bones would collide, Michael held her without saying anything, his heart beating against hers. Even though he didn't echo her words, she was certain he felt them. It was just more difficult for him to allow himself to love, to care.

Time passed as they shared secrets, longings, and once again passion, but not her true identity. It was with regret that she told him she had to return home. Carefully he helped her dress, seeming to be on the verge of confessing his own love. Too soon, they arrived at her home. She waited as he struggled with his words. Instead of speaking, he kissed her deeply before he left. Pausing at the doorway, she watched until the dark coach was out of sight, knowing he'd taken her heart with him. But it was a gift she gladly gave. Realizing dawn was but a scant few hours away, she walked inside, sure that tomorrow they would begin their path together.

NINE

MICHAEL STARED AT the machine in mounting fury as he listened to Finnigan's explanation. Despite the man's obvious wish to lighten Brianna's role in the deception, it was all too apparent. Evidently she wanted him to succeed enough to sell his pride to Etienne Giles for the price of one used printing press.

And why such a high wish for his success? Despite the memory of her soft body entwined with his, he could only think of one reason. He swallowed the bitter truth. Desperate for the money she knew he could provide if the firm flourished, she'd calculatedly made sure it would succeed and then assured herself of the bounty by sealing the bargain last night.

Wishing he could believe otherwise, he stared at the evidence confronting him. He'd seen the domestic, Mary, in the office yesterday. Brianna had somehow obtained education and breeding beyond her origins, but nonetheless was linked to that past.

"Now, Michael, I know what you're thinkin'." Finnigan followed him from the machine room to the front offices.

"Do you?" Michael stopped and stared at Finnigan. "I know you didn't go begging my cause to Etienne Giles. Why is that? Because you knew what it would mean to me? Because the money isn't that important to you?" Michael struck his fist against the nearest wall.

He flew around at the sound of the door being opened. Brianna's smile was simultaneously bright and shy. "Good morning, Finnigan, Michael." She spoke in turn to them, her smile faltering at the anger glittering in Michael's eyes. "Is something wrong?"

"You tell me," he gritted out as he left Finnigan and approached her. Closing his heart to the feelings she'd unleashed, he blanketed his emotions in steel.

"I'm not sure what you're talking about." She stumbled over the words, looking much like a trapped rabbit as her gaze darted between Michael and Finnigan.

"The machine, Brianna. Or have you forgotten how you sold my pride to Etienne Giles?"

Her face blanched. "But I only did it to help you. If you'd been here—"

"If I'd been here you couldn't have plotted and planned. Or did you decide to play me against Etienne and see which one of us would have the honor of winning you?"

Brianna's hand clapped over her mouth as she stared at him in horror. He almost regretted his accusation when the tears sprang to her eyes. Seeing the betrayal splashed across her features, he was torn. Certain she'd played him for a fool, he'd thrown out his anger, not realizing he'd feel a share of her pain. Scrambling with the handle, she jerked open the door and escaped before he could utter another sound.

"Well, that ought to get some of your pride back," Finnigan said in disgust before he disappeared into the adjoining area.

Alone in the hollow office, Michael stared at the still open door leading outside. He could easily go after her to beg her forgiveness. Realizing the insanity of the contradictions, he slowly shut the door, closing the piece of his heart he'd foolishly left open.

* * *

Stumbling up the stairs and into her room, Brianna fought the tears that threatened to fall. The pain that ricocheted through her rib cage refused to subside. She could scarcely sort through the maze of emotions choking her. Hurt, betrayal, and injustice fought for dominance. Feeling like a bride who'd been widowed on her wedding day, she entered the bedchamber to see the evidence of her earlier whimsy. Dresses were scattered about the room from her primping that morning. Unable to choose a flawless frock, she'd emptied her entire wardrobe in an effort to find the perfect one. Now the neglected dresses mocked her as she stared into the dismal gray of the winter morning.

"Brianna? What are you doing home so soon?" Virginia's voice of concern carried through the doorway. Entering the room, her aunt moved to her side, studying Brianna with worry. "What is it, child?"

The soft words unlatched the flow of sobs locked inside her. Virginia's arms flew around her as she led her to the bed. Perching on the edge, Brianna confessed what had happened—all but the previous evening's events. She couldn't share any of that with her aunt.

"I knew you shouldn't have sought employment. The class of people a woman must be exposed to in the business world is abominable. Well, you needn't worry. You never have to see that dreadful man again." Virginia's words only caused the pain to sink deeper, and Brianna battled another round of weeping. Tears couldn't erase Michael's words, and incredibly the thought of never seeing him again created the most pain.

Virginia offered another fresh handkerchief, and Brianna accepted it. "This is my fault. I should have provided suitable entertainment for a young lady. Since Robert's been so ill, I've given up my own social activities, but that doesn't mean you should have. I will send notes to my friends and tell them that you are receiving invitations and suitable callers."

"But—"

"There'll be no discussion about this, Brianna. Your situation is clearly my fault, and I intend to repair it."

Staring through the window, Brianna saw the first drops of cold winter rain falling outside. Her own image was equally bleak. A soiled debutante in love with a man who despised her.

The dance floor was crowded. Too crowded. Unfamiliar faces and names weaved through Brianna's vision and memory. Despite her unwillingness to attend, Aunt Virginia had insisted. Weary, despite empty days no longer filled with work, Brianna dragged herself to each social event. Night after night she socialized, forgetting men as soon as she was introduced to them. Her aunt's friends had been all too willing to draw her out. But Brianna's ravaged heart rejected overtures, and she discarded the pretense once out of sight of her aunt's circle.

Conflicting memories pressed about her each day, taxing her energy, exhausting her resources. Like a fresh wound needing to be cauterized, her emotions were raw and tender.

Tonight's dance seemed to blend with all the others. A parade of meaningless people talked about things she had no interest in.

"Mademoiselle?" The familiar voice made her look up in surprise. Etienne's dark eyes filled with concern as he gazed at her.

"Etienne, how good it is to see you." Brianna scrabbled to regain her poise which had been so badly shaken.

"You are here alone?" he asked in disbelief.

"Yes, except for my chaperon, that is. My uncle's been ill, and my aunt doesn't socialize because of the extended nature of his confinement." She deliberately omitted any mention of Michael and was relieved that Etienne's impeccable manners prevented him from asking.

"I'm sorry. I didn't know. Please extend my wishes to your uncle for a sure recovery." Etienne looked as though he wished to say more, but he politely withheld further comment.

"Thank you, I will." The social niceties grew more difficult, the obvious concern on Etienne's face harder to bear.

"If it wouldn't seem presumptuous, may I ask for a dance?"

She wanted to protest, to tell him she was unbearably weary of meaningless dances, but he had been very kind to her. Even though their transaction had cost her Michael's love, it had salvaged his hope. "I would like that."

Allowing Etienne to lead her onto the dance floor, she tried to remember the special times spent in his home with Michael, but walls of pain assaulted her. When the dance ended, she wished desperately for an escape.

Etienne's eyes searched her face, obviously seeing the signs of strain. "Allow me to get you a glass of punch."

Before she could protest, he went for the refreshment, and she sank into the nearest chair. Feeling as though she'd aged forty years, Brianna knew she was losing her energy along with her will.

In a short time Etienne returned, pulling up a chair beside her. "Are you feeling well?" he asked with concern.

"No, actually," she replied, grasping at the unexpected straw. "My headache is quite unbearable."

"Would you like to go home?"

"I believe I'll go lie down instead. I have to wait for my chaperon before I can leave."

Hesitation colored his expression. "But surely—"

"Really, Etienne. I'll be fine. But thank you for your concern. As ever, you've been a fine friend."

Refusing to meet the rampant concern in his eyes, she rapidly crossed the floor and disappeared from sight. But instead of climbing the stairs to repair with the gaggle of overly inquisitive women who filled the second-floor rooms, she hid in the shadows that lined the edges of the dance floor. She watched the guests, finding Etienne with ease. To her relief, he fetched his coat and hat, preparing to leave. His kindness was so laced with pity that it was almost worse than the indifferent flirting of strangers.

As he turned to leave, her attention latched onto the group of people near him. Spotting a treacherously familiar silhouette, she felt her heart leap in anticipation. But then the man turned. He wasn't Michael, not even a pale replica. Disheartened, she sank even deeper into the shadows, wondering how Michael could have so easily forgotten her, knowing she could never stop loving him.

TEN

THE WINTER HAD never seemed so dismal. Michael stared through the window into the bleak morning. Knowing if he turned around his offices would seem equally gloomy, he kept his attention on the street. It was almost as though if he looked long enough, he could conjure her up. Disgusted with himself, he abandoned the window.

A glance through the tiny pane of glass beside the door convinced him of the emptiness there. How strange. He hadn't expected to miss her laughter so much, the cup of tea she thoughtfully offered when the days grew overlong. Although she had been there such a short time, she'd made a far greater impression than he'd ever expected. Another memory gnawed at him, one he tried to keep carefully tucked away. One of ivory skin and incredible tenderness.

Michael shook the notion aside as Finnigan loomed in the doorway.

"What do you plan to do about the designs?"

Michael stared at him blankly.

"For the orders, Michael. We need an artist."

Despite Michael's anger, Etienne had insisted on carrying the note on the machine, allowing Michael to give him a percentage of the business in return. It had salvaged his wounded pride, but the cause was beyond repair.

And now they were again without an artist. It was as though he'd turned the hands of the clock backward.

"Brianna signed an employment contract," Michael mused aloud.

"You aren't thinkin' of holdin' her to it, are you, Michael?" Finnigan's facial lines deepened his frown.

"Possibly." Michael averted his face, not meeting Finnigan's gaze.

Finnigan shook his head slowly. "You couldn't hire another artist in time, but still . . ." His voice trailed off, leaving the obvious unspoken.

"Still . . ."

Brianna paced the confines of the office, unable to believe Michael's insistence that she fulfill her contract. Finnigan seemed to share her concern while Jimmy hadn't stopped smiling since her return.

"I can't believe you expect me to stay here and work for you." Brianna hoped her expression didn't reveal the flush of distress she felt.

Michael's face was somber, not revealing any emotion. "That is exactly what I expect. I cannot employ another artist on such short notice. And I have a considerable amount of orders to fill."

"My contract was only for sixty days," she reminded him, wondering how he could ignore what had passed between them. How could he think of designs when her heart was breaking?

"Leaving three weeks of your contract to be filled." Michael didn't flinch.

Swallowing, she resolved she wouldn't show her feelings, either. "And if I refuse?"

"Your obligation can be attached to your relatives."

Horrified, she drew back. She could scarcely believe the change in him; nonetheless she couldn't subject her aunt and uncle to the consequences of his anger. "Very well. I will complete the contract. But that is all."

Unable to discern the reaction that flickered briefly over his face, she turned to her old desk. Hiding her feelings was tantamount to hiding the Crystal Palace beneath a rug. Wishing she hadn't thought of the comparison, she took off her wrap with shaking hands.

Jimmy hurried to hang up her cloak and drawstring purse. Flinging a sketchpad down, she located pencils and oils. Finnigan was slower to approach her. Waiting until she was settled, he offered her a cup of tea, scratched his head as though debating whether to speak, then retreated to his own part of the building.

She felt a bizarre combination of homecoming and imprisonment. She caught sight of Michael staring at her more than once, but he always pretended absorption in his own work. She considered drawing disastrous designs, but knew she couldn't do it. Yet there were no more elaborate pictures of wedding rings. Even the thought intensified her pain.

Working the day away, she took only her designated lunch break. As evening neared, she readied her materials and put them away while Michael was occupied. Quickly grabbing her wrap, she escaped before he could notice. Out on the street she gulped in drafts of the freezing air, jostled by impatient pedestrians who had no patience for a weepy woman blocking their way.

She'd kept her feelings carefully reined in all day, allowing only her anger to surface briefly. Now all of her other emotions threatened to choke her. Disbelief, hurt, and unreciprocated love boiled within. Only her pride had kept them from erupting. Brushing away her tears, she kept her head upright until she reached the safety of her home.

Once inside, she ran up the stairs, avoiding the others. She might be able to carry on the charade all day, but she couldn't last out the night. Sinking onto the soft down mattress, she realized she had no safe harbor. She was a captive at the publishing firm during the day, and at night Aunt Virginia waited to send her off to yet another ball or party.

A knock at the door caused her to groan. "Yes?"

"It's me, child. May I come in?" Virginia said in a worried, muffled tone.

"Of course." Brianna sat up and tried to conceal the signs of her tears.

"You've been so quiet lately, my dear. I feel sure you've been worried about your uncle." Virginia settled next to her, and Brianna felt an immediate stab of remorse. Caught up in her own worries, she hadn't given Uncle Robert's illness a passing thought.

"How is he?"

"Much better," Virginia answered. "That's what I was coming to tell you. The doctor says he's on the mend. By spring he should be back to his old self."

Brianna threw her arms around her aunt, crushing her close. "I'm so glad!"

"I knew you would be, child. That's why I wanted you to know." Virginia rose from the bed and moved toward the doorway. "Now you won't have anything to worry about."

Brianna managed to return her aunt's smile before she left. *Of course. Nothing to worry about.*

The next few days passed much the same way the previous ones had. By the end of the week Brianna felt her nerves begin to shatter.

"Meeting." Michael entered the building without a normal greeting, just a command. "Get Finnigan."

Tempted to throw her sketchpad at him instead, Brianna clenched her teeth, found Finnigan, and together they returned to Michael's office.

"Good, you're both here. The order we've been courting is ours."

"The Walters contract?" Finnigan asked in surprise. It was the one big deal Michael was convinced would bring them back to financial success and beyond. None of them had thought the prestigious company would send their business to Griffith Publishing. It was the type of anchor that could drive them beyond their competitors. With such an influential client, banks would open unlimited letters of credit for the firm. Brianna and Finnigan both stared openmouthed at Michael.

"I had the same reaction. But this is it. A way to climb out of the coffin."

"When do they want delivery?" Finnigan asked.

"February first."

"But we'd have to throw over the Landry account to free the presses," Finnigan protested.

Brianna stared between the two men, slowly rising to her feet. "The orphanage order?"

"Yes," Michael answered shortly. "It's regrettable, but we have no other choice."

"Regrettable? Leaving children to do without the only few pennies they can earn? You call that merely regret-table?" Brianna's stifled emotions spilled into the mid-morning light.

"What would you have me do? Lose the only opportunity we have to put this miserable firm back on its feet?" Michael's voice and carriage were stern, unwavering.

"I would have you remember that first you are a human being." Brianna glared at Michael, Finnigan's presence forgotten. "And that you can extend both charity and love and that neither is a weakness."

"I don't need you to tell me how to conduct my business!" he shouted back, equal measures of veiled emotion unleashed.

"You took my loyalty and my love and you stomped on it and threw it away. I let you, but that's my own fault. But I won't be part of your plan to take food from children's mouths." The words ended on a blast and hung in the tension of the room. When Michael didn't answer, she turned to leave. "I pity you, Michael Donovan. You may become rich, but you'll be unhappy and alone."

Frozen by her words, Michael watched as she left, certain this time no coercion would bring her back.

"You're a fool," Finnigan said bluntly.

"Thank you. She didn't take enough of my hide with her."

"She's right, and you know it. You've made up a batch of excuses why you can't love her. She's smart and funny. Full of new ideas to put into this old heap. Then she goes and puts her heart on the line so you won't lose this business, not because she wants it, but because she knows how much you do. Pretty rotten, eh?" Finnigan put the full effect of his sixty-plus years into his stare. "They're all excuses. The real reason is she's Irish. And you can't get beyond that. Well, so are you, son. You can deny it. You can call yourself the son of Elizabeth Griffith, but you're still a child of Erin. And not lovin' that girl won't change you into an Englishman. Nothing will."

Michael sat in his office, long after Finnigan left, long after darkness filled the empty building. The evidence of his mistakes mounted to lay in silent accusation. Brianna's commitment to the orphanage proved she wasn't interested in the money. In his fervor to make certain he didn't repeat his mother's mistake, he'd made a far greater one. He knew he had hurt Brianna. He'd taken her innocence and sullied the memory. Her flash of integrity slashed through him. But could he give up all he'd worked for, all he'd dreamed of?

Staring into the darkness, he honestly didn't know.

By morning Michael had made no decision. Nor had he even bothered to go home and change his clothes. His last stirring of hope disappeared when all his employees were hard at work and Brianna's desk was still empty.

Not bothering with a coat, he left the building. Putting one foot in front of the other, he walked the overcrowded streets of the busy city. Hours slipped by as he stared into the ever-present crowd, somehow hoping for a glimpse of Brianna's face.

Aimlessly rambling, he stopped by the Astor, remembering his first dinner with Brianna. He loitered about the lobby until a floor walker's insistent gaze sent him on his way. Michael took to the streets again, the pull of the places they'd shared together drawing him to Wallack's Theater. He stared at the playbills proclaiming which new productions were to be performed, remembering with bittersweet pleasure how the evening had ended and then the unforgettable pain of the following morning. He hailed a hackney cab, and rode until he reached the Crystal Palace and Latting Observatory. Wandering the grounds, watching young couples who strolled hand in hand, he could picture Brianna's face, her delight in his adventure, her response to his first overture.

Darkness was descending, he realized suddenly. The whole day had disappeared. Deciding he had to see her, he found another cab and slowly made his way back to the city. Cursing the traffic and the press of the people blocking his way, Michael fought the urge to jump from the cab and walk the entire distance to Brianna's house.

When he finally arrived, he knocked impatiently at the servants' entrance. He recognized the woman he'd met before. "Mary. Is Miss McBride at home?"

"No, sir, she's not." He watched her puff up as though gathering both force and courage. "She's at the Grand Ball for the Prince of Wales."

"But that's only for the upper tendom." Michael wondered if the woman was daft.

"I'll have you know Miss Brianna is accepted by the

upper tendom, as is her aunt and uncle. This is their house. She's no servant."

"But—"

"And I'll thank you to not be knockin' at the service door anymore!"

Too dumbfounded to venture further questions, Michael turned from the woman and found the waiting cab. Inside, he wasn't certain where he wanted to go. Home seemed the only option. Why had Brianna sought work if she was a gentlewoman? That certainly explained her clothing, education, and breeding. But why had she kept her background a secret?

Arriving at his house, Michael paid the driver and unlocked the door. Once inside he came to the same conclusion Brianna had first sensed. This was a terribly lonely house to return to. Why hadn't he noticed it before? After the lamps were lit and the fire stoked, he sank to the rug, remembering the night they'd been together. He finally allowed the memory to be replayed genuinely, without the taint of the following day overshadowing it.

Finnigan's words rang in his mind. *Because she was Irish.* How true was the accusation? Was that why he'd overlooked all the obvious signs and believed her to be a servant in her own home? All the foolish excuses he'd told himself rose up to mock him now. He'd concocted reasons to explain everything about her that denied her true background. He'd told himself she must have borrowed her clothing from kind employers—the same employers who'd evidently educated her along with their own children. With a bitter snort he realized that such kind employers existed only in fairy tales.

Remembering his father's wasted life, Michael knew he couldn't pursue that path, either. The demise of his grandfather's proud and hard-earned empire still pained him, and the memory wasn't one he could simply set aside as though it hadn't happened. Michael stared into the flames that leapt in the hearth, trying to sort through lifelong beliefs and what he'd learned since meeting Brianna.

He could no longer deny that she had opened a portion of his heart and brought him both hope and magic. A log snapped, sending showers of sparks at the screen protecting the priceless rug that covered the floor. Was he like that screen, keeping the exciting sparks from reaching him for fear of being burned?

The quiet of the house settled around him. No voices would ring out to greet him, he knew. None to tell him that they believed in him as Brianna had always done. Instead Finnigan's words resounded in his head as they had through the long, confusing day. Had he so focused on the bad that he'd totally overlooked the good? To his way of thinking, Finnigan had always been an exception. Could Brianna be, also?

ELEVEN

SUMMONED BY HER aunt, Brianna prolonged the encounter by moving slowly toward the parlor. Upset by her niece's uncharacteristic sadness, Aunt Virginia was determined to cure the source of the pain by planning even more social events. But the teas, dances, and dinners only made Brianna's heartache worse. Comparing the men she met and the one she loved only made her realize there would be no other love for her.

Arriving at the archway leading into the parlor, Brianna stopped abruptly. Michael stood by the piano, looking at the family Bible, which was always on display. The faint rays of winter sunshine drifted through the lace curtains, illuminating Michael, who had positioned himself near the window.

She wondered if it was possible that her heart had stopped. The sudden pounding that followed convinced her that it had not. Before she could speak, Michael glanced up. For long, agonizing moments they could only stare. When he spoke, she found the use of her legs again, shakily moving forward to meet him.

"Brianna."

"Michael."

Like awkward strangers who wanted so much more, they yearned to be closer, but still stood stiffly apart.

"I've brought this," Michael began.

She tried to focus on the envelope he held. The beautiful

hand-decorated paper caught her attention. When he handed it to her, she found her hands trembling as she slipped the elegant envelope aside and stared at the incredible confection in her hand. It was one of the famous handmade valentines that Michael had always scoffed at. Decorated in lace with gold edging and beaded pearls, it was a treasure. She started to read the handwritten inscription, her heart trembling as well when she recognized Michael's handwriting.

The light of my love is a lass most fair
With eyes of rain-washed skies and midnight-colored hair.
As bonny as the dales of Erin,
She's beautiful, bold, and darin'.
She holds my heart in her hand.
Now I beg her to wear my wedding band.
Were I a knight, I would wish her for my lady fair.
Alas, I am but a Donovan. I await her answer with hope and care.

The tears trembled on Brianna's lashes as she held the precious words close. It seemed he had truly inherited the Irish gift for verse.

His voice held a husky tremor. "I believe the card asks a question."

Unable to speak, she nodded.

"And your answer?"

Stunned, she could scarcely utter a sound. Her voice was barely more than a whisper. "I don't understand."

He took her hand. "I realize how wrong I was about everything. It wasn't until you were gone that I knew I couldn't let you walk out of my life."

Hope was a new friend, one she wanted to embrace. "Do you mean that?"

"The most important question is: Do you believe me?"

"Oh, yes."

Suddenly she was in his arms, arms she'd despaired of ever holding her again. Their kiss expressed their rekindled passion, and when they finally broke apart, her eyes were bright with unshed tears. Still, she had to ask, "What about the orphans?"

"You were right." He cast his eyes downward, not revealing the anguish he'd suffered to give up his dream. "I suppose I knew it all along. I'll have to give up the big contract. It's apparent I wasn't meant to be a tycoon."

"You were meant to be a success and you will be." Her voice was fierce with love and determination.

"I see now the depth of your loyalty." One hand reached out to tenderly stroke her hair.

"I am your most faithful supporter, but you are destined, Michael Donovan. I believe it in my bones." She put her hand in his and felt the pressure of his touch.

"Said with the luck of the Irish. You almost make me believe it." A whisper of regret accompanied his words.

"There are thousands of ways to have the success you want. Valentines are wonderful, but why not expand and manufacture cards for other holidays? Christmas, for example." Her enthusiasm for the idea she'd given much thought to bubbled over.

"Who would buy cards for Christmas?" His tone was one of great skepticism.

"You can make it into a tradition," she suggested. He smiled indulgently, but she could see the thought taking root.

"Right now I want to concentrate on another tradition." He moved with purpose, and she easily let the subject go. There was time in the future to think on it. Right now she was inordinately glad that there would be a future with him. Only one thing stood in her way.

"I must tell you something," she began. He listened while she told him of her uncle's illness and her sense of responsibility to her family.

"You are to be lauded for your loyalty, but there's no need, Brianna. Your uncle's finances are in excellent shape."

Puzzled, she gazed at him. "What do you know of his affairs?"

"All that your aunt Virginia relayed to me." His expression held a combination of wisdom and relief.

"You met her?" Brianna's voice was a bit faint.

"She can't understand why you believe there's a monetary problem. Apparently they can retire comfortably anytime they want to."

"But Uncle Robert was worried about not working anymore!"

"Because he loves his work, not because he needs the money."

"Oh." Slightly deflated, she realized her aunt had been telling the truth all along. Money wasn't a problem, and apparently Virginia really had been too inexperienced to deal with their creditors. There had been no need for her to obtain a job. Brianna was inordinately glad that her stubborn nature had taken over, or she would never have met Michael.

"I know now that you're not related to the servants in the house," he added.

Ashamed that she'd never explained her situation, she stumbled over her words. "I intended—"

"We've had enough misunderstanding. Why don't we start with a clean slate?"

Relieved, she agreed. "Almost clean. There are some things I never want to forget." She met his gaze steadily, seeing a flame of passion leap into his eyes.

The memories they'd created together wouldn't be

erased; they remained the foundation of their relationship. Knowing that the barriers to his heart were gone, she knew the tender man she'd grown to know was hers forever.

"How soon do you think you and your aunt can arrange a wedding?" he asked, trying to disguise the raw emotion in his voice. He'd almost lost this incredible woman, and he didn't intend to take another chance.

"I've always fancied being married on St. Valentine's Day." Visions of white lace tulle couldn't compare with the image of being Michael's wife, spending every moment with him.

"That's less than two weeks away," he warned in a voice mingled with hope.

"I don't believe I could wait much longer," she whispered.

"I love you," he finally managed to utter, knowing the words would come easier now. Crushing her close, he realized she was right. He was destined for success. He'd just won the hand of the woman he loved.

Virginia and Mary backed away from the hall leading to the parlor. "I think you can dispense with the tea," Virginia whispered.

"Aye, ma'am," Mary agreed as they gazed at the couple.

Michael swept Brianna into his arms, and their kiss vanquished any doubt that St. Valentine hadn't blessed their union. Together Mary and Virginia tiptoed away, leaving them together. To their future.